Tapestry

ALSO BY FIONA MCINTOSH

Trinity Series
Betrayal
Revenge
Destiny

The Quickening Series
Myrren's Gift
Blood and Memory
Bridge of Souls

Percheron Series
Odalisque
Emissary
Goddess

DCI Jack Hawksworth Series
Bye Bye Baby
Beautiful Death
Mirror Man
Dead Tide
Foul Play
Blood Pact

Valisar Series
Royal Exile
Tyrant's Blood
King's Wrath

Luc & Lisette Series
The Lavender Keeper
The French Promise

Fiction
The Killing Words
Fields of Gold
The Scrivener's Tale
The Tailor's Girl
Nightingale
The Last Dance
The Perfumer's Secret
The Chocolate Tin
The Tea Gardens
The Pearl Thief
The Diamond Hunter
The Champagne War
The Spy's Wife
The Orphans
The Sugar Palace
The Fallen Woman
The Soldier's Daughter

Non-Fiction
How to Write your Blockbuster
On the Scent of Perfume

FIONA McINTOSH

Tapestry

Bedford Square
Publishers

First published in Australia in 2014 by HarperCollins Australia Pty Ltd,
Sydney, Australia

Second edition published in Australia in 2025 by Penguin Random House Ltd,
Sydney, Australia

First published in the UK in 2026 by Bedford Square Publishers Ltd,
London, UK

bedfordsquarepublishers.co.uk
@bedfordsq.publishers

A CIP catalogue record for this book is available from the British Library.

ISBN
978-1-83501-486-8 (Paperback)
978-1-83501-487-5 (eBook)

2 4 6 8 10 9 7 5 3 1

Typeset in 10.35 on 13.5pt Sabon Lt Pro
by Avocet Typeset, Bideford, Devon, EX39 2BP
Printed and bound in Great Britain by Clays Ltd, Elcograf S.p.A.

MIX
Paper | Supporting responsible forestry
FSC www.fsc.org FSC® C018072

The manufacturer's authorised representative in the EU for product safety is
Easy Access System Europe, Mustamäe tee 50, 10621 Tallinn, Estonia
gpsr.requests@easproject.com

For our Will,
also on a fantastical research journey,
into new frontiers of the mind

TAPESTRY

[HALF TITLE PAGE TO BE INSERTED]

PROLOGUE

London, summer 1715

HIS FINGERS REACHED HELPLESSLY TOWARD THE GLIMPSE of skin that had appeared when Nancy's shawl slipped off her shoulder. His eyes were closed, but he could see that plunge of soft, creamy flesh, a small valley nestled between proud breasts where the tiny medallion he'd hammered out of silver hung, warm and safe.

They were kissing in an apple orchard on the fringe of their hamlet, the sun only just lightening the sky on a bracing spring morning. The steam from their breath curled and twisted in the breeze when they pulled apart, and blossom drifted to the ground around them like the strewn rose petals that he knew she dreamed of for her wedding day.

Nancy looked down and he felt her hand press against his hard—

'Marvell!' boomed a voice.

The blacksmith snapped out of his reverie. 'Over here, Mr Fanning!' he yelled to his foreman above the clanging and ringing of hammers on anvils. He'd been banging out a length of iron and the repetitive work had allowed his mind to drift to Berkshire, where Nancy waited for his return. She had given him until the harvest in two years' time to marry her or she would allow Farmer John Bailey to woo her.

Marvell reached for a rag to wipe his face of sweat, and

with it thoughts of Nancy lying with John Bailey. He put his hammer down as his superior approached and pointed a thumb sharply in the other direction.

'You're wanted upstairs.'

Marvell frowned. 'I haven't done anything,' he said, knowing all too well that being called upstairs likely meant a docking of wages, or some other kind of trouble.

'I didn't say you had,' Fanning growled. 'Clean up.'

'Why?' Were they dismissing him? He'd been working so diligently and not spending any money on ale or betting. 'I've been here early every day this week, Mr Fanning.'

'Marvell, get your arse upstairs as soon as you've tidied up… and hurry!'

The man stomped away. It definitely sounded as though Marvell was up for a reprimand.

He went to the washing trough, scrubbed at the dirt with the gritty paste provided, and thought of his sweetheart again.

'Wait for me, Nancy,' he'd asked as he broke free of her kiss that spring morning. 'Let me find a journeyman's work in London and earn enough to give us a future.'

As he dried his face and hands, he remembered how she'd pulled him close, smelling of roses and the gingerbread she'd baked for him before their dawn meeting, and how she'd nodded at him tearily before she made him give a pledge. 'Go, William. But do not keep me waiting beyond the harvest festival of 1717.'

'I will bring home two fists brimming with silver so you can wear a dress of silk to our wedding, and we can host a fine feast and live in our own cottage from then on.'

He had kissed her fiercely and then turned his towering, brawny frame to begin his journey on foot to London, where at length he found work with John Robbins, the prized London blacksmith.

Now Marvell sighed away his memories, rolled his sleeves down and did his best to smooth his hair, but decided he couldn't help how he looked at mid-morning on a busy working day. He loped to the back of the foundry and trudged upstairs, anticipating a bollocking even though he had no clue why he should be in trouble.

'Mr Fanning,' he said as he knocked tentatively.

'Come in,' the man said. 'This is William Marvell, sir,' he continued with careful deference to an older man inspecting the main floor from the vantage of this upper level. Above him hung a sign wrought in iron: *By hammer and hand all arts do stand*.

Fanning turned to Marvell again. 'Sir George Moseley wishes to talk to you.'

Marvell blinked. 'Morning, sir.'

'You've certainly got a chest for your work, eh, Marvell?' Moseley remarked.

Marvell lifted an eyebrow. 'I've been swinging a hammer since I was twelve, and working the bellows since I was indentured at six summers, sir. I suppose my chest has shaped itself into this hard barrel over years of working at a smithy.' He shrugged, and tried not to look down at his hands and his arms, twice the width of Moseley's and bulging with muscle roped by thick veins. Marvell didn't believe he looked much different from any other journeyman, but he knew he had a lot of silver to earn to keep his promise to Nancy to come home with his huge fists full of coin.

'How long have you worked for John Robbins, son?' Moseley asked. He was in the uniform of a guard, which, together with his age, suggested to Marvell that he enjoyed plenty of authority. Marvell felt his mood turn defensive.

'More than a year now, sir. I planned to give it at least two before I return to my village in Berkshire.'

'And how goes your work here?'

'I work hard, sir. Stay out of trouble. I save every penny I make, as I'm engaged to be married. I'll open my own smith on my return to Berkshire, sir.'

'That's what I like to hear. A man with grit and ambition, earning an honest wage for honest work.'

Marvell didn't understand what the official's point was, but decided it was better to stay silent than risk appearing a dullard.

'How would you like to earn ten pounds for a single day's work?'

Not even in his daydreams had Marvell entertained thoughts of a job that might pay him so handsomely. His whole year's work at Robbins's smithy might amount to sixty pounds. He frowned at Moseley, feeling uncomfortable at the way his hair still dripped damply down his back, and wondered whether this job offer had a sinister side. It almost sounded too good to be true. The silence lengthened as he pondered this.

'Your apprehension shows, Marvell,' Moseley remarked, while Fanning glared at his employee.

'I don't know what that means, sir,' Marvell answered, 'but if you're asking whether I feel suspicious, then yes, forgive me, sir, I do not feel comfortable.' He wiped his sleeve across his mouth, knew it to be uncouth, but he was a smith. What could this man, resplendent in what he now realised was a military uniform, want with him, other than to ask for his horse to be reshod? 'I'm sorry, sir,' he began, 'I don't understand why I am being interviewed or being offered this kind of money.'

Moseley nodded. 'I like your honesty, Marvell, and you come recommended to me for your reliability. So let me enlighten you as to my mysterious offer. I'm tasked with the role of finding a new city executioner. Our last, after escaping prison for his debts, murdered a man and beat a woman so senseless I can't imagine her recovering from her injuries. Mr Price was the city hangman for a number of years and finished by swinging at the end of his own noose, having lived a life on the fringe of the law, it seems.' He gave a sardonic grin. 'I don't intend for that to occur again.'

William's mouth had gaped open as Moseley gave his explanation. 'You're offering me that job?'

'We've asked around. Blacksmiths tend to have the right skills needed. You have genuine potential as London's new city executioner.'

William began to reply, but he faltered and Moseley took this for acquiescence.

'We shall pay you for each hanging. Obviously they do not occur every day. We prefer to hang criminals in blocks of six or more out of Tyburn. I trust you're not squeamish about hanging women either?' He didn't wait for Marvell's answer before pulling out a snuffbox and moving rhythmically through the ritual of pinching the tobacco and sniffing it loudly. He cleared his throat, undaunted that two men waited on his words. 'I presume, Marvell, if you swing a hammer as well as your employer asserts, that you can also swing an axe?'

William nodded, still too stunned to speak.

Moseley shrugged. 'I cannot imagine when you might be called upon to use that particular skill, but I have to warn you that you may occasionally be required to behead a prisoner. Is that a problem for you?' Now he did wait for Marvell's answer.

'If the punishment befits the crime, then I can't imagine I'd hesitate to deal with a man who has sinned so harshly against our king and country.' He could see that his careful reply was what Moseley wanted to hear. It would have been so easy to jump in with a simple *no*, without considering the implications of that answer.

'Excellent. You will be paid more than you can imagine for such a job done cleanly and without sensation.'

More than you can imagine. William did glance at his large hands now, remembering his promise to Nancy. 'I can imagine a lot of money, sir.'

Moseley threw him a wry smile. 'Shall we say twelve pounds per severed head?' he offered. 'You keep whatever your victims give you… and their boots, of course. Any hangings of common criminals at Tyburn we will pay by six necks. Let's say ten pounds for each batch, shall we? The first of those will take place in the next few weeks.'

William Marvell found it impossible at that moment to swallow. His lips wanted to form the words *thank you*, his hand yearned to offer itself in a gesture acknowledging that a deal had been agreed. But he didn't trust his voice, and his hands had instantly become clammy, rooted to his side. It was all he could do to nod, dazed.

'Excellent. Congratulations on your new role, Marvell. You shall hear from me in due course. I would suggest you get some training in, learn to swing that axe accurately.' He grinned. 'Rumblings up north suggest we may need those skills sooner than later.' Moseley sniffed loudly again, chortling softly, before nodding at his companions. He tossed a tiny sack of coin at William. 'Get yourself some pumpkins and practise.' He strode from the room, Fanning following politely.

They left William blinking where he stood, pennies for pumpkins jingling softly in the leather sack in his palm.

ONE

Terregles, Scotland, August 1715

SHE KNEW SHE'D FIND HIM HERE, ON the roof, silent and lost in his thoughts as he stared south toward the river and beyond to the borders, where war beckoned.

'Have you made a decision?' She was careful to ensure there was no hint of reproach in her tone.

He looked down as she approached, but didn't turn. 'I have no choice, Win,' he replied, his voice gritty. He cleared his throat, which she suspected was to shift the tension he'd been feeling. Winifred, though she spoke with restraint, felt his sense of duty hurt her as keenly as if he'd delivered a blow to her belly. She could hear he was heavy of heart, no doubt struggling with his decision, but he still sounded as though he'd already made it.

Winifred stood close behind him and wrapped her arms around his chest, for her own reassurance as much as his. She felt small against his broad, hard body, as she rested her cheek on the velvet of his coat and wondered how she would find the courage to part with him. 'Ignoring a summons to Edinburgh doesn't mean—'

'It does,' he said, his voice raw. 'I've been named in the Warrant. A traitor to the Crown.' He shook his head and gave a soft sneer. 'The Act for Encouraging Loyalty in Scotland is very clear. I'm officially now a rebel. It seems I have two choices:

imprisonment, or join the call and raise my standard against the English king.' He turned in her arms and embraced her properly, kissing the top of her head where golden hair met pale, unblemished skin. 'I'm damned either way. Forgive me for bringing this upon you.'

She looked up into the face of the man she'd fallen helplessly in love with fourteen years previously at the French court of exiled King James III of England – the one the Protestants called the 'Old Pretender' – and was struck by how much more handsome she found him without his periwig, which he'd had to wear for the portrait he'd been posing for recently. She took a deep breath, knowing that no matter how much it grieved her to give up her husband to this dangerous rebellion, she couldn't deny her support for his courageous decision. 'William, one of the reasons I married you was because you shared our family's fierce belief in returning the true Catholic heir to the British throne.'

'Ah. And there I was, convinced it was purely because I was so irresistibly handsome,' he replied dryly, winning her smile. He turned back to look across the moors, but in that moment Winifred saw a terrible sadness behind his gaze and alarm rippled through her. 'Our children's lives are now at risk... yours too, my love.' She could feel his shoulders slump with heavy regret. 'The King of England knows me for a Jacobite. I don't hide my Catholic beliefs.'

'Nor I, my beloved,' she uttered, reiterating her support for his cause. 'Come downstairs and warm yourself. Summer is farewelling us, and if you're going to fight for the true king, we must not risk your being anything but hale.'

They walked across the rooftop and shared a poignant glance as Winifred recalled the exciting moment in France when that same blue gaze had rested on her for longer than was considered polite. She'd known of this strapping and stylish newcomer from Scotland. How could she not have, when all the Jacobite court's women were gossiping about an eligible bachelor who had arrived in Paris to pay his respects to the exiled British king?

'My, but he's handsome,' Queen Mary Beatrice had whispered to the impressionable nineteen-year-old Winifred from behind a fluttering fan.

Winifred remembered how the heat had flashed on her cheeks and her gaze had instantly dropped.

'No, no, my dear Winifred,' the Queen went on. 'Do not avert your attention. You do not even have to use feminine wiles to attract this one. He has eyes only for you and the court is ablaze with speculation, for he is a fine catch. Match his gaze and meet him in the gardens should he ask you to take a turn. I shall certainly be giving my permission,' she added, giving Winifred a conspiratorial smile.

Upon the death of her mother, who had been the Queen's loyal friend, Winifred had been shown valuable patronage by the exiled sovereign. She had even been permitted to accompany Queen Mary Beatrice on a week's visit to Versailles. They had arrived via the glittering Hall of Mirrors, which reflected the extravagant surroundings and attested to the wealth and power of the man who had built this palace; during winter he would burn hundreds of candles in chandeliers and their light would be boosted a thousand times over in the mirrors to make it as bright and sunny as an afternoon in July.

It was here in the court of the Sun King, Louis XIV, that Winifred had learned the sophisticated language of the court: how to say one thing but mean another; how to lie effortlessly and elegantly; how to use wit rather than acidity; and how to be exquisitely discreet as well as flirtatious and irresistible to men at all times.

As she regarded her husband, Winifred wondered whether he was also remembering how the women in the exiled court at Saint-Germain-en-Laye had chattered about the cobalt-eyed Scot, with his expensive and fashionably cut clothes and wig of dark, curling hair. William had been gracious to all, but even amid her nervousness Winifred sensed his gaze following her hungrily. He laughed more with her than with the other women and encouraged her views on everything from the Jacobite cause to King Carlos of Spain's appointment of his grandson as heir. She knew she also impressed him with her conversation, which ranged well beyond needlework and how to run a household.

'He is the laughter and song in my heart,' she'd finally admitted to Queen Mary Beatrice on the day that William had proposed marriage.

She recalled how the Queen had chuckled. 'Your acceptance of a marriage proposal will break the hearts of a dozen other lovely ladies, child. He is most eligible.'

'I have no desire to follow my sister, Lucy, into a wimple, Your Majesty,' she had replied.

'Then I insist you marry here,' the Queen had said with a smile.

Winifred Herbert wed William Maxwell in the quietly beautiful chapel of Saint-Germain-en-Laye. She had walked the sixty-two steps from the church entrance to the three stairs that led up to the altar with a less than demure smile that friends claimed refused to leave her blushing cheeks for days. Not even the near-to-freezing cold that clawed up from the pitted flagstones through her jewelled wedding slippers could chill the warmth that her bright expression brought to all the guests.

And then she had kissed her 'family' of nine years a fond farewell and sailed with William for Scotland, finally arriving at the Nithsdale family seat at Terregles in the border county of Dumfries. The house was a rambling affair of pale local stone and charcoal-coloured flint, where generations had added new wings and one had even built a tower, the rooftop William favoured. It afforded him a view across to the River Nith and beyond to the patchwork of fields that sprawled into England.

Terregles was part of the frontline of proud seats that straddled the invisible line dividing Scotland and England. It was from these border counties that raiders moved either into England or out of it, and the Nithsdales were expected to police these southern raids and deal with any daring Englishmen who wanted to steal livestock, chattels… or even women.

William had remarked to Winifred more than once that while the highlanders had a popular reputation for being the hardiest of the Scots, few realised how fearless and tough the border lords had to be in dealing with the regular skirmishes they were involved with. But William never disrupted her running of the household with news of the scuffles connected with the 'border reivers' and she made no fuss when bandaging his wounds, or helping to set a broken bone sustained in the fighting.

In the main she had to admit that life at Terregles had moved to a slow and happy rhythm, especially with the help of her Welsh friend and lady's maid, Cecilia Evans… Until now, that was. For William to speak of his misgivings so openly told Winifred that everything about this fight ahead was different from any her husband had fought previously.

It was only last year that the Hanoverian dynasty had staked its claim and George I had left Germany to sit on the English throne. Stirrings of rebellion had been simmering in Scotland ever since.

Now Winifred tried again to reassure him. 'News from my friends in the south suggests the Protestant king is lacking in conversation and appears "dull and wooden". He seems unhappy to be in London, misses his homeland.'

'George may not be a glamorous monarch, but my dear, I fear he is a fervent one… and so strongly Protestant that he will not countenance Catholic rebellion. My sources at Whitehall suggest the dutiful, often unanimated public mask belies the sharp intelligence of the private man.'

'Intelligence does not always go hand in hand with warmongering, surely?' Winifred wondered as she allowed William to help her through the doorway that would lead them off the rooftop, beneath the low lintel and down the creaking flight of stairs. She lifted her embroidered silk skirts and he assisted by gently crushing the hoop of her gown.

It was comforting to hear him chuckle. 'These rooftop openings were clearly never designed for women, my dearest.'

'Ah, but I am unlike most women.'

'This is true. Your heart is surely as stout as your petticoats.'

Winifred enjoyed being able to release her tension through amusement. She paused on the creaky steps. 'You could always make me laugh, William, no matter what.' She regretted how sad she sounded despite her smile.

William kissed her hand and his expression matched her tone. 'Our German monarch is determined to keep Scotland tightly manacled to England.'

Winifred nodded, feeling as though a fist of ice were closing around her heart. 'Then you must do as our true king asks, my beloved. He has called you to arms and your tenants and vassals will follow you into battle. I told you last spring that the curious eclipse of the sun Master Edmond Halley reported was surely of great portent for London which it darkened for several minutes. Maybe it is written in the stars that our family must follow this dangerous pathway if it is to remain spiritually true and rid Britain of the Protestant king. Never forget you have your family's pride and blessing and love at all times.'

Winifred took his hand again and led him down the narrow corridor, the timbers sighing beneath their tread. At a small landing beside the door that gave access into the house proper, she paused. They shared a glance, understanding that the entire household – including their daughter – waited beyond to hear his decision.

'Our Jacobite supporters in London may conspire, but they are indecisive. They will lead the clans to slaughter if their vacillating continues. And I am troubled over Lord Mar's battle prowess. He is not the right leader for the clan chiefs.' He sighed, looking deeply anxious. 'Oh, he'll unite everyone, of course. Scotland is a long way from London and it's easy to sound brave when highland lords are yelling their battle cries.'

'Will they rally?'

He nodded. 'We all will, because our king demands it. But Mar isn't Scottish nobility. The highlanders will struggle to follow him.' Will shrugged. 'It comes to naught; I will be required to raise my standard no matter who leads us. Alas, I fear we lowlanders know far better what we're taking on than do the highland chiefs.'

'I have faith that you will prevail, William.'

'You know this, do you?' he teased, arms reaching around her. He kissed her softly.

'I think I have seen it in my dreams. I promise you, you will not give up your life for James but, forsooth, you will offer it, beloved.'

Winifred watched the lines around his eyes crease as he smiled and felt the wintry fist squeeze her heart a little harder.

'Are you a stargazer, my sweet? Can you read the puddles, or the lines of my hand?'

She shook her head. 'I know only that I love you without limit, William Maxwell. I always have. I always will. And you will live a good life and die in old age when called. I feel it with a deep and true knowledge.'

He clapped his hands. 'My wife's a soothsayer!' he exclaimed, and she giggled.

'By Saint Mary, hush!'

'You shall have to find a way to hush me, then,' he said, treacherous fingers reaching for the laces that closed the front of her dress.

She batted away his hand. 'William, really!' But there was no heat in her voice and her movement was as harmless as the beat of a butterfly's wings.

'I can be very quiet if you distract me,' he continued, deftly loosening the laces now.

'You're not jesting, are you?' She chuckled, and then looked at the door. 'They're all waiting.'

William sighed, reached over and locked the door from the inside. 'There. Let them wait. Now we're alone, trapped in our tower, where no one can see us or reach us.'

'You would have me here?' she asked, amused.

'I would have you anywhere, Win, my love. But why not in my private tower, where you are now imprisoned and at my mercy, and where we can forget the woes of the Jacobites and Scotland?'

She laughed, looking down to see the sides of her dress fall away and her husband expertly undoing the clasps that held the exquisitely embroidered stomacher in place.

'I remember this dress. You were wearing it the first time I met you at the palace in Saint-Germain-en-Laye.'

'I'd spent many moons with my needle and thread making it perfect,' she said, watching the last of the clasps give way beneath his urgent fingers. She sighed with soft pleasure as he placed the embroidered panel reverently on a small table nearby.

'A stolen moment together,' he whispered, and she could feel his warm breath on her neck. 'Romantic, don't you think?'

'Up against a wall, my love?' she said, smiling, half surprised that she was permitting it, half delighted by his daring. 'You make me feel like a strumpet,' she told him, loading her tone with promise.

William grinned, fully loosening her undergarments so her breasts, still full and firm after two children, were bared. He groaned, bending to kiss each nipple. 'The sight of you like this chases away my demons, Win.'

She could feel his hard urgency, could hear it in his suddenly throaty voice. Her own desire matched his, and without another thought she surrendered to their combined lust and began helping him to raise her skirt and undo her hoop. All the while they shushed each other's laughter, lest they be discovered.

Later, as they sat on the floor like children, their backs against the dark panelling of the timber, holding hands, with her head resting on his shoulder, Winifred dared burst the amorous bubble they'd built around themselves in these last stolen minutes.

'Will you speak to our son in France?'

'Yes, I'll write to Willie today,' he said, standing and offering a hand to help her up. 'Let's get you back into your fastenings. I don't know how you women do it. Frankly, I think going to war is easier!'

'Don't jest, Will. I'm frightened for you.'

He lifted her chin and kissed her tenderly. 'Don't be. I will ride on your confidence and love. And you admit you saw it in the stars. I will not give up my life for my king, but I will offer it.' As she began to reply, he gave her a rueful look. 'Your words,' he reminded her.

'Which I stick by,' she said.

'And which I trust.' He stopped her from saying anything more with a final lingering kiss. 'Thank you for this. It helped to remind me about what is important. Not king or country... but family. I love you, Winifred Maxwell. And when I am confronted by our enemy and all looks hopeless, I shall remember our stolen lust against a wall at Terregles and I will think of us as carefree, reckless souls who dared to dream that a Scottish king will one day rule over Scotland.'

It was easy to fit her wide skirts through the doorway that led to one of the wings of the Scottish manor. The lowering sun farewelled itself through a large window looking out over the western moorlands, drenching the broad hallway in which they stood with a soft golden pink light. 'And when do you depart Terregles?'

'Early autumn, mayhap,' was all he would say.

Winifred flinched inwardly, but betrayed nothing in her expression. William always said she had the perfect face for 'trictrac', a game of strategy they had played regularly together in France throughout one particularly bitter winter.

'Just leave me a few people so I can run the estate.'

'Nay, my lady. This is an act of war we make. You and our daughter shall not remain at Terregles and be easy pickings for the government hounds. They will not use you or our children against me. We're fortunate that Willie is schooling in France, but we should warn your sister of my troubles in case we need her help. I'm sad that they're *our* troubles, darling Winnie.'

'I am ready for the task, William. Where will our daughter and I go?'

'To my sister Mary. Stay with my family at Traquair House and be safe.'

Will kissed her again, lingering against her lips, heedless that a servant might see them.

She must not weep. She swallowed her fear, and with it went any tremble in her voice as she pulled away from his kiss. 'Take pity on the family that will worry about you.'

'Be as stout of heart as I have come to know you. I would that you'd leave before the month is out.'

'Come, we must tell our daughter and send word to your sister at Peebles,' she whispered, her cheeks still flushed from their lovemaking.

She led her husband away from the tender sunlight, and toward an uncertain future of rebellion against the English Crown.

TWO

London, December 1978

William knew only one way to kiss her, she realised. Deeply, as he did now – the sort of kiss that made her see stars like a cartoon character, and trapped her attention in such a way that not even the grey drizzle of a freezing London morning could penetrate her awareness.

'Oh, get a room, would you!' a woman muttered as she pushed past them, breaking the spell.

Jane grinned awkwardly. They were standing at the Seven Dials intersection in Covent Garden, outside their hotel and very close to their lovely room.

'I'm going to marry her!' Will called to the woman, who was dashing off in the direction of Monmouth Street. They had been a momentary annoyance to her, already forgotten. If she heard, she didn't turn.

'Will, shh!'

'I want to tell the world,' he said, kissing the top of her head as he pulled her close.

Sharp guilt pierced the gossamer cocoon she'd allowed Will to build around them. It seemed that with each day they spent together he had spun a new layer of love and commitment… ownership, even. She wasn't really sure what to call it. But whatever it was, it was strong and binding, drawing her closer and closer, until the invisible, unspoken bonds had morphed into something tangible: a promise of marriage. Now she wore a crazily expensive diamond ring attesting to what he had just openly declared. So why did she hesitate? Why wasn't she showing the usual traits that a newly engaged woman might? How come she wasn't picking everything up left-handed all of a sudden? And why, when she caught sight of the glittering jewel, did her breath catch dully with a faltering anxiety... to the point where she found it hard to look at the spectacular ring?

Is Will the right one? The question finally burst through the silken bubble as her happily chatting fiancé led her to a café for breakfast. She barely followed his conversation as questions mounted like obstacles before her. *Is there enough between us to sustain a marriage, children, adversity, middle age, old age?* She swallowed the tumult of uncertainty that had leaped into her throat.

Maybe it was her old foe: that need to take control and to keep control of any situation. Her surrender to Will's innocent query had afterwards felt like a loss of control. 'Be mine,' he'd whispered, and his words had been filled with affection and tenderness. Yet now she heard those words in her head as proprietorial. At the edge of her mind, Jane knew it was paranoid to think like this, but still she was hesitant and unsure of him.

Until this moment, it had been only while he slept and she could steal utterly private time that she had allowed herself to confront her dilemma: was marrying Will wise? She'd decided to put it down to the natural nervousness of any bride. Even though Will exhibited none of the same hesitation, she told herself he would surely be vacillating as the enormity of this commitment began to dawn on him... particularly as family and friends were already celebrating.

They hadn't known each other that long. Tomorrow would make five months. In truth, there were days when it felt so right she could yell out her happiness, and these were the times she relied upon, but there were twice as many days when an inner voice demanded she search her heart. *Are you sure he's the right one?*

Or is he convenient? She was having one of those moments as Will grinned at her, muttering how hungry he was again for her body. The notion that she was cheating herself as much as Will felt suffocating. He wanted to kiss her again, she knew, as they waited to cross another narrow side street, but she pulled away casually, disguising her deliberate action by grabbing his hand instead.

'Let's try that new place up the road that the concierge told us about,' she said. He groaned. 'Well, you should never have planted the thought in my head about kicking off the day with a hot chocolate. I have to have it now.'

'I'd like to have *you* now,' he whispered, before linking his hand with hers and gauging the traffic snaking from the seven streets into the plaza, carrying people and cars into various parts of Covent Garden and beyond. 'Now,' he said, and they stepped out into the road, dodging cars and skipping into Monmouth Street.

Hopping over puddles, dodging other pedestrians, they arrived laughing at the café. It was painted black and overhung by a large awning, also black, that made the doorway appear like the opening to sin itself. As they moved deeper inside, the erotic fragrance of chocolate was punctuated by the exotic aroma of coffee being ground, making them both sigh theatrically with pleasure. Behind the front counter a young woman was cutting up a slab of chocolate cake, and one slice fell apart. She laughed, chopped it into smaller pieces and put them on a plate.

'Care to try some?' she urged, holding up the plate.

'Why not?' Jane said, tearing her gaze from the shelves that housed beribboned boxes of chocolates alongside bags of chocolate-coated everything and anything... liquorice, fruit, bite-sized biscuits, assorted nuts.

'Chocolate body paint?' Will said, holding up a small jar and looking at her with a question in his expression.

'Too messy for hotel guestrooms,' she answered, lifting an eyebrow at the grinning assistant before she took a plump cube of the cake, making rapturous sounds the moment her taste buds registered it.

'I'm beginning to understand that part of our marriage contract is that I must always keep you in chocolate,' Will said, gesturing toward the café area at the back of the shop.

'Then I shall love you forever,' she quipped.

As they eased into an empty booth, he fixed her with a gaze devoid of its former playfulness. 'Be sure, because forever is a long time.'

Jane covered her surprise at his sudden intensity by pulling his gloved hand to her cheek, then kissing it swiftly. 'Forever's not long enough,' she replied, instantly hating herself for flirting vacuously with a man who was so committed to her. She desperately wanted to be just as committed to him.

'A hot chocolate and a coffee,' Will said to the fellow who had shuffled up to take their order, entirely unaware of her dilemma. 'I'll have scrambled eggs with toast. And she'll have a slice of that rather decadent-looking cake, drizzled with chocolate,' he said.

'On holiday?'

Will grinned at the overly curious man. 'Working. I have a lecture to give in northern England. Is that the right terminology?'

The fellow glanced at Jane; she was yet to speak, but he'd clearly already picked her as a Brit. Maybe it was Will's bright yellow rain jacket, trimmed with blue, that marked him as a foreigner. It was far too jaunty for a Britisher in early winter, which pegged him as a tourist, and he was far too tanned or chatty to be anything but American. Of course, the southern drawl was also a giveaway.

'"Up north", we say,' she said, dragging off her brown, waxed jacket and smiling at the waiter.

'And after that I'm going to marry my beautiful sweetheart.'

Jane blinked in annoyance when the waiter glanced at her as if dryly amused. 'Congratulations. Busy time for you, then.'

She shook her head. 'It's a while yet before—'

'Make it a strong hot chocolate, would you? My fiancée likes it strong.'

Jane wasn't impressed with the look, loaded with innuendo, that passed between the two men, but let it go. She also didn't like having Will speak for her.

She peeled off her gloves and scarf, idly reflecting that the irritating but harmless drizzle of this morning would likely be sinister black ice by this evening. Hardly ideal for an American tourist, but then Will was hardly a sun and surf kind of fellow despite hailing from Florida. Didn't *everyone* in Florida live on or near the beach?

Will pulled off his gloves with even teeth that looked all the whiter against his effortlessly bronzed complexion and reached for her hands. 'Cold?'

She shook her head. 'Not any more.'

Will kissed her hand. 'Let's go back to bed after this.'

'We've only just emerged from two whole days in bed!' Jane reminded him.

'So make it three. Who's counting?'

'Your father,' she quipped.

Will laughed. 'Pops doesn't doubt our love. That comment he made was because he's concerned that we're rushing into marriage.'

'Maybe we are,' Jane said before she could stop herself.

He gave her a curious glance, but was still smiling as though he knew she didn't mean it. 'You and I are old souls, Jane. We were predestined to meet.'

'Is that so?' *Predestined to marry as well?* she wondered.

Will continued, heedless of her angst. 'I reckon we're two lovers who have always been together and we just keep dying and reincarnating to find one another again. If I wasn't predestined to fall for you, why would I have loved you the instant I fell over you?'

She started to laugh. 'All that stupid bloody gear you walk around with, perhaps? I'm sure we're staying at a hotel overlooking the Seven Dials and those seven streets because you can't be too far from anything resembling your precious ley lines.'

Will gave her a look of feigned injury. 'We prefer to call them "straight tracks".'

'Straight tracks, straight lines, ley lines... aliens, magic, spirits of people's past,' she mocked, then reached for his hands across the table. 'I'm only joking. You know I'm impressed by your research.'

'But you don't really understand any of it, do you? Even though I've spent the last two months trying to explain it.'

She sighed with pleasure as her cake was placed before her on a small wooden platter. She would have preferred something savoury for breakfast, but now it was here, her treacherous taste buds hankered for the sweet treat. The drinks arrived soon afterwards.

'Scrumptious,' she said, nibbling on the small slice, though sorely tempted to dig a fork into Will's oozy eggs. 'So what are you going to tell the boffins up north about your weird lines?'

'They're not weird,' he said good-humouredly.

'But they're not magic either, Will. Do you believe in magic, really?'

'As a geophysicist,' he reminded her in an exaggerated, lofty tone, 'my job is simply to explain the world around us through research and understanding.' He shrugged and became more serious. 'The straight tracks are yet to be fully understood, but there are many theories, ranging from the plausible to the comical. When something can't be fully buttoned up, there will always be some people who will look toward the supernatural. Other people, like me, look for ways to explain it.'

'Tell me about the stuff you're *not* able to explain,' she said.

He sighed, smiling softly. 'Many people believe that the ley lines connecting religious sites, ancient sacred monuments, Earth vortices are tapping into the phenomenon of abnormally high magnetic fields. They're known as "dragon lines" in China, where feng shui practitioners have referred to them for millennia,' he said. He put his knife down and transferred his fork to his right hand to shovel food neatly into his mouth while he continued talking.

'Some New Age groups believe – and we should not dismiss them as unhinged simply because they think beyond the reality of what scientists know – that these huge focuses of magnetic energy offer portals into other worlds.'

'You're kidding, right?'

He indulged her soft sarcasm with a smile, but gave a shrug of regret. 'You know, as a species, we're superstitious and spiritual anyway, so it's logical that when we can't explain something we want to imbue it with otherwordly qualities. My talk in Scotland lays out the world's varied research into ley lines.'

'Imagine if I hadn't been visiting folks in Cornwall and you hadn't been at Land's End…' Why did she keep saying stuff like this? Was she hoping this was going to turn out to be a dream, or some alternate reality? *Wake up, Jane*, a voice called. *You're going to be walking down the aisle and saying, 'I do' to this man any minute. Be sure before it's too late!*

But I'm not sure. Everyone is, except me, she answered silently, *and Will's dad, perhaps. And I don't know why I'm not as in love with Will as I think I should be.*

Tick tock, the distant voice replied, getting more distant as it repeated its words. *Tick tock, Jane.*

'But we *were* both there,' Will reassured her. 'A ley line brought us together and now we have a ley line running between our hearts, never to be broken across time or space.'

What a desperate romantic he was. 'Which ley line brought us together?'

'St Michael's,' Will replied, newly animated. 'It's vast. Runs from the tip of Cornwall and St Michael's Mount just offshore of Marazion – which many people believe is the oldest village in Europe – and continues across the country, heading north-east, cutting through various ancient edifices dedicated to St Michael. Coincidence? Planned? Divine?' Jane took a breath to answer, but Will continued as though he didn't require her response. 'There's another straight track that can be drawn, beginning in Ireland at the monastery called Skellig Michael, passing neatly through the Cornish holy mount, bisecting Mont Saint Michel in France and then off it goes, piercing other sacred sites such as the Sacra di San Michele and Assisi in Italy, and Mount Carmel in Israel.'

She blinked. 'No wonder the New Agers get off on this stuff.'

He nodded ponderously. 'My interest is in the facts, but the point is even the toughest sceptics might admit there's a special frisson, or energy, within these spiritually important sites, and they can be linked by a straight line.'

Jane shook her head as she pushed her cooling chocolate aside. 'Okay, I'll grant you it's fascinating.'

'Thank you. And it's why we want to explore the theories and learn more. It's why an international grant has been made available to me.'

'But what do you really believe, Will? That these supposedly amazing lines that crisscross the world have genuine spiritual significance? Is there a magical connection – is that what you're chasing?'

Will gave a soft scoffing sound, but she detected that it was a rehearsed response. She saw in the way he dropped his gaze that he wasn't totally dismissive, and then he surprised her by admitting as much. 'I don't know. I don't decide anything until my eyes see it or my research proves it, but I'm a great believer in staying open-minded. I love the notion that the spirit can show immeasurable strength, that faith in something can make one achieve what feels like the impossible... that magic just might exist.'

Jane frowned, surprised by this glimpse behind the rational façade that was the Will she knew. 'And you don't believe in coincidence?'

He smiled, raising his gaze from where he toyed with his last neat mouthful of egg on toast. 'I didn't think you were cynical,' he remarked playfully.

'I don't think I am. I'd love to believe in magic. Wouldn't everyone? The world needs it. But the reality is that no magic is going to stop wars or famine or death. If I could call on magic, I'd stop a lot of the bad stuff that happens in the world. I'd stop the culling of seals, I'd stop all the strikes, I'd stop the fighting in Northern Ireland and I'd find the Yorkshire Ripper.' She smiled. 'I'd certainly stop this ridiculously cold weather.'

'You'd call on magic to do all of that because you like to take control, Jane.'

She blinked. 'What do you mean?' she replied, buying time.

He shrugged. 'You're someone who likes control, that's all I'm saying. It's not a bad quality,' he continued. 'I envy it, to be honest. It's part of your charm.'

'A controlling personality doesn't sound especially charming,' she challenged.

He grinned at her, and she felt him stroke her hand. She realised he used his affection like a weapon, and most women, including herself, were likely defenceless against it. 'Because you're hearing it as a criticism.'

'An accusation, perhaps.'

Will shook his head. 'I'm saying it's a special quality. You don't need magic. You're someone who can make things happen through sheer force of will.' He gave her a searching look. 'Let's not get maudlin. I love you exactly as you are. We're planning a wedding.'

Should they be, though? 'Sorry.'

'I think bed is the best place for you,' he teased, and his deep blue eyes sparkled with mischief.

Jane felt a surge of something she hoped was love, but worried that it was, instead, plain sexual passion for this man who'd asked her to marry him just days earlier. She'd said 'Yes' immediately, caught up in the romance of his chosen setting – below the Statue of Eros in Piccadilly. People had whistled and clapped when Will lowered himself to one knee and cleared his throat, grinning unselfconsciously as he took his time digging into one of his pockets to withdraw a small, dark green velvet box. At his gesture a violinist had appeared and struck up a beautiful melody and then, on his nod, someone had pulled a string that unfurled a piece of red silk in the shape of a heart that hung from the end of Eros's bow with their names embroidered on the silk. 'I've never met anyone I've wanted to say this to until I met you, Jane. Marry me. Make me the happiest man on the planet. Be mine.'

People had roared with cheers and Japanese tourists had begun snapping photos. She remembered thinking that her face was registering shock, not melting with helpless adoration as it should have been.

'Will…' she'd croaked, looking around, embarrassed at the happy, encouraging expressions. 'I'm speechless,' was all she'd been able to say. She hadn't been lying either.

He'd undone the box and the crowd, getting larger by the heartbeat, leaned in as one and sighed at how impressive that sparkling rock looked against its velvet cushion. It was an enormous single diamond surrounded by smaller baguette-shaped stones, and winking at her as though it needed no sunlight to show it off, defying her to resist it.

She could have. But it was Will's tender look of love she couldn't turn away from.

Men had fallen for her in the past. She'd never had to go on the hunt for companionship: her looks had always attracted them in the first instance and something about her had kept them interested, although she had finally pushed each suitor away. One – dear David – she'd broken his heart. He'd just assumed they would marry because he loved her so much and they'd been together for nearly a year. What had been in his head? She'd enjoyed his companionship, his lovemaking, his friendship, but couldn't imagine a lifetime with him, although she had no idea what she *was* searching for.

Will was different. Even Jane, despite her unclingy ways, knew this was not a man to let go carelessly. There was nothing about him that she could point to as being incompatible with her; she was sure every girl standing within arm's length would not disagree that the tall, golden-haired, blue-eyed, all-American guy on his knees was a catch and a half. And, one more plus, Will Maxwell was obscenely wealthy, which was why the twinkling oblong stone she was being offered had to be three, maybe four, carats, and that was without the surrounding baguette-shaped diamonds. Dating a lovely Jewish guy from Hatton Garden's diamond-sorting community two years earlier had given her a strong appreciation of sizes and quality of stones. This was a big stone of clearly exquisite quality, even to her relatively untrained eye.

Jane recalled how the women around had begun nudging her, urging her to accept. *Why was she hesitating?* someone asked. *Yes, why?* she asked herself. She *had* hesitated, that was true.

'Don't make me ask again,' he'd whispered, almost as a joke, for she had seen in his gaze that he couldn't imagine her turning him down.

And so she hadn't. Reckless? Spontaneous? Defiant? Good or bad, those inherent traits of hers had formed an arrow shape and sped to the target of her heart. Jane had looked around at the smiling faces and nodded almost helplessly, too unsure of her feelings to say anything at that moment. Her silence had not mattered to Will, because he had scooped her into his arms and kissed her feverishly. She had heard the girls nearby squealing sentimentally, more cameras clicking and then the violinist striking up a new and jolly tune.

'I love you, Jane,' he'd murmured.

'I love you back,' she'd replied, breathless with surprise and hoping with all her heart that she meant it – it felt as though she did. Besides, that was what he'd needed to hear, wasn't it? It was what she'd needed to say to make everything feel right. She'd never told anyone, other than her parents, that she loved them. She couldn't even remember the last time she'd said it to either of them beyond school days when she went off on camps or excursions.

Now both sets of parents were in town, Jane thought with a slightly sinking feeling, as she swallowed the last chunks of the cake. The Maxwells had flown in three days ago for the small engagement celebration and her parents had done the same, hurtling down from Wales. It had happened so fast that Jane had felt as though she'd been caught up in a maelstrom with no control whatsoever.

Both mothers had put their heads together to plan a big summer wedding, just six months away. There would be the wedding itself in Wales, of course, and then another ceremony in Florida at Will's parents' beach house – if you could call a mansion that.

The fathers had made the sort of surface conversation that men who were still strangers did. Both slapped Will on the back and shook his hand. Will's father had thawed somewhat after meeting Jane's family and realising that Will was planning to settle down with a girl from what was clearly a good family that could match it financially with the Maxwells any day of the week. Jane had felt unnecessary as the wedding machinery whirred into full action.

Now she watched Will flirting harmlessly with the girl at the counter as he paid. She remembered how he had ticked off the list of pluses on his fingers, doing a fair impersonation of the conversation he'd had with his father: '*Not a divorcée, no children, beautiful in my opinion, young, fit—*'

'*Oh, these are all important qualities, Will*,' he'd said, frowning as his father must have. '*Most importantly, comes from good stock – people like us*,' he'd added in a deep voice, approximating his father's. '*She won't go mad with the money because she's used to it*.'

Now that she'd met John Maxwell she had realised it wasn't a half-bad impersonation.

The four parents were undoubtedly tentative that their beloved children seemed determined to hurry the important process of marriage. Yet it also appeared that Will had instantly won her parents' hearts and in turn she had scored highly in the minds of the Maxwells. Champagne glasses had been raised and clinked, a silent deal done across the fizzing nectar.

Now, in the café, Jane became aware of Will's tugging at her arm. 'Where did you just go to?' He grinned, deliberately allowing a sample of cake he'd accepted at the counter to squelch across his perfect teeth and make her laugh in spite of her mood.

'Mm?' She'd forgotten where they'd been in their conversation.

'I said bed is the best place for us right now.'

She had to agree. 'In bed with you is my safe place. Nothing can hurt us there.'

'Hurt us? Oh, Jane. You *are* being maudlin.'

'I thought I was being romantic.' She laughed.

'You have nothing in the world to fear.'

'I've never worried before,' she admitted. 'Until this moment, I've never had to consider anyone but myself, because I've never got serious about anyone. I've never really worried about anything much at all.' She pushed a hand through her dark blonde hair and held it there. 'Mum and Dad are so strong and generous, and nothing bad has ever happened, if you get my drift.' He nodded, but she still cast her gaze down. 'I've always felt safe, even when I've been travelling the world alone. But suddenly now that I have you in my life, there are fears swirling that I'd never imagined.'

Was that it? Was she frightened that something might ruin these wonderful feelings of brightness and hope? Did the fear make it impossible for her to embrace those feelings? Or was she avoiding what she was trying to pretend wasn't there – her reluctance to marry Will?

'Jane,' he began, full of appeal, 'nothing's going to happen to me, to us. We're forever. Come on, let's walk off breakfast.'

She let it go. 'So, bore me some more about the ley lines. Never let it be said that I was a bad fiancée who didn't listen attentively.'

Jane let him talk. He was passionate about his subject and she enjoyed watching his enthusiasm – the way he waved his long-fingered hands around. She blushed as she imagined those same fingers cupping her bottom when she moved above him. She liked his hair and its soft tickle against her naked skin – it was, in fact, the first characteristic she'd noticed about Will Maxwell, when he'd not seen her bending to tie a shoelace and had stumbled over her. His hair was thick and a rich golden colour, and fell in waves that did exactly as they pleased. He'd cut it to meet her parents, hoping to please her. Will preferred it longer and unruly until tufts flicked out behind his ears and around his beautiful oval face, which was currently unshaven and shadowed with dark prickles. She knew women watched him; even the café staff now watched them walk past.

It was Will's voice she would choose as her favourite feature of him. Mellow, not pitched too deep and capable of a deliciously sparkling laugh when she could provoke it. His American accent was addictive and contrasted with her Welsh lilt, which had been overshadowed, but not forgotten, by her years of attending a fine British public school. She could strengthen it as she chose, of course, but then she could also mimic Will's southern American English, or adopt her cousins' Cornish brogue with ease, because of a finely tuned ear for language.

'... black lines of negative energy, Curry lines of natural radiation, Hartmann lines of magnetic energy...' She let his soothing voice warm her, while she wondered which of the energies had aligned to bring him to her. She was twenty-seven, and had begun to believe her sister's quip that she was a serial lover without the love.

Finishing her history degree – specialising in late eighteenth century social and cultural life – had been a milestone in her life. She had enjoyed drilling down to understand the social mores of the era, its language and developments. But what was the benefit in knowing that soup was placed at one end of the table and fish at the other, and that custards and vegetables were never placed centrally; or about the introduction of vaccination against smallpox; or that John Wesley founded the Methodists in the late 1730s, and that the Royal Academy of Arts was founded in 1768? She'd studied the paintings of Gainsborough and Reynolds but preferred the work of Hogarth, whose dark, satirical scenes of life she found more intriguing. She had liked the enrichment her studies provided but truly, what good could they do her, other than enabling her to teach history, perhaps? Or become a historian? Neither of these options appealed. She hardly needed the money.

She'd returned to Wales for the long summer break, but had rejected her parents' suggestion to join them at their holiday cottage in Brittany in favour of taking up her cousin's invitation to visit Cornwall and enjoy some summery days in Penzance, where she could think and make decisions. It was there that she'd decided she would answer the nagging voice in her mind and set out on the journey that she'd not discussed with anyone yet: writing a novel. It was such an exciting notion it seemed truly all-consuming. She felt ready to sit down and write. It would be fiction, of course. Historical fiction? She wasn't sure.

She hadn't known what she wanted to do with her life four months earlier. Did she want a career? Did she want to remain in academia? Did she want to join the family retail business? Or did she just want to travel for a year? She could, for her allowance from her parents was generous, plus they'd offered to buy both their daughters a house or an apartment, whichever they preferred, in any city they liked. She was embarrassed that her life was so easy and had hesitated to go hunting for property, despite her father's urgings.

'London, New York, Paris, Rome… Cardiff,' he'd quipped over the phone. 'Just find what you want and let's get you settled into a place of your own.' She could hear her mother coaching him in the background, no doubt forgetting just how sensitive phones were today. Jane loved her for it, could hear how much her mum wanted to encourage her to spread her wings, even while feeling the umbilical cord straining, wishing she could keep her child close.

'… and dowsers are getting quite a following,' Will was saying beside her. 'But then, water is energy, and animals and birds have followed instinctive pathways for centuries. Which of us can categorically say that they aren't tapping into some energy line that guides them to a watering hole, or fruitful feeding grounds, or nesting sites?'

She blinked herself out of her thoughts, smiling at him. 'It's a tough one,' she said noncommittally.

'I don't believe you've heard anything I've said,' he chastised.

'I hang on your every word, William Maxwell of Nithsdale.'

'Have you been looking into my history?'

She shrugged. 'No, but maybe I should learn more. Do you know anything about him?'

Will paused outside a shop selling outrageously priced shoes and handbags. The shop had Jane's instant attention.

'Know about him? My mother dines off him, Jane. Scottish noble, fought at the Battle of Preston, thrown into the Tower by the King of England, sentenced to death as a traitor… yadda yadda.'

'You're kidding!' She turned from the black patent-leather loafers that she'd been studying in the shop window to look at her fiancé.

He grinned. 'I'm not.'

'So, yadda yadda?' Jane shook her head slightly. 'What happened?' His background had genuinely pricked her interest; which student of history wouldn't be sucked in by that ancestry?

'I'm bored with it,' he said, waving off her curiosity. 'My mother tells every girl I've ever gone out with that we're related to the famous Nithsdales. And you know how we Americans love even the vaguest notion of a royal link to Britain. I think some women have hung around me not because I was fascinating them, but because they loved the whiff of noble ancestry.'

'Sorry for mentioning it,' she said. 'Hate to be like all the others,' she added, feigning a pointed tone.

He ignored the barb. 'You're not like all the others. And that's why you're the one I love. You're the woman I want to spend my life with, have children with, grow old with and—'

'Trip the magical ley lines with?' she cut in, her humour returned.

'Absolutely. We're on a straight track together. Not even death can break it.' At her shaken expression he sighed. 'Come on, how do you fancy a tour of the Tower? And then I'll buy you a slap-up lunch at the Arts Club.'

She shrugged a shoulder. 'I've seen it many times.' She knew he'd also toured London previously. 'Are you a member of the Arts Club?'

'Fully paid up, of course, by my father. He knows about these things.'

A Porsche screeched to a halt at the traffic lights and a couple, not long past their teens and dressed in the aggressive clothing of the emerging punk movement, banged the hood. The driver, dressed in a dazzling disco-style burnt-orange shirt and burgundy jacket, had to be a stockbroker, Jane thought. And she imagined that the burgundy jacket had matching disco flares that would further offend his attackers. He glared, but wasn't prepared to say anything to the scary-looking pair in T-shirts bearing swastikas. The man's jeans were deliberately torn, she was sure, as were the girl's fishnet tights emerging from a too-tight, short leather skirt. *Must be freezing, that get-up*, Jane mused, noting the spiked cuffs around their wrists and the chains hung from their waists, but most of all the impressively spiky mohicans towering from their otherwise shaved heads. She didn't dare stare until she and Will were well past them.

The lights changed, the disco Porsche roared off and Jane had to wonder whether the political message of moderation was having an effect on any demographic. It was being called 'the winter of discontent': industrial disputes just seemed to be gathering more and more momentum, affecting every aspect of daily life. A general election was looming and that likely meant even more financial indecision and everyone feeling unsettled. Not only was a change of leadership for Labour in the air, but also the potential for Tory-led government and a new broom. Margaret Thatcher was exciting, her father thought, even though she was a woman. 'Now we'll see some change,' he had promised as the new Tory campaign began to yell that *Labour Isn't Working.* And, truth be told, it wasn't. Yet though Jane had no interest in politics, her history studies had shown her that no matter who was in power people always found something to complain about.

The rich just always get richer, Jane, one of her university colleagues had quipped. It was an oblique dig at her social situation, which she generally avoided discussing... but then, her brand of jeans alone said more than enough about her financial standing. She knew it was hopeless to join in political discussions. No one took her seriously.

They were now meandering out of the Seven Dials area, sharing a smile as they passed the hotel and their bedroom, overlooking the central point from which all the roads radiated, then wandered toward the Royal Opera House.

'This whole area is about to get a major redevelopment,' Jane remarked. 'I've always loved Covent Garden as it is, though. I hope they don't clean it up too much.'

The noise from the pubs they passed was relentless. She knew from her past experience of living in London that this area always seemed to be throbbing and full of people no matter what time or season it was, or which government was in power.

They strolled down onto the Strand, where double-decker buses ground past. She saw advertisements on two of them promoting *Evita*, with a little-known singer in the title role of Eva Peron. The singer, Elaine Paige, was causing a stir in the entertainment sections of the newspapers, she'd noticed, and besides, it was a Lloyd Webber musical – it had to be great. She made a note to get some tickets while she was in London.

Surprisingly agile black London cabs darted around them, in and out of the river of cars, searching for a gap to fill in the traffic. She and Will wandered around Trafalgar Square and along Piccadilly, ultimately joining the river of pedestrians flowing into the Tube station below.

It was to be a single-stop journey, then they could stroll to the Mayfair-based Arts Club through Green Park. Will was attracted to the linear clock in the station concourse, which was stretched across a map of the world. Jane had passed it many times and never noticed it.

'I might have guessed... another straight track?' she baited.

'Correct – time is a straight line to and from infinity,' he said, putting an arm around her shoulder and pulling her to him as he stared at the map. 'Look at this amazing clock, would you?' Will sighed. 'Somewhere in the world, the sun is always shining.'

'Of all the most powerful ley lines in the world, which would you like to visit?' she asked, reaching both hands around his waist so they were as close as two people could stand.

'Good question – but I think what you're referring to are the major Earth vortices, which are spots on our planet that some people consider of huge significance, where ley lines intersect and so on. Right?'

'I have no idea,' she replied, waving a hand. 'Pick just one.'

'Hmm. Rapa Nui – Easter Island – in the south-east Pacific is hugely tempting.'

'Where those amazing statues are,' she said, recalling seeing pictures of the Polynesian monoliths with their enigmatic expressions.

'Lhasa in Tibet is also somewhere I'd love to see.'

'Choose!' She grinned. 'Simple question.'

Will pondered the map for a few moments while Jane watched his neat, spare profile. He was frowning, seemingly taking her frivolous query very seriously. Finally, he pointed to the middle of a continent she had never visited. 'I think number one on my must-visit list of great Earth vortices has to be Ayers Rock.'

'Australia?'

He nodded and his gaze became distant, but there was a new sparkle in it as he answered. 'Every day I fight the urge to go with the New Agers and believers. They attribute huge spiritual and "special" energy to what the Indigenous people of Australia call Uluru.' He kissed her and his focus snapped back to alert. 'Besides, that particular monolith has always intrigued me. It's where important ley lines intersect which, if you follow the believers, gives it vast magical powers. I may be a scientist, but as I said I can't help but *want* to believe in the magic. Ayers Rock looks different at various times of the day and in its changing seasons, rising out of the great desert the way it does – an island mountain. I think I have to feel its magic, if it exists. That's the role of a sceptic, isn't it – to test those kinds of claims? And, more importantly, I'd like to climb it and write my name in its book at the top.'

'Really?'

He nodded dreamily. 'Ayers Rock is maybe three hundred million years old.'

'That seems like forever.'

He grinned. 'That's how long my love for you will endure.'

She gave him an affectionate punch. 'Come on, let's head down before it gets too busy.'

As they turned away from the clock, loud voices echoed around the station as a stream of young men, football supporters by the look of their similar scarves, ran through. When people stopped to let them by, they yelled at them, frightening many. Several of the football fans were pushing at each other – initially play-fighting, but then it became less friendly. Jane instinctively shrank back behind the strapping frame of Will.

Four of the young men – fuelled by alcohol, Jane could see now from the bottles in their hands – laughed and cajoled their way closer to the clock where she and Will were standing.

'Where the fuck are we? Does anyone know where England is?' one called out and pointed at the map. They laughed, and offensive name-calling was exchanged.

But then one of them turned and in that split second Jane connected with a gaze, angry-bright from liquor, sliding over her and Will.

'What are you fuckers starin' at, then?'

'Minding our own business, fella,' Will said amiably. 'We'll get out of your way. Come on, Jane,' he said firmly, and pushed her forward.

'Hey, Jane,' another mocked, 'can we have your purse, please? Me mates and I 'ave run out of cash.'

Jane ignored them and kept walking, but suddenly felt her bag being yanked off her shoulder. Comically, in that moment, all she could think about was how much money that bag had cost yesterday in Knightsbridge. And instinctively she yanked it back.

'Let go!' she snapped.

Will spun around. 'Hey, guys, really, we want no trouble,' he appeased, his tone even, his hands open.

'Yeah? But we do, mate! We want some trouble. I hate fuckin' Yanks too.' The man was bulky and the same height as Will. Jane thought he seemed older than most of the gang, and he looked like he worked out, if his thick thighs and biceps were anything to judge by. He seemed to be pulsing with unspent energy, like a stormy sky, with its constant grumble of thunder threatening to unleash a lightning strike. *Don't strike us*, she pleaded inwardly. *We're going to be married*.

It was wry indeed, she realised, how she embraced the notion so easily in this moment of fear.

More of the mob turned their way, and Jane could see commuters moving back, some heading for telephone booths – hopefully to call police – while others were craning around, no doubt searching for a glimpse of the station's security team.

Will shrugged, remaining impressively affable. 'I have Scottish blood, if that helps you hate me less…'

Jane believed he'd said it reasonably, humorously even, but she thought she saw the flash of a blade. The mood was spiralling downward and they were suddenly the target of the men's anger. Will would have to fight, but she knew he was capable of it. They might not have known each other long, but they'd filled that short time with endless conversations that stretched into the early hours. Will had been a jock at school, and beneath his expensive Barrymore-collar shirt and flared jeans lurked a body that rippled with muscles. He worked out with weights, he ran several miles each morning and he knew how to box – middleweight champion in his senior years, apparently. And he was also a martial arts expert, if all that business he'd told her about Japan was accurate. Nevertheless, she didn't want to see him prove any of it.

'Here, have it,' she said, pulling her old leather purse from the bag and tossing it at them. She needed a new purse and she wasn't carrying more than forty pounds in cash. Hopefully they'd take the money and toss the purse, but if they did take her Barclaycard, so be it. She could cancel it in a blink. Pity to lose the other guff she carried around, but suddenly she no longer cared.

They jeered and started to scatter everything from her purse on the ground, skimming her regular credit card, library card and the emergency American Express card that her father funded, and she'd forgotten about, at people like one might skim a stone across the water's surface. No one spoke; some people were frozen, others were shuffling away from the trouble. She envied the latter group as she and Will stood momentarily mute, knowing it was better to let them have their petty fun.

'Thanks, whore,' their tormentor spat.

'Asshole,' Will muttered.

Jane cut her fiancé a look of horror, but sensed the insult had slipped out before he could censor himself.

'What did you say, Yankee-boy?' the thief demanded, the tattoos on his arms twitching as though his muscles were spasming beneath them.

'Nothing,' Will replied. 'You got what you wanted. We're leaving.'

She didn't see it happen. Even when Jane felt herself pushed off-balance behind Will, she didn't know what had occurred. She was aware of Will's head whipping to one side and his layered hair flipping back. The crack of his neck sounded deafening, but worse was the second crack of his head against a pillar. He toppled like a tree being felled – Jane still clutching his arm – and she heard his skull hit the cream-coloured tiles of the station floor. His once-laughing face was now slack, his beautiful blue eyes closed, his mouth open and bleeding from where he'd bitten his own tongue.

The men ran off, laughing, but not before flinging her emptied purse back at her. Jane didn't care about anything except seeing Will open his eyes and smile at her again. She shut out the sounds of concerned voices, of a distant ambulance siren, and ignored the helping hands of commuters that tugged at her.

'Don't move him again!' she begged them, as Will was rolled onto his back and she caught sight of the depression on the side of his head where he'd cracked it.

The siren intensified in her mind and suddenly Jane could no longer breathe.

THREE

Scotland, September 1715

THE JACOBITE RISING HAD BECOME OFFICIAL WITH a public declaration by Lord Mar:

> *... having taken into consideration His Majesty's last and late orders to us, find that now is the Time that he ordered us to appear openly in arms for him, so it seems to us absolutely necessary for His Majesty's service, and the relieving of our native country from all its hardships, that all his faithful and loving subjects and lovers of their country should, with all possible speed, put themselves into arms.*

The Earl of Nithsdale stood on the steps outside Terregles House for the final hug that he dreaded. It would have been so much easier if none of the servants had lined up, his daughter had not been dressed in her Sunday best, holding hands with Cecilia, the lady's maid, and especially if his wife – oh, his wife – were not looking at him that way. He knew she was proud of him, but he also knew she was frightened for him. This was no reiver skirmish. This was war with the red-coated English Army, and their horrible drums and pipes and better weapons and battalions of well-drilled soldiers – not farmers and smiths, bakers and millers carrying hand-me-down weapons. William mentally shook his mind free of what he could not control, and focused on departing with a smile of reassurance to all those counting upon him.

Sparsely wooded areas clung near the grand home, but sprawling beyond was the heather-covered moorland, and right now those tiny bell-shaped flowers were in full pink and the earthy, herbal fragrance rode in on the soft breeze that charged into their small valley. William took a slow, deep inhalation of the aroma of his beloved heath around Terregles. 'I shall miss this.'

'You will be home soon enough, my lord,' his dear wife replied, squeezing his hand. 'Fare thee well, Will,' Winifred said, affectionately holding that hand to her face before kissing it. William suspected her sorrows had been wept in private, and was glad to avoid any unseemly display. He could always count on Winifred to be strong for them both.

'You knew it might come to this,' he whispered. 'Our situation was better suited to being the rebellious one.'

She nodded her understanding. Families around Scotland were dividing their loyalties. Even if they were wholly Jacobite, one side would opt to show its support while the other remained loyal to George. Winifred understood that in truth most didn't care who sat on the throne far away in London, but everyone in Scotland genuinely cared about allowing Scotland to rule itself. Winifred's staunch faith meant she had encouraged William to be on the side that raised the flag for King James, while his brother-in-law, equally patriotic to Scotland, would look to remain loyal to England.

Thus Charles, Lord of Traquair, would not be fighting with Mar, but would take responsibility and care for Winifred and the children. William was grateful for her assurance, her determination to send him off without any extra guilt beyond the crushing weight of what he was already experiencing. 'Charles has far more to lose financially, and a far larger family to protect. I know he will look after us.' That was

Winifred's way of telling him she understood, trusted his decision.

'And I know I can rely on your strength, Win.' He kissed her tenderly on her lips, uncaring that they were surrounded by servants as well as a gathering of vassals and tenants obliged to follow their lord into battle.

William finally broke the kiss to bend on one knee before a child. 'Darling Anne, be good for your auntie,' he said, pinching his only surviving daughter's plump cheek, grinning broadly to hide his concerns. 'And I need you to take care of your mother for me. Will you do that, precious girl?' Anne nodded and smiled shyly at her father as she clutched a knitted bunny.

Winifred had been determined that their son not be used as barter in any violent actions that might be destined to find them, for the region of Terregles was said to be the most Puritan region of the country, where Catholics were regarded as idolaters, their houses constantly searched. William was grateful for that foresight today, because getting young Willie away now would have been almost impossible with the new blockades in place.

William and his men finally departed in a slow, snaking trail. Among them were a few mounted men, but the rest were a raggle-taggle band of farmers who carried picks, pikes and the odd sword between them. William had learned that the Duke of Argyll – a firm supporter of the Hanoverian dynasty – had already arrived at Stirling Castle and was mustering troops and new volunteers by the day to slaughter into submission similar bands of men who were mustering to join Lord Mar.

Within two days William was in the thick of the action, gathered at Perth and enjoying some early success in the highlands. The clans pushed south, heading into the north-east of England, where sympathies for the Jacobites simmered. News was getting through that Lord Derwentwater, among others, had finally declared for James and had mustered men and was even now awaiting the arrival of his Scottish brothers.

A first real blow came with the death of the French king Louis XIV a few days after his seventy-seventh name day; the powerful sovereign surrendered to the excruciating agony of senile gangrene, taking to his bedchamber, slipping into a coma and dying at the start of September. His infant great-grandson was named his heir, while his effeminate son, the Duc d'Orléans, was appointed regent.

'He is a different animal from his son and has little allegiance to us,' William admitted to his fellow lords. 'I have no doubt he is cuddling up to the English Crown,' he added with disgust, knowing the English ambassador in Paris would likely be pressing hard to unload Louis's ships, which had been bound for the anxious rebels in Scotland. They had been counting on the French king's support, but with Louis XIV dead, their campaign felt on suddenly shaky ground.

FOUR

London, December 1978

JANE SAT HUNCHED AND MUTE BETWEEN HER parents in a surprisingly light-filled room, specifically set aside for relatives of patients. They could make their own tea and coffee, which was only marginally better tasting than the generic coloured liquid spewed out by the vending machines on the levels below the hushed, breathless corridors of Neurology's intensive care. But they were now two days into the trauma of Will's attack and used to the nondescript beverages and plastic cups that threatened to collapse with each sip.

'John said they'd get in around 2 p.m.,' she heard her father say.

'How far north had they gone?' her mother asked. Jane didn't think it mattered, but she suspected her parents were simply making conversation.

She felt her father shrug beside her and check his watch. 'Argyll somewhere... on the west coast, I gather. They were having a good holiday until a few hours ago. Apparently Diane was humming with excitement at visiting the ruins of Terregles House.'

'Oh, don't tell me – the Earl of Nithsdale's country mansion?'

'One and the same.'

'I'm sure she's desperate to see John's name in *Burke's Peerage*,' her mother remarked in a sarcastic tone.

'Don't, Mum,' Jane whispered.

'Sorry, darling. We're all tense.'

'This looks like the doctor,' her father murmured, and stood up as a bearded, middle-aged man approached.

'Jane,' the man said, offering his hand, smiling warmly from above his loud, wide tie and looking more like a cuddly TV presenter than an eminent neuro-physician.

Will had been transferred from St Thomas's Hospital, where he had first been rushed to the emergency rooms in the ambulance, unconscious and mostly unresponsive. The trauma team at St Thomas's soon decided that Will needed the specialist round-the-clock intensive care that was best provided by the Institute of Neurology in Queen Square, assuring Jane and her parents it was the best place for someone in Will's condition.

But to her it smacked of doom. Why wouldn't he just wake up, open his eyes, and tell her he was sorry he'd left her for a while? They were on holiday, for heaven's sake, planning a wedding and getting parents acquainted. Starting a life together, talking about Australia together. She would agree to climb his bloody rock for their honeymoon if that was what it would take. She hadn't lost that love of his dewy-eyed pleasure in the mysterious that defied his logic, his training, his knowledge.

Guilt gathered in her throat like a dam, holding back the waters of shame. Was the attack on Will her punishment for not loving him as he loved her?

She'd hated the way her parents had moved into the same hotel as soon as they'd received the horrifying news. And as lovely as he seemed, she didn't want to shake the physician's hand. She didn't even want to be talking to him, because it was like surrendering any hope that Will might suddenly wake up. She wanted to be walking around London with him, eating lamb shanks at the Arts Club, strolling through Green Park, or maybe travelling on the train to Scotland, where he was supposed to be giving his lecture next week.

Jane felt a pressure on her shoulder from the cuddly-looking doctor's hand. 'Shall we sit down in here?' he offered, gesturing toward a smaller room. She didn't even know she was standing, or that he'd already introduced himself to her parents, who were making polite conversation to fill the terrible gap between not knowing and dreading what might be coming. And now she realised she was seated, her gaze desperate to focus beyond the window-scape visible from whichever floor they were on; frigid, naked trees swayed in the winds of the worst winter since the twenties, or so the weathermen were speculating. Their branches looked like supplicants praying to heaven. *Please let him wake up!* she prayed with them. But Dr Harris – was that his name? – was gently calling her to attention.

'Jane, I need to explain to you what has happened to Will. It's important you understand.'

'Is he dying?' she asked, her emotions helplessly raw as she snapped her gaze back to his, challenging him, ignoring this gentle first push of his into the bubble within which she'd been trying to cocoon herself.

He didn't flinch, didn't look away or betray any sign of nervousness. 'In my opinion he's already dead,' he said, delivering the cruel words far too tenderly. 'Forgive me for my bluntness, but I suspect you would rather I was honest.'

Harris looked at the trio of shocked expressions, but was obviously used to facing such situations because he didn't apologise again, didn't clear his throat or fiddle with his flame-coloured tie, its pattern making Jane feel dizzy. Instead he marched on, laying out the facts.

'It was what we call a king hit, delivered by someone who, I suspect, knew exactly what he was doing.'

'But that couldn't kill him, surely?' Jane's father said.

Harris looked thoughtful. 'Yes, it could, but in fact it didn't in this case. What it did do was knock Will unconscious. The real damage was inflicted first when his head hit a pillar and then when it slammed into the hard tiles. It was a triple whammy, you could say.'

'Will's a fifth dan in karate,' she offered, trying not to sound angry, but knowing she did anyway. It was like trying to argue with a traffic inspector who'd already written out the parking ticket. Harris looked just as implacable as ever. 'I just don't understand.' She shook her head. 'He's breathing, right?'

Harris gave a small shrug. 'Yes, that's because we're keeping him alive, Jane. But I think a decision will have to be made when—'

'No!' She looked around at her parents. 'Absolutely no way! Will's going to wake up.'

'I doubt it, Jane, not in the short term,' Harris said in such a tender voice she wanted to beat her fists against him. 'My experience tells me that even if by some miracle he did wake, the damage might be unbearable for you, for his parents and no doubt for Will himself. You told me how active he is. Would you want Will to exist in a vegetative state? Because that's what the future could hold, whether he breathes for himself or we keep him breathing.'

Out of control, a voice whispered in her mind. Although she'd promised herself no more crying, because it made her feel weak when she most needed to feel strong, a treacherous pair of tears leaked down her cheeks at his words. She hurriedly wiped them away.

She found her grit. 'You are to keep Will breathing.' She stood, shaking off her parents' hands as they immediately reached out in concern. 'I want some air,' she pleaded, and opened the door before anyone could protest.

Behind her she heard Harris muttering placatory words to her parents, and then she was gone, hurrying along corridors, down stairways, through various doors, desperate to drag cold air into her lungs to shock herself out of whatever dulling stupor was telling her Will was going to be just fine.

She burst out into the hospital gardens and sucked in deep,

chilling breaths as she leaned a hand against the wall. Her engagement ring sparkled arrogantly. Designed by Will, of course – an academic who was creative and spiritual, a scientist who wanted to believe in the mystical... in magic! She shook her head. Despite her shock on that fateful morning beneath Eros, she'd loved his ring on sight – just as she had fallen for him on first sight, with his alarmed apology and loopy grin – and she remembered now that same crooked, delighted smile as he'd pushed the ring onto her finger after she had accepted his proposal so lightly and without truly meaning it.

Now they were telling her he was as good as dead. How ridiculous. She would have laughed out loud if it hadn't been so terrifyingly real. All her uncertainty had fled. She could love him; she would learn how. The years would do it. He made her laugh, he made her cry out when he touched her, he made her feel safe. They'd been meant to meet, meant to be together. If they could only be together, she would get as used to Will as a comfy old pair of jeans that hugged you close, but never constricted. It was her failing, not his, that she hadn't told him she loved him with all of her heart. Her hesitation was only habit, she was sure of it. Everyone knew she was not usually one to fully commit to anything. But she was certain now. She *did* want to marry him. She *did* want them to be together, forever, tripping the ley lines fantastic!

'Darling?' interrupted a trembling voice.

'Mum... I can't.'

Her mother, elegant as always, nodded. 'Nor would we ask that of you yet,' she said. The word *yet* was swallowed, probably so it wouldn't resonate too loudly with Jane that Harris had given her parents a time frame for consideration. She heard it, but was able to ignore it. 'The Maxwells are here,' her mother continued.

She nodded, weary and heartsick. 'Where?'

'They've gone directly to see Will. Are you up to seeing them, or should I...?'

'No, no... of course... I mean yes, of course I am. I must. They're probably feeling just as traumatised as I am.'

Her mother's hug threatened to make her cry again. 'We've got to keep being strong now for each other, darling. You need time to accept what has happened and then – only when you feel strong enough, I promise – we will help you formulate a plan. All right? No snap decisions.'

Jane could see her father hovering in the background. These were uncharted waters for her parents; they too were used to being in control. She'd never seen her father appear so hesitant, but it reassured her when he came up to her. 'Come on now, Jane. Show the spine I know you have. You've got a long journey ahead and you need to dig deep. Harden up. Take charge, my girl.'

She sniffed and nodded. It was what she needed. Her mother's sympathy only hurt her more. Her dad's gruff way was the right approach – always had been for her. 'It's too soon. I was hugging him, and the next moment he was unconscious. Dad, Will could have killed that man with his karate. I cannot switch him off.'

'You've got to put that to the back of your mind right now, Jane, or it's going to undo you. We're all praying,' her father said, his voice shaking slightly, but his expression gritty, 'that Will recovers.' Old Spice cologne wafted toward her and the familiar smell rallied her. 'But these are such early days,' he continued. 'We have to get you through the shock and out the other side, where you can think clearly.'

She wondered if Harris had used that phrase; they didn't sound like her dad's words. It didn't matter. Whether she was thinking clearly or not, she was convinced of one fact: she had no intention of taking Will's life support away. He was going to recover. She was going to find a way through to that moment when he would open his eyes and say her name again in that lovely voice of his.

Clustered with the others around Will's bed, Jane wondered

why they were all whispering, herself included. If anything, the nurses were encouraging family members to talk to Will.

'It can help,' one said to Jane, squeezing her arm, after changing Will's dressings. She wore a badge that told Jane her name was Ellen. She was about Jane's age, and no blousy uniform could hide the attractiveness that shone from a sweet, round face with a dazzling white smile. She was tanned too, and that heightened the glow she cast about her.

'He looks so young,' his mother remarked, unable to stem her tears. 'I can see him as a boy, just like in that photo we have on the piano.' She began to weep again quietly.

Jane swallowed, looked away from Ellen and took her mother-in-law's hand, hoping it would help. 'The nurses say it's a long road ahead for everyone. Don't think about yesterday, they tell me. Just think about today and achieving tiny improvements, small milestones.' She glanced at Ellen, who nodded encouragingly.

'And the tomorrows will take care of themselves,' Diane said, nodding as she pressed an embroidered handkerchief to her nose and glanced at Will's father, who was grinding his jaw, staring at his son in such deep shock he was yet to say anything.

But as if his wife's sniff were the cue, at that moment he unleashed his anger. 'My son was a walking weapon, damn it! Fifth dan black belt!' he spluttered. 'No one could do this to him – no one! What the hell happened down there, Jane?' he snarled.

Wrung out, Jane could think of nothing to enlighten or comfort his family. 'It's a blur, John. I didn't see what happened because Will pushed me behind him. It happened in the blink of an eye. I think he was protecting me, and so was unable to protect himself.'

'Will is a master practitioner,' Maxwell snapped, his expression disgusted. 'He chose not to help himself and that has always been Will's problem. He's weak! A walking lethal weapon who won't pull the trigger!'

Jane closed her eyes momentarily to draw some calm. 'Will sees his karate as a philosophy – he uses it for spiritual guidance, not as a weapon.'

Maxwell glared at her. 'It's a fighting craft, Jane. It's there to be used so you can protect your own life *and* the lives of those you love!'

Will's mother gasped and wept a little harder. It was obvious Maxwell was used to winning in everything. Jane couldn't have cared less about him and his anger at this moment, but she was perceptive enough to realise it was the raw pain of a father talking, with little rationality behind it. So she said nothing, simply sighed and nodded.

'Well, he can't stay here,' Maxwell growled, as though the silence had finally broken through whatever barrier had been holding him back. 'I'm not leaving my son in this place.' His American accent sounded suddenly harsh, aggressive.

Jane's father blinked. 'What would you suggest, John?' his singsong Welsh accent a foil in its mellowness.

'He can come home.'

Startled, Jane glanced at her parents, then shook her head at her mother, who seemed ready to launch a counter-argument. 'The decision's mine, surely?' Jane wondered aloud to her in-laws. *Does a fiancée not count?*

'I've made a few calls,' John Maxwell said, as though she hadn't spoken. 'I've contacted one of the top neuro guys in the States and he wants Will brought to Johns Hopkins in Baltimore. My boy is going to get the very best care that money can buy.'

Jane's mum spoke with appeal in her voice. 'The people here are very—'

'It's our son lying there, Catelyn,' Will's father cut across her mother. Rather savagely, Jane thought. 'If you were in the US right now and this was Jane lying here, wouldn't you want her at home?' His voice cracked.

It was a fair point. No one could deny his logic.

'We want to get him the very best help,' Diane whispered, as though the obvious needed further reinforcement to the dullard English around them. 'Johns Hopkins is the top neurological hospital in America.'

Jane was glad that none of her family responded to that statement. She saw Ellen watching her from the nurse's station, some distance away. Ellen gave her a 'stay strong' sort of smile.

'Listen,' Will's father continued, jabbing a finger into the air, but fortunately pointing at no one in particular. 'I've spoken to the folk here. They want to pull the plug. Well, no way, mister.' He shot Jane a searching look and she helplessly nodded to indicate she couldn't agree more. He seemed to take heart from this; his hostility dissolved and his tone softened as he turned to address Jane's parents. 'There's some cutting-edge research going on at Hopkins.' He shrugged. 'I want to give your daughter back the husband she wants. These kids – well, they may be young in our estimation and they've only known one another a few months, but there's no doubting that Will is besotted with Jane and I have to presume she loves our boy just as hard.' Jane felt a fresh wave of guilt break against the shore of her pain as John Maxwell continued. 'Hell! Diane was just eighteen when we married, not even twenty-one when she had Will. Who are we to preach? We have to do everything we can to give these kids a future so they bear us grandchildren.' He fixed them all with his glare. 'We all want the same thing, surely? Now, Diane and I can handle this better at home. They're not going to do anything more for him here – you folk need to understand that. I'm not stealing him from Jane. I'm going to find out how to cure our son and then give him straight back to her.'

He was challenging Jane and her family to argue differently, pursing his lips and sticking out his chin, which turned even more square.

She looked at Will's own slack jaw, where a dribble of saliva had followed the line of the breathing tube and left a thin stain against his darkening beard. She remembered how that beard had been stubble a couple of days ago, and how, in his enthusiasm to show her something he'd once seen done in a movie, that unshaven chin had rasped against her belly, making her buck and giggle and spoiling any potential for serious passion, because then Will had pursued her ticklishness and the whole hotel had heard her begging convulsions of laughter. Yet now the stubble had grown, testimony to the life ticking over behind the unconscious mask.

'When do you see this occurring?' she asked, working to achieve a reasonable tone and a steady voice.

John Maxwell didn't flinch. 'As soon as the hospital allows that he can be safely moved.'

'He's stable now. Would you take him away from me tomorrow?'

'I would, Jane,' he said without hesitation, 'because he's absolutely no use to you right now. He's no use to anyone. We might as well flick the fucking switch.' Jane shrank back, but Will's father clearly didn't care how brutal he sounded. 'The Institute medical team isn't exactly filling me with hope, so I say we give Will his best shot at recovery… and it's not here. It's in Baltimore.'

'Jane, dear, you know you can come with us, of course,' Diane said, as though everything had already been agreed.

Jane glanced at her parents, both of whom looked stricken, but kept their own counsel. She loved them for their silence. She hadn't realised she'd let go of Diane's hand, but she reached for Will's hand now; it was unnaturally dry to the touch.

'Diane, John. I'm going to the hotel now to take some sleeping tablets and try and rest my shattered mind for just a few hours. Please let me sleep on your plan.'

John nodded once. 'Good girl. Thank you. I realise that's not a yes,' he said, when Jane took a breath to respond, 'but I'm glad we're on the same page.' He leaned over to kiss her brusquely. 'Get some rest. We'll stay with him tonight.'

Jane turned and cupped Will's face – all the more beautiful to her in repose – and kissed his lips, feeling the slippery sensation of lip balm, which she'd seen Ellen gently smear on earlier.

'See you in the morning,' she whispered to him.

Ellen caught her eye as she left with her parents. 'Dr Evans, our most senior neuro, is coming to assess Will this afternoon. You'll meet him tomorrow, probably, and I know you'll really like him. He's a forward thinker, all for giving the patients the time and space they need.' She squeezed Jane's arm. 'He believes patient knows best. Trust him.'

Jane nodded, hopes rising. 'Thanks for looking after Will.'

'Oh, that's the easy bit. He's worth fighting for. I'll kiss Will goodnight for you too.'

Jane smiled weakly at the joke and imagined that Will was probably going to enjoy it.

FIVE

Scotland, autumn 1715

As Winifred's coach emerged from the cover of the royal forest of Ettrick, where deer roamed aplenty, she and Cecilia caught their first sight of Traquair House, built on a rise above the River Tweed. Formerly one of a series of defensive towers built along the line that protected the Scottish borders against English invasion, it was now the family home of Charles, Fourth Earl of Traquair, his wife Mary – William's sister – and their brood of children.

Winifred recognised in Mary the features of her brother, and she also found Mary's warm, sympathetic nature immediately endearing. It was obvious to their new guest how much in love this couple were.

'I am so glad to welcome you here, dear Winifred,' Mary said, clasping her sister-in-law's hands between her own. 'You are to make Traquair your home in dear Will's absence.'

And so life settled down for Winifred as she and Cecilia fell into the rhythm of Traquair's routines and the demands of helping Mary with the household management, which included everything from hiring staff to ordering shopping from Edinburgh.

'Two new moons have come and gone,' Mary mentioned one day. 'Hard to credit,' she added, shaking her head.

Winifred didn't need her to say to what she referred, for

William strode around her thoughts every moment she was awake and roamed her dreams as she slept. 'I try not to think about it,' she lied, and quickly changed the subject. 'We must add some mace and cloves to our list, sister. Here, let me write that down.'

Mary's expression showed she understood her remark was being deflected. She nodded. 'And I must not forget to procure my husband's grey writing paper from Messrs Gordon in Canongate. Upon my word, he'll be in fair wrath if I forget.'

Winifred sent Mary a look of dry amusement. 'Your dear husband couldn't be angry with you over anything, Mary. He worships the very ground you tread.'

Mary grinned. 'Why don't we travel to Edinburgh and do the shopping ourselves? You could use a diversion.'

Winifred leaped at the opportunity. 'Oh, yes, and then we can choose the candles ourselves! You said you didn't trust the cotton wicks they've been sending.' She bent her head over the list again. 'I'm adding starch blue. The laundrywomen will need fresh reserves if they are going to work through the linens to put away for winter.'

They had their trip to Edinburgh, autumn began to surrender and Winifred grew increasingly glad that Will was a reliable correspondent. When his letters came, she sat down with Mary and read parts of them aloud. Anne would giggle at the little stick pictures he drew at the end of the letters, usually of himself and Anne picking apples, riding horses or holding butterflies.

The latest had greeted them after Winifred had spent the day in the dairy overseeing the making of cheese. It was Mary's son, Linton, who had been sent with the message.

'Aunt Win, it's another letter from my Lord Nithsdale,' he said excitedly.

Winifred picked up her skirts and ran with her nephew back to the main house.

Mary and Cecilia soon scuttled in after her. 'I heard.'

Winifred tore open the letter, not even pausing to seat herself. She began reading aloud, hungrily devouring the words like a woman famished.

'*My dear hearte...*' And now she did pause, blushing slightly as she skipped over her husband's endearments and enquiry as to her health and Anne's.

'*What news of Willie?* he asks,' she said, looking up at her sister-in-law, who smiled benignly. Cecilia nodded encouragement. 'I must tell him that our son took his first hunt.'

Winifred continued reading aloud. '*Mar's army is moving south through the winter like a great snowball, gathering up more men as we travel. Behind us Perth is captured, as are all the towns on the north side of the Forth. Our standard flies o'er the kingdom of Fife, Forfar, Kincardine, Aberdeen, Banff and Moray. Even Inverness is proudly Jacobite. Lords Kenmure and Carnwath and I took Moffat, and now we journey to Dumfries.*'

The three women exchanged a look of nervous relief. Mary smiled encouragingly. 'He is safe,' his sister murmured.

Winifred read on, her shoulders visibly relaxing. '*Regrettably our Jacobite army failed to capture Edinburgh Castle, foiled at the last by stupidity, but we stay hopeful that our monarch, King James, will arrive hitherto with much needed men and arms from France. We are assured a dozen ships are docked at Le-Havre-de-Grâce, loaded with men numbering two thousand and well equipped with weapons ready to sail to Dumbarton.*

'*Mar's army is camped at Perth. The highlanders number nearly five thousand. Lord Argyll's forces are outnumbered sorely, and I am one of those who believe we must take our chances and overpower the English now, for we are scarce of weapons and ammunition for prolonged battle. Our spirits remain high, dear Win, but keeping our men's minds on the fight and their tinder dry is the challenge. Even you knowest the mindset of the highlander. His attention wanders, and if we do not keep him amused in fighting and marching, he will become bored and be consumed by other amusements.'*

''Tis true,' Mary agreed.

Winifred turned the page. '*The weather is infernal and the terrible roads we travel are scarce more than bridle tracks. I should avoid them like the devil in any other situation. We are frozen most of the time and often so soaked to the skin that nary a fire can dry us, but we are heart-full of optimism, my love. I shall write again soon – my next letter surely from England and more triumphant.*'

Her voice broke slightly as she began the next sentence but steadied swiftly at Cecilia's soft squeeze of her arm. '*Kiss Anne for me, my best to dear Mary and Charles, and I send this with all my love, and my urgings to you to stay cheerful and strong. I do love you with—*'

She blushed and shrugged.

Mary hugged her. 'Let his sweet words be yours alone, Winifred. Come, Linton, we have work to do.' Cecilia followed them.

Winifred stood in the front doorway of Traquair House, her hands still chilled but aching, as they had begun to slowly thaw from being indoors. She used the murky sunlight filtering through cloud to read again the letter from her sorely missed husband, especially his declaration of love for her and their son and daughter.

He was unharmed and still optimistic, and these things were all that mattered to Winifred. She cast a prayer, her eyes closed, his letter clasped to her breast. 'Oh, dear Lord, please let Will live,' she whispered.

SIX

London, December 1978

In the taxi Jane could have sworn she heard faint words, as if from a great distance. She accepted that it was probably the echo of her own fervent hope, communing with her in prayer. 'Please let Will live,' she repeated in her mind, and snatched away a tear that had just welled up and threatened to spill down her cheek.

She stared at the shops passing her by and realised everything was suddenly irritating her – especially everyone else's tears, their stolen glances of sympathy, the pity that seemed to permeate the bubble of chaos she walked around in. Even her parents' whispered mutterings in the taxi were getting on her nerves.

'Darling?' her mother said as Jane asked the cabbie to pull over. That word *darling* could mean so much coming from her mum – everything from a question, to an admonishment, to the endearment it normally expressed.

'I'm going to walk back to the hotel,' Jane said. She tried to sound affable, but even she heard in her tone a warning for them not to argue.

It didn't faze Catelyn. 'It's miles. Plus it's raining.'

'Mum... please. We're on the Strand. It's not miles. It's about ten minutes and it's always raining in London. I have an umbrella.'

'You're sure?' her dad offered, but only because her mother had glared at him to say something.

Jane reached for an excuse. 'I just want some air.'

Mercifully, her mother seemed to understand that what her daughter really wanted was to be alone. 'Don't get lost, darling.'

'You need some rest, Jane,' her father cautioned out of the taxi window. 'By that I mean sleep. Total switch-off.'

She gave him a sad, tight smile of agreement, saying, 'I won't be long,' and lifted a hand in farewell as the taxi eased back into the traffic. Absently aware of her surroundings, she walked without purpose or direction, wandering in the footsteps of whoever happened to be in front of her. Right now she was following red sneakers, but she had spotted some black heels clicking along; their loud clatter might help keep her focused. Her mind was uncharacteristically empty. She was aware of having no desire to think, or even to look up from the pavement, to which her gaze remained riveted. She switched to the black heels as the red sneakers veered off to beat the lights before they changed and cross the busy Strand.

Just walk, she told herself.

The rude clangour of a sudden ambulance siren dragged her from the stupor where neither today's Will nor the world could reach her. She was walking in a haze of memory. Will's kiss, Will's love, their laughter, their lovemaking... all rolled into a warm fug in her mind. The screaming siren pulled her from the thin bubble of safe blankness and threw her straight back to days ago in the Tube station. The police were searching for the attackers, and if Will died, a senior officer had explained to her father, they would be looking for men to charge with manslaughter.

But Will was not going to die, and she couldn't have cared less whether they found the perpetrators or not; revenge was not on her mind. All she wanted was for her life to wind back to that morning when she was kissing Will at the Seven Dials, eating chocolate cake for breakfast, talking about magic and seriously contemplating another day in bed… Why hadn't they done that? Why had they passed the hotel?

A leaflet was thrust into her hand by someone she barely noticed, and only now did she realise it was one of five she was clutching: ads for a new pizza restaurant, a small show that was running just off Drury Lane, a pub that had introduced its winter menu, a Christmas market that was the new rage in London; and now, this last one, on lilac-coloured paper, inviting people to a session with a clairvoyant. The first five people who visited and carried a leaflet would have their reading provided free.

Got questions that need answering?
Confused by your life's path?
Need to make a big decision?

The address was in Covent Garden. Why not? It would be a good distraction. She could have answered 'Yes' to each of those questions. Maybe just listening to a stranger would help. She snapped back to alertness and threw the other leaflets into a nearby litter bin, turning off the busy Strand to make her way back into the market area.

The clairvoyant's room was at garret level, straddling a Moroccan restaurant and an outdoor clothing shop. It was a tiny room at the top of two tall flights of stairs and as she entered the smell of frying spices wafted up the stairwell.

Jane glanced at the time. Her parents wouldn't be wondering about her yet; she reckoned an hour at most was all she had, though. She knocked on the thick, gloss paint of the creamy-white door and waited. As she knocked again, the door opened and a man of indeterminate age looked back at her from pale, searching eyes that she thought were blue. His mid-brown hair was trimmed close to his head and his oblong face sported a close-cut, precisely shaped beard, as though from another century. *You'd look perfect with a sword in your hand and a cloak tied at your throat*, she thought, relieved that she could feel amused by anything. On this first glance, everything about him struck Jane as spare, from his lean frame to his neat, symmetrical features. Surprise must have been reflected in her expression.

'Expecting an old crone?' he wondered with a wry glance, his tone playful.

In the heartbeat of her hesitation he smiled, transforming as amusement sparkled in his eyes and fizzed in his voice. Attractive creases appeared in his face and a warmth seemed to radiate from him. She presumed he was gay from his slightly effeminate way of speaking and, while she inwardly fought the stereotyped assumption, his narrow, small stature and precise, well-fitting clothing reinforced her presumption.

'I *was* expecting a woman,' she admitted, finally finding a voice.

'Sorry to disappoint. I do it deliberately, though – I mean not telling people my name is Robin on the flyer. Would it have put you off coming?'

She nodded.

He grinned, and the effect was bright and disarming. 'You see? I was right to leave it off!' he teased. 'Why don't you come in?'

'Um...'

'What's to lose?' Robin challenged gently. 'You wouldn't have trekked up those stairs if you didn't have questions. Let's see if I can guide you to some answers.' He beamed at her. 'It's free, remember? You're the first of the five. What's more, I'm very, very good at what I do.'

She smiled at his persuasive manner. 'Why free?' she asked, stepping in and allowing him to close the door behind her and take the coat she shrugged off. 'Wow, it's lovely and warm in here,' she remarked before he could answer. She was delighted by the light and airy studio office. 'I love your windows,' she said, pointing toward the tall arches with coloured squares of pale glass at the top.

'They're mesmerising, I agree,' he said.

As she went on admiring them, she pulled off her scarf and he took that from her too.

He seemed able to read her thoughts. 'I know you were probably expecting a gypsy tent with lots of drapes and crystals… perhaps even some incense.' She hoped she wasn't blushing as she registered the truth of his words. 'But I like a clean space to think in,' he said gently, placing her coat on a wooden hanger and draping her scarf around it with care before putting it on the wall hook. 'Coffee? It's real and exceptionally tasty. Here, have a seat and get comfy.' As he spoke, he moved quietly around a small kitchenette. 'How do you like it?'

'Small, strong, but with milk and sugar, please.'

'Italians would call that "caffè macchiato".'

Jane blinked. 'Never heard of that.'

'It will definitely be your new vice.'

She found Robin warm and charming – a balm for her state of mind. Since she'd set eyes on him, her misery hadn't once encroached on her ability to talk.

'My name's Jane.' He threw her a smile of welcome. 'Do you live here?'

'No. But I don't live far from here. I like to keep home and work separate.'

Jane couldn't fathom how a clairvoyant made the kind of money needed to work out of a chic office such as this and live not far from Covent Garden. Perhaps he was extremely wealthy and happened to have a psychic talent. Or maybe he was a trickster who gave the perfect illusions to troubled people searching for answers. 'How on earth do you make a living?'

'I have regular clients who pay an awful lot of money for me to tell them exactly what they want to hear. I also have regular clients who pay an equal amount of money to learn the truth.'

Neither of them spoke while she watched him grind the coffee beans before heaping a few spoonfuls of the grounds into his percolator. Within a minute or two, the giveaway sound of bubbling coffee and the seductive fragrance of the brew had him reaching for a tea towel to lift the jug off his small stove.

'I bought this in Italy,' he explained. 'I prefer it to filtered coffee, which tastes flat to me. You'll love this,' he said, placing on the side table a saucer bearing a napkin, a shiny teaspoon and a small, fluted glass. *He has style, that's for sure*, she thought. She'd only ever drunk coffee out of a glass in Turkey.

'I've warmed the milk too.'

'Thank you – that looks good,' she admitted.

'It is. Better in Italy, of course. Enjoy.'

Jane quietly stirred in her half-teaspoon of sugar from the sachet he'd supplied, and as the rich, liquoricey flavour hit her taste buds, she felt her shoulders relaxing from what had begun to feel like a permanently tensed state.

Robin joined her, sipping and smiling. 'Tell me that's not delicious.'

She couldn't help herself. Her first real smile in days broke out. 'It's yummy, thank you.'

'So if nothing else, I've made you smile and given you a coffee you'd gladly pay for,' he said, once again mysteriously echoing her thoughts.

'So why, if you have these rich, happy-to-pay clients, do you need to take wanderers like me off the street who give you nothing, but cost you in time and coffee?'

He cocked his head to one side and shrugged. 'Well, it's a bit like being a lawyer. I have skills that everyone needs from time to time, but not everyone can afford them. I've led a blessed life, but when I walk the streets I see so many unhappy people. At each season's change I give away five sessions, and if any of those people want to return, I will see them at a fraction of my normal rate for as long as they wish. I think of this consulting in the same way as a lawyer might consider his pro bono work. Important, and one must make time for it.'

'That's very... um... community-minded.'

'It means I have no trouble sleeping,' he said in answer, reaching for his coffee and swallowing almost a third of the glass neatly in one gulp. He used the small paper napkin to dab his beard free of any milk froth. 'How are you feeling?'

'What do you mean?'

'Since arriving here.'

Jane was instantly on guard again. 'Er... fine, thank you.'

He smiled softly and she watched again, marvelling at the infectiousness of his amusement and how it lit up his face.

She looked down. 'Does it show?'

'That you're looking for answers? Or that you are in deep shock?'

Her gaze snapped upward. 'Both.'

'Yes.'

'Yes? Yes... what?'

'I'm answering your question. Both of these elements have formed a dark companion – a shadow that follows your every move. There's a third element too.'

'What's that?'

'Guilt.'

The word hung between them as she searched Robin's face, unconcerned by the lengthening silence, whereas normally she would have rushed to fill it.

'So you don't need to look at tea leaves, or study my hands—'

'Or hold your stunning new engagement ring,' he interjected wryly. 'No.'

She flinched at the mention. 'I suppose everyone can see it's new,' she said in a sceptical tone.

'Yes, of course. But would everyone know that the person who gave it to you is gravely injured?'

Jane gasped. She clapped her hands across her mouth to prevent the shriek that sprang to her throat. The treacherous tears that leaked down her cheeks told him he was correct. But then he sat there in his neat, self-contained manner, with a slightly amused and not fully readable countenance, and it seemed to Jane he believed he already knew everything he needed to know about her.

'Forgive me. That was my ego getting in the way. I am no charlatan, but many would view me that way. I would very much like to help. How can I help you, Jane? What is it you need to know?'

She didn't care how or why he knew about Will; that he undeniably did was shocking, but at the same time strangely comforting.

Cooing pigeons suddenly lifted off somewhere above the coloured panes of glass and the battering of wings felt symbolic. Jane allowed her most important question to take flight. 'Why am I feeling guilty?'

'Well, only you know the complete truth of that, but I sense your guilt is not cynical. I believe you are questioning the meaning of love.' Jane swallowed, but hoped she'd disguised it. 'I sense that you have never been in love before, although you have been associated with enough men not to be called a prude.' He eyed her and she took a visible breath but said nothing. 'Now you find yourself at a crossroads in life. This is a man that any single girl of the right persuasion would fall easily in love with.' She blinked. 'And you do love to be with him. You love being loved by him. Physically, financially and sexually you're both highly compatible. Mentally you are curiously well matched too. Although he is something of an academic, he is also a dreamer, while you, Jane, are more realistic, certainly practical, probably the stronger-willed. You balance each other. So, with this compatibility swirling about you and his clearly stated and demonstrated love for you, you are a little scared by the nagging question of whether you're ready for the commitment he wants... and you certainly don't trust the compatibility. Your subconscious, I suspect, is telling you it's too neat, too perfect, too... easy. Maybe you believe that the love you dream of should be harder to attain, that you need to work for it, earn it, *risk* something for it.' He stared so intently at her during those final few words that she caught her breath. And then he smiled, again instantly shifting the mood. 'Crystallising it down,' he continued in a more light-hearted way, '*he* wants you and no other. Meanwhile, *you* would prefer to be together for a while without the ring, the marriage, the fuss, the declarations of undying love.'

She nodded, feeling horribly transparent. 'Is that wrong?'

'Why don't *you* tell *me*?' he offered. 'Just speak whatever's on your mind.'

'Well, you said it all. Will has so much going for him, so much to offer. We fit together so well. What's more, he loves me and shows it constantly. I just can't imagine a woman alive who would turn Will down if she were me.'

'You haven't turned him down.'

'But I don't love him the way he loves me, Robin.' *There*, she'd said it aloud. 'I want to. I just hesitate to say it, to show it, to allow myself to feel it.'

'Why do you think that is?'

She shrugged.

'That's not good enough, Jane. You have to sort this out.'

She drank her coffee, not enjoying being cornered in this way. 'He orders for me.'

Robin lifted an eyebrow but waited.

'We might be in a café and he'll just order what we're having.'

'And you don't say anything?'

'It feels petty. Besides, he usually gets it right.'

'But you don't like that power being exerted.'

'No. I'm used to being in charge of my own life. By wearing Will's ring, it's as though I've suddenly yielded my freedom.'

'Dramatic,' he said with a smile. 'But then, you have in a way, haven't you?'

She pulled a face. 'I'm not going to become a doormat like his mother!' And there was another truth spoken. It felt like a heavy load being lifted.

Robin watched her, waited. 'Your natural need to manage

situations is one of your strengths, I suspect.' She flinched as he pressed the emotional bruise. 'If you bend your mind to something or someone, you usually get it.'

She shrugged. 'I've not thought of it that way.'

'Did you bend your mind to getting Will?'

Jane lifted a shoulder. 'I wasn't aware of it.'

'Do you believe in love at first sight?'

'I want to.'

'It didn't happen between the two of you?'

'I think it might have for Will,' she answered, looking away, embarrassed.

'Tell me what you think love is, Jane... at its core.'

'Chemistry,' she replied. 'My personal take is that there's no accounting for it. It just happens. Invisible, powerful, irresistible. No rhyme or reason. You look at someone, talk to them and you find yourself helpless in their presence, but you can't explain why.'

He smiled. 'Go on.'

'Will's brilliant at everything,' she continued. 'It's hard to live beneath that dazzling glow.'

'You feel overshadowed?'

'No... I wonder if I can live up to his ideal of me. I'm wilful, but he reads that as strong. I'm independent, but he reads that as my being someone with fathomless courage. I'm not like any other woman he's been with, I think – plus I helpfully tick a lot of other boxes he and his family desire.' She shook her head. 'I'm making this sound clinical. It's not like that. But...'

'It's how you feel?'

She nodded. 'I'm not impressed by his wealth, family name, connections.' She slapped the chair arm lightly. 'We were having fun. Why did he have to make it serious?' Robin said nothing, watched her carefully. 'I feel like I'm in therapy,' she added, cutting him a rueful glance.

He lifted a shoulder. 'It could be viewed that way, but it's doing neither of us any harm. Keep talking.'

'Will is everything I should leap at: intelligent, academic, kind, owns an amazing loft apartment in New York's most wanted street and a holiday cottage upstate.' She gave a moue of regret. 'He's keen to start a family, but only when I'm ready. He's talking about buying us a big place at somewhere called East Aurora.' She eyed Robin. 'He adores my body, worships at its altar most nights, laughs at my prickliness, understands my mood shifts and he loves the spontaneity that my parents have always considered a sign of my reckless spirit. Nothing made them happier than to hear about a ring on my finger.'

'Are you worried he'll become too much like his father?'

'I didn't know his father until a few days ago, but yes, now I'm nervous that he'll become overbearing. Will calls me "she". I hate that, but I think it's an American thing.' Robin nodded. 'But now Will's dead… technically. It's as if I wished it, brought it upon us. Is that possible?'

He didn't answer her question, only sighed. 'And you want to wind back the clock.'

'Of course.'

'Could you rid yourself of your reservations if you could go back in time?'

Their gazes met and locked. Jane couldn't answer that. 'You're the stargazer. Tell me, why can't I commit?'

'You're holding back, Jane. That's all.' He sipped his coffee silently, watching her over the rim of his cup.

'Yes, but I feel like an impostor. Tell me why I'm holding back.'

'Pure caution. Some, like me, might admire you for questioning the relationship. Marriage is not easy. I'm sure anyone who's been married or is still married would admit as much. The early flush and excitement of love are not enough to sustain a marriage.'

'So I'm being cautious?'

'Maybe you're making sure that he is definitely the one.'

'I've accepted his ring. We're planning the marriage. How

am I making sure? It's not as though I'm planning to trawl bars and nightclubs to find other options.'

Jane could hear the traffic building as more horns klaxoned the news that rush hour approached. She knew she should go. Robin was talking again.

'I agree that true love is mysterious. There's no telling why, or with whom it will happen. I personally believe it's out of anyone's control – including yours. Two people who appear compatible and perfect for each other in every way might meet and simply not connect. Others, who seem laughably disconnected on many levels, find each other irresistible.'

She nodded. 'Okay, I get that. I know people you'd never put together for various reasons and yet they have fantastic relationships.'

'Exactly.'

Jane sensed he was waiting on her, that she must drive their conversation forward. She took a nervous gulp of her coffee, while her most vital query felt as though it were choking her.

She cleared her throat. 'Will he live?'

'That is up to you,' he replied calmly, ready with a smooth answer as though he'd been waiting for the inevitable question.

She sucked in a breath, took the paper napkin he'd placed under her coffee and dried her eyes. She blew into it, suddenly untroubled by the impolite sound in front of a stranger.

'Up to me? You mean, whatever decision I reach.'

'Life is all about decisions. Every minute of the day we make decisions, some of them minute, others more daunting, but each leads us to where we find ourselves from that moment on. You are here today because of a series of decisions that probably began days previously.'

She swallowed, remembering Will's deep kiss in the street, the woman pushing past and snarling at them, breakfast… her sense of indecision. Jane returned her gaze to Robin to break the string of memories. She'd relived them too many times already.

'Ah, there's the guilt in your eyes again. Now you feel his

terrible accident has changed everything. You feel you must commit. You believe you do – or should I say *could*? – love him as he loves you.'

'I'm certain I want Will back as he was and us back as we were,' she bleated.

He regarded her with his head inclined slightly to one side. 'Mm, interesting that you neatly evaded the statement I posed, qualifying it in your own way.'

'What does that mean?' Jane knew she sounded offended.

'That it is revealing.'

'Robin, I don't know what to think any more. I'm confused, I'm rudderless… isn't that why your leaflet urged me to come here?'

'You're right,' he said.

Jane felt herself easing off the hook he'd just caught her on. 'So here I am. Tell me what to do. Help me!'

'I'm a clairvoyant, Jane. Do you know what that means?'

She shrugged. 'You look into my future?'

He laughed, but there was nothing mocking in it. If anything, she heard only affection. 'A French word,' he said. '"Voyance" is about vision. And "clair" means clear. All I do is help you to see your options more clearly. I cannot make decisions for you.'

'All right. What can you see ahead for me?'

Robin lifted a hand and held it out. 'Death and misery,' he said, before opening up the other hand. 'Or life.'

'Two happy lives?' she asked, staring at his second hand, not wanting to be tricked. Suddenly she saw Robin as one of those cunning pixies of folktales, trapping their victims with seeming truths but playing with semantics. She wanted to be sure she understood his meaning precisely.

'Oh, certainly I mean more than one,' he replied evenly. He swallowed his last mouthful of coffee and put his glass down. She still hadn't lost the feeling that she was being manipulated. 'Don't let yours go cold.'

She downed the final contents of the small glass.

'Why don't you tell me what's directly ahead of you,' Robin encouraged.

'As you already said, I face a decision,' she said.

'Go on.'

'Which I'm glad about, in a way.'

'Why?'

She shrugged. 'It allows me to take some control of the situation, I suppose.'

Jane watched the glimmer in Robin's eyes intensify. It was as though he were smiling behind that even façade. 'Ah.'

She blinked. 'What?'

He sat back, his expression one of innocence. 'Well, I think we're getting to the crux of your internal dilemma.'

The pause lengthened. Perhaps she'd always known it, but the truth felt more obvious when an outsider called her on it. 'I admit, life's easier for everyone if I'm in control.'

'Good,' he replied, and she wasn't sure if he was congratulating her on her candour or on passing some sort of test of his, answering the question correctly. 'So what is the decision before you?'

'Whether or not to let my fiancé return with his parents to America, where they feel he has a better chance of recovery.'

'Does he have a better chance over there?'

She frowned. 'I can't be sure, but they're offering us no hope in the London hospital. In fact, they want me to consider switching off life support.'

'And across the pond?'

She bit her lip. 'They want to try some things. The doctors at a top hospital in Baltimore say there are some cutting-edge therapies that might help Will.'

'I don't understand why you have any dilemma,' Robin responded.

The comment was delivered gently, but it was a bald statement that made her feel instantly remorseful that she had ever hesitated. 'Well… er…'

'You want him to survive, surely?'

'Of course,' she said, injured that he had even mentioned it.

'Then why wouldn't you do everything in your power to give him that opportunity? If London isn't and Baltimore is, surely you should grab the chance that someone is prepared to try new methods and therapies to bring him back to you.'

'I would do anything for Will. I'd risk my own life, if that was what it took.'

Something deep and knowing flashed in the pale gaze of her companion. 'Anything?'

Now he really was sounding like a Rumpelstiltskin sort of character... was that a cunning note in his voice?

'Yes,' she whispered. 'Anything, if it gave him back to me whole.'

'You just want him back?'

She nodded, initially too unnerved to answer in case it was a trap; it felt like one. 'I want Will to be safe, and if there's something I can do to achieve that, I will do it.' That sounded clear – a bottom-line statement that no one could misinterpret.

Robin nodded. 'Your loyalty will serve you faithfully, Jane.'

She frowned. 'What does that mean?'

He sat forward, ignoring her query. 'Where is Will's special place?'

Her puzzlement deepened. She shook her head. 'I don't know what you're getting at.'

'Well, it's a simple enough question. Of all the places that Will might know and love, which is the most special to him?'

'Wherever I am, of course,' she answered flippantly, trying not to let irritation creep into her tone.

It wasn't so much a dismissive look at her response – even though she wanted to interpret his slight smile in that way – but more that, as he regarded her, she felt only his sympathy. Something told her that he wasn't playing with her heartstrings, he was testing her. She felt this truth simmering behind that gaze – he was making her reach toward something, but she had no idea what that something was.

'Of course it is. He loves you, Jane. He knows you would do anything for him; that he can count on your love, your resourcefulness and your independence to pull you both through – that you will be strong enough for both of you, and that you will seize control when everything feels hopeless.'

'Is it hopeless, though?' she pleaded, unsure of whether they were talking reality or in riddles. It felt like the latter.

Robin shook his head slowly. 'Never hopeless. But his life depends on your strength, your imagination, your ability to let go of things when needed, embrace others that you don't necessarily understand and make decisions that might feel strange or dangerous. His future life and potential happiness also depend on your honesty.'

She felt utterly confused now. Was he talking about the American therapies? 'You mean I should let him go with his parents?' she asked. 'Back to America?'

Robin shrugged. 'I can only show you the pathways. You must wrestle with what you know, and reach a decision alone as to which path you should walk. I am merely a guide.'

'A guide to what, though?'

He smiled sadly. 'To the great tapestry of life.' She looked at him and realised tears were welling again. If he noticed, he didn't react. His gaze had turned dreamy. 'We're all connected in various ways and our lives touch and affect one another, but the most powerful link is through the blood that connects one generation to another. Blood is the golden thread that runs through life's tapestry.'

He was losing her. Blood… generations… threads? What was he talking about? She tried again, making her question specific. 'Do I send Will to America for treatment?' She was aiming for a yes or no response.

'He's no use to you in a coma,' Robin replied evenly, returning from his dreamy state, his gaze alert and twinkling again.

Did she trust him? 'That's what Will's father said.'

Robin shrugged. 'He can lie here unconscious, or there unconscious. It doesn't bring him back to you, keeping him in London. Besides, I imagine you can afford to hold his hand in either country.'

'Whatever makes you say that?' she asked, her tone brittle, ever touchy about her family's financial position.

'If you were only wearing a vintage Chanel coat, Jane, I'd allow that it might have been something you'd saved up for, or perhaps something given to you. The fact that you shrug it off so carelessly along with your Hermès scarf, and barely cast a backward glance at either, suggests you are used to wearing fine, thoroughly expensive clothes. The jewelled, harlequin leather Chanel hobo slouch, however, is a dead giveaway.' She could feel the blush rising from her neck. 'No one carries that sort of thing around London, unless she's some sort of celebrity with lots of minders, or someone like you with access to money that she cares little for. Those three items alone amount to thousands of pounds and most people couldn't hope to afford them.'

She had the grace to show her embarrassment by looking down at her hands. How curious it was that he could recognise her styling choices.

'Yes, all right.' She cleared her throat. 'I could sit by his bedside in London or in America.'

'Nevertheless, how thoroughly pointless,' he said, flicking away a piece of lint from his thin, sea-green V-neck. She'd thought his eyes were blue when they met, but she realised now they were green, echoing the soft, woven Italian yarn sweater. He touched the knot of his multicoloured silk tie. It was a Paul Smith, so maybe she shouldn't be surprised he recognised Chanel when he saw it. She'd bought Will the identical tie, but hadn't given it to him yet. She didn't want it to be the tie he wore to his own funeral.

'So, what?'

He blinked. 'That's up to you. You can either accept, or you can act.'

'Robin, I don't know what you're talking about.'

He grinned. 'Irritating, isn't it? But that's my role. As I say, I can only show you the paths.'

'I don't see any.'

'I've already given you a clue. Consider where Will would most like to be right now.' He winked at her. 'Apart from awake and in your arms.'

'I can't imagine,' she said, frustrated. 'Anywhere but where he is. I don't know.'

'Think about it.' He handed her a card; she didn't even know he'd been holding one. Then he stood up. Clearly the free session was over.

'You haven't shown me the path,' she said, as he went off to fetch her belongings.

He slipped the coat onto her shoulders. 'When you arrive back at your hotel, your mind will feel clear, I promise. It will allow you to go back over what we've discussed and realise that I have given you the information you need to see a clear path. A straight line,' he said meaningfully. 'Trust your instincts, Jane.'

She turned to face Robin as she knotted her scarf and slung her bag over her shoulder. She held out her hand. 'Well, thank you… for your time. It has been interesting.'

'Enlightening, I hope.'

She smiled. 'We'll see.'

Robin shook her hand. 'You came to see me. Use what you learned. Use what you know. I promise, you alone have the capacity to keep William safe.'

William. Jane never called him by his full name. She could feel the ball of emotion rising through her throat. 'I… I wish I knew how.'

He held her hand between both of his. 'Search within. The answers are there, and even though you don't feel it, I promise you I have shown you the path forward. And I know you need that self-assurance, that control. It's up to you now to walk that track. It won't be easy. One more thing to bear in mind: there's a push and pull in life always.' So did he. Jane gave a perplexed shrug. 'For every action there's a consequence,' he said.

'Yes,' she replied, trying to show him she was following his line of thought.

'Drop a tiny pebble into still waters—'

'And there's a ripple effect,' she finished. She understood the concept, but not the application of it to her circumstances.

'Good,' Robin said, as though pleased they'd got that out of the way. He smiled sadly. 'There's always a price, isn't there?'

'Robin, I...'

Then she shook her head. He really did sound like a mystic now, and maybe that was for the best. She hadn't really expected answers. She'd come here for a diversion and he had certainly provided that. She glanced at her watch. Her parents really would be worried now. 'I must go.'

He nodded, and again she saw the knowingness in his gaze. As though he understood her perfectly... knew her thoughts, anticipated her actions, felt her sorrows. 'You have my card. Perhaps we'll meet again.'

She smiled sadly. 'You've been sweet to a stranger. I hope what goes around comes around.'

Robin chuckled. 'Never a truer phrase. Take care, Jane. There's a bumpy road ahead, but you're a survivor. Always remember that.'

She left, lifting a hand in farewell as she disappeared down the flight of stairs, wondering at the strangeness of Robin, but also at how curiously powerful he'd made her feel during the short time she'd spent with him. She needed to hold on to that feeling of security – feed off it, if she could, in the difficult times ahead.

SEVEN

Scotland, autumn 1715

At the beginning of September Mar's troops had seemed unstoppable, and the Duke of Argyll had been sent to Edinburgh to take command of the English government's army in Scotland, which was hopelessly outnumbered by a rolling mass of Scots, increasing by the day in numbers and confidence.

But within a month, William's words had returned to haunt him and his fellow lords. The new French regent turned out to be far more determined to remain on good terms with George I in England than to support the Jacobite cause, and as William and his fellow rebels had feared, the French ships and their precious cargo of weapons intended for Scotland were unloaded, to be held in France indefinitely.

As October drew on, their exiled King James III of England was no closer to returning triumphant to Scotland, no matter how much his Catholic supporters proclaimed his name in various towns and how many English-based Catholics joined their marching throng.

The highlanders stood firm for independence, but while Lord Mar might have a way of gathering men, he was rapidly proving he was no strategist and certainly no army commander.

'His indecision will get us all killed!' William growled as he sat beside the fire. They were camped at Perth, where food and accommodation were poorly organised. He glared at the two other noblemen sharing his meagre meal of rabbit and ale. Their faces looked ghostly in the glow of the flames and their expressions told him he was saying nothing they didn't already know. He pointed behind them to other small campfires where men sat morosely hunched in groups, a few singing quietly, some playing dice by candlelight, but most silent. 'There's our army. Hungry, frozen and drenched, while the redcoats are fed, warm and well-drilled. How can we expect farmers to sit around here while their animals and families starve through the coming winter because of our leader's absence?' No one bothered replying. William pressed his point. 'I shall write to Mar this night. He has no grasp of what lack of direction, and ultimately boredom, will do. To a highlander especially.'

But William's declaration fell on deaf ears; he didn't receive even so much as a reprimand for his forthrightness.

By month's end, with winter now nipping at their heels, a smaller force of Jacobites had completed a fatiguing march into England, and it felt to William as though this must be the final push.

Wednesday, 9th November dawned slate-grey, with fierce, drenching rain and a chill that clawed beneath the highlanders' tartan plaid to make even the most robust of them shiver. The sombre weather lowered the mood within the Jacobite ranks as the army moved out on what it hoped would be another triumphant march.

One of William's vassals, a bastard of the Pollock family, with which the Maxwells had been aligned down the centuries, drew his horse alongside his lord's. They plodded slowly in the bedraggled column of Scots. 'I don't know how we're doing it but we're doing it, My Lord. The men believe we are touched by magic.'

William laughed aloud. 'Nay, Pollock. We are told the Almighty works in mysterious ways. Remind the men that we are witnessing a demonstration of that and tell them to cleave to their faith. It is beyond me, too, how we've come this far with so little support, and with even our own commander dithering so much he might effectively be our enemy.'

Pollock grinned at the dark humour. 'Perhaps, My Lord. But we will follow you into the very maw of the redcoats.'

William shook his head, hating the responsibility that burdened him day and night, and especially the sense of foreboding that seemed to build within him on this twenty-five-mile march to Preston through slick and treacherous mud.

'Urge the men forward, Pollock. Rally our boys' spirits with the reassurance that we shall take the city of Liverpool next.'

William arrived in Preston to the cheerful news that two troops of government dragoons had left the town on discovering the Scots were approaching. Whispers among the Jacobites quickly turned to open chatter, and ultimately into the belief that the King's men would not be giving them any opposition.

'Well, isn't this a surprise!' a fellow rider remarked, as they walked their horses unchallenged into the city centre.

William nodded. 'I had no idea Preston possessed such fine buildings,' he observed, noting the fine Town Hall and mansion-like residences of the local landed gentry.

'I think at last the men can enjoy the spoils of their success.'

William wasn't convinced it was time to celebrate just yet, but kept his own counsel on this. 'This city must not be destroyed. I must talk to General Forster about instructing our men not to pillage too enthusiastically.'

But it soon appeared that there was no threat of this, as General Forster, a Tory politician who was in command of their smaller force, decided to spend the next couple of days relaxing and enjoying the delights of the town, and encouraged his men to do the same.

By the time the General had recovered from his convivialities and crossed the Ribble Bridge with his fellow nobles to reconnoitre the region, he was astonished to see government troops gathering in numbers.

While William had little faith in Forster, he trusted the man known as Old Borlum. William Mackintosh, the Laird of Borlum and uncle to the clan chief of Mackintosh, was in charge of two thousand of the most hardened and brave highland souls. It was his men who had inflicted most of the damage that had been giving the Jacobites cause for cheer until now.

William found himself drawn to Old Borlum, particularly as the older man had served with Louis XIV's army and had visited the palace where he and Winifred had met, fallen in love and married. He passed up a night of revelry with his fellow lords in favour of a drink with the highland clan in a copse on an incline overlooking the English Army's encampment.

'The sumph! That man's soft in his head,' the older man said of Forster. 'He's as timid as Mar in making decisions. He should be protecting the bridge.' Mackintosh growled as he stomped up to where William was sipping an unhappy wine. He pointed. 'That's our weakness, Maxwell! If they take the bridge, they have us.'

William nodded. Old Borlum was making sense. 'We've had the men working on putting the town in a state of defence all afternoon as you instructed, Mackintosh. Lord Derwentwater has been giving the soldiers extra money to encourage them.' William hoped this would give Mackintosh some reassurance as to their readiness.

William's neighbour nodded in agreement and added, 'The Earl even pulled off his coat and rolled up his sleeves to help, My Lord. He was most energetic.'

Mackintosh gave a sneer. 'Meanwhile, Mar lingers in Perth, impressed to learn that the Frasers, MacDonalds and Mackenzies have rallied.'

Tomorrow would tell them whether the bridge would hold. William chose to sleep on the ground with his men in a barn. When Pollock protested, he hushed him.

'In war we are equal, Pollock. We all bleed.'

The next morning – as cold as its predecessor and, though not raining, just as sodden underfoot – William sought out Mackintosh, leaving instructions for his men to be ready to move at the given order.

Old Borlum saw him coming and spat on the ground. William looked out across the fields to where the English Army was also readying itself.

'Do you worry about the target you make?' he asked, gesturing at the bright green, blue and red tartan the older man wore.

The gruff highland leader curled a lip. 'Aye, I might well have a target painted on my back, but I'd rather take a pike through my tartan than die in soft velvets.'

William cleared his throat and grinned disarmingly. 'The highlanders are certainly a force to be feared.'

Old Borlum scowled. 'Mar has received more men in the space of a week than all of Argyll's army put together, and still he hesitates. He'll get my highlanders slaughtered.'

'Our barricades are strong at four points,' William said.

'Then pray it's enough, laddie, for they'll be over that bridge by midday, ye mark my words.'

EIGHT

London, December 1978

JANE THREADED HER WAY BACK TO THE hotel at the Seven Dials, banishing memories as they erupted.

The concierge opened the hotel door. 'Good afternoon, Miss Granger,' he said sombrely. Obviously word about Will had spread around. 'Your parents have left messages.'

She hurried through the foyer, deliberately not making eye contact with any of the counter staff, who tried to capture her attention with notes. Then she walked briskly around the corner to the lifts. The trip up to the fifth floor felt like an eternity. Back in her room, she flopped onto the bed, still in her coat, and closed her eyes to prevent herself from crying. She took slow, deep breaths until her heart felt as though it had stopped racing.

Robin was right. What was she fighting it for? She would let Will go with his parents. There was nothing to be done for him here. The decision was made and it felt like a monstrous weight had lifted from her burdened shoulders. Before she could change her mind, she reached for the phone and called her parents.

Her father was silent until she'd finished speaking. 'You sound very sure.'

'I *am* sure, Dad. I don't like the alternatives. I'm going to give him this chance. If it doesn't work, I'll face the next big decision then.'

She heard him sigh and whisper something, presumably to her mother. 'Are you back in the hotel?' he asked.

'Yes. I'm going to try and sleep once I've spoken to the Maxwells.'

'I suggest you sleep on that decision before you share it with them. But in the end it's up to you, love. Your mother and I would really like you to go and see someone called Hollick. He's been recommended by Uncle Dick.' She knew her parents had been muttering between themselves about seeking some professional counselling for her.

'Dad... is this a psychiatrist?'

'Pyschologist,' her father corrected, as if it made all the difference.

'I'm not mad, Dad. I'm sad.' The rhyming made it sound comical, but neither of them laughed as they might have in another situation.

'I didn't say you were mad,' he replied quickly, not entirely masking his frustration. 'In fact, you're one of the most clear-thinking people I know. It's why I've trusted your decisions all of your life, even when you wanted to marry Will in such a rush.'

'What does that mean?'

'Jane...' he began, sounding dictatorial. Then his voice softened. 'I've never known you to be anything but your own girl. Will seemed to smother your natural inclination to be...'

So her dad had also noticed. Typical! They were too alike. 'To be what, Dad?'

She heard him sigh gently. 'To be you. He speaks for you, I noticed.'

'Isn't that how it is when people fall for one another? They begin to think for their partner?' She knew she sounded defensive.

'Of course, love. Sorry, I'm just used to outspoken, darling Jane. I'm not used to you deferring to anyone.'

'I'm not, Dad. I promise.'

'Good. Don't let Maxwell senior bully you either. Do this because you want to. Anyway, I do think talking through your pain with a professional will be helpful.'

She didn't have the strength to argue. Besides, it was another diversion. 'When?'

'Your mother made an appointment for tomorrow at 10.30. He's in Harley Street.'

'Of course he is,' she said, not meaning to sound as sarcastic as she did. 'All right, Dad,' she said softly. 'If it brings you and Mum some peace of mind.' She pictured them sitting side by side on the hotel bed a floor below, both listening in.

'It would.'

'Fine. Don't worry about me for dinner.'

Her mother chimed in, proving Jane's suspicions correct. 'Darling, please, you have to keep your strength up and your sister's arriving this evening. She'll want to see you.'

'I just want to rest. Please don't worry. If I wake up at a reasonable hour, I'll call. If not, I'll see you tomorrow for breakfast.'

There was a pause and the sound of scuffling; her father must have taken back the handpiece. 'We'll check in on you later, Jane.' Clearly they didn't trust her state of mind. 'You take your time... rest.'

'Thanks, Dad. I love you.'

She heard the click of the phone. Distantly she registered the hum of the hotel lifts, the sigh of the heating in the room, the faint growl of traffic below, but mostly she was aware of the coo of the doves – or were they pigeons? – fluttering and landing intermittently on her balcony. One pair marched up and down the railing, male wooing female intently, cooing and begging her to capitulate. Was it true that doves mated for life? She wasn't sure, but she liked the notion that they might. She knew some birds did give their lives to each other. Swans did, she was sure. And if one died, the romantics believed the other would grieve itself to death.

Her mind was drifting. *Will isn't dead*, her internal voice assured, refocusing her. *He's sleeping, waiting for you.*

But waiting for her to do what?

She heard Robin's question in her mind. *Where is Will's special place?*

Where indeed? She sat up, balancing on her elbows, too troubled to sleep and yet too tired to think about being anywhere but quietly here in bed. But life had taught her that action was better than inaction in most circumstances, and certainly in this instance.

She remembered Will's parents and immediately rang their hotel, Claridge's. She had to leave a message, realising now that they were both probably still at the hospital.

'Yes, thank you. Can you tell Mr Maxwell that I've reached a decision? Please ask him, or Mrs Maxwell, to call me when they can.' She waited for the inevitable question. 'Yes, it's Jane.' Pause. 'No, just Jane. They know.' Another pause. 'Yes, they have it.' She was sure Will's father would already have spoken to her parents at this hotel.

She pulled off her coat, scarf and boots and looked around the room, which was still scattered with Will's belongings. She was planning a shower, but absently moved around touching his things, even smelling one of his sweaters to inhale his cologne. She ran a finger across his old leather briefcase, stuffed and overflowing with books and files containing his notes. She sucked in a breath, suddenly remembering the talk he was giving in Scotland. Had someone let them know up there? She dug around in the briefcase to find his diary.

Several minutes later she ended another call, trembling from the stress of having to explain to the event manager, and then again to a professor at the university, what had occurred. They'd both heard the reports about the attack, but no name had yet been released.

She ran a shaking hand across her face, recalling the shocked silence of the woman on the other end and how, eventually, her lovely Scottish accent did its best to give the appropriate responses. Jane understood it was all anyone could do, yet the words felt hollow, fell so very short of the mark in easing her pain. The sympathy, the gentle voice, the wishing for everything to become well again just made it worse, in truth.

Snatching two tissues from the nearby box and sniffling into them, she opened a folder from Will's briefcase, flicking through the pages of the speech he'd laboured over. She felt a deep pang as she remembered how he'd anguished over hitting just the right note for this presentation and would never give it. In a brief flash of bright-coloured madness, she toyed with the notion of delivering the talk on his behalf. Rationality returned as she realised that she wouldn't make it through the first few sentences of his presentation without breaking down. Besides, she didn't know anything worthwhile about ley lines, and hardly anything about his research project as a whole.

Her gaze absently scanned the carefully written words, the letters large so he could refer to the notes easily.

However, Alfred Watkins, an amateur archaeologist who coined the term 'ley line', meant it as a way of describing a clearing. From a height, Watkins could map clear straight tracks, which he claimed were ancient trade routes. New Agers, UFO believers, dowsers, witches and warlocks claim they hide a mysterious energy, which only a few can tap into. And now our concept of the ley lines has expanded to include what are known as Earth vortices – places on our planet that hold enormous and inexplicable natural energies. The major 'Earth vortices' include Sedona in Arizona, Mount Everest in Nepal, Nazca in Peru, Stonehenge in England, and my personal favourite, Ayers Rock in Australia. 'Uluru', as I prefer to call it out of respect for its Aboriginal custodians – the Anangu – is believed to record the Dreaming activities of the Anangu's ancestors from thousands of years ago. It connects the Anangu with their forebears and glows red like the blood that still runs—

Her reading was interrupted by the shrill ring of the telephone on the desk where she was sitting. She snatched it. Predictably, it was Will's father.

'Hello, John.'

'Jane, sorry, darlin'. I've only just been able to pick up your message.'

It annoyed her briefly that he suddenly sounded so like Will. It was just the American accent, she assured herself. Yet she also realised they were sharing an awkward pause, and although it was barely more than a couple of heartbeats in length, in that time everything about her miserable situation shifted from confused to sparklingly clear. Jane could almost hear chimes in her head as a crystal light winked and seemed to take her hand and guide her in a straight line.

Will must go to America to be saved.

And Jane would go to Australia to save him.

Where is Will's special place? Robin had asked. She hadn't been able to answer then, but she could now.

He would want to go to Uluru, where some insisted that one of the Earth's greatest magical vortices existed. She knew from his excited chatter that it was a site of immense sacred significance to its custodians. It was the destination he had chosen when she asked him a question nearly identical to the one Robin had posed! How could she have forgotten Will's answer?

Perhaps waiting there in the desert were more answers for her. Was that what Robin had been getting at? Was that his clue, the pathway that he was trying to show her… the straight track to Uluru and redemption? Would she find deliverance at this vortex? If the realisation hadn't been so traumatic, Jane was sure she would have found herself laughing. She was even thinking in the right terminology.

'So, Jane, you... er... you said you'd reached a decision,' John murmured awkwardly at her ear.

She blinked herself out of her roaming thoughts, surprised by the sudden *release* she felt.

'Yes. I... I agree he should go with you. He must have this chance.'

She could feel his relief sizzling down the phone.

'Thank you, Jane. Wow, you impress me. I want you to know, kid, I truly believe this is the right path to take.' His words resonated. 'Will you come with us?'

'No.' She hadn't meant to sound so convinced or answer so fast. 'Er... I'm going to be doing something else for Will.'

He couldn't hide the surprise in his voice. 'Not coming? How can you help him if you're not with him? You're his fia—'

Don't say it! Don't undermine me. She forced her voice to sound positive. 'Will wanted to go to Ayers Rock.'

'Ayers Rock? What, that huge monolith in *Aussie*?' *Americans never quite grabbed on to that terminology correctly, did they?* she thought absently as she formulated her excuse.

'Central Australia was on his must-do list. He wanted to take me there.'

'So?' Now he just sounded belligerent.

'So, I'm going, John. I'm going for both of us,' she pressed, more firmly now.

'Why?'

I don't know why! Robin seems to think it's the right path! her internal voice screamed at him. 'Because it's what he'd want,' she said instead, sounding softly exasperated. 'It was going to be our honeymoon destination,' she lied, grabbing at the only plausible excuse she could think of. 'I have to do this. It's where he wanted to go – it was one of the last things we were talking about before he... Anyway, my mind's made up,' she said, sounding far surer than she felt inside. 'I'm going to take something of him with me and go there for him.'

'He didn't tell me he was marrying into Heaven's Gate.'

She didn't know what Heaven's Gate was, but it sounded like a slap, an insult. However, she didn't back down, her father's warning burning in her mind. 'And he didn't tell me his father was so narrow-minded. Now, I'm giving you and Diane what you want—'

'I should think we all want the same thing,' he cut in.

'... But I'm no help to Will in his present state.'

'You don't know that. I'm sure the doctors would like the love of his life nearby, talking to him, trying to get through to him.' He couldn't disguise the sarcasm in the words *love of his life*. She loathed him in that moment, and wondered how a man with his personality had produced such a gentle soul as Will. 'How does rushing off to a fucking big, red rock in the middle of Australia help my son?'

'Listen, John, swear at me again and I won't take your calls – as well as which, I may just refuse you the freedom you want with your son. Remember the Baltimore adventure is your idea, not mine.' It felt good to assert herself. This was the Jane she preferred. 'I'm supporting you because I agree we have to give Will every possible chance. He may be your son, but please don't forget that I'm entrusting you with my fiancé. And while you're putting your faith in science and medicine, let me balance it up with the potential healing of the spiritual plane.' She was breathing hard, feeling the anger creeping past her defences. She didn't believe in Will's hippy-trippy stuff either, but now she definitely wasn't going to back down. Either she defied Maxwell, or became his doormat. 'Don't ever think Will wasn't into it,' she added as a final barb. 'He was a researcher who demanded fact, but he also loved the notion of the mystical.'

'Prayers, you mean?'

'Yes,' she said, because it gave him a simple explanation for something she suspected he would never even try to understand or engage with. Despite Will's determination to find hard research-based evidence for the ley lines, she knew he was still drawn to the magical qualities they possessed for some people. She could hear it in her mind while reading his notes... portals to other worlds. 'I'm going to say a prayer for him in a special place that was extremely important to him and his work. Since he can't go there, I'll make the pilgrimage for him.'

'Mumbo-jumbo bullshit, Jane. You surprise me. You really didn't strike me as one of those lunatics. But you've said okay and that's what matters to me, kiddo. Just be at the hospital tomorrow to sign the paperwork we need to release Will.'

'I have to be there, anyway. The police have more questions. They will have interviewed all the potential witnesses; there will be plenty of people who saw what happened.'

He waited, and when she said no more he continued, but in a softer tone. 'Listen, honey. He chose you to be our daughter-in-law. We haven't had a chance to get to know you, but in time I think we'll understand each other better. I'm sorry if I sound unreasonable; my boy comes first right now. If you want to go off on some madcap lark that helps you get your mind straight, that's fine. But come back to him soon – he'll need you. You may be the one who saves his life.'

That's what I plan to do, she wanted to say, but instead cleared her throat. 'This is something I have to do. And now the decision is made it feels right. You yourself said we have to try everything we can to save him. Well, I'm trying everything – I'm letting you take him away from me and then I'm going in search of answers.'

They exchanged strained goodbyes, but once Jane had hung up, she felt a fresh energy racing through her. *Uluru.* At least now she had a plan; she had some direction. Back in control! She was going to climb to the top of the great Earth vortex and she was going to write Will's name in the book at its summit. And then he would open his eyes and speak her name. She knew it was a curious thing to believe, but somehow it felt right. This was what Robin had been referring to, she was convinced. At last she was thinking clearly – or rather, seeing clearly.

She refused to take notice of the little voice that told her she was behaving like a woman possessed.

NINE

GEOFFREY HOLLICK WAS YOUNGER THAN SHE'D ANTICIPATED – probably early forties – and attractive in a neatly parted-hair and clean-shaven way. She suspected he had grown old before his time, and had never done anything that could have been termed overly youthful, or that might have disappointed his parents. He wore a loudly striped tie, which he'd loosened in a weak attempt to show he was not at all starchy. Yet he seemed to possess a genuine smile that had enough of a glow to warm not only him, but the person on the receiving end too.

He invited her to sit down and offered her a cup of tea, which she declined with a smile to his secretary, followed by a glass of iced water, which she accepted. He poured it for her himself from a jug on the sideboard behind him. It gave her the opportunity to strip off the clutter of outdoor clothes, while she listened to the ice rattle into the thick tumbler with satisfying clunking sounds.

They were seated in deep club chairs, facing each other across a small table. He had no pad or pen, which was reassuring. She could see he was resisting the urge to steeple his fingers, although she sensed that was his default position. Introductions and the obligatory twenty seconds of small talk about the weather were now behind them.

'Your mother explained what has occurred, Jane, and I'm glad you felt open to coming along today. Talking is a great release valve, obviously.'

He waited.

'Sometimes there can be too much talking, Dr Hollick.'

'Oh, please, call me Geoffrey,' he said, then decided even that wasn't quite hitting the right demographic for her. 'Actually, Geoff is fine.'

She smiled at his smile. It really was his key weapon, but she wasn't sure he knew it.

'I've done nothing but talk… and think, Geoff. If anything, I want to shut my mind down. Will's coma is all-consuming and there are times when I can barely breathe for the unfairness of it. "If only" is the phrase that I turn over and over in my head.'

He nodded gravely. 'I want to see if I can have you leave here today a little better equipped to handle that crushing emotion. I fully appreciate how it must feel… like the walls are just closing in.'

It was her turn to nod. 'Everyone means well. Everyone's pulling in the same direction, but my parents' sadness for me is suffocating. I love them, Dr Hollick… er, Geoffrey… Geoff…' She blinked, smiled, gathered her thoughts. 'But they can't help. I feel I can only seek the cure on my own.'

'Cure?'

'For how insecure I'm feeling.'

'Which is why you're permitting Will to return to America with his parents for cutting-edge treatment.' At her surprised gawp, he nodded. 'Your mother mentioned it when she called me.'

'But what she didn't tell you – because she doesn't even know yet – is that I don't plan to accompany Will. I have my own thoughts on how to kill my pain.'

He had been regarding her almost blithely, but at this point his gaze intensified. 'Jane, this is why you're here today,' he said with a note of urgency. 'It's important you accept that your mind, and every aspect of your emotional self, have taken perhaps the greatest shock that could be inflicted on them. And—'

'Surely no one's more aware of that than I am.' She cut across whatever he had planned to say next. 'I can't do anything but accept. It doesn't make the grief any easier to deal with, though. I need to distance myself from the pain.'

He cleared his throat. 'And how do you plan to do that?'

And it was then, seeing the concern turn his pleasant face into a mask of anticipation, that Jane realised how her words must sound.

'Dr Hollick, I'm not suicidal.'

He blinked. 'Well, no one's suggesting—'

It made sense now. Why hadn't she realised her parents were worried about this? 'Yes, I think they are. I suspect my parents are anxious I may be so unbalanced that I'll do something reckless. I think they thought my way to kill the pain might be to kill *myself*. This is why they've sent me here,' she said, her tone filled with dawning comprehension. She gave him a look of reassurance. 'I am going to see Will open his eyes and say hello to me again. But in the meantime, I'm distancing myself and trying to be proactive by going to a place we had planned to visit together. It's a sort of pilgrimage for Will.'

'Oh, I see... um, may I ask where?'

She explained patiently. The plan seemed to enliven him.

'That's actually rather marvellous,' he admitted, as she finished with a shrug. His words surprised her. She'd expected professional disdain, but now his gaze was full of sparkle and admiration. 'I wouldn't call myself a believer, but the older I get, the harder I find it to discount the power of faith. And faith in anything – each other, for instance – can achieve remarkable results.' He shook his head. Jane liked him all the more for revealing something of himself. 'And you feel strong enough – I mean emotionally – to make this journey?'

She sighed. 'I refuse to sit by his bed here, or there, and watch him sleep while doctors poke him with needles and measure his brain activity. I also refuse to accept that Will is done with this life... and I'll be damned if I'll let anyone switch off his life support without a fight. I share your faith in others, Geoff. I believe the mind is far more powerful than we know, and I'm going to test mine and push its barriers. I'm going to a place I know Will's soul yearns for and I suspect has fled to. I know that sounds crazy. But I'm going to find him and wake him up.'

Now Geoff did steeple his fingers and looked comfortable at last. 'You know that big question you've been casting out into the universe... the one about "If only"?' She nodded. 'I admire your plan because you're turning "If only" into "What if". There's a very positive response from the body and the mind, and a change in a person's whole attitude, when they refuse to be a victim and start taking action.' She smiled, wanting to hug him in that moment. 'I am all for people taking action, taking responsibility for their emotions – staring at the beast in front of them and roaring loudly straight back at it.' At this point he even shook his fist. Jane wanted to grin but restrained herself. 'And that's what you're planning to do, Jane. You're roaring back at the monster. Listening to you and your passion for Will's special place, and hearing about his desire to see it, I think your plan is the perfect fuel for the fire of your love for him. If you feel healthy, if you feel strong, if the motivation doesn't wane and you keep the trip brief and perhaps agree to being contactable, I can't think of a single reason to discourage you.'

'Thank you.' She didn't know what else to say. She reached for the tumbler and swallowed some of the chilled water – flavoured with a squeeze of lemon, she realised.

He shook his head. 'I wish more people would fight back like you're doing. It's very hard, though, to have this attitude when you're feeling battered and drowning in grief. I suspect you'll return from Australia changed, in a good way.' He grinned. 'I've read about the old straight tracks,' he admitted.

'You have? What's your opinion of them?'

He shrugged. 'Only that they have to mean something, and the fact that we haven't discovered what that could be is our failing, not a reason to sneer at any theories. Personally and very privately, I rather like the notion of magic. Never quite lost my fascination with European fairytales, I'm afraid.' He chuckled as he momentarily lost himself in childhood memories. 'But, I'm a psychologist, Jane. I counsel a number of prominent people who would likely curl a lip at any suggestion of the ethereal. My role is simply to be your guide in your decision making, to help and be sure you are seeing clearly.'

'To show me the pathway?' she asked, deliberately echoing Robin.

'Precisely.'

'Do you think I *am* seeing clearly?'

'Yes. I don't think self-harm or even self-pity is a factor here. I sense fury and courage instead… and a desire to right the wrong. I don't even hear a note of revenge. You haven't once referred to the men who did this to Will.'

'They were cruel and stupid, and most of all drunk. I have nothing to say to them. I have no desire to waste a moment of my life thinking about them.'

'You're marvellous. An inspiration.' He stood. 'Promise me you will take very good care of yourself while you're away.'

'I promise,' she replied, standing and shaking his hand. 'Thank you for believing in me.'

'When will you leave?'

'As soon as I can after Christmas. Maybe in a week's time. I can't see my mother allowing me to leave before then.'

'Good luck, then,' he said.

'I'll need it when I explain this to my parents,' she said with a sigh.

TEN

Lancashire, November 1715

The Preston parish church had become the Jacobite force's headquarters and the spire was used as the main lookout point. Lord Derwentwater and his reserve of mounted gentlemen volunteers set themselves up in the churchyard. A flat-roofed mansion belonging to Sir Henry Houghton was taken over by threescore highlanders from Mar's regiment, affording them a clear view down the narrow lane to the bridge. At other strategic barrier points, different groups of Jacobites answered to different commanders, and each had his own opinion of how to fight the battle before them. Old Borlum was now openly defying General Forster's orders.

William knew this fragmented command spelled disaster, but found himself with no choice other than to join the fragmentation. With a small group of a dozen of his own men, all well armed, he took over one of the big houses on Church Street, the main thoroughfare, where the first assault from the English Army began.

Yelling above the sound of nearby shooting from cellars and windows, William urged his men to hold their fire.

'On my mark!' he bellowed. 'Wait for a target, then line up your man.'

Anxious fingers desperate to pull triggers were stayed by Maxwell's command, but finally, as red-coated men poured through the barricade, he ordered them to unleash the fusillade. Unable to get a clean shot, he soon led his men out of the house in a noisy charge, not dissimilar to the berserk yells of their highland cousins, and into the streets for hand-to-hand fighting.

In the midst of battle he felt, for one rare moment, in control, as the fighting began in earnest and the Jacobites started to inflict heavy losses. His sword could do no wrong and his men fought bravely alongside him, riding high on his inspiring confidence.

The English attempted to burn the town, but the winds would not conspire against the Jacobites, although the smoke of the fires gave the redcoats much-needed cover. General Wills's troops were then able to infiltrate the alleys that led behind the bigger houses and gradually more and more of the stately homes were captured by the English, including Patten House, which had commanded the best view for William's men.

Dusk was falling and William ordered two scouts, one of them Pollock, to bring back information on what the English were planning for this night.

'Should we not wait—'

'I'm not waiting for anyone, Mr Pollock. Thanks to the smoke we have no communication any more, so we must make our own decisions.'

Pollock disappeared into the smokescreen and returned at nightfall, dodging muzzle flashes that briefly illuminated the town in ghostly red.

'The English have been told to light a candle in the front window of every property now held by government troops,' he explained.

'Then let's confuse them and light some of our own,' William said.

Pollock looked dubious, but William, preferring action, personally took charge of stealing from house to house, dodging intermittent fire and crouching behind anything that afforded him cover when explosions of light threatened to show him to the enemy, to light a candle in any location where he knew Jacobites held firm.

'Capture any redcoat who trespasses,' he counselled them with a wink.

While William risked his life to baffle an increasingly confident enemy, his commander, Forster, retired to bed.

William spent his night congratulating the pockets of Jacobites on their few casualties. He dealt with the smell of blood on his clothes and its metallic taste clinging to his throat by washing them away with wine, and dozed sporadically propped in the corner of some poor Preston noble's drawing room.

Sunday, 13th November brought a new scenario, however, as General Carpenter arrived in the town with his three units of dragoons to bolster General Wills's numbers, and the tide started to quickly turn against the wearied Scots. The English soldiers began to encircle them, barricading them in the besieged town.

No one dared call William anything but a hero when he urged his leaders to plot their army's escape. 'Live – fight tomorrow and the day after. Do not give our freedom cheaply,' he pleaded, at the risk of appearing cowardly.

But it was already too late. Carpenter's mounted infantry had blocked the road to Liverpool, effectively surrounding the plucky Scots completely. A council of war was held and, in a toxic atmosphere of accusations and threats, Forster and Mackintosh slugged it out until a murky dawn broke over Preston, the weather matching William's dismay as Forster capitulated on behalf of the mostly furious Jacobites. He sent out their surrender, caving in to the English Army's demands.

'Why?' William growled to his elder.

Old Borlum sighed. 'Because the redcoats have it over us, son. I was one of the hostages they demanded while brokering terms. Wills told me if I broke faith he would raze the town and spare not a single one of the rebels. This way we follow your logic: perhaps we live to fight another battle.'

William didn't believe this, but it was a moot point now.

By the following day, more than fifteen hundred of William's compatriots were lined up, heads hung low in defeat, to be paraded before General Wills and his men in the Preston market square and required to yield their weapons. William could hear the redcoats laughing, exchanging jokes at the pitiful pile of pikes, swords, bayonets and muskets alongside pitchforks and axes.

'The farming tools certainly kept you cowardly dogs at bay for long enough!' he yelled, knowing it was pointless and would only bode badly for his future.

'My Lord!' Pollock begged, pale with fear for his superior. 'Your family, sir!'

'If I should die, let my son know I spat in the face of the Protestant whoresons,' he cried, filled with righteous defiance.

A shot rang out so close that William looked down at his body to be sure it wasn't he who had taken the wound. He was whole. Pollock was no longer standing beside him, though; he was on the cobbles, blood pooling beneath him as his eyes stared upward with a glazed expression.

Shocked, William crouched by his side, taking the dying youngster into his lap. 'Pollock…' he groaned.

'I'm sorry, My —' Pollock's head fell to the side as his life slipped away and William felt empty rage grip his insides.

'I didn't want to shoot you, my Lord Earl,' an English officer said smoothly. His voice was slightly effeminate, his tone taunting. 'General Wills assured me you are too valuable. Even so, such blatant insubordination will not be tolerated, even from a prisoner of noble rank. It required punishment as an example to the Jacobite peasants.' He spat for emphasis, near to where William kneeled. 'So I let your man – like a good and loyal vassal – bear the punishment for you. I'm sure you will explain to his family… make good with them.'

William stood up, trembling with rage. The General walked his horse over. 'Don't be an ass, Nithsdale. For every action you take that offends my men, I'll have them kill ten of the peasants who follow you.' William locked gazes with the General, who stared at him coldly, unblinking. The Englishman shrugged. 'I can assure you the good people of Preston would prefer to have ten fewer mouths to feed.' He grimaced and turned to his men. 'Take the nobles away.'

Cowed and helpless, William allowed himself to be shoved along, feeling sickened as he witnessed the Jacobite officers handing over their swords in the churchyard. William and his fellow peers were directed to the Mitre Inn, overlooking the city square.

'So you can endure your humiliation in privacy,' the officer was saying, but William wasn't paying attention.

He did hear Lord Derwentwater's mutters, though. 'Best not to enrage them any further. It's hopeless now, Maxwell. I suspect they shall send us off to our stately homes shortly, and we will have to comfort ourselves with the knowledge that we risked our lives for our true king.'

They were led into the low-beamed, panelled inn, where the smell of old beer and tobacco gave way to the pungent tang of sweat and despair as General Wills supervised their line-up, a look of deep satisfaction evident in his gaze.

'Where is Mackintosh?' William asked, as the dozen or so smug English officers present to witness the surrender of the nobles stilled the clanking of their swords.

'You'd know if he were here, my Lord Nithsdale, by his smell,' Wills replied coolly. 'His ancient cladding – cloak by day and bedding by night, and likely tablecloth and napkin too – makes for a hostile aroma.' His fellow officers laughed. 'He's being sent to Newgate Gaol,' the General continued conversationally. 'And you'll be following his path to prison soon enough, my Lord Earl.'

'I thought we were to be returned to our homes, sir,' Derwentwater bristled. 'My family will pay—'

'Your family, sir, could not pay even close to the price of treachery to your sworn king. No, Lord Derwentwater, I am under instructions from His Majesty to bring all of you rebel lords to London so he might gaze upon your traitorous faces before judgement is passed.'

'You jest,' Derwentwater said, a helpless note in his voice as he threw a worried glance at his fellow lords.

William knew he shouldn't have been surprised, but still his heart raced at the terrifying news that King George would be exacting a different sort of punishment for their disloyalty. He was breaking with tradition; perhaps that was to be part of the mark he'd leave on England: brutality.

'I do not see how any of us could be called traitors, General, when we also were under the instructions of our king. Our true King of Scotland.'

Wills smiled at him. 'I applaud your courage, Maxwell – and your slippery Scottish rationale – but I doubt whether either will save your neck.' He rested his gaze on William a moment longer with relish, and William felt a cold finger of fear trace a line down his spine.

'You plan to hang lords of the realm?' he said in astonishment.

'Did I say "hang"? My apologies if I misled you, sir,' Wills said, and blinked slowly, knowingly, raising his gaze to lock with that of William. 'I will supervise the handing over of your weapons now, gentlemen… if you please. Shall we begin with you, my Lord Nithsdale?'

When all the pistols, swords and daggers had formed a pile on the table before Wills, he graced his prisoners with a fresh smile. 'Thank you.' He turned to his offsider. 'A cup of ale, perhaps, to drown the rebels' sorrows, Mr Cotesworth, then I'll see them on their mounts with one of our foot soldiers to lead each horse. I will not permit them to ride proudly into our great capital. They will arrive booed by the crowds as the traitors they are, with ropes around their necks and hands pinioned behind their backs, sir.' He glanced once more at the lords. 'Enjoy the King's ale, gentlemen.'

ELEVEN

London, December 1978

THE STARS ARE ALIGNING, JANE THOUGHT TO herself as the doors on the Boeing 747 closed and she could finally relax, knowing there would be no chatty fellow passenger seated next to her. The business-class cabin was only scarcely populated, so it promised to be a peaceful trip to Singapore.

The stewardess seemed to drop in on her thoughts. 'Nice and quiet for the next fifteen hours,' she said. 'Though it will get busy out of Asia and into Australia,' she added, placing a glass of apple juice down on a paper coaster. 'My name's Pearl. I'll be looking after you for the flight, Miss Granger.'

Jane admired the straight, slippery dark bob of the smiling woman. She just knew Pearl's hair would look as sharp and glossy in fifteen hours as it did now – unlike her own, which didn't take kindly to perspiration or the static on aeroplane fabric. She was still wearing her dark glasses to hide her eyes, bruised and sore due to tears and lack of sleep. 'Thank you, Pearl. I plan to sleep most of the way.'

The exquisitely made-up attendant nodded and gave her a gentle smile. 'Do you want us to wake you for meals?'

Jane shook her head. 'I've taken half a sleeping pill.'

'Are you sure I can't get you anything to eat before you go to sleep, Miss Granger? Perhaps a snack as soon as we're up?'

She found a smile. 'I'll be fine, thank you.'

Pearl tore a blanket free of its plastic bag and handed it to Jane with lovely hands that sported perfectly shiny plum nail polish that contrasted with her uniform. Jane hoped Pearl hadn't noticed her ragged nails. She'd not attended to them in a fortnight.

'I'll be back with a toiletries kit if you want to kick your shoes off and put on some socks and a sleeping mask,' the hostess said in a soft, breathy voice, her gleaming white smile warmly seductive. 'We won't be turning off the lights for a couple of hours.'

Pearl drifted away, sensing Jane's need to be left alone, and at some stage over the following minutes of taxiing to the runway and her empty glass being cleared, Jane noticed that a small bag of goodies had quietly arrived, along with a menu… just in case.

She was already feeling drowsy, though, and looked forward to the release of enforced sleep and quiet time. Until that release happened, she busied herself with doing as Pearl had suggested: kicking off her shoes, positioning the pillow and getting comfy beneath the blanket. Soon she'd push back her business-class chair as far as she could, but for now she turned her head toward the glittering lights of Manchester Airport, blinking into the inkiness of the drizzly night. She had no intention of getting off at Changi Airport, even to stretch her legs. She'd stay on the plane and let them clean around her before the seven-hour flight into Sydney.

Jane had convinced herself that the sleeping tablet was necessary to make herself rest, as once she hit the Sydney tarmac there would be a swift connection to an Ansett Airlines domestic flight to Alice Springs. And from there, she'd already organised a rental car, anticipating that she'd have her second wind by then to make the three-hour drive down to Uluru.

Jane figured that Will would already be in America, sleeping quietly in the hospital in Maryland with his parents at his side, so she didn't want to waste another second in keeping her promise and fulfilling this curious, almost manic desire to climb Will's rock. To be on the ley line, to stand on one of the Earth's most highly charged vortices according to the New Agers.

To tap into the spiritual power of the world and its magic, her consciousness thought, but she heard it in Robin's voice. *Blood is the golden thread that runs through life's tapestry,* she heard him say again in her mind. She'd not understood where he'd been going with that part of his conversation, but then her time with the clairvoyant had seemed unanchored, as though he knew things that he wanted her to discover for herself... about herself and about Will. That was how it felt, but whether she bought into it she was unsure. Perhaps she already had, or why else would she be travelling many thousands of miles to the other side of the world, on a whim... a fairytale-like belief that she could change the outcome of a life – or lives, as Robin had slyly suggested?

It certainly sounded crazy, but a new energy was powering her. Her parents, predictably, had baulked at her plan and Jane had Hollick to thank for somehow convincing them not to overreact or argue. She had promised that they would know exactly where she planned to be each day; they had codes and numbers for every move she was making, from flights to car rental to her motel beneath Uluru. Her father had organised for a limousine to meet her at the international terminal in Sydney and drive her to the domestic one, which was clearly overkill, but she was not going to argue. She was under instructions to call them at the beginning and end of each day. To show them how reasonable she was about their concerns over this madcap idea, she agreed to all of their demands – or near enough. The offer she felt obliged to make to her sister to accompany her was politely refused, much to Jane's relief. She and Juliette genuinely loved one another but were wildly different, and her sister's look of disbelief when Jane announced her intentions would have been comical if she hadn't also accused Jane of being selfish and childish… and Jane seemed to remember the words *ridiculous* and *laughing stock* being bandied around too.

She thought of Will, who'd spent Christmas Day in his silent world as doctors hovered, measuring vital signs and essentially preparing him to travel. She hoped that when, on Christmas Eve morning, she'd whispered to him her intention to depart on 27th December and where she was headed, he'd heard it somewhere deep in his consciousness and was even cheering for her.

'When I return, you're going to wake up and be Will again,' she'd whispered.

She thought about her frigid Christmas, hastily spent in Wales and mostly in whispered tones. Had her mother cooked a turkey? She didn't think so. Couldn't remember, didn't care. Ah, that's right, she'd baked a ham… 'Best not to waste it.' Jane didn't want to relive those two difficult days. She'd slept through most of Boxing Day and had not emerged downstairs to meet the visitors who'd come to pay their respects and share their sadness.

Jane felt herself being shaken; she wanted to grumble at her mum for disturbing her, but Catelyn never called her 'Miss Granger'. She pulled off the eye mask to find that Pearl was keen to collect her blanket and pillows, as they were making their approach into Singapore. Jane obliged. Fifteen or so hours of Will's suspended life had slipped by as she'd slept.

After touchdown she yawned as eager fellow passengers packed up and disappeared. The crew smiled indulgently at her and now even Pearl was leaving; a new crew would take over from Singapore. Jane felt guilty that a cleaner in blue overalls, a vacuum pack on her back, had to work around her. She stood to stretch before taking time to neaten her hair and clothes and put on her shoes. She wanted to brush her teeth, but knew she'd have to wait until they were airborne again.

Jane watched as a couple of familiar faces returned, but before long the business cabin was near enough full of new ones, including a man in a suit who became her neighbour. She was grateful that he obviously didn't want to engage in conversation, as he nodded hello and then ignored her, burying his head in a book. Perfect. She would do the same on this second leg.

The flight passed painlessly because of the adventures of a man called Jason Bourne, who had all sorts of problems after suffering from amnesia. It made her wonder, as she caught her first glimpse of the sparkling white city that Sydney showed itself to be, whether Will might have memory loss when he woke – she refused to add *if he woke*.

The sunlight winked off the gently moving water of the harbour and glittered on the mirror-like finishes of the city's skyscrapers. She'd had no idea that Sydney would be this modern or sparkling; after the grime and weariness of London it looked positively surreal and fresh.

Glimmers of new hope fizzed through her, making her heart pound a bit harder as they hit the tarmac on a sizzling hot 28th December morning. She hated the fact that Will would be kicking off his New Year's Day sleeping strapped to a bed. Maybe she could sign his name and her own in the book at the top of Uluru before the New Year ticked over, and call on all the energies – spiritual, magnetic, astral, ancient – to help return her to the pathway she and Will had been on.

At the Institute in Queen Square, Ellen was still feeling the effects of Christmas festivities. Phew, she'd had a little bit more of the 'merry', as her family called it, than she'd planned. And coming in today, back on shift after a few days' holiday, had been tougher than she had imagined it would be. But she was glad to see Will again. Poor man… such a handsome guy too, and lost in his prime. She smiled sadly at his slack, blank face before she glanced at his file.

'Hi, Ellen,' one of the other intensive care nurses called.

'Oh, hi, Gail. How was yours?'

'I worked.' She shrugged. 'It was okay. The kids spent it with their dad. It was his and the wicked stepmother's turn. I'll see them tomorrow and they'll be with me after their New Year's party.'

Ellen gave a sympathetic nod and squeezed her colleague's hand. 'So we're together on the ward for New Year's Eve, then?'

'Afraid so.' Gail laughed.

She got down to work. 'No change here, I see.' Ellen nodded at Will.

Gail shook her head. 'Nothing. They're taking him next week. He's off to America.'

'So soon?' Ellen asked, surprised. Her friend nodded. 'Wow, I've lost track of time.'

'Sad. I mean, they're going to put him and themselves through that traumatic journey and anyone can see he's not coming out of this soon.'

Ellen frowned, leaning her head to one side. 'These cases are always baffling... none of us knows for sure what might happen.'

'The father is such an angry sod,' Gail said, looking over her shoulder. 'I'll bet he beats his wife.'

Ellen gave her colleague a look of reproach. 'I don't have children, but I can't imagine what it feels like to look at your child, injured, potentially dead, and feel so helpless. I can forgive his rage. He's trying to do something, at least. Will could sit up next week and that angry father of his could shake a fist and say he was right all along.'

Gail nodded, then cut Ellen a wicked glance. 'I'd keep him like this if he were my husband, though.' She winked.

Ellen admonished her with a click of her tongue. 'Bad girl. But he *is* gorgeous. How's his fiancée doing?'

'Gone!' Gail nodded, mischief twinkling in her eyes. 'His mother told me that – um, what's her name?'

'Jane,' Ellen offered.

'Jane, yes. Well, apparently Jane isn't coping and has decided to take a journey to the other side of the world, to... oh, find herself or some other mystical thing.' At Ellen's surprise, she added, 'I'm not lying. She's gone.'

'That's not what I mean. I spoke to her on the morning of Christmas Eve and she was really strong, I thought. She did say she might be going away briefly, but I thought she meant to Wales – that's where her family comes from.'

'Well, apparently it's Australia. Anyway, I'd better be off. He's all yours tonight, you lucky thing! I get Mr Stephens while you get Mr Fabulous.'

Ellen returned to Will's side, observing the prone man, the offer that his parents had made on Christmas Eve still burning in her mind.

'Come with us to America. You know how to care for him, Ellen,' Diane had bleated.

The angry father had shrugged. 'Just help us get him to Baltimore. Then stay on, all expenses paid, for a holiday. Come back whenever you want.'

Ellen had thought of nothing else over the last few days. The idea of taking a break from the humdrum was more than tempting. She had thought she might talk it over with Jane and was surprised to hear she'd gone overseas. It sounded heartless of Jane, but in the few days Ellen had known her, Will's fiancée hadn't struck her as anything but heartbroken.

Well, it looked like she'd be making the decision alone. It wasn't a hard one. She was due so much holiday leave that the hospital would probably make it easy for her to take a long vacation. She'd always wanted to visit cities like New York, Chicago, perhaps even Los Angeles and San Francisco – see where some of those TV shows she watched were made. And she would be paid for it! She sighed, suddenly excited. She'd say yes to the Americans when they came in later tonight.

Ellen focused back on Will. He'd lost weight, but his frame was still broad, muscles still defined, and his formerly burnished skin was yet to pale completely. She thought about her own boyfriend, Adam, with his paunchy belly and freckled body and those almost comically skinny legs. She didn't really love him. Their thirteen-month relationship had long ago lost its romance and now just felt like habit. Comfortable, but boring. Would she hurt him by leaving, or let him off the hook? Both, probably.

'I'll take such good care of you,' she murmured quietly as she sponged Will's face. She liked to talk to her comatose patients. She reached for a comb, having paid attention to how Jane would straighten his damp hair and then tousle it again.

'He doesn't like it tidy,' Jane had explained to her, barely holding back the tears.

'There, just how you like it, Will,' she said, admiring her effort. 'It's the coldest day of the year today. The weather has decided to have one last blast at us before the clock ticks over into 1979.' She spoke in a bright but soft voice, just for him. 'I reckon it will snow tonight, which is no good for me because I'm on the bus tomorrow morning. Mind you, the shivering may do me some good. I ate far too much over Christmas. Now, before we turn you over to prevent those sores, let's just do the vitals again.' She reached for his wrist. 'Yes, I know you're hooked up to clever equipment, but I like doing some of this stuff the traditional way. Besides, maybe you can feel it.' She grinned at him. 'Now shush, I'm counting!' she joked at Will's impassive expression.

Ellen was concentrating on the second hand of her watch, lightly feeling Will's pulse tap against her fingertips, when out of the corner of her eye she saw his brow suddenly furrow, as though he were concentrating intensely. It happened so fast that she was sure she'd imagined it; his forehead had smoothed in a heartbeat. But she didn't imagine it when his fist suddenly clenched and relaxed, because she felt it.

'Will?' she said, excited. 'Will? Can you hear me? It's Ellen, your number one fan! Come on, Will, show me you can hear me.' She reached over him and pressed the call button on the wall.

Soon enough, others arrived. She was glad it was Dr Evans on duty. She had enormous respect for him, plus he too was easy on the eye and made the long night shifts more enjoyable.

'Ellen?'

'Will just moved and it was deliberate.'

'Describe what occurred,' Evans said, reaching for the printout from the machine that was keeping track of the electrical output from his patient's brain.

She told him concisely.

He nodded. 'Yes, I see it here.'

'I was talking to him, but I don't think he reacted to anything I said. When he frowned, it was as though he were concentrating on something distant.' She shrugged. 'Sorry. I can only tell you what I saw, how it struck me.'

'No, it's valuable,' Evans assured her. 'We don't take enough notice of visuals sometimes. I think we rely too much on this sort of stuff,' he said, flicking the printout. 'Well, that's very positive. Okay, I think we should get stuck into a bank of tests and see if we can provoke another reaction. He could be surfacing from the coma.'

She nodded, feeling a thrill of optimism for Will, but sensing her grasp on the trip to America slipping. 'Do we say anything yet?'

Evans shook his head. 'No, let's not give his family false hope. If we can stimulate that response again, then maybe we'll have something to go on.'

'Come on, Will. Hold that thought, whatever it was,' she whispered. 'Whatever you felt, whoever you were thinking of just now, find it again. Make my New Year!'

TWELVE

Uluru, December 1978

JANE WAS STAYING AT A MOTEL THAT squatted in the shadow of Uluru, and the rock towered above it like an ancient sleeping beast. The motel operator – who'd introduced himself as Baz – had told her as he took her breakfast order, in an accent she had to really concentrate on to understand, that the government was 'doing away with' the accommodation she was currently enjoying.

Enjoying? Jane had never stayed anywhere so basic. Then again, though not glamorous, her room was spotlessly clean and tidy. She was comfortable and had, in all truth, slept her first peaceful night since the attack; her sleep hadn't been disturbed and she had no memory of dreaming. It was also the first morning since Will's attack when she'd woken and remained dry-eyed. The night had been clear, cold and lit by a billion stars glittering against a velvet dome. Most importantly, it had been silent, save the scuttle of small creatures outside and the odd haunting call of a bird. Yes, it might well be basic – this was, when all was said and done, one of the most remote tourist outposts in the world – but Jane genuinely had no complaint. Besides, she had her eye focused on the prize alone and didn't care what it took to win.

'Yeah,' the owner murmured, as he came back to slam down a thick, squat cup containing weak-looking coffee that she just knew was going to taste awful. 'They're building a big new complex – a bloody village, they're calling it,' he continued. 'A resort with swimming pools and the like, and bloody fountains and staff in uniforms, but get this...' He paused dramatically so he was sure he had her complete attention. 'It's fourteen kilometres away! None of this stepping outside and nearly breaking your neck looking up at the Rock. We'll have to bus you lot in from bloody miles away!'

She shrugged, and said, 'It's not a bad idea to turn it into a national park,' before realising her comment was likely to fan the fires of discontent. She hastily added: 'Because it's so, so beautiful here.'

'Yeah, well, can't stop progress, can we?'

She shook her head. He wasn't shifting. She blinked and waited, sipping her coffee, and it was every bit as horrible as she'd anticipated. The air conditioner thundered in the background like a jet. She was one of only four people in the dining room and the laminated tablecloth beneath her elbow felt sticky from last night's meal; she didn't want to check.

'Most people don't come at this time of year,' he continued, scratching his belly. 'It's a bit too bloody hot right now – be careful, it can get up to forty on the Rock midsummer. I'm surprised you're here, although maybe I shouldn't be. You Poms pull off your clothes to sunbake when it's bloody fifteen degrees.' She smiled faintly, unable to translate from Celsius to Fahrenheit, but she grasped his meaning. 'You climbing today; is that why you're up so early?'

She nodded. 'I want to sign the book at the top.'

'Yeah, righto. But it's much harder than it looks. I've done it loads of times and I can tell you it never gets easier. Take my advice: you hold on to that chain for dear life. But I'm not even sure today's the day for it.'

Jane frowned. 'Oh? Why's that?'

'Storm brewing. Probably hit later on.'

Jane pressed a paper napkin the colour of egg yolk to her

lips, realising only now as the cheap tissue stuck slightly to her mouth that it had been chosen to match the plastic daffodils in their fake terracotta pot just near the faux crystal plastic salt and pepper shakers on her table. 'How much later on?'

'Ah, winds'll probably hit this arvo or maybe midday, they reckon, although I don't think it'll wait that long. And we've got some rain coming.'

She looked crestfallen. Why hadn't she thought to check on the weather? Wasn't it always ridiculously sunny and drought-ridden in Australia? Wasn't this a desert? 'When is rain forecast?'

'Tonight, they're saying. Maybe early tomorrow.' He gave her a faint look of sympathy as he began to clear her plate. 'It's the wet season, luv. You gotta expect it.'

'So, windy this afternoon, stormy tomorrow?'

He shrugged. 'That's what the bureau is saying, but those clowns never get it right. My arthritic knees can warn me better.'

She tried to smile. 'And what do your knees say?'

'That she'll be blowing earlier than this afternoon.'

Jane glanced out past the stiff net curtains hanging across the window close to where she sat. It was closing on 5.45 and dawn was easing her way across the sky with bright pink fingers of light that reached toward the hulking shadow of the still sleeping Uluru. 'What about the others?' she said, nodding toward his guests.

'Film crew from Tokyo. They won't climb. They're interested in the ancient rock paintings. They've got a guide arriving any moment.'

She weighed up the odds of his caution. 'It's still so early. I mean, the sky looks happy enough to me.' Her mouth twisted as she wrestled with the dilemma. 'You reckon it's an hour up and another hour back?'

He shrugged. 'Depends on how fast you climb and whether

you hang around at the top, but that's about right. Someone once did the ascent in seventeen minutes.'

She looked again at the serene skies, which had lightened in the last few moments while they talked. 'I'll take my chances. I'm used to trekking around Snowdonia.' He looked unmoved, clearly ignorant of where in the world that was. Jane didn't think she'd mention Wales and open up a new conversation; she stood instead. 'I'll head out as soon as dawn breaks and be back before nine.'

'I'm headed to Erldunda, but don't worry, I'll have them put the kettle on at nine for your morning tea,' he said with a wink. 'Oh, yeah, I promised the kitchen I'd ask: will you be wanting lunch? It's just that the film crew won't eat here and that leaves only you.'

Jane shook her head, giving him the answer she knew he wanted. 'I won't either, though thank you. I might try and stay ahead of that rain and head back to Alice Springs when I return from the Rock.'

He raised an eyebrow. 'That soon? Okay, no worries. Climb carefully. Drink lots of water.'

'I will.'

She nipped back to her room to grab a light waterproof jacket and filled an old soft-drink bottle with water, which she then thought better of carrying with her. She drank half of it instead, gasping at the volume of water. She was dressed in shorts, stout sneakers, a T-shirt that covered her arms to avoid sunburn and a hat with a flap to protect her neck. She remembered the block-out that Baz had recommended when she checked in, and smeared some of the white zinc paste onto her nose.

Jane felt energised, excited even, as she clambered into her rental car to drive to the car park, from where a path led to the spot where all climbers began their ascent.

'This is it, Will,' she murmured at the wheel as she unhurriedly guided the car into a parking space. She knew she was well ahead of the tour buses, which would arrive in about one hour's time. She wanted to be on the summit before anyone else, wanted no distractions, no other voices to interrupt her peace – especially while allegedly on the ley line that connected with the vortex that was Uluru.

She turned off the engine and stepped out of the car, immediately struck by the powerful silence. Uluru waited for her, still clothed in its purple robe of night. Even though she shivered in the pre-dawn shadows, Jane could already sense the tiptoe of warmth across the desert. Any moment now the sunlight would steal across the dark brown earth, urging it to red, and Uluru would stretch, shake off that robe and glow in the first of the morning rays.

Jane saw a large gecko with striped, scaly skin skitter across the sand nearby. It paused as if listening, waiting. She watched its tongue slip out to wipe its large, bulbous eyes. She returned her gaze to Uluru and decided that photos she'd seen did not do it justice. She began to appreciate Will's fascination; it really did appear to rise majestically – and somewhat incongruously – from the flat earth, as though magically conjured.

From a distance it looked perfectly smooth, but the edifice had folds and creases as well as intriguing weathering marks showing curls and striations. Jane fancied that the elements had battered the Rock in order to write their stories on its canvas for people to interpret and pass down from generation to generation. She wondered if the ley line that crossed this point passed through her as she stood here; she hoped it did. Hoped she was standing right on it, and that it would connect her with Will's lost mind.

'Find your way back,' she said, imagining his spirit latching on to the ancient straight track into her soul. They were old souls – he'd said that, hadn't he?

She looked over her shoulder as a breeze ruffled her hair. A few clouds, newly gathered, were illuminated pink like pillows of fairy floss, attesting to the bureau's forecast of rain on the way. However, for now they looked harmless enough.

Pink sky at night, shepherd's delight; Pink sky at morning, shepherd's warning, she heard in her mind. An old adage her grandmother had been fond of quoting.

She wasn't worried. The clouds were far away and she was too close to Will's salvation to let grumpy skies turn her back. *Walk*, she told herself. *Don't linger another moment.* Tiny birds chirruped and flitted and she could hear the prattle of insects as they woke up. Tiny footprints were impressed on the fine, glistening sand. Lizards, birds, mice, snakes… they'd been on this old, old seabed long before her.

Jane realised the dawn chill had disappeared. It felt like a perfect temperature now – neither hot nor cool. It had reached her blood's warmth, bathing her in a womb-like sense of peace. She fancied she could hear Uluru sighing at her approach, wanting to commune with her. She knew the locals preferred that tourists not clamber on their sacred site.

'Just me,' she whispered selfishly. 'If not for Will's and my names at the top, you'll hardly know I've been here,' she promised.

At the base she stared up at the fiery, pockmarked sandstone, at its clefts and folds, which looked like part of a thick rock blanket that Uluru had pulled over the ancient knowledge it hid.

Since she'd arrived at Alice Springs, people had been sharing warnings.

It's over three hundred feet high.

You're too light – if the wind's high, you could get blown off.

The climb will fool you. I hope you're fit.

Don't disrespect the Anangu. Would you clamber over your local church's altar?

Take a pen.

Well, she had her pen and she'd made peace in her mind with desecrating a holy site, through the rationale that she was saving a life.

She began her ascent, emptying her mind of everything but Will and her desire to bring him back to her. Somehow, between taking off in London and the present moment, the notion had slotted into her mind that this trip was her salvation too. Hopefully she would return a changed person, with a new attitude to Will and being in love.

Jane soon passed a cluster of red boulders that were no doubt the 'chicken rocks' Baz had joked about the previous evening.

'Chicken rocks?' she'd repeated.

He'd grinned. 'Yeah, they're where most people chicken out… long before they even reach the chain!' he'd chortled.

Now she pushed past them, determined not to be like most others. The chain was there for a very good reason, Jane discovered, after about ten minutes of using it. Uluru was deceptively steep and smooth enough that she didn't feel entirely secure even with the traction her sneakers were giving her. She found that she was relying heavily on the thick, solid metal chain to haul herself up each slow step. The sun was smiling fully now, and despite the effort it took to climb, it felt empowering to be here in the desert with only its creatures and its spirits for company. The breeze was pleasantly cooling and Jane felt strong for the first time in what felt like an eternity of misery. She cast her thanks to Robin and Geoff for their encouragement.

Jane knew that the ascent was over one and a half kilometres long, but even so she was taken aback when she finally reached the end of the chain at the close of what was presumably the toughest section, only to find she had covered what looked to be merely a third of the climb. The edifice was taunting her, it seemed, and had hidden most of itself when she looked up at it from the base.

The breeze had stiffened at this height too – she felt exposed now – but for the moment she revelled in its cooling of her damp face. She paused to pull off her waterproof windcheater and tie it around her waist and wished she had thought to bring the water, but took a deep breath and headed upward. This section definitely wasn't as steep, but she was wearier now and suspected she would have to maintain her pace and energy for a long way yet. She knew from her treks around Snowdonia not to look up. The trick with climbing was to focus just on the next step, placing each foot carefully and securely, covering the distance steadily but surely.

She could hear the whoosh of her blood thumping rhythmically near her temples. Her breathing was coming harder, but she smiled: the exertion made her feel alive again. She should, however, have tied her hair back, she realised; the wind was having fun whipping it around her face. She paused again to tuck it inside the back of her T-shirt. Not terribly effective, but it would have to do.

Jane stole a glance around her, marvelling at how high she had climbed and the boundless view the height gave her of the surrounding desert. She could see the scrubby spinifex grasses, wattle trees and spindly desert oaks that she'd read about in the guidebook she'd bought. The wildflowers of spring were long gone, but Jane could imagine how beautiful they must have looked against their burnt-orange canvas.

She stepped up and onward, emptying her mind again of conscious thought, but exquisitely aware of minutiae: how her muscles were tensed in her calves, how she was perspiring and could feel the prickle of the wet patch on her back, how her normally soft blonde hair was curiously itchy against her skin because of the dampness. She could taste saltiness on her lips and her eyes stung a bit from her sweat. She'd forgotten sunglasses and felt fortunate that so far this wasn't one of those achingly bright days, like yesterday, when it almost hurt to look up at the sharp, sunny sky.

The cry of an eagle caught her attention, dragged her from the void of her mind. She shielded her gaze, looking for its dark, distinctive shape hovering overhead. There it was: a wedge-tailed eagle, called walawuru locally, she'd read. Its cry was lonely and haunting, like a woman's shriek, echoing her own feelings. Odd. Just moments ago she had been feeling so upbeat. Why had this bird's piercing cry stirred a sudden, inexplicable feeling of dread and dislocation?

Jane sat down to take a breather. It was warming up fast, and the atmosphere was turning muggy. Totally different from how it had felt on arrival yesterday afternoon. The humidity had been gathering without her sensing it while she'd climbed and she could hear the wind now, like a lion's roar against a cliff-face. Somewhere below her it was whistling shrilly, as though hurtling through the hollows of the ancient rock.

The gusty conditions had crept up on her too, and she noticed they were no longer comforting or pleasant. They had strengthened enough that she was yearning for the chain again. But she was close now... too close to consider anything other than pressing on. She touched her pocket, reassuring herself that her biro was there. The eagle was back, its shriek even more ghostly as it challenged the cries of the wind, which had torn some of her hair free from its attempted trapping.

Desertion in the desert, the eagle called at her as it hovered high, directly above her.

Jane ignored the fanciful notion that the bird was mocking her. She wished again for something to anchor herself to. There was no doubt in her mind any more that the claim of people having been blown off was not a fantasy. Her nine stone certainly felt light enough on this precarious angle that she believed she could be blown away. There would be nothing to grab at, or hang on to, if she lost her footing. She forced herself not to look down or even across the landscape until she was on the summit's plateau. With each step she planted her feet as solidly as she could, leaning almost at right angles into the wind, which wanted to knock her sideways and tumble her across the face of Uluru.

You shouldn't be here. You shouldn't climb our sacred site, the eagle baited.

Jane trudged on, much more slowly, taking great care to ensure each footstep was secure, hands tensed like claws very close to the Rock's surface so that she was almost on all fours. She was no longer perspiring. Instead she was cold, cold with fear. Where had that come from? When had fear penetrated? Voices were whispering now on the wind, nagging at her. She couldn't make out their words. *It's just the wind*, she told herself; *your imagination is running away with you. This is the right choice. Robin told you to seek the path; this is it.* This was the ley line that connected her to Will. This was the vortex that would deliver him back to her and her to him.

Finally, unbelievably, she scrabbled over the last few feet and hauled herself onto the summit, lying on her belly, panting. It shouldn't have been this hard. Why was she so exhausted? Her parents had tried to tell her that she was fragile; *brittle*, her father had said. Her mother had railed that she hadn't slept, had lost weight, that her body was fatigued and ravaged by grief. Her sister had tried to counsel that, physically as well as emotionally, she wasn't strong enough right now. But she wouldn't be told. Had refused their advice.

Jane had dutifully called her parents from reception on arrival and the connection had been scratchy enough that she was all but shouting down the phone. Still, she'd managed to produce a breezy tone, which wasn't all feigned, so they were probably feeling secure in the knowledge that she'd reached her destination, even though they didn't understand her journey or her driving ambition to climb to the summit of a massive rock in the middle of Australia.

It did sound peculiar. No longer daft in that amusing, 'What a funny loony you are!' kind of way. She lay here with the wind growling around her, knowing there was no help at hand should anything happen to her. It was madness of a dangerous kind. Only Baz knew she was here. He wouldn't be back at the motel for hours to raise the alarm should anything occur. *Nothing's going to happen*, she admonished herself, looking up toward where the book awaited her. *Sign our names and down I go.*

This was an unhinged idea, she finally allowed. *Everyone's right. You're lost in guilty grief and making poor decisions.* It was as though rationality were only just seeping through her mind, past the craziness of the last few days... the preoccupation with magic and miracles... and only now was she appreciating the peril she'd put herself into.

She tried to stand, but immediately went down on her knees as the wind gleefully began to tease her with its strength.

I can push you off, it whistled. *You could become a statistic. There've been quite a few deaths already of foolhardy tourists who didn't pay attention to good advice... who ignored the sacred site... who wanted to trip the light fantastic of the ley lines.*

Jane yelled aloud – no words, just pure emotion.

Then she began to talk aloud to herself. 'Ignore everything,' she calmed herself, glad to hear her own voice, even though the wind tried to steal that as well. 'Sign and go home!'

Baz had warned her to make the descent *like a donkey*. 'Take a winding path down – longer, but safer. Don't be tempted to descend in a straight line. And don't be too proud to slither down on your arse,' he'd added with a wink.

Jane rallied despite the sky's suddenly ominous aspect, the sinister clouds clustering directly above. They'd crept up on her – in partnership with the wind in their silent, hasty stealth. The gusts began to intensify further now that she was on the summit and vulnerable. On her knees she half crawled, half staggered to the book, flesh protesting at the hardness of the rock, bones grinding. She was trapped between the pressures of nature and gravity, one of which, the wind, wasn't giving a smidgen.

Her shaking hand reached for the biro that was tied on to the book with a piece of weathered string. Normally, somewhere like this, she would have read previous entries, but now she was too distracted and frightened.

She pressed the pen down onto the lined paper to enter the date in the appropriate column. The biro dimpled the page but made no other mark; it had run out of ink. She scratched with it, made frantic squiggles on the page, but it refused to write for her.

'Shit!' she yelled, flinging it aside and digging into her pocket for her spare pen. Oh, how sound that advice had been.

She dragged it out, her breath coming raggedly now, and after pulling off its plastic lid with her teeth she once again put nib to paper. But just as she was about to scrawl the date, Jane screamed in fright as something – a coach driver who was just pulling his tour bus into the car park would later describe it as a rogue squall – howled and shoved angrily against her.

At ground level, where lizards capered and birds flitted, that same wind blew hats off and made some people squeal as they felt hurried along, but mostly it provoked laughter and a decision not to risk climbing today.

Yet on the exposed summit of the great Uluru, that same rogue squall hit a vulnerable woman at nearly three times the speed as had entertained the other tourists. And as it knocked away Jane's already tenuous hold on the smooth surface, easily flicking her legs from under her, she screamed for help, but her cries were yanked away, borne on the winds into the desertscape beyond.

Jane rolled several times, feeling the unyielding surface bruise her flesh, and then she was suddenly scooped up and shot close to the edge of the massive red rock. She was half running, half falling, aware that she was now headed for certain death. She should have listened to the advice of those who loved her.

She'd let Will go to America and now she was even further

from him, and most likely going to die before he did. What a tragic couple. *A modern Shakespeare would love it*, she thought as she toppled. His parents would keep him alive, believing it was devotion and love while they witnessed him wither to a husk of himself. Better he died than lived the life of a seeming corpse. But still she clung to hope.

Stretching before her was the vast central Australian desert, full of secret knowledge. Was this what the powerful Earth vortex wanted? To lure her here, only to kill her? Relentlessly pushed and toppled and scooped closer to the killing edge, she screamed at the magic that so many believed had existed here for millennia… in this place of ancient cunning.

'How can I save you, Will?' she yelled in desperate rage.

You'll need courage.

The response was a thought. It had no voice, but rode on the wind and pushed into her mind fiercely enough to make her gasp.

Do you have it, though? demanded the thought. *Do you, Jane?*

For Will, I have the courage of every brave man or woman who's walked this Earth, her mind growled back.

Magic exacts a price.

I'll pay it! she shrieked. *Make him safe!*

And the wind keened like a wolf howling as the clouds broke over Uluru and turned the hulking rock from red to purple-grey beneath the sheet of rain that engulfed it, sending cascades of rivulets and tiny waterfalls pounding down its crevices, turning its surface slippery.

But Jane felt none of it. She was aware only of falling as the wind got its way and shoved her off the giant edifice. Her screaming faded, until there was only the silence and a void as death beckoned and opened its arms to her. And what consumed her was that she had never signed Will's name or hers in the book. Neither of them was real any more… they had both winked out of existence and all she could hope for was that their spirits would meet on the ley line down which she fancifully decided she was hurtling, on an ancient and cosmic straight track to her death.

THIRTEEN

Peebles, November 1715

DISTANTLY, JANE HEARD WOMEN. FIRST, THE CHITTERING sound of excitement and then a single voice, firm in spite of its gentle tone.

'She's swooned. Hurry, Cecilia, fetch the smelling bottle.'

The rank smell of ammonia startled her into full consciousness and she coughed and spluttered, pushing away the hands that fussed, vaguely aware of being dressed in frilly clothing and not understanding why.

'She's all right, Mary, thank heavens.'

Jane gasped a new breath, her eyes startled open. 'Where am I?'

There were two women; she recognised neither and kept blinking, confused as to why they were dressed in period costume and leaning over her with worried expressions. One of them was holding her hand.

'Feeling better?' that one said. She had eyes like liquid chocolate and coarse dark hair parted in the middle. It was pulled back loosely beneath a small linen cap trimmed with lace, leaving a modest festoon of curls around her squarish face. Jane would have described her as handsome rather than pretty.

Her companion, however, clutching the offensive bottle, was doll-like by comparison, with large blue eyes, hair the shade of ripe corn silk and a smile to melt hearts. Her hair was swept gently behind her head and was without a bonnet.

Both looked trapped in a costume drama.

Jane, confused, nevertheless lost interest in the women, her attention snagged by her surroundings as she took in the rich timber panelling, the moulded stone fireplace and the bookshelves that lined the room. The pervading smell, apart from the sweet timber burning in the grate and the lingering ammonia, was leather, possibly from the covers of the books.

'Where am I?' she repeated.

'In the library, dearest,' the doll said. She had a roundish face and wore no make-up or jewellery, but she was dressed exquisitely in clothes that the BBC costume department would surely appreciate having returned.

'Who are you?' Jane whispered.

'It's me, darling Winifred. Mary. Don't you recognise me? You fainted. The news was a shock, I know, but you must take heart.'

'Will...' Jane began.

'Yes, Winifred dear, we know,' the bonneted one – not called Mary – said, taking charge. 'Please be still. You have been so unwell. We know you've been worried about him, and now this turn of events. But William is not injured.'

'He's woken?' she asked, shaken by where she found herself, but thrilled by the news that Will might have returned to consciousness.

But neither answered, as they had both turned at the sound of someone entering the library. A tall, dark man in a long, chestnut-coloured wig strode toward them. Jane gave a small gasp – half amusement, half shock. 'It's cuts and bruises, nothing serious,' he said wearily, in answer to the question in their combined gazes. 'However, the situation is serious. He will be taken to London, apparently.'

Jane frowned, realising she too was dressed in strange silks and was showing off most of her chest in a gown with a rounded, low-cut bodice. Uncomfortable pressure was emanating from an upside-down triangle of embroidered linen that held the dress tightly against her breasts. And she was lying down on a sofa.

Was she dreaming? Dreaming had never felt this real. 'Why is Will back in London? He's meant to be in—'

'He's not *back* there yet, sister,' Mary said. 'He's on his *way* there with the English Army. I beg you not to fret. Your health has been sorely weak; you know how anxious we have been for you.'

Jane blinked in deep consternation. All right, this was a dream... must be. She had to get out of it; she tried to wake herself, but failed. Vague memories of climbing up the face of a huge rock, being smashed around by a terrible storm and then falling began to filter into her mind. She clutched at these images, reaching toward reality, hoping to drag herself from this dreamscape. But her recollections were disrupted by the tall, slim woman – she possessed an achingly sweet smile, Jane thought irrelevantly – who perched herself on the edge of the sofa and took Jane's hand... again.

'Winifred, you've always been the strong one. I know you'll be strong now for Will, for the family.'

What on earth was this woman talking about? Who was Winifred? And more to the point... 'Who are you?' she repeated, frowning.

The woman stared back at her with a flustered expression, her eyes misting. 'It's Cecilia. Cecilia Evans, your lady's maid and oldest companion. Why don't you recognise me?'

'I don't recognise any of you,' Jane admitted frankly, sitting up.

Cecilia pursed her lips. 'It must be the fever,' she said to the others before returning her gaze to Jane. 'We thought we'd lost *you* a few days ago; now it seems *you've* lost your memory.'

Physically, Jane felt as though she'd had one wine too many and her mind were dulled, filled with cotton wool. 'I don't understand where I am, or why I'm dressed in these ridiculous clothes, or why you're talking to me as though we're straight out of an Austen novel, or how you know Will, or most of all why he's in London.'

Cecilia blinked back at her in clear consternation. 'Oh, Win, dear. 'Twas such a devil, this fever of yours. You look stronger… though I daresay the sickness has muddled your mind.'

Mary was back. 'Winifred…'

'I am *not* Winifred. I'm Jane. You're all potty. Is this some sort of weekend with the Georgians?'

Mary and Cecilia shared a glance of fresh concern.

'Did she fall? Hit her head?' the man asked.

'No, Charles. She was resting on the couch when the messenger came. She read the letter lying down. Upon my blessing, though, dear Winifred looks to have some colour back in her cheeks at last.'

Charles and his huge wig hove into view, the better to see for himself. 'Indeed, madam, you look ten times better than you did yesterday. The fever is broke, and your strength is returning, it seems – which is a blessing, for you must be especially strong of heart for what must now be endured.'

Jane couldn't hold her laughter in any longer – not now that he was hovering above her with fat, chestnut curls dangling about his head. 'That truly is an outrageously large wig, Charles. Don't you feel ridiculous?'

He stared at her as though she might have regained her health but her mind was surely lost. 'You'd better call the physic, Mary. Mayhap she needs to be bled.'

'Bled?' Jane repeated in horror. She rallied and stood up, pulling and scratching at the silks that rustled with every movement. Her hand went to the stiff bodice that held her tight, and only now did she become aware of the huge, hooped skirt billowing beneath her waist. 'I can barely breathe in this get-up. Someone will have to undo it, or I really will pass out.'

Mary glanced pointedly at Charles, who took his leave. 'Yes, of course, dear Winifred,' she said, and moved to Jane's back to start undoing buttons. 'We'll loosen the stomacher.'

'Can someone please tell me about Will?' Jane asked. 'All of it!'

It was Cecilia who obliged. 'I shan't spare you, Win, for I know you prefer candour. Your lord husband wrote that the men were divided. He was imprisoned with his fellow peers, including the Englishman Lord Derwentwater; they handed over their swords and other weapons at the Mitre Inn in Preston and were put under guard.' Jane was still registering *your lord husband*, her expression clouded with fresh confusion, by the time Cecilia paused for her to say something, and when she didn't Cecilia continued. 'When the messenger left Lancashire with this letter, William had been kept at Preston for several days, although four of the regular officers had already been court-martialled and executed, as we understand it.'

Jane blinked at her. She had no grasp of what they were talking about, but neither did she care. All she wanted to know about was Will.

Cecilia again continued after leaving a polite pause for Jane to say something. 'We've been told that the prisoners were divided up and that William, together with the other peers, was put into a carriage and taken to Wigan under the escort of dragoons.'

'Wigan,' Jane repeated with laughing disbelief, desperately trying to make sense of this onslaught of information.

'But they're definitely on the way to London,' Mary continued from behind her, where she was loosening the ties on Jane's bodice. 'They paused at Middlewich and William was able to get the letter away to you. I think you swooned before you finished reading it, so I took the liberty of reading it instead. He needs you to send some money via a messenger to Barnet.'

'He also thinks you should endeavour to travel to London,' Cecilia added.

Mary reappeared in front of her and Jane felt she could breathe again now. Both women smiled hesitantly, waiting.

'Listen to me now, both of you,' Jane said slowly. 'I think you have me confused with someone else. I am talking about Will Maxwell.'

They both smiled sadly. It was Mary who spoke. 'Yes, dearest. William Maxwell, Earl of Nithsdale. He is my brother, your beloved husband and the father of young William and Anne,' she said encouragingly, as though willing Jane to agree. When Jane didn't respond with more than blinking confusion, Mary continued hurriedly, golden curls dancing around her face. 'And though my heart wants to be light, for your sake, I think I must say what's in it, dearest. He's in trouble most keen with the English king. King George will seek to make an example of the highborn who promoted this rebellion.' She paused, seemingly keen for Jane to grasp the import of her words. 'The government has six nobles as prisoners.'

'The Earl of Nithsdale,' Jane repeated slowly, her tone filled with incredulity, as though she'd heard nothing since Mary had uttered those words. This was the forebear Diane Maxwell was so proud to be associated with; it was the very man Will's parents had been researching in Scotland when their son had been attacked. Will had never given her the full story; he'd waved her off with *yadda yadda*, bored with the family connection his mother dined off. What had happened, though? He'd never told her what had happened to the man who had been accused of treachery!

'This is not happening,' she murmured, feeling unbalanced.

Another confused glance was exchanged by the women.

Cecilia spoke first. 'Winifred, you really must have hit your head. How did we miss that?'

Jane took a deep breath and, before the others could notice, pinched herself as hard as she could. She could feel her nails digging into her flesh, and instead of waking up, she discovered that she was still very much here in the musty-smelling library with these strangely dressed women who were clearly trying to be kind, but were only confusing her further. She reached for the only real fact that might help her. She'd set out on the morning of 29th December 1978, to climb Uluru. 'Will you tell me the date, please?' she asked.

Mary frowned. 'Of course, dear. It's 19th November.'

Jane blinked. That couldn't be right; how had she jumped back a month? '19th November 1978,' she murmured.

Both women chuckled, but not happily, by the sound. They both appeared concerned. 'No, dearest, not the year 1978. Heavens, we'd all be long dead. The year is 1715, of course,' Mary assured her.

Jane gasped. *What?* '1715,' she repeated and watched them nod at her with worried looks. 'It can't be.'

'Here,' Mary said, handing her the letter and ignoring her babble. 'William says he has no one to work for his release and is not permitted contact with the outside world. He needs you to travel to London on his behalf.'

Despite her internal chaos, Jane forced herself to accept that everything would explain itself shortly. For now, dream or reality, these people were her only lifeline. She must play along until she could work out what was happening to her... and especially to Will.

'Am I allowed to see him?' she asked, hearing her own voice as though it were coming from a long distance away. She had never felt so confused or dislocated from reality.

'Yes, they would not deny his family.'

'Will you come too?'

Mary looked surprised. 'I dare not, dear sister. You know that Charles and I must appear to support King George. We discussed this. Surely you remember?'

'I... I...' she began, and as she stammered her response it was as though some of the mists that had clouded her mind thinned slightly. And now, finally, Jane did latch on to a memory... it wasn't hers, she was sure of it, but perhaps it belonged to this person called Winifred whom the women were sure they were addressing. She reached toward the memory and could now recall a man wearing a wig who didn't look like the Will she kept in her mind's eye, but he was certainly called Will and he was her husband. He was explaining the family's decision to deliberately split their loyalties. The conversation was filtering through and she remembered her fierce agreement that the Nithsdales of Terregles would support the Jacobites, for they had less to lose and were more committed in their support of the Catholic claim. She could hear the echo of her voice.

Charles doesn't care who sits on the English throne, so long as London doesn't interfere with his business concerns in Scotland, Winifred had said; Jane could hear it now repeated in her mind.

Aye, that's why it's best we raise our standard for our exiled King James, then rely on my sister's family for help, William had replied, in a voice similar enough to her Will's tone for her to wholly believe it might be him, although the rich Scots accent was not her Will's. And now that she saw the Earl in Winifred's memory, there *was* something familiar in his smile, wasn't there? Didn't that slightly crooked grin remind her of the grin of the man lying in the hospital bed?

They are both your men, whispered a thought.

And now other memories began to crawl into her mind of a life spent with William, Earl of Nithsdale. Of lost children, and agonies of sorrow for the babies they'd named and then buried. But there was a healthy son, being schooled in France and occasionally visited by her sister. Not the sister she knew, called Juliette, who had scorned her plan to visit Uluru, but a sister in this alternative world she found herself in. She and William Maxwell, the Earl of Nithsdale, also had a surviving daughter called Anne.

These were real memories, real thoughts. They belonged to a woman – not herself, but the woman she'd become. She sensed the presence of this other woman, lost like a shadow but watching from a distance. The woman was frightened, confused – and weak, as though sickening. Worry for a child broke through the strange link and became part of Jane's thoughts.

'Where's Anne?' she suddenly said.

'By my faith! Winifred, you've remembered. Bravo!' Cecilia exclaimed. 'We have sent Anne to our friend Bess. She is safer with her. I did not wish her to see you sickening and confused in your mind. But if you remember your beautiful child, surely you remember us…'

The two women waited, as though holding their breath. The terrible fright for Jane – or Winifred, as she felt herself fast becoming – was that she *did* remember now. The clouds were clearing rapidly. She recalled everything about this strange world she was in, but she didn't understand why she remembered, or how she'd come to be here.

'I do, dear sister Mary. And Cecilia – a better friend one could not wish for,' she finally said, even the formal words coming easily now.

They hugged her, making soft noises of relief.

Mary shook her head. 'As I live and breathe, your recovery is astonishing. The doctor had you for the grave last week.'

'Truly?'

They nodded together.

'All we could do was make you as comfortable as we could. And you insisted on being dressed,' Mary said.

Cecilia grinned. 'You said if you were going to die, then you were going to do so in your silks, looking out the window to where Will was, and not languishing in a bed.' She clapped her hands. '*Now* look at you. Bonny and bright as ever!'

'So I must travel to London, you say?'

Mary nodded. 'But are you strong enough, I wonder?'

'I feel hale,' she admitted, marvelling privately at how that word had bubbled up, when she had never used it before. 'I could do with some air after days inside. I think I'll take a walk.'

Mary looked doubtful, but Cecilia seemed to agree that it was a fine idea. 'I'll fetch your cloak. Just a short stroll down to the stream, mind. Do you wish for some company, Winifred?' she asked.

Jane shook her head. 'Thank you, no. I just want to clear my thoughts.'

Jane knew they were watching her, but she pretended otherwise. Rugged up against the biting cold in a scarf tucked into the neck of a heavy velvet cloak with a dramatic hood, she felt every inch Lizzy Bennet. Fur-lined gloves, fur muff and heeled, laced boots completed her look. She could convince herself she was off across the fields to meet Mr Darcy – although this era she found herself in was too early – but, bemusement aside, she also needed to get away and think through this surreal situation as best she could.

Good sense demanded that this was a dream, but her heightened awareness told her she was not going to wake up. Something had happened while she had been on Uluru and, impossible though it seemed, apparently she was in Scotland in the early 1700s and her husband, William Maxwell – she gave a small but vaguely hysterical choke of laughter as she thought of this – was in grave trouble. Wouldn't Diane Maxwell have been thrilled! Jane was meeting the forebears whom the Maxwell seniors were so proud to mention. They had gone off to learn the history, knowing nothing more than that John Maxwell believed himself to be distantly related to the Earl of Nithsdale from Scotland.

But why had she become Winifred Maxwell? And what had happened to the real Winifred? They'd said she'd been for the grave. Had Jane's health brought Winifred back from the brink of death? More importantly, how was she going to get back to Jane Granger's life?

Jane walked without purpose and realised only as she was arriving at the wash house that she had absently followed the path down to the leaching lawns where, Winifred's memories told her, she regularly supervised the hired labour as they carried out the laundry duties. She could see only two women working today. There would be no treatment with lye and laying garments out on the lawns for bleaching under the sun today, she thought. Apart from the dismally cold weather, there were hens scratching about. Winifred's memories told her that they only bleached twice a year – mid-spring and at the end of summer, when sunshine and dry weather could be counted upon.

One of the women straightened from where she had been rolling linen through a mangle and stared at Jane intently. The other stepped forward and curtseyed on her approach. 'Good morrow, My Lady. You are much better, I see.' She said it with such surprise that Jane laughed. 'We thought you were for the grave; forgive me for saying it.'

Jane smiled. 'It seems I have recovered.'

'Heavens be praised,' the woman said. Jane recalled her name to be Aileen. 'We're nearly done getting the table linens readied for Hogmanay.'

'Aren't you cold, Aileen?' she asked, noticing the bare arms, with only a shawl between her and the elements.

Aileen chuckled, but there was vague confusion in her expression. 'I don't think on that, My Lady,' she replied, and Jane realised she had stepped over an invisible line of etiquette. She smiled to cover her confusion.

'You make me feel overdressed, that's all,' she said, knowing she was making it worse, but feeling embarrassed now.

Aileen was gracious. 'Well, My Lady. You've been sorely ill. You should na' be out for long. And we can manage here – we're almost done.'

Jane nodded. She stepped into the small stone shed and ran her hand over the mangle, admiring its simplicity and effectiveness. She smiled at the petite second woman, younger, and yet it was hard to define her age. Her skin was flawless, her greenish eyes clear, and she was still eyeing their visitor with deep curiosity. Something about her pricked at Jane's memory.

'It's surely a miracle,' she suddenly remarked, and there was something in her tone that caught Jane's attention.

'Don't mind Robyn,' Aileen said, coming into the wash house. 'She's new. Murdina is sickening, so I called in a friend of hers who offered to work.'

Jane frowned, still looking at Robyn. 'Have we met?'

The woman smiled and there was something knowing in the expression. She returned to her mangle and Jane noticed how raw her hands were, no doubt burned by the caustic lye the household used to bleach its sheets.

She wasn't sure how she suddenly knew these facts, but decided she must let go and allow Winifred's knowledge to fuse with hers if she were to survive this challenge… whatever it was. Without it she understood now that she was doomed to walk this strange landscape in constant confusion. Only Winifred could provide the clues to her role here.

Suddenly Jane realised she had been staring at Robyn in silence.

'If you'll excuse me, My Lady…' Aileen said, sounding awkward as she gave another quick curtsey. 'I have to take these back to the main house for airing.' Jane saw her arms were laden with slightly damp linen, ready to be ironed.

'Of course,' Jane replied, nodding politely.

Aileen left and Jane knew she probably should too, but she felt compelled to remain with Robyn a fraction longer. She was sure the young woman had some kind of knowledge about her. Robyn had returned quietly to her work, but there was a tension in the air.

'Is there something you wish to say to me?' she finally said, embarrassed by the long silence that had managed to stretch between them.

'I suspect *you* have a question for *me*, My Lady.'

Jane blinked. 'Yes. I've already asked it. Have we met before?'

'Not in this life,' Robyn said without hesitation, and her words made Jane suck in a breath.

Robyn eyed her intently. Jane's mouth opened, but she couldn't speak for a few moments. 'You're Robin? The... the clairvoyant?'

The woman shrugged. 'I am but a washerwoman, as you see.'

'You brought me here?' she asked, shocked.

Robyn shook her head and found a sad smile. 'No, my Lady Nithsdale. You *are* here.'

'But you know me as Jane. My fiancé is—'

'I know you are on a strange journey, My Lady. But the pathway is yours. You chose it.'

'You guided me to that path!' she snapped.

Robyn shrugged. ''Tis true you were given insight. But the decision was yours alone.'

'And what now?'

'Walk the path,' Robyn challenged.

'The man I'm marrying is lying in a coma in hospital.'

'Nay, My Lady. Not yet he isn't. Not for a couple of centuries. Right now, your husband is a prisoner of King George I of England.'

Jane could feel the cold snagging at her toes through the thin leather of her boots. Even so, she felt pathetic for noticing it while Robyn stood bare-armed, her raw hands immersed in what had to be freezing water. Her strangled breath billowed out in curls of steam.

'Would you like to come inside?'

Robyn shook her head. ''Tis no place for me, the main house.'

'The kitchen, perhaps? Or one of the outhouses? I must talk to you, but apparently I've had a fever. I can't risk getting sick again. And you should warm your hands at least. I insist.'

Her companion agreed with a shrug. They walked the short distance back to the main house in silence. Jane instinctively knew its layout and forced herself not to question this fact. *Go with it*, she urged herself. *Walk with Winifred*. She led Robyn to the yard at the back. 'Wait in here for me,' she said, ushering her companion into the stables, where two horses and a donkey seemed to be residing. Inside, it was dry and surprisingly warm, and the straw smelled sweet and fresh.

Jane hastened to the parlour and found a maid. 'Bring a mug of sweetened tea to the stable, please.'

The woman looked at her as if Her Ladyship's mind had loosened.

'Do as I ask,' Jane added. 'One of the washerwomen is feeling faint.'

She didn't wait for a response and was soon back in the stable, eyeing Robyn with fresh disbelief. 'Who are you?'

'Exactly as you see, My Lady.'

Jane suspected she would never get to the truth of this woman… man… whoever he or she was. But Robyn had answers, she was sure of it. She didn't want to waste time on what didn't matter to Will's life.

The donkey brayed into the tense silence, then quietened just as abruptly.

'Will needs me,' she bleated.

'Both Wills need you,' came the reply.

Jane blinked. 'I don't understand.'

'Try.'

They heard footsteps. 'I said you were feeling faint,' Jane explained.

Robyn nodded, and leaned against a stall affecting a dazed expression.

'Thank you, Catriona,' Jane said, amazed by how quickly she was getting used to retrieving information from Winifred, including giving orders. She took the pewter mug from the tray.

The housemaid stared. 'What ails you such that you'd involve Her Ladyship?' she sneered at Robyn.

'Never you mind, Catriona,' Jane cut in. 'Back to your duties. I'll take care of this.'

The servant curtseyed and left. Jane didn't imagine they would have long before Catriona's gossiping ensured that others, equally curious, came to snoop.

'I'm not dreaming this, am I,' she said. It was a statement, rather than a question, but Robyn shook her head all the same.

'No. You travelled to a place of great power.'

'It was a pilgrimage. I wanted to do something tangible, something positive for Will.'

'You challenged one of the great Earth vortices. You stood on the ley line and yearned for its magic. Your plea was answered.'

'Here? I've been flung back to 1715, nearly three centuries before my own birth, and you want me to believe that this is where answers are to be found?'

'I promise you that the answer to your yearning is here,' Robyn replied cryptically, speaking with irritating calm. 'Most importantly, this is where the journey toward saving Will begins.' She sipped her honeyed tea and regarded Jane. 'Lady Nithsdale was dying, Jane. Emotionally, Winifred has always been strong, but physically she is rather fragile. You must fight that fragility if she, you and both Williams are to survive.'

'How is my Will involved?'

'Will is a direct descendant of William Maxwell, the Earl of Nithsdale.'

Jane nodded her head, unsurprised. 'So what?'

'The Earl has been accused of being a traitor,' Robyn said, warming her hands around the mug. 'He is on his way to London for trial.'

'But why does that affect my life, and Will's life?'

'Because if the Earl of Nithsdale is executed, your Will is going to die too. They are inextricably linked through blood.'

'What!' she gasped.

'Blood is the golden thread in the tapestry of life – do you remember my saying that?'

'You... he... yes, but...' She began to whimper, not understanding any of it.

Robyn looked over Jane's shoulder. 'Hush now, My Lady. You need to stay strong.'

'Will is going to die?'

'Yes, unless you save his kin. You must save both of them – William and Winifred – if you want to see your Will again. Time travels differently here, but I warn you it is also contrary. A few minutes in the world you left can be many days – even weeks – in the world you find yourself living in now, but sometimes time speeds or slows. I cannot gauge when that might occur. It is the nature of the magic you are using.'

Jane barely heard anything Robyn had said except for *if you want to see your Will again.*

'Why is this happening to me?' she asked, reaching for a wooden railing to steady herself. The donkey shied, unhappy at her closeness, snorting its warning.

Robyn pulled her to the doorway. 'You went to Ayers Rock looking for answers. You wanted to do something to change the course that life had put you on. You would have done anything to save Will's life.'

'But—'

'But nothing,' Robyn cut across her. 'You have the power now to make history. You alone can decide your future, Will's future, Winifred's and William's futures. Your choices craft four lives.'

'I didn't ask for this! My trip was meant to be symbolic!' she lied.

'Maybe that's what you told family, but privately you believed your pilgrimage might change the outcome of Will's situation.'

'Yes... but this?' She looked around her. 'This is just madness!'

'Hush, My Lady. There are others coming. I did warn you that magic exacts a price. The price it chooses is not up to you or me to decide. And you have called down a mighty magic for your own ends. It is no use whining that it is frightening, or too hard.' Robyn put her mug down on the ground and shook her, and Jane felt limp in the washerwoman's grip. 'Listen to me, Jane, for it is vital you understand.'

Jane lifted her head to meet Robyn's gaze. The servant gave a sad smile. 'Magic's favour is never given lightly. You are now Winifred, the Countess of Nithsdale. Jane is not yet born. And unless Winifred's husband, William Maxwell, can be spared the axe of Tower Hill...' Jane gasped, her hand flying to her chest, where she could feel her heart pounding against her fingers, 'then the life you want to return to can never be.' Robyn took Jane's hands. 'You must live as Winifred, and if you succeed in what you are about to do, then Jane Granger and Will Maxwell will meet again. The rest will be up to you.'

'You're sure?' she asked breathlessly.

Robyn nodded. 'Just worry about today. Tomorrow comes soon enough... I must go.'

'Robyn!' Jane gripped the woman's fingers. 'I can't do this!'

Her companion smiled warmly at her this time and it gave her a glimpse of the male Robin. 'You will surprise yourself as to how strong you are. It's why you're here, Jane. Take control! It's why Winifred needed you and why Will is counting on you – both Wills. But now people are coming. Unless you want to explain what will sound like insanity to your sister-in-law and your friend, it is best we part.' Robyn unlocked her fingers from Jane's grip. 'Be brave.'

Jane let her go, a sob trapped in her throat as loneliness and fear crowded her mind. She heard voices calling for Winifred and felt her resolve harden. She was helpless in her real life but she was not helpless in Scotland, in the depths of winter, 1715.

She had a man's life to save. She didn't know this man, but Winifred did. Had Winifred died when Jane arrived? She wished she'd asked Robyn. Perhaps her soul remained and now both of them were one.

'Winifred!' Footsteps clattered across the cobbles. 'Dearest one, there you are. I was told you were with the washerwoman. There's no need to be doing that now.' Jane heard Cecilia's anxious voice, then saw her figure outlined in the doorway of the stable.

'Yes… sorry, I was… I was thinking about Will.'

Arms encircled her. 'I know. And you must realise that as your beloved friend, I am here to help you. Whatever must needs be done, we shall do together.'

'Do you mean that?'

Cecilia, taller than most women, with a strong jaw and kind expression in her rich brown eyes, smiled softly at her. 'Truly,' she confirmed, and hugged her. 'I will go with you to London if you wish it.'

'Thank you.'

Her friend's face grew serious. 'We will need to get organised if we're to journey from north to south in winter. Come, let's get you inside where it's warm. We shall take a few days to plot our journey and make a plan. I'm sure Charles and Mary will want to help. And I'm sure our friend Mrs Mills will be full of gladness to put us up in London for as long as we need.'

You can't escape this, Jane, she schooled herself. *So save William Maxwell. Save yourself. Save Will!*

FOURTEEN

THE NEWS OF TOTAL DEFEAT REACHED THE Earl of Nithsdale from the sarcastic lips of his old foe – the slightly effeminate senior officer who'd shot Pollock – as William travelled south in a carriage that he shared with three other peers, including Lord Derwentwater. They were surrounded by dragoons, who were determined not to lose their noble prizes. Other prisoners followed on foot.

'I'll leave you to ponder your fates, gentlemen,' the man said, taking the four lords in with a sweeping look through their carriage window from his horse's back. He lingered on William, though. 'Safe travels.' He cut away from the column.

'Indecision brought us to this,' William growled, thinking back over the street-to-street fighting into which their battle in Preston had degenerated. 'I am sorry for you especially, sir,' he said to Derwentwater, who was hailed as the jewel among the captured prizes. William was aware that he had never enjoyed more than a cursory conversation with the young peer. 'Your good father was kind to my wife's family at Saint-Germain-en-Laye.'

'We didn't meet there, did we, sir?' the younger man asked. 'I was born there.'

William shook his head. 'I would remember if we had.'

'I have no regrets,' the younger man said without bravado. 'I fought for king and faith.'

'I do not fear for you, My Lord. You are young, wealthy and

a vital power in the north. King George would do well to curry your favour.'

Yet William had begun to worry for his own family... and neck.

'Have you requested help from your kin?' Derwentwater enquired.

'Aye. I hope my good wife Winifred has received my letter urging her to meet me in London.'

'That is much to ask of a sweet woman, My Lord, during this cruel winter.'

William nodded. The boy was still of the romantic notion that this situation had not turned serious. But William had seen the truth in the guarded eyes of the officer who had just taunted him, and the other soldiers were licking their lips in anticipation of retribution.

He suspected that it would not be easy now to escape the King's justice. He responded to the young man's words. 'My wife is the person I trust most in life, and she alone possesses the powers of persuasion to seek the right support.'

'Will the Crown get busy punishing the men we left in gaols in the north?' Derwentwater wondered.

'Nay, he'll use the nobles to promote the message of intolerance of Catholics,' Kenmure said, joining the conversation. 'It's exactly what King George craves. We are the example to the rest of the Jacobites.'

At Barnet, Lord Derwentwater summoned the officer in charge of their escort. 'Where do you take us?'

'Marshalsea and Fleet for most; next in quality to Newgate Prison, where the highland lord and some of his sheep-fucking followers have been sent. But for you, My Lords, it's the Tower, on the King's orders.'

'I'm assured we'll be on horseback from the morrow,' Lord Winton, another of their party, muttered.

The following day, William noticed their escort being changed and a beefing up of the guard surrounding them.

'They're taking no chances of allowing sympathisers to come to our aid,' he remarked, feigning a casual tone. However, looking at the huge crowds that had begun to gather to watch this procession of the damned, he had no doubt that their situation was becoming more and more dire. Soon enough their hands were bound.

'How are we supposed to hold the bridles of our horses while uncivilly trussed like chickens?' he demanded with astonishment.

'You won't be holding anything, not even your broken pride,' came the acid reply from the closest officer. 'Just stay atop your mount, if you can,' the man taunted.

They were tied like slaves and escorted between a party of horse grenadiers and a platoon of footguards, their progress into the capital designed to humiliate: jostled by the crowds lining the streets of London, whose odours blended into one unclean, jeering breath. Meanwhile, their escort moved in time to the irritating sound of drums beating a victory march, and pipers added a jolly tune that had the audience banging on everything metal they could carry.

William dryly noted several bedpans joining the loud clangour of instruments as Londoners chanted: 'King George forever, no warming-pan bastard!'

He grimaced. Even now, so many years on, people believed the vicious rumour that Queen Mary Beatrice, who had struggled to become with child, had never actually given birth to her son. Protestants clung to the notion that King James, born at St James's Palace in front of a host of onlookers, had been somehow smuggled into the Queen's labouring bed within a warming pan.

He let go of his ire; there were more immediate worries. Despite the cold, the atmosphere was choked with the noise of the crowd and its chants for revenge.

At Tower Hamlets, William was informed that he and his fellow peers would be housed in the Lieutenant's Lodgings and tomorrow would be brought to Westminster to begin examination.

Find me, Winifred, he cried inwardly. *Only you can save me now.*

Traquair House was in a state of flux as Winifred prepared for her journey to London. Jane had begged off food and company that evening, desperate to have time alone to think.

Everything about her elegant bedchamber was familiar to her through Winifred… the sage-green colour scheme, the silk brocade drapes enriched with the gold thread favoured by the weavers of Lyon, the thick oriental rug that she suspected was one of her sister-in-law's wedding gifts. The walls, panelled with wood to dado height with pretty green trefoil wallpaper above, the intricate plasterwork on the ceiling… she knew it all. And yet, though it appeared like a set for a period drama, there was nothing fake about it.

Jane could hear the creak of boards elsewhere in the house, voices drifting up from the drawing room and the dim ringing and clatter of pans from the kitchen and scullery. It was a living, breathing, working mansion of the early eighteenth century and she was still feeling tremors of shock shake through her every now and then. They made her think of her childhood fox terrier during a thunderstorm. Pixie used to shiver as if cold, her teeth even chattering in her fear, and nothing Jane did or said made a difference. Jane felt like that now. It didn't seem to matter what amount of soothing these strangers offered, or how much she tried to remain rational… the shivering seemed to be a rote response to her shock.

Finally she gave her arm a pinch. This was it – if she had dreamed everything, including her conversation with Robyn, she would know it.

'Wake up!' she whispered, squeezing so hard it made her eyes water.

She watched the whitened area of her skin flood back to its

normal colour and the flesh retract to its original state. She touched the area absently and could feel a protest of soft pain. At last she resigned herself to being trapped here until she could work out how to escape.

She sat at a mahogany desk near the window and watched the twilight close to dusk as the sun sank on this incredible, frightening yet somehow exhilarating day of her life… was it her life, or was it Winifred's life, which she'd stolen? *Winifred.* The name didn't suit her. She moved to the dressing table to study her new self in the mirror and do some digging into her host's knowledge.

Searching her newfound memories, Jane discovered Winifred was thirty-five. The mirror told her she was slender and blonde, with a gentle face of soft, regular features, which she realised belied the Winifred whose thoughts she was getting to know. Winifred might have a fragile constitution, but she was made of stern stuff emotionally. Already Jane could feel Winifred's passion rising; her host was worried for her husband, but she was also angry that the Catholic push was in tatters.

After concerted but gentle probing, Jane decided that her host was not dead. Winifred had simply let her in. Perhaps she had been too weak to resist her, given that she had been close to death. Maybe it was because she'd needed physical strength when she'd realised she was dying. Or possibly fate had chosen for her. Whatever had occurred, Jane understood she now had to live as Winifred in order to keep both of them alive.

'It's 1715,' Jane whispered, close to the mirror, watching her breath steam upon it. Into the steam she wrote her initials, just to remind herself that somewhere out there in the fabric of the cosmos, Jane Granger existed.

She allowed the peril of her situation to distil down into one thought now. If she didn't live as Winifred and attempt to save William Maxwell, Fifth Earl of Nithsdale, then Will Maxwell of Florida was not only not going to make it, he wasn't even going to be born. What was more, was if Winifred died, so would she, and no one would be any the wiser.

'Get your act together, Winifred!' Jane growled softly to her new reflection. 'We have a big task ahead.'

She now understood that she was somehow going to have to make a passionate plea for William's life. And the only way to do that was in person.

She shook her head and spoke to the hidden self behind those blue eyes of her host. 'Come on, Jane, you have to think like an unemancipated woman of three centuries ago. You have to be Winifred; behave dutifully, act demurely and don't swear!'

There was a gentle knock at the door. 'Winifred, dear?'

It was Cecilia.

Jane walked across her room, feeling the drag of her long, voluminous dress and tight bodice, which had now been rebuttoned. *Why couldn't I have fallen into 1790*, she wondered, *when dresses were cut high under the bust and flowed loosely?*

She opened the door and Cecilia beamed at her with a worried smile.

'You must have so much on your mind, dear Win. But I urge you not to worry about Anne.'

Anne hadn't even crossed her mind beyond that first moment of anxiety bubbling up through Winifred. 'I'm not worried about Anne and Willie,' she said, remembering the boy's name. 'They are both safe and with people who love them. All I can worry about now is my lord husband,' she said, amazed at how politely the words were flowing.

'Did you write to Mrs Mills in London?'

Jane tried not to smile at the memory. 'Yes, I have the letter here,' she said, returning to the writing desk where she had laboured using a quill and dipping it in ink, grateful for that course in calligraphy all those years ago. Amazingly, though, once she'd opened herself up to being Winifred, the skills had flooded into her consciousness, and scratching with the nib had felt relatively easy and normal. So had the polite, stilted language required for letter-writing. But the urgency was there and hopefully Mrs Mills would have rooms.

'The rider is here. Let me take the letter from you.'

'We might beat it to London,' Jane wondered aloud. Winifred's knowledge told her that mail took days, weeks even, unless a single messenger on horseback was paid to take the letter directly to the recipient, door to door, come hail or shine.

'In this snow? I fear not, but should our luck bring us such providence, then it will matter not who reaches London first. I'm sure lodgings will be gladly provided for us, given our cause.'

Jane nodded. 'Thank you, Cecilia. I don't know what I'd do without you.'

Her friend smiled, squeezing her hand. 'Rest now, dear. I shall have a warm jar of posset sent up.'

'No spice,' Jane said, delighted that she even knew to say this.

'Egg, treacle and no nutmeg in the milk, I promise. It will help you to sleep.'

'When do we leave?'

'The day after tomorrow. Charles is readying the carriage, and organising a groom to travel with us.'

'Very good. I must thank him. Goodnight, Cecilia.'

She undressed, relieved to be rid of her gown, and buttoned herself into a sensible but exquisitely embroidered cotton nightgown. The maid came in with Jane's posset; she had also delivered a warming pan hours before, so the chill in the bed had been beaten back. A modest fire had now burned to embers in the grate. But Jane could sense the frost clawing at the small panes of glass in the windows and it made her wonder about the journey that lay ahead. It looked as though it could be difficult to travel the entire distance by coach. The snow was becoming very deep. Fortunately, she'd learned to ride as a child. She had always been pretty good at it too, but she was glad it would not be *all* the way to London on horseback.

As she slipped beneath the sheets, sighing at the unexpected pleasure of the feather pillow, Jane thought about Winifred's husband. Where would he be sleeping tonight? Was he cold? Was he frightened?

As her lids began to feel heavy and she prepared to welcome the escape of unconsciousness, a sudden thought bubbled up from Winifred. Jane's drowsy eyes blazed open with panic. There were incriminating papers at Terregles. They had to be hidden. She had to beat the government officers to the Nithsdale family house and get rid of anything that might endanger William, or indeed their family, even further. They also needed to hide some money and jewellery, and other papers that should never fall into Crown hands.

Within moments she'd banished that safe, drowsy state she craved and was running down the stairs barefoot, with no care for her unpinned hair, and only a hastily grabbed dressing gown for modesty. She began calling for her friends and all three came hurrying out of the drawing room, their expressions filled with worry. In Charles's case, his face was also plastered with mortification at seeing his sister-in-law so underdressed.

'Winifred!' Mary gasped. 'What ails you?'

'I crave your pardon…' she began.

'Are you sickening again?' Cecilia asked, rushing to meet her on the stairs.

'No, no. Forgive me this disturbance, but tomorrow I must leave for Terregles.' At their looks of shock, she pressed straight on with explaining her reasons.

'You make a good case, Winifred,' Charles said when she had finished. He looked far more attractive, she thought, now that he was devoid of the wig and stripped down to his waistcoat and breeches, shirt unbuttoned at the collar. He had a small sherry glass in his hand. 'You should leave tomorrow. Waste not a moment.'

'Oh, my dear, can you be ready?' Mary asked.

'I could leave right now if I were permitted,' Jane replied.

'Good. I shall have the carriage prepared for you to leave after dawn. You can be at Terregles by sundown,' Charles assured her.

She glanced at Cecilia, who nodded encouragingly.

'Thank you, all of you.' She covered a yawn, realising again how wrung out she was. If only they had any idea of the journey she'd travelled already. 'Good evening,' she whispered with an embarrassed smile.

William Maxwell sat hunched in a tiny chamber pondering his fate. The English had split up the noble prisoners, although what they thought any of them could do while gaoled in the Tower of London was beyond him. The campaign to return the rightful Catholic heir was smashed beyond all hope.

William realised the Earl of Mar and the king in exile in whose name they had fought would likely suffer no further, whereas the brave border lords and the English Jacobites who had rallied would bear the brunt of the English Crown's wrath. He tried to banish the thought but it surged through his defences, and he had to face the fact that he might have to give his life to appease King George.

He met one of the other lords while both were permitted a dawn stroll on the rooftop walk, which the senior yeoman guarding him assured him had been a favourite with the young Princess Elizabeth when she was imprisoned by her half-sister Mary. It didn't impress William; he was Catholic, after all, and cared little for the footsteps of a famous Protestant queen.

'If one's life is to end now, then to die on a battlefield, weary, blood-spattered, yet burning with the fire of one's convictions and yelling the name of the true king would be a good death,' he said to his fellow lord. 'But to languish in a cell, awaiting the humiliation of a trial that will be nothing more than farce, is soul-destroying.'

'I suspect this is the easy part,' his companion, Kenmure, lamented. 'I overheard the guards saying that the King's revenge will be to see us led to the mound at Tower Hamlets so the crowd can jeer and throw rotten fish and fruit, while we suffer in the most horrible way that a man can, and to such an undignified end… with our heads on spikes outside the Tower.'

William blanched inwardly, but his voice remained steady. 'Do not speak of this to Derwentwater if you meet him. He remains cheerful that his release is near guaranteed.'

Lord Kenmure nodded. 'I hope it shall be. By the way, did you hear the news that Old Borlum escaped?'

William actually gave a small gust of laughter. 'Truly?'

His companion shrugged. 'My gaoler likes to talk. Even Newgate couldn't hold the old dog.'

'The highlanders were our bravest warriors – had the most to lose too. I wish him well.'

Now, back in his cell, William stared out of the tiny window, cut from the otherwise impenetrable walls of the Lieutenant's Lodgings where he was being kept, and felt the weight of dread at the cruel death that probably awaited him. In fairness, the Constable of the Tower had been gracious enough to provide each of the lords with what could only be described as half-decent lodgings, given that they were within the most feared prison in the land. William realised he could have been flung into one of the damp dungeon cells, to share it with the rats that swam in at high tide. And although he was in a locked chamber, it was dry, and had soft floorboards and access to fresh air – even a view, albeit only of Traitors' Gate.

He stared at that view now, remembering how his gut had twisted as they'd been rowed down the Thames on a barge at dusk, halting at the huge wooden doors of this infamous water gate. Hulking above it was the heavy masonry of its arch, which he estimated spanned more than fifty feet, possibly sixty. He'd heard as a youngster that the arch over the gate had collapsed twice previously and, like fellow schoolboys, had imagined it haunted by the wretched souls of those sent to their God once they passed beneath it. As he and his fellow prisoners had glided past, he had shuddered at the imposing bulk of the Tower, looking like a stone monster whose jaws opened slowly and ominously to swallow him just as they had another Catholic, Sir Thomas More, whom he had long revered. Nearly two centuries ago, this infamous councillor to King Henry VIII had made an identical, uncomfortable and unnerving journey down the river to pass beneath the gate. He had emerged from his cell, down in the freezing, dank depths of the Lieutenant's Lodgings, only for his execution. William tried to ignore the stabs of dread that the same fate awaited him.

He and his fellows lords had been invited to dine with the Constable on the day of their arrival and had been told they would join him each evening for a meal for the duration of their stay. It was a courtesy befitting men of their rank.

Nevertheless, while 'stay' sounded innocent enough – as though they were honoured guests – in fact the Crown would be pushing to have their heads removed from their bodies as soon as it could. Poor Derwentwater. He was such a young man, and though he'd fought bravely enough, William had learned that the youngster had only joined their cause because of the haranguing of his wife, who had all but suggested she'd think him a coward if he didn't. He was handsome, utterly charming and stunningly wealthy, but none of those attributes would help him to keep his head, William feared.

William's thoughts moved to the youngsters in his own life: his two children. He remembered Willie's earnest look when he came to his father one day with a runt from one of the dog litters. William had set his quill down and taken the linen that held the pup and rubbed and rubbed until the angels had smiled and breathed life into the pup. His son had looked at him with such awe and adoration he would never forget it. Willie believed his father invincible. How could he let his boy down now?

And cherubic Anne, a delicate child with the sweetest temperament to melt any father's heart... He dug into his breast pocket, where he kept her first attempt at embroidery. She'd insisted on forming his initials on a sampler and given it to him as a gift. He'd promised her he would carry it with him into battle and it would bring him luck. He kissed it now, beseeching it to do just that.

As his gaze absently followed a lantern's light aboard a small craft plying the River Thames, once again his thoughts shifted to Winifred, and a fresh burst of anxiety assaulted him. He shivered, this time from the bone-aching chill of his room. Winifred's health was often frail through winter and he felt the weight of guilt pressing on his conscience at the challenge he had set her. It would be hard enough for a highborn woman to traverse the country in agreeable weather, but in this fearsome cold he wondered if she would even survive the journey. His sister and brother-in-law could only offer invisible help; physically, Charles would be forced to distance himself from his 'wayward' Jacobite brother.

It was too late to regret his request. Already several days had passed. With God's mercy, Winifred should have already received his letter, and knowing his wife as he did, he was sure she would not have wasted a moment in indecision. He smiled grimly, imagining her flinging down the letter, impetuously grabbing her cloak and leaping onto a horse to head south without a care for the consequences. In his mind she was fearless. William took strength from that, and knew he must remain as outwardly cheerful and confident as he could... for her sake.

FIFTEEN

WITH WINIFRED'S FAITHFUL MAID AND COMPANION CECILIA riding next to her, Jane had left Traquair House at the first glimpse of sunrise. Since then they'd fallen into silence and she'd had the luxury of her private thoughts, going back over her first morning in eighteenth-century Scotland.

As she'd dressed, she'd felt embarrassed that anyone should have to assist her – she would have to stop thinking like a modern woman. Besides, she did need help from Cecilia to tie herself into her whalebone corset. She'd once again stared hard at the reflection in the mirror of a highborn woman, terrified for the life of her husband. She presumed he was interred in the Tower of London. Jane had toured the Tower several times during childhood, but more recently had actually been a guest there. One of her closest friends during her university days had been the daughter of a senior military officer who, upon retirement, was given the ceremonial office of Constable of the Tower, which meant Emily's family called the Tower of London home. Jane had spent many a happy weekend roaming the Queen's House, built by Henry VIII, which had housed Anne Boleyn and Elizabeth I among its famous prisoners. It had been exciting to have a private viewing of the Crown Jewels and walk around the spaces that were cordoned off from the thousands of tourists that tramped around the Tower every day. But Jane had been acutely sensitive to its role since the eleventh century, as a gaol and place of oppression as much as a fortification and palace. If Emily's dad had been the Constable in the Middle Ages, he would have been one of the nation's most powerful men, a key defender of the capital and its sovereign.

Her favourite memory was the nightly Ceremony of the Keys. This ritual locking of the Tower of London by the Yeoman Guard had been occurring nightly since the Middle Ages, without exception – other than a single occasion during the London Blitz. With seven hundred years of tradition behind it, it was now accorded the pomp that her countrymen did better than any other nation on Earth. Emily's mother was forever chivvying her husband to get dressed into his full ceremonial outfit for the occasion. Jane often stood behind Emily's dad, trying not to giggle at the dancing plumage on his ceremonial hat, while he took the salute of the Chief Warder. The wide-eyed tourists would click their cameras as the watchman made his ritual way down Water Lane, to be halted by the sentry and given the challenge: 'Who comes there?' Then the monarch's keys were handed over, the Tower was considered secure for that night and the haunting 'Last Post' was played.

She'd sit out on the rooftop of the Queen's House and smoke with Emily. She'd listen to her whinge about a new boyfriend who only wanted sex and didn't take her anywhere exciting, while she privately mused about moving in the footsteps of Elizabeth I.

How many times had she lounged in the window seat of the family's drawing room, after an exam or exhausting week of study, sipping on a mug of tea that Emily's mum had handed her, for which she'd sighed her thanks? She'd loved that spot the most, looking over the illuminated Tower Bridge and onto the Traitors' Gate, which had welcomed many a doomed man.

As Winifred had stared back at her from the mirror, she'd realised that the Earl of Nithsdale had probably been rowed through that very gate and passed into the hands of the Yeoman Guard. She had moved away, unable to hold Winifred's fearful gaze any longer.

It had still felt like night when she heard the huge French clock on the landing join with a cockerel outside and begin to sound its deep chimes. She'd counted five. She had tiptoed across the thick silken rug to open the curtains and seen a tiny slash of pink at the far edge of the winter sky. Her breath had steamed against the windowpane and once again she'd caught herself scrawling *JG* with a fingertip against the chilled glass. Winifred's body had shivered – no, *her* body had shivered in the cold, and she'd faced the new humiliation of having to use a chamber pot. She would never again take for granted the conveniences that she'd previously barely noticed.

Dressed, her hair neatly pinned, and a small cloth bag packed with one other gown, she'd stood before the mirror again and made a promise to the woman who looked back that she would *be* her. No more Jane. She would breathe, live, think as Winifred from now on. It was her only hope.

Now the carriage wheel bounced over a rut, her teeth smashed against each other and Winifred was rudely pulled from her thoughts.

'Nearly there, dear,' her companion said, squeezing her arm.

It was true. She recognised the surrounding countryside... surely just minutes to go now.

'We have to be very careful, Cecilia. The government men might already have raided the house.'

Cecilia nodded, rapped on the ceiling.

'Yes, My Lady,' came the muffled reply of the driver, unaware it was the maid who was trying to win his attention.

Cecilia thrust her head through the window. 'Can you see any men milling about, or horses gathered outside the house? Any carriages?'

There was a pause before the man answered: 'All quiet, My Lady.'

'Very good,' Cecilia replied. 'Drive on.'

They glanced at each other. Cecilia, to all intents and purposes, was her maid, but they'd been friends since childhood and now she was also her accomplice. How could Winifred ever repay this loyalty?

'What's your plan?' Cecilia asked.

Winifred shook her head. 'I have none to speak of. Charles and Mary have insisted I close up the house to save on expenses, and my dear brother-in-law has kindly lent me as much as he dare so I can employ a lawyer to plead my lord's case. Mary has promised to collect Anne from our friend Bess and she will keep her safe in my absence.'

'Then you have no need to fret on this last matter.'

'No, other than my fear of making darling Anne an orphan.'

'Hush, now! We shan't speak of such nonsense,' Cecilia admonished.

Winifred nodded, turning her mind to more mundane matters. 'I shall keep on our grieve, for our farm still needs managing… and the byre-woman must keep tending our cows. Mayhap I shall instruct the gardener's wife to light fires now and then so the house suffers no damp during this fierce winter.'

'Who will oversee the finances of the estate?'

'To be truthful, Cecilia, I am more worried about William than his estate right now… 'Tis too late to send money to Barnet as he requested. I just hope I have sufficient for London.'

'Terregles, My Lady!' the man yelled from above as they passed through the grand wrought-iron gates of her former home.

The two women nodded at each other, as if willing themselves to remain composed and strong. The wind howled at their bonnets and tore at their skirts as the groom helped them from the carriage and the head maid and housekeeper rushed from the huge front door, shocked to see the pair.

'Oh, My Lady, welcome home. We are heartsick with worry for you and my Lord Nithsdale,' the housekeeper said, gathering up the two women like a clucking mother hen and ushering them into the glow of the hallway to gain respite from the chill wind.

Winifred caught her breath. 'Sarah, it's a fleeting visit, I fear. I must travel tomorrow to London.' Sarah looked shocked, but held her tongue. 'I must needs reach my husband.'

'Of course, My Lady. Let me get you out of these cloaks and I'll have some tea brought into the drawing room. And a tray of food – just cold ham, but you look too tired to wait for much more. Shall I light the fire?'

'I say we do not stand on ceremony and go to the parlour instead, Sarah. It is always warm there. Besides,' she added, to lighten the dread surrounding the trio, 'I need to see Bran and Gordy and they always have muddy boots.'

The housekeeper smiled. 'Gordy's been in the high fields today, My Lady. He is staying at the hut tonight because the weather is too fearsome.' Winifred nodded, having guessed that such might be the case. 'But I can find Bran easily enough. Come, let me put a pot of water on for you. You should both warm your fingers by the hearth.'

Sarah let them sit in comparative silence while she gave her mistress a report on the household. Winifred learned that old Lady Nithsdale was so fragile now that she needed a lot of physical help, and with the house being run by so few staff, she had gone to stay with relatives. Most of the servants had now been laid off and Sarah had wisely taken it upon herself to shut up many of the rooms. Though head of the household staff, she was tackling the menial jobs now, and Jane couldn't help but admire her as she ladled food that she had cooked herself into earthen bowls.

They tried not to feel forlorn, but Winifred was sure they looked it as they swallowed Sarah's cock-a-leekie soup, sweetened and thickened with prunes. She chewed on a heel of bread, thinking hard on what was ahead of her.

'Does Gordy think it may snow again tomorrow?' she suddenly muttered to Sarah, who was busy making an oatmeal posset even though Winifred had said she wouldn't need it.

'Aye, he does. They say it's three feet thick in places already.'

She glanced at Cecilia. 'I cannot take Charles's carriage south. It is too dangerous.'

'Surely you do not mean to go on horseback!' Cecilia exclaimed, her hunger momentarily forgotten as she dropped the spoon into her bowl.

Winifred shrugged. 'We must be brave. I cannot risk not getting through. If it means riding bareback, Cecilia, you know I will. We will ride to Newcastle mayhap, and take a coach from there to London.'

Sarah put a mug down beside her. 'There now, My Lady. Get that into ye. It's got a shot of whiskey in it that should give you a good night's sleep. You too, Miss Cecilia. Here's yours.' She placed another mug down. ''Tis a fearsome journey ahead tom—' A door slammed. 'Ah, that'll be Bran.'

An old man in a muddy kilt brought a swirl of icy air with him as he entered the parlour, banging his boots free of snow. He stood in a small pool of water, pulled his cap from his tatty grey hair and bowed. 'My Lady, I am sore sorry for the news.'

'Hello, Bran,' Winifred said in a tired voice. 'Thank you for coming so quickly.'

'I be here to help however I can, My Lady,' he said, bowing his head before nodding silent thanks to Sarah, who had pushed a warmed mug of laced milk into his icy fingers.

Winifred sipped the posset out of politeness and felt the liquor hit the back of her throat, its fumes rising off the hot milk, stinging her eyes. She had to admit that she felt more alive for it, and took another slug before putting the mug down. 'Bran, I need your help to bury the family papers. I can't let them fall into the hands of the Crown. If nothing else, they will protect our son.'

'Aye. I might have just the right spot, My Lady. Whenever you are ready.'

She smiled. 'Finish your mug, Bran.'

Soon the pair of them were trudging down the grassed terrace at the back of the house. The ground was now iced with a foot of snow, which crunched beneath Winifred's footsteps as she tried to lift her skirts with her free hand. With her other she clutched tight the family's documents, including the deeds to the house and the paperwork attesting to the transfer of estates to their son. She'd be damned if she was going to let King George confiscate Willie's birthright. She had also stuffed in some jewellery and coin as a precaution.

Bran carried a lamp and a shovel, offering her a helping arm when she stumbled. She trusted this old man and Sarah with the family's lives, for both had been with the Maxwells since William was a youngster, and both were fiercely Jacobite.

'Here,' she said suddenly. 'That was seventy-four steps I counted.' When Bran looked wryly at her, she even found a small grin. 'One for every year of the Earl's and my ages.'

'I won't ask how many of them belong to you, My Lady. You look as young as the day Lord William brought you home.'

She felt her eyes water, pretended it was the cold and hoped the lamp hadn't highlighted it. She pointed to the spot to distract Bran's gaze. 'Right here, then. Can you cut through the turf, Bran? I fear it might feel like stone in this weather.'

'I shall try,' he assured her, and with Winifred's urgings he bent his back to his labours. A while later, when even the cold wind had been forgotten, they stood before a small but deep enough hole dug into the near-frozen earth. Bran had cut the turf neatly into three squares and set them aside so they could be replaced later. 'Will that do it?' he asked, wiping his leaking nose on his sleeve.

'It will serve us fine, Bran.' Winifred gratefully lowered herself to her knees, uncaring of the mud or snow, and placed the precious documents, wrapped up with waxed linen stored in a box, into the earth vault they had created. 'Now cover it up.'

He did so. The hiding of the documents went faster than the digging and within minutes the hole had been filled.

'Now replace the turf in precisely the same divots as they

came out and no one will be any the wiser, save us,' she instructed.

She carefully handed him the three squares of turf, which he reverently returned to their original spots before he banged down on them with his boots.

Winifred smiled. 'Perfect, Bran. They are to be dug up only on my instructions and their whereabouts must not be shared with *anyone*. I trust you in this.'

'You can rest easy in that trust, My Lady. I will not forsake ye.'

She squeezed his bony shoulder. 'Seventy-four steps north, in a straight line, from the great urn.'

He touched his cap. 'It is already forgotten, My Lady.'

Winifred smiled grimly in the dark. 'May it protect our family and yours, Bran.'

Jane was dreaming, and this time, deep in her subconscious, she knew it. But was it a dream... or was it a glimpse into the reality she craved?

Sarah had done her best to make her mistress comfortable, given that she'd arrived unannounced. Her old bedchamber had been considered too large to heat and hadn't been aired, so it was not only freezing but also smelled musty.

Instead, Winifred had chosen Anne's tiny nursery room. After a thorough prodding of the fire to coax the flames into a merry dance the two women had finally left her alone. Cecilia had covered Winifred's hand with her own. 'I shall wake you at dawn, I promise.'

Jane listened to the soft hiss and crackle of the wood and to the haunting cry of a nighthawk on the wing. With her feet resting on the warmth of the 'bedpig' to prevent the chilblains Winifred sometimes suffered, she felt herself drifting. Fever niggled on the rim of her awareness and seemed to launch her into a plane that was neither sleep nor wakefulness. And there she saw Will in his hospital bed in London – not America?

– with several people working busily around him. Dr Evans, whom she'd met and liked instantly, was reading a printout. He looked intrigued rather than concerned. Jane tried to reach out to them but the window into her own world began to fade as she drifted into a fitful sleep.

When she woke in the initially strange room, it shocked her. Gradually, familiarity seeped into her consciousness and she remembered it was Anne's nursery, she was at Terregles and she was still Winifred. She woke up fully and realised Cecilia was shaking her gently. But that wasn't what was making her teeth chatter.

'Oh, my dear, I fear we will not be journeying anywhere today.'

Recalling her vision, Jane was blazing with determination as brightly as her cheeks blazed with fever. 'With or without you, Cecilia, I am going to Newcastle today! Now, help me up.'

'Wait!' her maid and friend urged. 'Let the fire catch properly. I have lit it for you.'

Jane nodded, wondering at how achey a thirty-five-year-old, eighteenth-century body could feel, with some early twinges of arthritis in her hips and the punishment of childbirth taking its physical toll. She sat up, dizziness her most obvious companion, and sensibly waited for the initial light-headedness to pass. Jane knew her friend was watching her keenly.

'I cannot wait to recover,' she explained before Cecilia could comment. She sneezed. 'Every minute counts.'

'If you die of a fever on the way, it will not help the Earl.'

'Yes, but I would rather die than not try to save him,' she said passionately, also thinking of Will in his hospital bed in her dream. People had been flitting around him, the neurophysician looking intrigued as he read a printout. Amazed that she could remember this dream so vividly, Jane wondered what had happened. Perhaps he'd shown some signs of real life. Yes, that must have been it. The expectancy around him was probably excitement. Had he fluttered his eyelids, or had his toes suddenly flexed? She'd got tired of doctors and nurses, even orderlies, warning her not to read too much into twitches. *They're just reflexes* was a phrase she'd learned to despise over the days in the hospital.

Cecilia was offering an arm and she took it now, hobbling to the fire to warm herself. 'I shall be fine. I need to relieve myself, dear, and then I need to wash and get myself readied.'

'Sit here for a moment or two by the fire. I am going to fetch some hot water and a sponge.' Cecilia must have seen her nod because she left quietly. Jane knew she must rally... and fast.

'Come on, Winifred, dig deep,' she muttered beneath her breath. 'For both our Williams.'

Something in her determination worked, because when Cecilia returned with a jug of hot water, soap and a flannel – as well as a strange grey paste – she remarked that Winifred did indeed look stronger, although Jane was hiding her shivers well. Staying close to the fire, she sponged herself and then considered the tacky grey paste before her.

Toothpaste, Winifred's memories assured her. Jane lifted the small porcelain dish and smelled. Fresh mint hit her first; she could see it chopped up finely in a mix that she now tasted on her tongue. It was slightly abrasive, from salt and she didn't know what else. Dipping the corner of the damp flannel into the paste, she scrubbed Winifred's teeth as best she could, taking care to massage the gums in a circular action.

'You'll thank me for this in years to come,' she said ruefully to her reflection in the mirror, 'when your teeth don't fall out as quickly as your friends' teeth do!'

She opened her mouth wide. Winifred's teeth weren't a perfect white, but they weren't rotten either. Clearly, being highborn, her host had enjoyed the benefits of a healthier diet than most people of this era.

Later, dressed, she felt a fraction better for the luxury of donning fresh undergarments that nevertheless itched, and tying up her hair for the journey. Most of all, she was pleased to pull on a riding habit, and although she was going to rely on Winifred's ability to ride like a lady, she was thrilled at the close-cut, comparatively non-fussy attire she was now wearing. There had been another option in a heavy brocade that screamed French overkill but she'd preferred the dark green tailored jacket and matching long, narrowish skirt. The floppy sleeves irritated, as did the frilled lace that Cecilia tied at her neck, but Jane did not complain.

She had begun to sneeze. And when it was obvious that the fever was giving way to the real enemy, Cecilia went running for 'the elixir', as she called it. She returned bearing a largish, squat, cloudy-green bottle with a thick cork stopper. Jane could read *True Daffy Elixir* embossed on the glass, which was half filled with dark liquor. In her other hand Cecilia clutched a huge silver spoon.

'A dose of Daffy's will fix the ague,' Cecilia pressed enthusiastically. 'I ordered some for the Earl and left it here many moons ago. He was grateful for it. It is best for the colic and the bowel-gripe, but I myself have used it for bad digestives as well as for the night sweats.'

Jane fought the inclination to reel back. 'Nay, Cecilia, I fear I may return it.'

It didn't take much of Jane's deductive power for her to appreciate that the tarry-looking medicine was most likely a laxative. One glance at the bottle told her it was indeed laced with all manner of ingredients, from aniseed and senna to rhubarb and guaiacum wood chips... all geared to help the bowels loosen their load.

She shook her head and pursed her lips. 'I prefer not,' she finally said, the runs being the very last complication she needed in her life right now. 'Truly, it is best if I don't add to our woes by needing the privy too often on our journey.'

'What will you take, then? Perhaps some menthol vapours before we leave?'

Jane nodded, mainly to appease her friend. 'I think I shall

just fetch a few things for my lord husband from his chamber. He will surely need a fresh shirt,' she said, impressed by her own ingenuity in managing to escape without giving further offence. She squeezed Cecilia's hand. 'I shall be down shortly,' she said, then added, 'I'm looking forward to some porridge,' although it was a lie. Eating was not on her mind; in fact, partly due to her anxiety over facing the commode – which was in the dining room, of all places – she had no appetite at all this morning. Oh, the horror of it! Who would empty the pot? Cecilia, of course! Childhood friend, devoted companion... but paid to attend to her mistress's many needs, from running errands to emptying the chamber pot into the cesspit at the bottom of the garden.

Jane shuddered inwardly as she now made her escape down the short hallway to where William had his own suite of chambers. Winifred guided her to the right door and the key was already in the lock. The rooms were a cacophony of styles, she now recalled. William had resisted renovation in his bedroom and only allowed his wife to cover the original paintwork with blue-grey striped paper; but the two big tapestries he'd insisted on rehanging looked rather incongruous against it.

The bed was a huge four-poster affair with richly brocaded drapings that Jane remembered was one of the vast array of wedding gifts presented to them by Queen Mary Beatrice in France. It didn't match the curtains, but Jane felt the mixture of styles worked in a pleasingly eclectic way, probably because she was experiencing Winifred's surge of pleasure at being in her husband's room again. She could smell a lingering hint of the pomade he used on his hair when not wearing a wig, and she couldn't help but run her fingers over his brush and comb.

Jane opened drawers and cupboards, suddenly determined to learn about this man Winifred was married to. She touched his shirts and held his soft scarf to her face, inhaling his smell. She ran her hands over the velvet and brocade jackets, but knew that he was happiest in his riding gear, or his 'farm clothes' as he'd called them. Memories flooded in as she rode on Winifred's swell of love.

Yet it was the tiny portraits painted on porcelain that captured her longest span of attention. She remembered now that Winifred had commissioned these as a special gift to William for a recent anniversary. There were four ovals, two large, two smaller: the immediate Maxwell family. She recognised each member of the quartet now. There was Willie, adopting the rather serious and proud stance of the adult men he emulated; and Anne, looking appropriately reticent and supremely pretty. Her hair fell in a cascade of golden ringlets not unlike her aunt's, but she certainly resembled her mother too. Winifred smiled only slightly in her own portrait, yet Jane knew Winifred was capable of joyous laughter, usually in the company of William. And there he was, the Fifth Earl of Nithsdale, staring out at her from the last porcelain oval.

The curled wig aside, Jane was struck breathless momentarily by the likeness to Will she saw in this portrait. The man in this small painting seemed to hold back his smile, but the humour was there in the firm gaze, which seemed to stare into her soul. Intelligence lurked in his expression, and just a whiff of boredom at having to pose. He was romantically painted, wearing armour – odd, but compelling all the same, given that Winifred had lost her William to a battle he was duty-bound to engage in, and Jane had lost Will in a fight he had not gone looking for either.

Jane covered Winifred's face with her hands, trembling again and it was not from fever. Everyone was counting on her to stop some leather-hooded executioner from chopping off William Maxwell's head. It was terrifying!

She opened one of William's drawers and found a small tower of neatly folded and ironed handkerchiefs, embroidered – by Winifred, of course – with his initials. Two others featured the family crest. And one, she noted, had some very poor embroidery: a sampler attempted by Anne, she remembered.

She took that and one other of simple, embroidered linen, and after dabbing her streaming nose she tucked them into her pockets.

She relied on Winifred's good sense to grab a shirt and undergarments. When she finally descended the stairs and found her way to the parlour, she was genuinely feeling stronger, but feigned even better health to ensure that Cecilia and Sarah stopped fussing. Enthusiastically tucking into the thickened oat gruel from the shallow pewter porringer that Sarah placed in front of her seemed to appease them. The housekeeper had pointed at the salt bowl, as if she might like to help herself, but Jane declined.

'I might take some honey if we have any, Sarah.'

Sarah walked gladly into the pantry, returning with a pot. 'I would have warmed it had I known. It may be set.'

The sticky sugariness made the gruel more palatable, along with the fresh, rich milk, from which Sarah had skimmed the cream for her mistress. Jane wished she could mix up a honey and lemon drink for her sore throat, but knew a lemon in 1715 Scotland would be as likely as the arrival of a train to whisk her down to London.

'Ale or tea?' Sarah interrupted her thoughts.

Ale? 'Tea... thank you.' It was served strong and stewed, with no sugar and only a dash of milk. It didn't matter; it warmed her insides, and would keep the fever at bay.

She quietly mentioned the commode to Cecilia and that remark sent her friend scurrying off to the dining room.

Bran arrived. 'I brought this for My Lady, as ye bid,' he said to Sarah, handing her a silver case.

Winifred knew what it was. She took the case from Sarah and felt the warmth through her hands immediately.

'Tha' should last ye for a few hours, My Lady,' Bran said, pulling his cap off and hovering at the parlour entrance.

'Thank you, Bran.' She smiled, appreciative of the neat hand-warming case filled with warmed charcoal, which she could slip into her cloak pocket. 'I do believe the fever has broken,' she added truthfully. Yes, she was definitely feeling stronger for the food and drink.

'The horses are readied, My Lady,' Bran told her.

'I still think I'm too well dressed,' Jane remarked to Cecilia.

Her friend bit her lip, which seemed to indicate her agreement. 'What do you suggest?'

Jane dipped into Winifred's memories. 'I need a long cloak that covers me fully. This one I'm wearing is too fine and too short. Something as unremarkable as possible.'

'There's the blue one. That's long.'

'And extremely eye-catching with its pink satin lining! No, that won't do.'

'Wear mine,' Cecilia offered.

'Tosh! You need it.'

'I have a very old, dun-brown cloak, My Lady,' Sarah offered, slightly embarrassed at joining the conversation. 'I only use it to go out into the paddocks. If you want to travel unnoticed, I daresay it will do the trick if ye can bear it. It's awful long.'

'Bear it? I'd be glad to swap it with this one.' Jane pulled off her own crimson cloak.

'Nay, My Lady, I could not.'

'Oh, Sarah. This cloak is meaningless in the scheme of what I set out to do. Here, take it. Stay warm when you walk the paddocks and think on me. Please, fetch me that old brown one of yours. I recall it well.'

Sarah hurried away, returning trailing a shabby velvet cloak and trying to dust away the grime that had gathered at its base.

'Yes, it is perfect!' Jane exclaimed as she caught sight of the garment and its wide floppy hood. She took it from Sarah, who was blushing slightly to have the beautiful crimson cloak pushed into her hands. Jane twirled the cloak around her shoulders and tied its ribbon at her neck. She looked down and was thrilled to see it drop to her boots, skimming the top of their leather. She raised the hood and fastened it with the small clasp. 'How do I look?'

'Like a peasant,' Cecilia exclaimed with a mischievous grin.

'Wear your oldest clothes, my friend, and then we shall make a good pair,' Jane retorted, glad of the momentary light-heartedness that released the tension of their departure.

'My Lady...' Sarah began.

'Not another word, Sarah. This cloak is thick, warm and precisely what I require to travel as inconspicuously as I can.'

The housekeeper held her tongue.

'It's time,' Jane said, looking around at her trio of supporters.

Not long after, sniffing into Anne's handkerchief to stem the flow of her obviously running nose, she watched Sarah press a linen parcel into Cecilia's hands. 'I don't know what My Lady is sickening from, but make sure she is well nourished.'

Cecilia smiled at the housekeeper.

'Wish me luck, Sarah... Bran,' Jane croaked as Winifred expertly eased her horse away from the stable to the side gate, and onto the road that, to her, was little more than a path.

SIXTEEN

THE GOING WAS TREACHEROUS. JANE'S PALFREY STUMBLED twice, losing its footing momentarily on the ground's thin coating of ice beneath the fresh fall of snow that was more than a foot deep in places. But her horse was brave of heart, she knew from Winifred's memories, and it would ride until that brave heart gave up if its mistress asked.

How glad Jane was now of the riding lessons her mother had encouraged her to take since she was old enough to sit a horse! But right now she was drawing on Winifred's knowledge, because although Jane had ridden in a few exhibitions using a side-saddle, it was Winifred's competence that would get her through this trial. She remembered from her lessons, rehearsing for the Regency Exhibition, that she must align her spine with the horse's, which would prevent her from putting too much weight onto one side of the animal. The saddle, though strange for her, was well worn in and felt curiously comfortable as Winifred's skills came to the fore, enabling her to find the perfect position and balance, as well as the all-important correct draping of her skirt.

Now, though, a couple of hours' riding into their challenging journey south, Jane wasn't sure she could feel her face; it was too numbed by the chill wind howling gleefully around them. She reached up and pulled the woolly scarf back over her mouth and nose, tucking it in around her collar as best she could. The cloak was far thicker and warmer than her own had been, and she silently blessed Sarah for suggesting that she take it. Nevertheless, she could feel the morning frost biting through the fur lining in her gloves and clawing at any skin on her face that was bared to its cruelty.

Jane had always believed that snow possessed the magic to turn even the most barren topography of her Welsh homeland to a fairyland. And right now all the fields and hills were iced in white, sparkling and glistening beneath the winter's thin sunlight. In different circumstances this would have enchanted her, but right now it presented a trial she feared. Were they moving quickly enough? Would fresh snowfall just hamper them, or would it block them in? Would their horses survive? Would they survive?

Cecilia seemed equally apprehensive. 'Mayhap the direct way would have been more sensible, dear Winifred,' she suggested over the wind's howl.

Jane shook her head and yelled back. 'Bran said to avoid Dumfries and Carlisle. They are teeming with government troops.'

'How far away is Newcastle?'

'Twelve hours at this pace, mayhap,' she finally admitted.

There was a pause as her friend absorbed the horror of that truth in silence.

'Then we must hasten, Winnie.'

'We shall stop at the nearest inn we reach once we are past the warmest part of the day.' She threw Cecilia a wry glance and, mercifully, Jane could see her friend's eyes crinkle with amusement as she grinned back beneath her scarf, for there was nothing remotely warm about today.

The wind gradually dropped, until they moved in near silence punctuated only by the occasional snort from their horses and their own coughs or loud breathing. The respite was short, though, as one of God's furies was soon replaced by another: snow. The soft flakes began to drift around them, gentle at first, but gaining in intensity over the following hour; the temperature had fallen, and Jane could only just make out the road ahead, thanks to the spikes of hedgerow peeping through the snow. They met only one other rider, who tipped his hat at the women and passed by saying nothing, which suited Jane. It was too cold to talk and it was obvious that the cruelly frigid weather had imprisoned most by their hearths.

An hour or so later, they came upon a family with six young children huddled together in the back of a cart like a bundle of old rags, and were happy to stick with this group as they reached the villages surrounding Newcastle.

'My husband has work in the city,' Jane thought the woman said. Her accent was almost too thick for even Winifred to decipher.

She nodded. 'We go in search of work too,' she said breathlessly, for want of other words.

'What are you seeking?' she guessed the woman asked while she rummaged beneath her clothes to feed the mewling infant in her arms.

'We both desire a role as a governess,' Jane called, hoping that sounded appropriate but vague enough. Her cloak notwithstanding, she couldn't fully pass for a peasant, riding as she did on a decent horse and wearing fur-lined gloves. The now-cold tin of charcoal reminded her that she was far from an ordinary traveller as she looked around at the shivering family and at Cecilia, who did not have her level of comfort either. Jane decided she would not use the hand warmer again.

Oblivious to Jane's surging guilt, the woman nodded, losing interest as they rounded a bend in the road. Fortunately the town of Rothbury came into view and everyone's attention was suddenly diverted – first by the sickening smell, and then by the ominous sight of a gibbet at the crossroads leading into the town.

The children laughed and pointed. The other women looked away, but Jane found her gaze helplessly pinioned to the sight of a decaying corpse displayed in a cage. A nasty, sweetish smell, like rotten eggs and rotted meat, made her heave. The scene was made all the more revolting by the carrion birds that pecked through the bars of the cage.

'Who would that be?' Winifred of course should know this, she realised, but the question was out.

Her eyes continued to water at the overpowering stench as Cecilia, more composed, shrugged. 'A highwayman, I suppose. You always did have a faint belly for it. We must get some more menthol,' she muttered. 'This won't be the last.'

Jane took a deep breath of the icy air and it helped settle her stomach. 'I had better get myself used to it, then,' she replied, and urged her horse on quickly to put distance between them and the executed man.

Ellen was lurking behind the physician, Evans, when Will Maxwell's parents were shown into the ICU. She thought his father seemed set to explode, while his mother appeared pale and thin-lipped.

The social worker who was escorting them looked frazzled. Other professionals had been gathered, each with a personal and, more to the point, vested interest in Will's case, including the dietitian, respiratory therapist and physical therapist, a specialist pharmacologist, and sundry nurses who took care of Will's daily needs. Only the registrar and the hospital chaplain were missing – though Ellen would not have been surprised if Father Wiley popped by, for he had taken a keen interest in Will's situation and recovery.

'What the hell is this all about, Evans? You promised me—'

'Mr Maxwell, calm down, please,' the physician began, his tone reasonable, his hands open in appeal.

'Calm down?' Maxwell roughly pulled his arm free of his wife's. 'Why don't you go fuck yourself, *Dr* Evans?'

Ellen shared an uncomfortable glance with her colleagues, but Maxwell's reaction came as no surprise. He wasn't the first father to lose his composure under these circumstances.

'John, don't,' his wife pleaded.

Robert Evans – built like a toilet block, with a ruddy complexion and a rhythmic Welsh lilt – didn't react, Ellen noticed. She felt quietly proud that no one else in the team so much as flinched. They were used to emotional explosions, and nowhere in the hospital were emotions rawer or more ragged than in the intensive care unit.

'Don't what?' her husband snapped. 'Don't tell these priggish English medicos that they wouldn't know if their own asses were on fire?'

Evans waited for John Maxwell to round on him again. But Maxwell had begun to look embarrassed when no one fought back.

He tried again, though. 'Come on then, *Dr* Evans!' he snarled, his tone dripping with sarcasm, his face turning red with his rage. Could she really travel with these people? 'Tell me why you can't release my son today. You've delayed us for two days already!'

'Mrs Maxwell, would you like to sit down?' Ellen offered. Diane was looking ready to break.

'No, she wouldn't!' her husband thundered, desperate for a fight. *He won't get one here*, Ellen thought. 'I demand the release of my son *today*. He's going to the US, where they can offer us some hope.'

'Actually, there's some encouraging news,' Robert Evans began conversationally. 'I didn't want to raise any false hopes too soon, but I think it's fair to say that Will is showing some indications of surfacing.' His language was carefully chosen, Ellen noted: nothing dramatic, but just the right note of optimism.

Diane Maxwell reacted first, crumpling into tears, her hand clamping against her mouth to stop any sound of weakness. Her husband glared, but Ellen glared back as she helped Mrs Maxwell to a chair beside her son's bed.

'You never wanted us to take him back home, did you?' John Maxwell accused.

All of them knew that anger was often the favoured mood of desperately upset parents in the early stages of the grieving process. As shock gave way, the bitterness took over. Depending on how long their child was in the ICU, eventually that passed too, and emotions usually settled down into calm resignation. Ellen wondered if John Maxwell would ever reach the calm stage.

Evans ignored the bait and pressed on as though he had parents standing in front of him who were eager for his news, rather than parents filled with fear and doubt. 'Let me explain.' Firmly, and in layman's language, the physician began to outline what Ellen had first witnessed from their son two nights before. It had led to a range of tests and almost round-the-clock physical monitoring, as well as twenty-four-hour automated checks.

'… false hope, but I'm feeling confident, now that we've had a chance to monitor the subtle changes, that Will's body has its own plan.'

Maxwell had calmed slightly, his body language more docile, but a belligerent attitude was still present in his expression. 'Why should that change *our* plans? If Will's going to wake up, he might as well wake up on American soil, where he belongs.'

'Well, that's certainly one way of looking at it,' Evans said carefully. 'Except my experience suggests that this is an intensely fragile, but incredibly important, time for Will's body. If I can explain it thus: it's as though his body is reaching toward something, so to alter the status quo would be putting this positive change at risk.'

'Or is it just that you smell the chance for some success when so far you've failed my son?'

Anyone else, Ellen thought, would have shown some flicker of offence. But if Evans felt angered by John Maxwell, he betrayed nothing in his expression. Frankly, there was only so much slack the hard-working, mostly unacknowledged nursing team would cut a man who couldn't find a single kind word. Ellen wished Evans would slap Maxwell with his ace card.

The physician spoke again and his voice was gentle and generous… but he must have heard her thought because he played the ace. She had heard him speak of it only once before; she didn't think many of the other staff were even aware of his family background.

'I understand your despair, Mr Maxwell. I myself have lost a son in tragic circumstances. Even with all of my know-how I couldn't bring him back from the disease that took him. I have never felt more out of control than I did when we were losing Charlie, but one thing I never gave up on was the medical team that was working around the clock to save him. To a terrified father it never looked as though they were doing enough, when in fact they were giving one hundred per cent.'

Maxwell's puffed chest deflated slightly, Ellen noticed, and his mouth hung open a little. Evans had shocked him. Good!

The doctor continued even more gently. 'Now, I accept that the American team may have something different to offer and I am all for exploring new avenues. However, right now, right here – as Will gives us the first glimpse that he may be pulling himself back to you – my professional opinion, from over two decades of working with head traumas, is that changing Will's environment, moving him around, bringing in a new team that hasn't been with him from the start, would create unnecessary risks.'

Everyone watched John Maxwell take an angry breath, but, inwardly cheering, Ellen also watched her favourite physician press on and ignore him. 'I would go so far as to suggest that to do anything other than let Will's body quietly continue on this pathway to consciousness – which I firmly believe he is on – would be tantamount to risking his life.' Diane Maxwell gasped and her husband looked apoplectic. 'I know this is a shocking thing to hear, but my belief is that your son is balanced on a precipice. No one is better equipped than the patient to know the right time to start reaching for consciousness. Will alone knows when his body is ready. We have cared for his body, ensured he is comfortable, and the team here continue to talk to him as a gentle stimulation, so my advice is that you leave Will as he is until we can see where this phase in his recovery is headed.'

'Are you saying that to move Will now *would* kill him?' Mrs Maxwell asked in a shaking voice.

'Not *would*. But it's a real and very definite risk, in my opinion,' Evans answered, but looked firmly at Mr Maxwell as he said it. 'The decision is yours, of course. So it's up to you now to tell us what you wish. If you want Will moved, we will follow your instructions and have him readied for travel.'

Ellen wanted to applaud the way Evans had masterfully and politely heaped the guilt onto Maxwell senior's shoulders. If John Maxwell defied the physician now, Ellen would eat her uniform. She wanted to see America, but not at Will's expense. In all the days she'd tended him, he'd never looked so handsome; how marvellous if he woke up in a day or so and she were the first person he saw. *Stop that, Ellen*, she berated herself.

'How long?' Maxwell snapped.

Evans shrugged. 'It's up to Will. I told you his fingers twitched two days ago. Last night, Ellen and one of the other nurses heard him groan and saw his toes curl in what we believe was a voluntary action. The energy output from his brain is changing too. We are monitoring him constantly, but of course we have to remain patient. As I said, this is a delicate stage – it could go either way.'

Maxwell nodded. 'Well, either way, Dr Evans, I'm taking my son back to America after New Year's Day. You have him until 2nd January.'

Three days, Ellen thought. *Come on, Will, wake up for us!*

SEVENTEEN

As the Maxwells were leaving the hospital, Big Ben was striking the hour of eleven. Jane's mother dashed from the garden to grab the phone at the Granger family home in Welshpool, on the border between Wales and England. She'd been plucking some chervil, the only herb growing in the garden right now. Catelyn liked nothing better than fresh chervil sprinkled on her scrambled eggs. She'd missed breakfast, so brunch would have to do, and if she had not been sure that this was Jane calling from Australia, she would have let the phone ring out and not permitted her eggs to toughen.

As she grabbed the receiver, she glanced at her watch and estimated it had to be eight-thirty in the evening in Alice Springs. Jane was surely calling to confirm that she'd carried out her crazy yet admirable goal to write her fiancé's name in the book at the top of that rock. Jane had found a picture of Uluru and shown it to her parents. They'd tried hard not to criticise, not to laugh out loud, not to share a look of horrified suspicion that their daughter might be going mad with grief.

But Catelyn knew Jane too well. She was grieving, for sure, but she was showing that same gritty determination she'd had when she'd told them she was attending a university in London and not Cardiff or Manchester, or even Durham. And she'd had that same sense of composure when she'd told them she was going off travelling around the world, taking a year off to fend for herself and learn a bit more about life. She'd been gone for two.

Jane had always set herself goals and been driven by an internal discipline that couldn't be swayed once she'd switched it on. And travelling to central Australia had been one of those occasions when her mother, certainly, had known better than to try and dissuade her. It hadn't made Catelyn any less frightened for her daughter, of course. Hopefully this call was to give them her return flight details. Catelyn cast out a wish as she spoke into the receiver.

'Hello?' There was the familiar sense of speaking into a cavernous space. She heard the echo and her heart did a flip of joy. 'Hello, Jane?' she said again. 'Is that you, darling?'

'Is this Mrs Granger?' It was a man's voice. He had a thick Australian accent and sounded as though he were speaking from the bottom of the sea. He pronounced their surname wrongly too, which vaguely irritated Catelyn.

She frowned. 'Er, yes... this is Catelyn *Granger*. Who's speaking, please?' Her words were repeated in an annoying echo.

'Mrs Granger, my name's Barry—'

The doorbell interrupted what he was saying. 'Oh, just a moment,' she said. 'There's someone at the door. Sorry... Mr, er, sorry, could you hold the line, please?' She didn't wait for his response. Whoever it was who had rung the doorbell had hastily done so again. It sounded urgent. Through the glass side panel of the front door, she could see the outline of at least two people. One of them now rapped on the door.

'I'm coming!' she called, her irritation at the phone call now morphing into indignation. Her husband had needed to go into Cardiff, her other daughter was probably soaking in yet another bath, and the housekeeper was still on her Christmas break. Why was no one else ever around? Someone on the phone, someone at the door, her eggs were surely like rubber by now, and she was still clutching the fragile heads of chervil.

She opened the front door and was astonished to see two police looking back at her. One was a woman with a pretty face and strawberry-blonde hair that was neatly ponytailed. It was the policewoman who spoke first.

'Mrs Granger?' she asked, mercifully pronouncing their name properly. She didn't sound Welsh, though. Irish, perhaps?

'I – I'm on the phone,' Catelyn said, pointing weakly over her shoulder to the grey-green 'trimphone' sitting on the hall table. They really should get one installed in the kitchen, she thought bleakly, so she didn't have to run from the garden, although suddenly she wished she hadn't made it to the phone and definitely wished she hadn't answered the doorbell. The policewoman had continued speaking, but Catelyn hadn't paid attention.

'Would you mind asking the caller to ring back?' the policewoman suggested. Catelyn knew she'd been told her name, but she hadn't been listening, lost in thoughts of scrambled eggs and trimphones.

'I think it's a call from Australia,' she bleated. 'My daughter… she's…' And it was in that horrid moment, trapped between her visitors and her phone caller, that Catelyn Granger understood they were all contacting her about Jane. Something must have gone wrong, or Jane would have called herself.

'Mrs Granger…' the policewoman began gently. 'May we come in?'

'Oh, no. No!' Catelyn shrieked as chervil fell and scattered on the pale, beautiful flagstones of the hallway, to be crushed underfoot as the police officers moved swiftly to steady her.

Eggs hardened in the kitchen and a soft hint of aniseed wafted up as Jane's mother collapsed.

Winifred and Cecilia spent an uneventful night at the Three Half Moons Inn at Rothbury. As far as the innkeeper was concerned, they were travelling governesses on their way to Newcastle to seek work.

The morning dawned brighter than yesterday's, and it had not snowed overnight, but a white blanket remained thick over the market town and their horses' hooves crunched on the crystalline carpet that led them south-east toward Newcastle. The mug of whey Jane had felt obliged to drink that morning was sloshing around her belly and making her feel nauseous. 'Cold turkey pie for breakfast does not agree with me,' she admitted.

The two women set a brisk pace and within four frigid hours they had entered Newcastle upon Tyne and had beheld two other criminals who had suffered the same treatment as the man outside Rothbury. By the third corpse, Jane had taught herself to hold her breath and cover her mouth with Anne's handkerchief as they passed... and not look up.

Newcastle was showing its prosperity from coal haulage, but also its loyalty to the Crown. Reward banners for information leading to the arrest of 'rebels' were posted everywhere they looked as they moved slowly through the broad streets and past tall houses built from brick and stone. Snow had been swept to the sides of the roads in great drifts and the remaining slush was fast turning to small rivulets or crusty patches of ice. The unremarkable garments and hoods pulled low in the face of such wintry conditions conspired to detract attention from the pair, who paused only once to ask a trio of servant women the way to the coaching inn.

Heartbreak was to follow as they forlornly listened to the coachman explain that every seat had been booked.

'But an urgent matter requires me to be in London without delay, sir!' Jane said, increasingly drawing on Winifred's sensibilities to handle such discussions. She was very glad now that Winifred possessed no trace of Scottish brogue in her voice. She left Cecilia to look after the horses and organise for them to be stabled indefinitely. Winifred's brave palfrey was not for sale.

'And I feel sorely bad for you, Miss Granger, but everyone is in a fury to escape the north, it seems. This winter is cruel indeed.'

Jane felt rising panic. 'I *have* to get to London!' she cried. 'It's a matter of life or death!' It slipped out in her wretchedness, and she hated herself for letting him know this much.

And not just him. She was aware of a gentleman waiting patiently not too far away, and he'd glanced at her when her voice had risen. She hadn't paid attention to him, but now their eyes met and she felt embarrassed to see sympathy in his dark glance. She did not want to arouse anyone's interest right now.

'Oh, Miss Granger, now you make me feel entirely responsible.'

'It is not my intention to burden you, sir,' she said quietly.

'Well, now... The next coach is not due to leave for three days.' As Jane opened her mouth to protest, he held up a hand. 'Do you ride, Miss Granger?'

'Of course,' she said, hoping she hadn't sounded as indignant as she felt, given how sore Winifred's right buttock was at present.

'And you have access to horses?'

'We rode in haste to Newcastle from Rothbury,' she said in answer. 'But, yes, our horses will be refreshed overnight.'

He nodded. 'Then dare I say, ride on, Miss Granger. You and your companion must travel to York, where I think you have a far happier chance of finding seats to the south.'

'York?' she exclaimed. 'That has to be several days' ride from here, sir!' Jane knew her voice had a note of high anxiety in it.

'Indeed,' he said, looking apologetic.

'Madam...' interrupted a new voice. She turned to regard the gentleman who had been standing aside. She watched him now as he removed his tricorne hat and bowed slightly. He couldn't be far off Winifred's age, Jane could see now that he had stepped closer – perhaps around forty – but he was disarmingly attractive in an unconventional way. It stemmed from his eyes, liquorice-coloured in this dim light and broodily intense in the way they regarded her. Spare, symmetrical features were dominated by the deep colour of his brow and hair; the latter, to Jane's great relief, was worn neatly scraped back and secured in a tight queue, completing a darkly handsome face. If he had confronted her in full periwig right now, she was sure her anxiety would have given way to laughter. She sensed, though, that this man was not prone to following the fashions of the day, if his greatcoat was any giveaway. He wore it in a careless manner and had none of the frills and fripperies that she'd noticed on other men. 'Forgive me,' he said in a softly spoken tone, 'I could not but help overhear of your plight.'

She waited, taking in his slimly cut, unadorned riding coat more carefully now that she faced him. It was of a sand-coloured worsted and not the heavily brocaded long coat favoured by most... yet the air he gave off reeked of wealth.

'You do not sound hale, if you'll pardon my forwardness. I doubt you should be travelling anywhere.'

'It is just the cold affecting me,' she lied.

He blinked, betraying his confoundment. 'Even so, perhaps waiting for the next coach—'

'I appreciate your concern, sir. But I have no choice in the matter. I must be in London by the fastest means.' She smiled, hoping to allay his frowning expression by making light of her situation, adding, 'I could well wish for a pair of wings.'

He didn't return her smile. If anything, he looked even more troubled by her determination. Why was he making this his problem? She wished he'd take his imposing frame and handsome face several steps back to where he'd been lurking previously.

'Well then, I am travelling to York myself,' he continued, 'leaving immediately. I too wish to get myself to London by carriage.'

'How does this help me, sir, I wonder?' she asked, still keeping her tone light.

He cleared his throat. Perhaps he wasn't used to women who were quite so direct, she thought. *Remember, Jane... 1715, not 1978.* She'd missed what he had begun to say.

'... So I shall surely reach York before you gentle ladies can,' he said, nodding toward the door and beyond to where Cecilia waited. 'I have no intention of stopping, not even for sustenance, until I have my seat on that coach. Perhaps, if it helps your cause, I might save you two seats on the same coach?' He looked over her shoulder. 'Coachman, when does it leave York for London, did you say?'

'On Friday, sir.'

'You have four days to get there from here. I shall make it in two if I'm fortunate, but likely three.'

She was taken aback. 'Um...' Now she felt flustered. 'Well, that's extremely generous of you, sir,' she said, slightly lost for what else to say.

He shrugged. 'It is no burden, madam.' He gave his short bow again, finally finding a tight, brief smile that was gone as fast as it came. 'Julius Sackville.'

'Er... Miss Granger,' she said, hesitating only slightly in her lie, and the pause she believed she covered well enough with a smile. It would not do any good to tell the truth to someone who might be in a position to hurt her cause. 'I am deeply grateful for your offer of help. My companion and I will do our utmost to arrive for that coach.'

His undistracted gaze unnerved her. She wondered if that gaze had seen right through the lie, and not just about her name. It felt as though this man's eyes looked right into Winifred's soul and could see the real lie – the impostor who lived beneath. Jane realised she'd been holding Winifred's breath, deliberately preventing herself from saying anything more that might reveal the truth. 'Good day, Miss Granger,' he said at last. 'I wish you both uneventful travelling, although I fear the weather will punish you. And I shall hope to see you safely in York by week's end. I should warn you to leave early on the morrow, as I gather there is to be a public execution in the market square.' He looked over at the coachman, finally releasing Jane from his hold. 'Good day, sir.'

'Lord Sackville, sir,' the man called after him, and tugged his cap in farewell.

Lord Sackville. Jane took a deep breath and turned to the man behind the counter. 'I trust you can accommodate us this night?'

He nodded. 'Yes, Miss Granger, of course, although you are fortunate. The execution Lord Sackville spoke of is that of a popular rebel. People will be travelling from far and wide to see the spectacle.'

Jane winced, turning back to say farewell, but Sackville was gone.

'What time is the execution?' she asked, amazed that it sounded as casual and conversational as if she'd just asked what the weather might bring tomorrow.

'On the stroke of nine I heard, miss.'

'You may have our room by seven. We will be dressed with the cockerel's first cry, I suspect.'

EIGHTEEN

JANE HAD NEVER EXPERIENCED WEATHER LIKE THIS, not even during her childhood, when she'd spent winter holidays with her cousins deep in Snowdonia. Coming from Wales and used to a harsher climate than in southern England, she considered herself hardy at the very least. But this journey was throwing up challenges she had no wish to tackle, she realised, as she and Cecilia held on to one another and gingerly navigated their way through the snow from their accommodation to the stable. From behind the scarf that now covered most of her face and was tucked back into her hood, Jane wondered at the wisdom of travelling on horseback in blizzard conditions.

After listening to what the stableman had to say and despite Winifred's suspicion that he was after making some extra coin at their expense, the Countess's good sense prevailed. They made the decision to keep their own horses stabled, to be retrieved at a later date, and hired two sturdier mounts. Jane had seen reflected in the stableman's expression – though he likely thought he'd disguised it – his conviction that he was dealing with a woman on the edge of madness, asking Jane repeatedly if she was sure that she shouldn't just wait for the next coach out of Newcastle.

Although the deal was done and he had just buckled on the second saddle, Jane admired the way he gave it one last try. 'By the time you get to York, miss, the next coach will be leaving here.'

His reasoning was clearly sound, and if lives had not been depending on the speed of her journey to London, Jane – and she was sure Winifred too – would have taken his advice. Instead, she dropped the coin into his reluctant hand and thanked him for his concern.

'I cannot count on that coach through here,' she countered, hoping she could make Winifred appear more rational in the stableman's eyes. 'The roads could be so snowbound that the coach does not even reach here, and then precious days will be lost.'

'No language lessons or music tutoring can be worth risking your life for, miss... if you don't mind my saying,' he had said in a final attempt.

'I am grateful for your concern... truly.' She felt sorry for his deep frown of worry and immediately took back her cynical notion that he was profiteering from their difficulties.

The stableman cleared his throat. 'In that case, would you wait a moment, miss?'

She threw a worried glance at Cecilia as he limped into the shadows of the stable, returning a minute later with a folded parchment.

Large, clear handwriting that sloped to the right spelled out:*For Miss Granger.*

'I was asked to give you this, miss, should you insist on riding to York.' The stableman held out the paper, which had been neatly folded and sealed with wax.

'By whom, sir?'

'By Lord Sackville. He was here yesterday and said I should do everything in my power to discourage your journey, but should you insist on leaving for York I was to ensure you were given this.' He shrugged. 'I wouldn't disobey my Lord Sackville.'

She eased a finger under the wax and after exerting some pressure felt the paper spring away from its first fold. Jane gave both her companions a glance before she moved to the doorway of the stable, where it was lighter, though not as warm.

The same assured handwriting gave a brief introduction followed by an equally brief list of four inns.

My dear Miss Granger,
If you insist on making the perilous journey to York, please consider these inns as safe and reliable accommodation.
Yours,
Sackville

Cecilia and the stableman tentatively approached her. She shrugged and gave leave for Cecilia to read the note out, including the list.

The stableman nodded. 'That first is twenty-five miles from here. He likely did not think you would make it much further than that today.'

'Oh, did he not?' Jane snipped.

The man blinked, unsure.

'And how far away is this next one?' she asked. He looked where her finger pointed and the silence told her he likely couldn't read. 'The Crown and Sceptre,' she said.

'Oh, that is just north of Durham, miss.'

'Well, I might surprise Lord Sackville and make it that far today.' She folded the note. 'You've been most attentive. Thank you.'

He touched his cap in a clearly habitual gesture. 'I'll fetch the horses.'

While they waited, stamping their feet to keep at bay the deep chill that was already clawing at them from the frozen earth, Cecilia cast her friend a look of anxiety.

'Dear Win. Truly, search yourself and ask if this is a wise course.'

'Cecilia, I would not think badly of you, not for a heartbeat, if you remained here until the next coach came and took you back to Terregles. But don't ask me again, my darling friend, because you see, unlike you, I have no free will in this.' She said it again, slowly, pausing slightly between her words. 'I have no choice.'

Cecilia gave her a pained look. 'You could die on this journey.'

'Then I will die, but Will could never say I didn't love him,' Jane said, hearing the real fear that lay in the heart of a desperate woman, searching for the truth of herself.

Cecilia hugged her. 'We will face this trial together. I would never leave you.'

The stablemaster returned leading two large, sturdy horses. 'I've blinkered them, miss. Helps against any skittishness in this weather.'

Within a few hours Jane was so bitterly cold she couldn't feel the sensation of Winifred's fingers on the reins, was sure she was no longer in control of her horse and felt distant gratitude for the beast's gentle temperament. To breathe hurt her lungs and even to lift her head to see the way ahead stung her eyes. Cecilia was surely faring no better, but her loyal companion never complained.

Despite her early bravado and Jane's best will, the Crown and Sceptre evaded them and the women collapsed into a shared bed five miles north of Durham at the very inn that Sackville had recommended. She hated him in that moment for being right, but worshipped the innkeeper for having a fire burning and hot tea to warm her frozen insides and the smell of roasted poultry scenting the air for an evening meal.

Sleep came hard and fast; they hadn't even needed to burn the candle in their room for more than it took to step out of their top layers and collapse onto their thin mattress using each other for extra warmth.

After another exhausting but less stressful day in the saddle, the formerly elusive Crown and Sceptre in the next market town was a grateful sight. And by day three out of Newcastle Jane had high hopes of making it as far as Ripon, because the day had dawned frosty, but with clearer skies. They were travelling at a good clip and both in fair spirits. Even the horses had a friskiness in their steps that boded well. Cecilia was recounting a time in their childhood when Winifred had decided she was going to run away from home. They were laughing as Winifred's memories dredged up the scene for Jane, and it was amusing to recall Winifred's packing essentials that included her father's small fruit knife, which she'd appropriated and believed would be required for chopping down branches.

'... to build your evening's shelter, you said!' Cecilia chuckled.

Jane was grinning at Winifred's memory of this halcyon time when she and Cecilia became aware of two men on a cart approaching. The pair of women had got used to being alone for long periods on the roads these last few days and Jane didn't know why, on this occasion, she wouldn't welcome the chance to nod at a fellow rider passing by, but something about the way the men watched them unnerved her. Maybe it was her modern mind, conditioned to be suspicious of just about everyone when travelling alone. It wasn't her imagination, though. Cecilia had noticed their interest too, and all humour had fled from her friend's expression.

'Do not slow down or break stride,' Jane muttered.

But as Cecilia glanced her way in agreement, Jane noted a third man, previously hidden by his companions, jump down from the cart, thus blocking Jane's and Cecilia's passage.

'Well met, ladies,' he said.

Jane forced herself to nod, allowing Winifred's instincts to guide her. Now she had no choice but to slow her horse in case, startled by his sudden movement, it might skitter and rear. She had no intention of engaging in any conversation with these men; their general raggedness aside, they possessed a hungry look that Jane's worldliness recognised and suspected had little to do with food. Trills of fresh alarm electrified her; robbery was no doubt on the horizon here, but only now did it occur to Jane how vulnerable they surely were. The warnings of everyone who had tried to advise her gathered like ravens on a winter tree, as though lining up to bear witness to her lunacy, muttering that *We told you so.*

A fresh fear crept up her spine that rape might also be on the minds of these men. They were highwaymen, her instincts told her, opportunists who preyed on unsuspecting travellers. If she could have made herself and Cecilia easier targets, she couldn't imagine how. *Stupid!* she growled angrily to herself.

Jane could almost hear the thoughts of the men. *Why pay for it if you can just take it on a lonely road in the middle of winter from two silly women travelling alone?*

She jumped when the man on foot spoke again. 'Where are you headed, miss?' he said, making Jane's horse shy back as he raised his hands.

'I am not sure that is any of your business,' she said, risking Winifred's loftiest tone, hoping it would scare off these opportunists. Her instincts were klaxoning at her that wickedness was surely on their minds. Why else would this man be deliberately blocking their passage?

'Ah, don't be like that,' he said, waving his arms again so Jane was forced to haul on the reins. She was aware of Cecilia doing the same.

She could see the stablemaster's concern in her mind's eye. How many times had he tried to dissuade her? And now she was convinced that Julius Sackville was behind it; had probably paid the man extra coin to try and put her off the madness of her journey.

'Would you step out of the way, fellow?' she said, adding terseness.

'Why don't you step down instead, miss?'

The cart had stopped, the other men leering and grinning, catching on quickly to what their friend had in mind.

'Shall I be forced to gallop over you?' Jane said, raising her whip.

'And leave your friend to us?' he said, feigning astonishment. Jane felt Winifred's mouth turn instantly dry. He was no longer hiding his intention. 'She looks worried, miss. To be sure, you would not leave without her. I could jump out of the way by the time you got that beast going, then me and the boys here could encourage your friend to stay behind.'

It wasn't often that Jane had experienced true panic in her life. She could recall occasions of anger or high anxiety – losing a passport, missing a flight, taking the wrong train, having a wallet stolen were situations that sent any traveller into what they might describe as panic, but there were always people or services around to assist. There were formal processes and there were credit cards to get one out of most jams, and in her case a wealthy family to fall back on.

But the times when she'd felt utterly out of control in a dangerous situation she could count on two fingers.

The first was seeing Will loaded unconscious into an ambulance and hearing the siren scream above them as they were raced to the emergency department of the closest hospital. She had been flung back into a corner of the ambulance while two men worked anxiously on her fiancé and the lack of control had sent her into a feeling of blind panic.

And the second occasion was now. She had no experience to draw on that was going to tell her how to handle this… and neither did Winifred. These were not men who were going to see reason, she presumed. They clearly lived in a lawless world, where no mobile squads of uniformed police were patrolling the roads with back-up close by. Winifred's fear was telling her that she and Cecilia had neither the strength nor weapons to keep these men back and that this man was right: one of them might get away, but the other would face all three hungry men.

'I would caution you to think very carefully about what you do next, sir!' Winifred's haughtiness came to the fore before she could censor it, for her host was used to being obeyed. But

Jane was keenly aware that men who lived above common laws did not follow any pattern of obedience, no matter how noble or wealthy their victim.

'Sir?' He laughed. 'I am so far away from a sir, miss, that I doubt you should think of me in that way.'

'I think of you not at all. And I would ask you to give me the same courtesy.'

'Ah, now, I am afraid I cannot do that, miss.'

'Why not?'

'Because I am lonely and it is nice to meet people to talk to on this long and wintry road.'

Jane sat as high as she could in the saddle as Winifred retreated; it seemed her host's rush of anger had been shortlived, for Winifred was weak. Jane could feel her host slipping away, and wondered again quickly whether Winifred would already be dead by now if not for Jane's strange and timely arrival in her body.

'*I* am not lonely. And I have no time to pass the day, for I have urgent business in York. Now, let us go by.' She wished her voice hadn't revealed that note of fear; she hoped she was the only one who had heard it. 'What is your name, man?'

He looked away, clearly bored now by the banter. 'Let us proceed with you kind ladies giving us your purses.'

'I will do no such thing, you wretch!'

The man approached, scratching his crotch. 'Ah, there we go. From "sir" to "wretch" in a breath.' He chuckled. 'I think I preferred "fellow".'

'You would do well to leave us alone,' Cecilia finally spoke up. 'My companion is not who she may seem.'

'Seem? Who does she seem to you, lads?'

'A servant, methinks. On her way to seek work in York in a fine household, Tom,' the youngest said.

'Aye, my guess be she is a maid to a noblewoman,' the other man in the cart added, clearly enjoying the confrontation as much as watching the women shrink back toward each other.

Tom put his head to one side, breath rising in lazy curlicues of steam, although he showed no sign of feeling the cold. 'Nay, I think she considers herself higher than that. Housekeeper, or – no, wait, lads. A governess, mayhap? She sounds like she has education. Either way, I think, miss, you are too tightly laced into your corset. Maybe we can help loosen it for you?'

All the men sniggered.

Cecilia clearly couldn't help herself as their intentions became more obvious. Jane heard her friend murmur a plea to the heavens. Her prayer only made them laugh harder.

But Cecilia was not to be put off. Suddenly numbed hands and wind-chilled face were forgotten as blood rushed in anger to warm her cheeks. 'You loathsome fellow!' she snapped. 'You are lacking in even the commonest sense of the commonest folk. This is no maid! Consider your neck being snapped on the end of a noose if you take another step toward her!'

Jane shook her head at Cecilia, believing her wrath would only inflame the situation, which was already teetering on a precipice. She looked around desperately, hoping for inspiration.

'I want your purses,' Tom insisted, and his voice had lost any politeness.

Jane felt incensed at the unfairness of what was unfolding here. The gold she had on her was mostly borrowed from Charles as it was and she would be damned if she was going to hand it over to a highwayman. She blinked. Well, Winifred was wrong. Between Cecilia and her they *did* have a weapon. Old Tom in front of her, who had to be fifty if he was a day, was about to earn an appreciation of what happened when a woman from another world turned angry. Jane Granger was engaged to someone who was a black belt in karate at fifth dan level. *Will is a master practitioner*, as his father had spat at her.

She'd loved it when Will had explained that his martial skills were a spiritual part of him, rather than the weapon they could be. Will's parents had taken him on holiday to

Japan when he was nine and he'd told Jane that by ten he was travelling a round trip of sixty miles three times a week for lessons with the only karate teacher of note in his region, who was ninth dan level. Once Will had mastered the moves, his teacher had taught him more of the philosophy. Will had then lived for two years in Japan in his teens, refining his technique but also progressing on his spiritual journey. Jane had begged him to show her, teach her; Will had agreed to train her in three classic moves so that she could defend herself if she were ever mugged. Well, she knew exactly which one she would use now, as it appeared that 'if ever' had arrived in the shape of a raggle-taggle highwayman with rotten teeth and an itch in his pants.

Jane unhooked her leg from the side-saddle and leaped down off her horse.

'O-ho, mayhap she's taken a fancy to you, Tom Wyatt!' one of his companions jeered. Tom growled a curse, hissing at the man for speaking his full name.

He watched her untie her cloak and fling it off; she could see he was confused by her action and was licking his lips, pausing to consider what she might be up to.

'Winifred!' Cecilia called.

'Be quiet!' Jane snapped as she locked gazes with Tom Wyatt.

Her skirt slowed her over this terrain. It would hamper her movements too if she chose to kick. Without thinking on it further Jane tore off the skirt; she felt buttons pinging into the snow to lie like dark eyes watching her next move. The jacket had to stay, but most of the fussy Georgian garments were now gone. She had good kicking boots on and she doubted Tom had ever confronted a karate block, or a front kick to the ribs.

The men were momentarily speechless at seeing her stripped down to her underskirt and she could hear Cecilia's shocked, gasped warnings from behind her. Jane was horribly aware of wearing no knickers as a modern woman would, and could feel the cold gnawing at the tops of her thighs through the thin cotton. If they ripped off her petticoat now, she would be naked from the waist down. Ludicrously, what flitted through her mind as she teetered on the brink of being violently assaulted was the thought of what Winifred would make of a bikini wax. The mirthless smile that this caused curiously helped her to focus, and her next thought was that she would let Winifred, and herself, die before she'd let this man overwhelm her sufficiently to rape her.

'Winifred, do not—' Cecilia began, her voice now small and tight, laden with horror. But it was cut off by Tom's laughter, his initial shock now passed.

'I think Winifred fancies me, boys! Her sweet ripe arse is shortly going to feel the chill of snow!'

'And the burning warmth of your prick, Tom!' the young one said, impressed enough by his jest to begin laughing uproariously into the frigid stillness. Jane could tell the men were excited now. They reeked of violence and lust and they smelled that both options were theirs for the taking.

Jane turned Winifred's expression into a sneer, ignoring everyone but Tom, who was just steps away. 'I am Lady Winifred Maxwell, Countess of Nithsdale, and you do not want to bring down my noble family's wrath, Tom Wyatt. Hanging will be the least of your troubles by the time my husband and his men have finished with you.'

'Do not lie to me, miss,' he said, although she noted he faltered, his eyes darting around. 'You have no rings or fine jewellery and you are dressed like a servant.'

She began to circle him, testing her weight on the ground for balance and ensuring there were no snags or branches to trip her. 'Looks can be deceiving.' Perhaps she should have worn Winifred's rings instead of burying them with the rest of the prized jewels. 'You admitted I do not sound like a servant.'

He glared at her. 'Whoever you are, I am hungry and I need your purse.'

'I shall give you money for food,' she offered, regretting that she needed to sneeze twice at this juncture.

It was his turn to sneer. 'You do not sound well, miss. You might catch your death, undressed as you are – not that I'm complaining to see a good-looking woman near-naked!' She could tell he was still perplexed by her actions. *Fine! Let him stay on the back foot.* 'And if you are as rich as you say, I should rather take your gold than your charity.' Then he grinned. 'But I shall take your chastity, because it seems to me that you are offering. Perhaps your noble husband does not service you often enough!' His friends enjoyed the jest.

Jane ignored the jibe. She'd fight him all the way, even if Winifred was frail. 'I did not say I was rich. I simply told you who I am.'

'Highborn, aye. And if you are, which I can only take your word for, you have money, all right, or we would not be standing here and arguing over it. Take 'er, lads!'

Jane stiffened and then instinctively moved into the fighting stance that Will had taught her. *Balance is everything, Jane*, he'd explained, moving her legs apart gently so that one was diagonally apart from the other. *And here*, he'd said, folding her arms into a flexed position. *You have to be loose, but your muscles must be ready to tense and unleash their power. I know that sounds like a contradiction, but I'll show you and you'll understand.* And she had.

But Tom's henchmen were not suddenly leaping down from the cart for her, she realised. Instead, they hauled Cecilia screaming off her horse and hurried her away from the road, slipping and sliding on the treacherous ground underfoot. Jane could see the deep furrows in the snow where Cecilia had been dragged. She'd put up a struggle, at least.

'Not up against that tree, lads,' Tom called in an irritated tone. 'Go behind those bushes, and for mercy's sake, stuff something in the bitch's mouth to stop the terrible screeching.'

'I've got something to stuff in her mouth, all right,' the younger one said, still trying to impress his leader.

'Fight them, Cecilia!' Jane yelled.

But the trio disappeared and Cecilia's screams turned muffled, and then there was a momentary silence. Jane could hear more scuffles in the background, followed by a man's yelp, which she hoped was Cecilia connecting her boot with one of them, but her attention was on Tom now. She had to deal with him before she could get to Cecilia.

'Maybe young John was as good as his threat and your friend has bitten him,' he wondered aloud, sounding amused by the man's yelp and the instant silence.

She whipped her head back to Tom. 'You'd better tell them to take their fucking filthy hands off her,' she snarled, all modern Jane now as Winifred shrank away altogether.

He actually put his hand to his chest in laughter, enjoying her swearing. 'No, you're no highborn lady, miss, not with a tongue like that,' he said, 'and I'm going to enjoy feeling that filthy mouth on my cock.'

He leaped at her. She was ready for him, though, and had none of Will's qualms of conscience at using her lethal skills. Shifting her weight onto her back leg, Jane executed a near-perfect roundhouse kick. Her thigh swung at right angles up near her hip, while her lower leg shot out and used her flexed foot as a weapon, empowering the heel to do the intended damage as it punched like a piston, driving into the soft and vulnerable flesh of Tom Wyatt's crotch. He doubled up with a shocked exhalation of breath, but Jane had to be sure. *If you ever use this move, make it count. Don't let them get back up*, Will had tutored. Her balance already regained, Jane's other knee now whipped up; she hoped to smash expertly upward into the bent-over attacker's jaw. But she missed as Tom Wyatt – stronger than he looked and certainly streetsmart enough to dodge a second blow – straightened, clearly hurting, but still with sufficient wit to grab her raised leg and flip her over.

Jane felt the squeaky crunch of snow beneath her; it felt as if all the wind had been punched from her lungs and she lay there for a moment, dazed and hurting. She blinked, remembered her dire situation, and instantly forgot the painful landing on her tailbone as she tried to rise. But she was a fraction late. Above her stood a heavily breathing Tom Wyatt. Steam was billowing from his mouth into the cold air and snot was dangling from his nose. She could smell vomit nearby; she knew his groin was hurting far more than her tailbone and she was frankly amazed by his resilience.

'You bitch!' he lisped, wiping the snot on his rough coat sleeve. 'I bit my fucking tongue too.' He spat and she watched a rotted tooth land nearby, a blood-bright gob against the virgin snow. 'I am going to kill you for that then rape your corpse.' And before Jane could take another breath, his boot had closed on her neck. 'I want to watch you die slowly, though.'

Jane believed him, and as the pressure increased and she could hear her breath rasping, her body struggling to take in air, she felt the life leaving Winifred. *No!* she screamed inwardly. *Hold on, Winifred!*

But her host's fragility wouldn't permit it and she knew her invisible companion was letting go. She could feel icy damp dragging her gleefully to sleep, her eyes bulging, and as darkness closed in Jane was sure she heard pistol-fire sound like a thunderclap in the frigid air.

Her last conscious thought was of seeing a flock of startled birds lift noisily from the bare tree nearby in a peeping, chattering, collective flutter. But it could have been the ravens in her mind… or perhaps Winifred's soul and hers.

NINETEEN

JANE'S NUMBED FAMILY SAT IN THE LARGE kitchen of their home with the phone inches from where her father sat slumped on a stool. The police had finally left and now it was just the three of them, coming to terms with the news that Jane hadn't returned from her climb up Uluru. The report was sketchy and the police assured them that she had only been missing for a few hours. In fact, the only reason they'd decided to make the visit was because the motel operator in Alice Springs was threatening to use the number that Jane had left him should anything untoward occur.

'That was him on the phone when the police arrived,' Catelyn remarked into the silence. 'I told him to hold the line.' She began to weep again.

'The policewoman spoke to him, Mum,' Juliette assured her. 'It's all right.'

'Yes, but I wish *I* had now. I have questions. He's there, on the spot. They aren't. How much can they know here in Wales?'

'Now, stop,' Hugh growled. 'They've repeatedly told us these are still the earliest hours. Jane is not registered as officially missing. You heard them. She could have returned, taken a tour, gone for a walk, hired a guide...' He shrugged. 'She could be anywhere, love. You know how independent she is. She might have decided to take the hire car and see some other sights, and forgot to let the motel know.'

'Jane's not like that,' her mother wept.

'Dad, they found the car at the base of the Rock. She's still in the area.' Hugh gave Juliette a soft glare and glanced her mother's way. Juliette realised she'd said too much. 'Jane's hardly herself right now, Mum,' she continued, in the hope of distracting her mother from thoughts of the car. 'She's confused, she's grieving, she's probably out of her mind with worry for Will. I know she didn't see it our way, but it was always madness her taking off like this.' Juliette shook her head. 'I can't believe we let her do it. I should have gone with her like she asked.'

'Don't you start,' her father cautioned.

'I should have. She needed one of us with her.'

Her father stood up and started to pace up and down. 'Jane is a sensible, practical and above all fearless girl, as you well know. If she took the precaution of leaving that motel owner our number, then we know she will have taken other sorts of precautions. Sometime soon the phone's going to ring and it's going to be our Janie. And she's going to be embarrassed, and probably even angry, if I know my girl, about all this fuss.'

'I'll make some tea,' Catelyn said. It was obvious no one wanted another pot made, least of all her, but it was something to do, something to focus on and be distracted by.

'Our Jane should have been born a boy,' her husband continued.

'What does that mean, Hugh?' she said in a watery voice as she spooned leaves into the teapot.

He shrugged. 'Even at school she wanted to be better than the boys, didn't she? She hated us sending her to a girls' school. Jane's tough, especially here,' he said, tapping his temple.

'Yeah, and you gave her the pretty genes too. It's not fair that she gets to be the fearless daughter and ridiculously beautiful with it.' Juliette mocked herself, trying to lighten the leaden conversation, but it didn't work. Her observation sounded sour and she knew it as soon as she'd said it, shrugging at her parents' surprised expressions. The self-mockery stopped and the truth emerged. 'What? Looking the way she does, Jane could have anyone she likes. And then she snares Mr Amazing and when she should be at his side pulling him through, she's off on a crazy adventure. This is typical Jane. Everything has to be on her terms.'

Hugh Granger frowned disapprovingly at his daughter and shook his head. 'No, that's not it, Juliette. Jane's always been searching for something – maybe she hoped Will would provide it, but...'

'But what?' Catelyn demanded. 'I hate us talking about her like this.'

'I think she's always been looking for a man who was stronger than she is,' Hugh said, as though finally releasing a great secret. 'But Will overwhelms her, takes away her control by making decisions for her.' He sighed.

'Oh, Dad, that's ridiculous. Which right-thinking girl wouldn't want Will Maxwell weak-kneed for them? Jane's a nutter if she found that anything but charming. And Will's a bit of a dreamer – that's what made him so interesting. He has the attributes to be a womanising playboy, but from what I gather he's the opposite.'

Hugh looked vaguely embarrassed at having revealed his thoughts. He cleared his throat, and in a more no-nonsense tone, took control of the conversation again. 'Anyway... you heard that the Australian police won't be calling it a disappearance until at least twenty-four hours have passed. It's only been eight since she left the motel.'

'You're right. She's going to arrive back at the motel and be livid with everyone for overreacting,' Catelyn said, pouring water into the pot.

The phone rang, startling them. Jane's mother gave a small shriek as her father grabbed the receiver after one ring.

'Hugh Granger,' he snapped, clearly apprehensive.

Juliette and her mother reached for each other and held

hands, waiting, expecting him to grin at them as he heard Jane's voice. He didn't.

'Oh, hello, John,' he said, looking vaguely guilty. 'Sorry. Er, yes, we were waiting to hear from Jane.'

He listened.

'No, it's hard to keep track of the times in Australia.'

Another pause. The women let go of each other, exchanging a look of disappointment. Catelyn returned to putting a cosy on the teapot.

'Yes, well, I hope she gets over the bee in her bonnet soon too,' he said, glowering for the sake of the women watching him. 'We too would be far happier if she were here. How is Will? Any change?' He waited. 'Really? But that's positive, surely?' He nodded, listening, nodded again. 'That's marvellous. I know... yes, I know you did. All right. If she calls – I mean *when* she calls – I'll certainly let her know. Yes, I'll have her call you too, although it's a bit difficult from Alice Springs.' He waited. 'Yes, from Sydney, then. Listen, John, that's great to hear about Will. Thank you for letting us know. I will. Yes. Best to Diane too.' He put the phone down and looked at them.

'Has Will woken up?' Juliette guessed.

He shook his head. 'No, but John was ringing to say there are some encouraging signs.'

'How encouraging?' his wife asked.

'Enough that John and Diane have agreed to hold off on taking him to America for a bit longer,' he replied, rubbing his eyes as the women shared a look of relief. 'They've postponed the trip until after New Year, as the doctors in London want to keep Will undisturbed in case he is surfacing. That's the word John used – he didn't say "waking up".' Hugh sighed. 'They were hoping Jane might be on her way back.'

Jane's mother nodded. 'She should be with Will, especially if her presence might help him.'

'I deliberately didn't say anything about Jane being

uncontactable at present. They've got enough on their plates.'

'Why don't we ring the motel ourselves?' Juliette offered.

'The police said they'd let us know.'

'Mum, you're so obedient! I'll ring the motel. What's that man's name again?'

'Let's not muddy the water. We'll give it a few more hours and if we haven't heard by midnight, I agree, we'll phone Alice Springs ourselves,' her father said.

Jane became aware of a soft breeze against formerly numb cheeks, and she felt strangely weightless. As full consciousness returned, she realised she was being carried, and she blinked open her eyes to regard a dark blue gaze that belonged to the last person she could have expected to see.

'Miss Granger?'

'Lord Sackville!' she croaked.

'Be still a moment, if you please.' He said this softly, but she also realised it was not a request. He carried her effortlessly and his hard body against hers sent warmth and security coursing through her. Although she felt vaguely ridiculous being carried, somewhere deep down there was a mingling of pleasure and relief that not only had she been saved from Wyatt's attack, but also that it was Sackville who had saved her.

She raised a hand to her neck, which felt tender.

'Do not test your voice, Miss Granger,' he said, so tenderly that she smiled. And just for a heartbeat she was sure she saw a grin flicker in his expression, its effect – even after it had disappeared quickly – warming his coolish gaze. 'I am glad you are safe,' he murmured for her hearing alone.

'Thank you, Lord Sackville,' she whispered, impaled once again by the intensity of his gaze. She felt like a butterfly specimen, pinned and helpless, while an admirer drank in the beauty of his captured prize. 'Is Cecilia safe?'

'I am, dearest,' came the familiar voice as her friend hove into view. She appeared dishevelled but smiling. 'Lord Sackville came to my rescue before any damage could be done,' she said, glancing with gratitude at the newcomer.

Sackville's eyes, however, hadn't left Winifred's, and Jane felt a curious sense of affinity pass between her and her rescuer as he placed her gently down into the welcoming embrace of Cecilia and turned away. Jane swivelled her head to follow his movement and her gaze fell on Wyatt, who was kneeling on one leg, seemingly recovering from having been knocked out.

'What happened?' she rasped, still trying to find her voice again.

'Lord Sackville clubbed him unconscious with a blow from his pistol. He'll have a sore head,' Cecilia whispered.

'Less than he deserves,' Jane murmured.

Julius Sackville unhurriedly checked his pistol before he took aim and pointed the barrel at the heart of Wyatt. 'I'm a terribly good shot,' he warned, his tone even, his expression untroubled. 'One of your blackguard companions is dead. The younger has run away, suffering, I suspect, from a broken jaw – I certainly hope so. But I've had time to reload just for you.' Wyatt threw his arms up hastily. Sackville shifted his stormy gaze to Winifred. 'Are you sure you're all right, Miss Granger?'

Jane drew a steadying breath. 'I'm fine; a bit bruised, perhaps.' She realised she was in her petticoat and how transparent it must be due to her dampened behind.

'Let's get you dressed again, my dear,' Cecilia muttered, but Jane was fully distracted by the conversation between the men.

'No harm done, then?' Tom tried, overly bright, but his voice shook and his eyes were fixed on the pistol. His gum had bled from the missing tooth and a trail of bloodied spittle ran down his rough, unshaven chin.

'Really? Do you think so?' Sackville asked wryly. 'I'd suggest you start running and don't look behind you.'

Jane turned to stare at their rescuer. 'You're not going to let him go, are you?' She looked back at Wyatt, who was stumbling to his cart.

Sackville squinted and pressed the trigger and the flintlock discharged, terrifying two rabbits out of a nearby burrow. Both women shrank back at the explosion of flame and smoke while Wyatt yelped and leaped into the air. Sackville had deliberately missed, Jane thought, going by his amused expression. Wyatt couldn't know that, but his confident sneer surprised her.

'You're not such a good shot after all, Master Sackville, and I can be gone before you reload.'

Sackville smiled humourlessly. 'Just getting my eye in.' He withdrew a second, matching, pocket pistol and pointed it at his no longer sneering, but genuinely frightened, target.

'This one is already loaded. I won't miss on my next shot, Mr Wyatt. I said start running. No cart. And remember this: I know your name. And when I have seen to these ladies, the constables of every parish will know it too and receive a description of you and your attack. Mark me well: you'll have your day in front of the magistrate even if I have to hunt you down myself.'

Wyatt slipped and tripped, arms flailing, as he staggered out of firing range and finally disappeared from sight.

Sackville turned to Jane now, but declined to look directly at her. 'Miss Granger, it is entirely unseemly to be kicking and flailing about in your petticoats, plus you will catch your death.'

'Fetch my skirt and cloak, Cecilia,' she pleaded. She addressed him again, refusing to be embarrassed. 'Is the man who attacked Cecilia really dead?' she asked, as her friend returned with her clothes and a handful of torn-off buttons.

'I watched him drop dead from the pistol shot,' Cecilia answered for him, 'although I care not. If you hadn't happened along…' she said, turning to Sackville, but didn't finish her thought.

'You must not think on that, er, Miss…?'

'Evans,' she said.

'Why *did* you happen along?' Jane asked, reclothed, her

skirt held together by its two remaining buttons. Her pulse had returned to something akin to normal and all her former adrenaline had leeched away, leaving her feeling vulnerable again. She hugged herself beneath her cloak. It was turning colder again, she was sure. 'I thought you were bound for York.'

'I was. I have come from there,' he replied, walking away from them to begin unharnessing Wyatt's horse from the cart.

She shivered. 'I'm not sure I understand.'

Sackville didn't look at her. 'I came back for you.' He cleared his throat. 'For you and Miss Evans, that is.' His gaze finally fixed on her again.

Jane blinked in astonishment. 'Why?'

He straightened and looked slightly baffled as to the right answer. Jane found his obvious discomfort at being questioned like this to be disconcertingly attractive, particularly as it broke through his otherwise controlled bearing. 'Because while those louts couldn't tell the difference between a woman of high social standing and a peasant, I certainly can!'

'So if I were a simple peasant, you would not have rushed to my aid?' She was shocked by how terrible his rationale sounded, but reminded herself that she was not in an age of equality. Women would have to wait another century or more before any sort of reform began.

'I did not say that.' Her terse silence forced him to continue. 'Let us not maintain this charade. I understand you are Lady Maxwell, Countess of Nithsdale, as you named yourself.'

Jane couldn't hide the surprise in her expression but didn't reply.

'She is, My Lord,' Cecilia took it upon herself to admit, and did not dare meet Winifred's gaze. 'And I am her companion and maid.'

He fixed Winifred with a fresh stare. 'I could not in good conscience, My Lady, leave you to make this journey alone. Such travel is hard enough for a foolhardy man such as I, but…'

He trailed off. 'It's bad enough that you have had to make it this far without an escort. When I learned that my coach to London had been delayed, I thought I should come back and escort you to York.' He seemed to gather confidence the more he rationalised; his control was firmly back in place. 'Now, four miles down this road is a respectable inn, where I suggest we abide overnight. We shall be on a coach tomorrow if the weather holds.'

Jane was acutely aware of a man lying dead behind the hedgerow. 'You seem to care more for a carthorse than a man, Lord Sackville,' she said.

'I don't care about that man at all,' he snapped. 'I do care about this horse, which gave no harm to anyone. It deserves a stable of fresh hay and a feed. Its driver, I hazard, deserves nothing more than for the wild animals to pick at his crime-ridden carcass.'

'I have to agree, Winifred. The man's a sorry wretch who falls upon unwitting travellers. You know how William feels about highwaymen and reivers.' Cecilia gave a satisfied sigh as Winifred nodded. 'Lord Sackville is right too: you'll catch your death if we stand here much longer. We all will.'

Jane could no longer feel her hands or toes. 'So we just leave him?'

Cecilia looked at her as though she were losing her mind. 'By my honour, Winnie! He attacked me! He would have taken you after that Wyatt fellow had! Lord Sackville killed the man in self-defence. You've witnessed him let the other two go. Don't think on any of them again – each nothing more than a mindless, thieving cur.'

'Well said, Miss Evans,' returned Sackville.

It was shocking. Yet Jane allowed herself to be led back to her horse.

Sackville was suddenly at her side. 'Here, let me help you,' he offered, lifting up Winifred's slim body easily, so Jane could once again seat herself in the side-saddle. His hand rested on her boot, and she could feel its warmth and its pressure through the soft leather. She was not imagining it. Sackville was communicating silently with her, passing her strength and encouragement. 'Are you strong enough to ride, Lady Nithsdale?' he asked aloud.

She nodded, disarmed by the concern in his expression and that dark, penetrating gaze of his, and perhaps by what he was not saying while he touched her with such tender familiarity. 'Please, call me Winifred,' she said. 'In fact, call me Jane,' she added, and when Cecilia threw her a frowning sidelong glance she shrugged. 'It's best we don't bandy around my true identity. Jane Granger is easier to hide behind.'

'Jane,' he said, and bowed his head, but not before she felt another slight squeeze of her foot.

She swallowed, angry with herself but not entirely sure why, as she watched Julius Sackville mount easily. He'd tied the carthorse to his own and the party headed away, neither of her companions even vaguely interested in checking the contents of the cart they had abandoned on the roadside.

They covered the journey swiftly, with Sackville riding ahead in silence. Later, at the coaching inn, all the horses were safely stabled. While Cecilia supervised a copper bath being poured for her, Jane found herself alone with him over the remnants of a pigeon pie. The rhyme of 'Four and Twenty Blackbirds' was humming through her mind as she tried not to stare too hard at her dining companion.

'Are you recovered… Jane? No delayed effect from today's events?'

She snorted softly. 'No, I am well, truly. If I could stop sneezing, I would say I was completely in fine health, although my rear is sore from where I fell.' He nodded, but there was no lightness in his bearing. She barely knew him, but couldn't imagine how he might sound if he laughed delightedly. She had to wonder if he ever had allowed himself such freedom. 'So what do you do, Lord Sackville?'

'Do? I do not *do* anything and yet I seem to keep busy with plenty of things,' he answered, looking slightly perplexed by her enquiry. He shrugged. 'For the most part, I live at the Martlets in the north and run my estate.'

'Are you married?'

'No,' he said brusquely, then softened, staring into his goblet. 'I was.' Jane blinked, held her tongue. 'She died. We were very young when we met and were still far too young when she left me. And it was so painful to lose her that I choose not to put myself into that position again.' His eyes had misted over, but suddenly he looked directly at her. 'And here you are, hoping to shift a mountain in order to save your own husband an early death. I have heard of his probable fate.' As he watched her expression crumple, he instinctively reached for her hand. When their skin touched, they both reacted as if burned and pulled away quickly, but his kindness remained. 'Ah, forgive me. That was insensitive. I meant—'

'I know what you meant. I am not offended,' she assured him. 'I was saddened at the thought of someone else I know who has turned to the mystical in order that she might save her husband an early death.'

He frowned. 'What is wrong with him?'

'He hit his head and has not regained consciousness.'

'A stupor? Did he fall from a horse?'

'Something like that,' she said, feeling deeply sad for lying about Will. She wished she could tell Sackville the truth.

'I am sorry for your friend. I have heard of this affliction; some name it apoplexy. Few understand it, although I have heard of people who have woken up a long time later, with no memory of the incident that prompted their sleep but no worse for it.'

She gave a small shrug, keen to move away from the topic. 'I haven't thanked you for what you did for us today.'

'I should hope any gentleman would do the same,' he said, swishing the sweet wine around the goblet he had been sipping from. He dropped his voice even though he was already speaking quietly. 'I am no Catholic, but I consider Lord Derwentwater among my closest friends.' He cleared his throat. 'I am concerned for his well-being. I hope to bear witness for him – to speak up for him.'

Her attention had been riveted on his large, well-cared-for hands as they twirled the stem of the goblet. Now her gaze flew to his earnest expression. 'What have you heard?' Jane knew that the Earl of Derwentwater was one of the important captives who had been taken with Nithsdale.

'Only what everyone knows... that he and his fellow rebels, including your husband, will shortly be put on trial.' He looked down. 'I'm sorry for you. I don't see a happy outcome for my friend or your husband.'

'Don't say that,' she begged in a whisper.

'Forgive me,' he murmured again. 'I am out of practice at attending to the sensitivities of a gentlewoman.'

She wanted to laugh. If only he knew. 'Oh, I think you have been highly sensitive to my situation, and most generous.'

'Because I killed a man for you?'

She stared at him, shocked, then realised this was wit. 'Good gracious, Lord Sackville, you made a jest. I admit I was not ready for it.'

He nodded ruefully. 'Something else I am out of practice with.'

She didn't deny his statement this time, but when he raised a sad expression to meet hers she felt a warmth prickle through her, beginning as low as her lap, where her hands now fidgeted. The heat rose, infusing her, until she was sure she blushed. She hoped that in the flickering, shadowy lamplight of the inn he would not notice, and then realised she was holding her breath. She let it out with an exaggerated sigh. 'There is still such a long journey ahead.'

'I shall see you safely to London. I give you my word.'

'Julius... er, may I call you Julius?'

'I want you to,' he said, staring intently at her, and the

way he said it made Jane momentarily lose her train of thought.

'Er… thank you,' she said, hardly daring to look at him. 'I was going to say that it is not my intention to make you feel in any way responsible for our safety. You have already been a more than generous friend to us both.'

He continued studying her until his nearness and their silence became unnerving. Just when she felt obliged to say something more, he spoke.

'Friend. I like the way you said that. Thank you.'

She frowned and gave a small shrug. 'I just do not want you to feel obliged to help us further.'

'I can assure you, obligation has nothing to do with it.' He surprised her by standing, surprised her further by taking her hand and, for the first time in her life, Jane watched a ridiculously handsome man elegantly kiss her hand. Except it wasn't her hand; it was Winifred's soft, pale skin that Sackville's eminently kissable lips were gently pressed upon. She watched the scene unfold as if she were outside it, yet felt his warm lips touch the flesh she inhabited. It was weird, it was disarming and if she were honest with herself, it was exciting.

That last one was hard to admit, but Jane could no longer ignore the fact that Julius Sackville affected her in ways she couldn't understand right now. That warmth, for instance, which made her feel anxious as he now straightened and prepared to leave her company. She didn't want him to leave, because she found him compelling; but she wanted him to be gone, sensing a sudden new complication rising on the horizon of what was already a complex situation.

'Good evening, Jane,' he said politely. 'I do hope you sleep soundly after your eventful day.'

She felt a fresh frisson thrill through her at the lingering touch of his knowing gaze, and at the sound of his voice speaking her real name with such intensity.

'Good evening,' she managed to stammer out, still not meeting his eye.

'We leave tomorrow at dawn.'

'Thank you. Cecilia and I shall be ready,' Jane said, finally raising her gaze, but Sackville had turned and Cecilia was approaching, smiling at him as he passed and nodded to her.

'A hot bath, a warmed bed and a honey posset will do you a power of good, Win, I'm sure. And I must mend your frock.'

Jane allowed herself to be led to the chamber that she was sharing with Cecilia and permitted her friend to undress her, feeling a sense of release as layers were stripped away and then the comforting embrace of warm, sudsy water as she clambered into the copper tub.

She told herself she was experiencing conflicted feelings because she was frightened, confused and completely removed from everything familiar. But now she almost wished that Julius Sackville had not been honourable enough to come back for them. She felt embarrassed by her hyper-awareness of him. For instance, why had she noticed his complexion, devoid of the smallpox scars that even Cecilia possessed? Why had she noticed the way he'd threaded the horse's reins through his gloved fingers? She could see them now: long, blunt-ended, with perfect half-moons on well-kept nails. Why did she struggle to meet his intelligent eyes, while her gaze focused on his neatly shaped lips and the tiny silver scar at one side of his mouth?

How did he get that scar? How did his wife die? It suddenly seemed important to know.

Her thoughts fled to Will, and she wished she had a photo she could look at. She didn't want to lose the memory of his smiling face, his lean, hard body, his smell, his touch. Will suddenly seemed a long way away and she was struggling to see his features in detail the way she could construct Sackville's.

She closed her eyes against the tears that inevitably stung the inside of her lids, and she cast a prayer for Will to hang on, and for Julius Sackville to ignore her tomorrow.

TWENTY

The Black Swan Inn where they'd overnighted was a twin-gabled, two-storey structure with a jettied upper floor, and overlooked a water meadow. It had been owned by a merchant, the innkeeper's wife explained, but was now a meeting point for stagecoaches between London and York. Cecilia had discovered from the staff who had delivered the tub and hot water that the inn was haunted; they intimated that the women should not be overly alarmed to see a man's pair of legs descending the staircase.

Perhaps that was why Jane had dreamed that night of dismembered arms floating around Uluru, carrying the head of the Earl of Nithsdale. She woke with a start to the sound of a distant cockerel heralding the pre-dawn. Cecilia stirred next to her, mumbling that the coach was leaving at five, not six, and that they must rise immediately. Dressing swiftly, still yawning, Jane realised she had little appetite, but was feeling brighter than she had in days. The bath the previous evening had certainly eased her aching hips and, strange dreams aside, she had slept deeply from the effects of the brandy-slugged posset.

Now, with her precious few belongings stowed above, Jane was being introduced to the discomfort of riding in one of the earliest forms of public transport: a stagecoach which she shared with seven others. If she had been asked at this moment whether she would consider swapping the carriage for a horse, she might have said yes, for Mr Bailey, the old man sitting diagonally opposite her, possessed fetid breath that managed to cross the divide and almost make her wish to tear open the window and let the wintry air in. His long, unfashionably curled wig was powdered so heavily that in the right light she could see its dust floating through the space his breath was fouling. His wife, meanwhile, fussed constantly over her husband, the tiny yapping dog on her lap, her cloth bag and her equally unfashionable hair, which was combed to stiff attention, standing high above her forehead. What was more, they were both overly curious about the two women and their male companion, and Jane suspected the wife was a gossip.

Cecilia, next to her, appeared more adept than Jane at the art of pointless discussion, so Jane feigned a headache and let the dull chatter twitter back and forth between them. Mr Bailey did his best to engage Julius, seated next to him, in the vapid conversation, but Sackville was blunt, repeatedly claiming he had no opinion on anything they were discussing, whether it was the King's determination not to converse in English, or whether his mistresses – unkindly nicknamed 'the Elephant' and 'the Maypole' – should be tolerated, or how the rift between the King and his heir, George, Prince of Wales, might affect the throne's future.

While Jane refused to show any engagement with the conversation, she was vaguely intrigued by talk of the King. But she noticed that Sackville turned to stare gloomily out of the window as the snow-covered scenery passed by too slowly for both of them. After several hours of having Sackville ignore her as studiously as he did their fellow passengers, she felt reassured that the apparent intimacy of yesterday had been in her imagination. That relief, however, came with a twinge of private regret, which she pretended didn't exist.

There were two other passengers in the coach: Charles Leadbetter, a middle-aged gentleman, and his young niece, Eugenie, who played with her doll and hummed songs to it.

Her uncle took snuff and, after a series of explosive sneezes, returned to reading a battered book – although how he managed to read as they bumped and bruised themselves along the road Jane could not understand.

The smell in the carriage soon became cloying from Mrs Bailey's overly sweet perfume, which was sharply at odds with her husband's sour breath, wig powder, leather, infrequently washed clothes and rank personal odour.

Jane had achieved a cramp in one leg from having it pinioned in the same confined position for several hours and her teeth were being juddered against each other because the journey on wooden wheels without any suspension smashed into every pothole on this notorious stretch of highway between England's north-east and the capital.

When Jane finally looked around the carriage, after hours of watching rural terrain blanketed by an endless carpet of snow, everyone else appeared to have fallen into a doze, including Mrs Bailey's dog. She could hear the crack of the coachman's whip above and his muffled curse, now and then, at the horses as he coaxed them through the thick snow drifts. The only other noticeable sound was Mr Bailey's snores. Sleep evaded Jane, but the relative silence and her sudden solitude did provide the chance for her treacherous gaze to slide toward the one person in the carriage she was keen to surreptitiously study.

Julius was beautiful in a way that men could be without appearing in any way effeminate. His proportions were perfect – from the length of the legs to the breadth of those shoulders contained beneath the dark frock coat he wore today. He was again without adornment. There was no jewellery, no wig, no frills. His hair was once more neatly secured into a queue with a small black ribbon. Winifred's memories told her that William Maxwell detested wigs too, but Julius seemed to lurk at the furthest edges of what was acceptable. His hat was in his lap, loosely held by those hands whose warmth and pressure she could still feel beneath the leather of her boots. The disloyal warmth pricked again, low in her belly, and she flicked her gaze from Sackville's lap to his dark lashes, and thought about the disarming gaze of the dark eyes hidden beneath them. She recalled their previous evening's conversation and his poignant admission about his dead wife. Jane began to imagine what she might have been like. She no doubt came from a highborn family, and was accomplished in all the same arts as Winifred, the perfect partner for a wealthy landowner. Jane could see the woman in her mind's eye: ringlets of blonde hair, silk ribbons, milky complexion and dewy eyes, with a soft giggle and an even softer body that yielded beneath his hard—

'Uncle, if we are stopped by highwaymen, do you think they will take my dolly?' the little girl to her left suddenly blurted out, and everyone stirred.

Sackville's eyes opened, his gaze already focused on Jane, but she'd jerked her glance away to the child in time not to be caught staring... and yet she couldn't shake the suspicion that he could eavesdrop on her thoughts and knew why she blushed. Why was she thinking like this? *We come from separate worlds*, she assured herself, trying to allay her guilt.

The uncle looked alarmed at his niece's sudden enquiry, but tried to disguise his reaction with another pinch of snuff. Its fragrance lent a welcome scent to the air even if the explosive sneeze that ultimately erupted did not. 'Er, no, my dear,' he said, dragging a large handkerchief to his nose. 'Do not trouble your pretty head with this matter.'

Mr Bailey, awake and straightening his gargantuan grey wig, gave a scornful grunt. 'The coachmen are armed with flintlocks anyway,' he rumbled.

'Bandits tend not to rob travellers headed south. The more organised thieves move fast on horseback, usually in pairs, and prefer to dip their hands into the wealthy pockets of hapless travellers headed north out of the capital.' It was the first words that Julius had spoken in nearly four hours of bruising travel.

And he immediately looked away from his fellow passengers, although his gaze brushed briefly over Jane.

'That's a very agreeable snuff, sir,' Cecilia said in her easy, conversing way, clearly anxious to get off the subject of highway robbers and opportunists.

'Spanish. The best,' the uncle replied, replacing the small tin in his waistcoat pocket.

'Cinnamon,' Jane observed, airing her thought aloud, even though she hadn't meant to; she'd been searching for the name of the ingredient that was spicing the air so pleasantly.

'Yes, indeed, Miss Granger. Bravo! I have my tobacco sent from a snuffmaker in Seville.'

'I prefer the German snuff,' Bailey said, entering the conversation. 'What about you, sir?' he said, giving Sackville a dig in the ribs. 'If you were to side with the wretched French, then we could while away the boredom with a debate on the merits of each, what?'

'I don't partake of snuff, Mr Bailey. It ruins the sense of smell… mayhap you hadn't noticed,' he said, his tone innocent, though the wry dig was unmistakable. He glanced again at Jane, who had to disguise her grin. Poor Julius. The smell of old Bailey must be intolerable at such close range.

The next two days followed a similar pattern: hour after hour in the uncomfortable coach; overnighting at inns with lumpy beds and even lumpier food on offer. Jane and Cecilia continued to share a room to keep costs at a minimum. On the second night, unable to sleep and with her belly rumbling from lack of food because she had not been able to stomach the greasy pork on offer, Jane tiptoed from their chamber, pulling her cloak around her nightgown. She hoped she might steal into the kitchen and find a crust of bread, or perhaps a few cubes of hard cheese.

She soon found both in the surprisingly silent kitchen, hacking off a modest hunk of cheese that she was sure would barely be noticed. She hurried into the main dining room, where the embers of the night's fire still glowed and would doubtless be shortly coaxed back into life with fresh logs. She stood as close to the fire's thin warmth as she could and blew on the dying embers, but no flame erupted as she'd hoped. She swallowed the morsels of bread and cheese, and urged herself to move away from the fire.

As she turned to begin the draughty journey back upstairs, she saw someone move in the shadows. She gasped, missed her footing slightly and then righted herself, but not without a small stub to her big toe, which hurt like fury. She recognised the familiar figure in the meagre firelight. 'Julius!' she hissed, her exclamation intensified by the pain. 'What are you doing brooding here in the dark?'

'Exactly that, Miss Granger. Standing by the fireplace just like you. If I had announced myself I might have frightened you, and I did not wish that. I thought it best that when you moved, I should too.' He looked dauntingly large in the dimness. He was still dressed, but the frock coat was gone, his shirt open to reveal a triangle of his chest. She felt her cheeks warm in the gloom, pleased that the light was low. 'Again I find myself asking for your pardon,' he continued.

She cleared her throat. 'You did startle me. There seem to be ghosts at every inn we pass through.'

Jane sensed his smile, though she could not know for sure, as he was still couched in darkness.

'You could not sleep?'

She sighed. 'No. Rest eludes me.'

He loomed forward into the soft glow of the fire and she saw that his hair was untied, falling near his shoulders.

'I never sleep easily,' he admitted.

'You seemed to slumber fairly well on the coach trip yesterday,' she remarked dryly, meaning it lightly as a parting jest before she drifted back upstairs.

'Did I? Then I was pretending,' he said, and the look he gave her was unnerving. 'And what were you thinking, Jane,' he said, the use of her name making her flinch, 'as you watched me feigning sleep?'

'I... er, I wasn't watching you. I simply noticed that you were dozing. I was pleased for you.'

'Why?'

'I wished I could switch off from the noises and smells of the others.'

'You simply had to close your eyes and pretend.'

'I am not so adept at pretending.'

He said nothing, but regarded her with amusement.

She wanted to stop the words, wished she could remain silent as others did when they felt cornered. 'I was thinking of your wife, actually,' she said – immediately regretting it, already knowing she had just opened a box that should have remained closed.

'My wife?' he said evenly. 'But you did not know her to think on her.'

Jane smiled, hoping she could rescue this awkwardness by saying something pleasant and polite and then quickly extricate herself. 'I just imagined how she might be.'

'And how did your imagination paint her?'

Jane shrugged, pulling her cloak firmly around her. She glanced toward the door as an indication that her departure was imminent, but she could not be rude. 'Um... well, let's see. I imagined her to be statuesque, an accomplished musician, a fine dancer, clever with the needle and beautiful, of course, with a pale porcelain complexion. I saw her with cascading ringlets of golden hair and eyes like sapphire.' *There*, she thought, *that should speak to his ego.*

'She was nothing like that,' he said in a leaden tone. 'Your imagination has conjured up society's image of the perfect woman – one I do not subscribe to, and the likes of which I am rarely attracted to. No, my wife was not statuesque. She was petite and raven-haired, with eyes that looked like wet shingle on the beach... sometimes dark as pitch, sometimes flinty grey.

She was Venetian – you might even have described her as olive-skinned – but yes, she was beautiful to me. Exotic, mysterious… even dangerous at times.' He shook his head as if in private thought. 'That temper of hers…' he murmured, then blinked, returning himself to the present. 'She did not fit the mould of English society at all. She laughed at it, in fact. She did not sew or paint or make great music. She did not come from a grand Venetian household either. She was my translator when I was on a tour of Europe, fluent in several languages, but it was when she whispered to me in our bed in Italian that I loved her most of all.' Jane felt her colour rising at his sharing of such intimacy, and for a heartbeat felt a prick of jealousy. 'She made me laugh – a rare talent, as far as I am concerned. And she made me weep. I have neither laughed aloud nor cried since her death, for those two extremes belong to her; they are the parts of me she stole and took with her to the grave.' Jane hardly dared to take a visible breath while he spoke so passionately.

They stared at each other and Jane felt momentarily frozen beneath his gaze, helpless against whatever power he held over her. She knew it was coming, should have pulled away, or made some movement to break the spell. But she did none of those; instead, she welcomed the tender kiss when it came. Soft and soothing, it made her feel safe, but as Julius lingered, his ardour intensified, became more searching. Although Jane tried desperately not to return the emotion, she could barely believe it when she saw flashes of intense light burn and burst like bubbles behind her closed eyelids. That had never happened to her before with anyone. Was this what was meant when someone said they had seen stars?

But just as she thought this, he pulled away, and she felt his parting as a sorrow. 'Heaven forgive me,' he said, his voice momentarily broken as he gathered up his feelings and neatly locked them away. 'That was utterly indiscreet of me.'

'I found it comforting,' she said, to placate his dismay, and disguise the truth of her own feelings.

He relaxed, sighing as he moved away from her. 'I am clearly in a weak frame of mind to take such advantage of you.'

It was only a kiss! A few seconds! She'd experienced worse on a New Year's Eve at the disco, when every bloke decided there was a free pass to a slobber and grope just because they'd counted backward from ten!

'I... I wish it were not so painful for you,' she stammered, ignoring the voice – Winifred's, perhaps – that told her Julius's kiss, although brief, had been as intimate as any act of love between two people.

'To what are you referring?' He frowned.

'The memory of your wife.'

He shook his head. 'On the contrary, I welcome the pain attached to the memory of my wife,' he admitted in a rueful tone. 'It reminds me that I'm alive... for there are occasions when it seems otherwise.'

'I know that feeling,' she admitted.

His brow knitted. 'How can that be?'

'Right now,' she confessed, 'I am confused, fearful and charged with...' She was going to say adrenaline, but knew it would be an alien word for him to hear and for Winifred to utter. '... with fury that my husband's life is under threat.'

'Indeed; I have a friend under the same threat. But a man who picks up a weapon and raises his standard against the ruler has surely already agreed to risk forfeiting his life, whether it is on the battlefield or later in a court of law?'

She closed her mouth on whatever was about to fly out of it, because of course Jane heard only truth in his words. But Winifred's ire was up, weak though she was – mainly because Jane had allowed Winifred to be unfaithful.

Jane took a slow breath, overrode Winifred. 'You are right, of course, Julius. But that does not stop me from desperately wanting to help him to safety. Given what you have shared with me, I am sure you understand my desire to protect him.'

He surprised her by gripping her arm. 'But what do you

believe you are going to achieve by rushing to London like this? Risking your own life? What do you think a gentlewoman of your standing can accomplish at the palace or in Parliament?'

She looked to where his hand held her. 'What do I think a woman can achieve?' She paused, then looked up and gave him a tight smile. 'Absolutely anything a man can.' And she saw the surprise flash in his dark gaze, and felt his grip loosen as he gave a soft groan of anguish.

'Your love is surely fierce, My Lady. Again I ask your forgiveness for my behaviour.'

'We shall not mention it again.'

He stared at her from the other end of the mantelpiece, but it might as well have been from the other end of the world. The gulf between them was wide now. 'Can we pretend it did not occur?'

Jane was not sure how he wanted her to respond. Would he be sad if she said yes, or would he be angry if she said no? 'We can try.'

'What do you plan to do in London?'

'Anything it takes to secure his release.'

He nodded. 'You are a brave woman, Winifred Maxwell… and your husband is the luckiest of men.' He released her from his gaze. 'Once again, I am in your debt. Goodnight.'

'Goodnight,' she whispered and watched him disappear through the door and up the stairs, already feeling the loss of his presence keenly.

TWENTY-ONE

JANE DID NOT GET BACK TO SLEEP, instead counting off the hours in her mind until she heard the first peep of the earliest bird. She was the first person dressed and downstairs into the darkly panelled dining room and had first pick of the morning meal, which today was hearty and appetising.

She knew the food would keep Winifred's fragility at bay, so she ate the warmed rolls spread thickly with butter and fruit conserve, and decided she would try the hot drink of chocolate, which turned out to be frothy and extremely tasty, if a tad gritty; the depth of flavour told Jane it was made with melted chocolate. The serving girl held out the sugar bowl to her as though it contained gold. She didn't let Jane touch the sugarloaf, but clipped off a chunk from the cone and dropped it into Jane's mug.

Jane bided her time, looking around the room at the pictures hung on the walls of country scenes depicting farmworkers ploughing fields or building haystacks. There was a study of children fishing in the river and a few still lifes. The perspective was way off in most, but she felt comforted looking at these simple glimpses of ordinary life. The candles in the room were lit, because dawn was yet to break fully across the purple-inked sky, and they guttered now as more people created draughts with their arrival.

Mrs Bailey bustled in, kissing her precious dog and demanding a saucer of fresh milk for it. Jane grimaced and swallowed the last of her warmed chocolate.

'Oh, good morning, Miss Granger. Did you sleep well?'

'I did, thank you, Mrs Bailey. And you?'

'Oh, I can sleep anywhere, dear, although Mr Bailey did his utmost to keep me from my slumber with his incessant snoring.'

Jane smiled weakly and was about to make an excuse to leave when Mrs Bailey reached for her arm.

'Have you seen Lord Sackville this morning?'

'Er… no, no, I haven't,' she stammered, angry at herself for the thrill of guilt and feeling that she was in some way lying. 'Why?'

'Oh, nothing important. It's just that we have a son trying to make his way as a merchant and we rather hoped that Lord Sackville might offer him some advice, as he is such a successful businessman and property owner. Our James is living in London now and mayhap the two of them might meet.'

'I see,' Jane replied, smiling encouragingly even though she held little hope of success for Mrs Bailey.

'He is just such an intolerably unfriendly sort, though. It is very difficult to know how to approach such a subject with a man who offers one no welcome for conversation, no easy opening for discussion of any sort.'

'Yes, he can be prickly,' Jane agreed, more for something to say as she planned her escape from Mrs Bailey.

'I am glad to have caught you alone, though, Miss Granger.'

'Why is that?' Jane replied, flicking her gaze back to the plump woman, for the first time noticing the clumps of powder in her wig. What on earth did she and her husband use?

Starch, came the answer from Winifred's memory. *Or cypress powder for some; it adds a pleasant scent.* Jane blinked. There was little that was pleasant about Mrs Bailey's stale-looking wig.

'Well, you seem to get on rather well with him,' Mrs Bailey answered.

Jane hadn't paid attention and ran the woman's words back in her mind. 'Pardon me?'

'Well, you and Lord Sackville seem to be on cordial terms.'

Jane instantly sensed where this conversation was headed. 'We are strangers, Mrs Bailey, simply being pleasant to one another while we share such confined space.'

The woman wagged a sausage-like finger in front of her. 'Strangers, mayhap, but he likes you, Miss Granger. I've seen the way he watches you with that hungry look in that imperious face of his.'

Jane felt as if her belly had flipped over. 'What fiction! I mean really, Mrs Bailey, I do think you're sorely mistaken.'

'Nay, I've seen enough of the world to know a man who wishes to make love to a woman.'

Jane began gathering up her scarf and gloves as a way of deflecting attention. 'That's scandalous, Mrs Bailey,' she contradicted as politely as she could. She nearly said she was married, but that would have opened up an alarming new conversation. 'I am promised to someone I love most dearly and I would not encourage any man to seek my affections. Besides, whatever you think you may have noticed, I can assure you I have not. Lord Sackville has been attentive and courteous, but only to the level of politeness that I would expect from any gentleman. He has not made any improper advances to—'

'Oh, my dear, nor am I suggesting he has or even will,' Mrs Bailey huffed, looking taken aback by the accusation. She shrugged. 'I did not know you were promised. I suspected that a single woman with your obvious attributes would hardly fail to catch the eye of one of the north's most eligible and, I might add, pursued bachelors. But Julius Sackville is glacial, to put it mildly, when it comes to the fairer sex. If they didn't know of his passion for his departed wife, many might believe him to be a frequenter of molly houses.' At Jane's shocked expression – for she needed no explanation of what a molly house was – the woman gave an indulgent chuckle. 'Of course, we know better. He neither looks the part, nor acts the dandy. Frankly, my dear, he doesn't seem to partake of an interest in anyone, male or female, and yet he pays you attention and care.'

'Mrs Bailey,' Jane began in a slightly haughty tone, 'Lord Sackville happened upon Miss Evans and me at Newcastle and took pity upon us as we travelled alone in winter. He simply offered to ensure that seats awaited us on the coach to London.' She made sure to soften her tone. 'That truly is as far as his interest and our friendship extends,' she lied, trying not to remember how close he had stood to her only hours earlier. If she'd so much as given a flicker of a smile, or fluttered her eyelids, or simply regarded him differently, Jane was sure he would have risked going further. Her throat constricted just remembering that moment of resistance on both their parts and being grateful for the hesitation. 'He has been a true gentleman,' she said, ignoring the memory of that deep, delicious and frustrating kiss that ensured no sleep came to her through the night.

'Indeed – although are you not just a little intrigued by him?'

'No. I am concerned only with reaching London and my place of employ,' she lied, desperate to get away. She began to stand. 'Now, if you'll—'

'You know most people believe he murdered his wife.'

Jane sat down again, stunned. 'What?'

Mrs Bailey's chins wobbled. She pressed a finger to her lips as food was placed before her, but she regarded Jane with a mischievous look. 'Put the saucer on the floor for Chester,' she said, pointing. The girl glanced at Jane, who threw her a sympathetic glance, but the servant obliged, clearly used to the idiosyncrasies of wealthier guests.

When the girl had left them, Mrs Bailey began tucking into her warmed rolls with cheese and marmalade. She was taking coffee with her breakfast and, though trying to be polite, Jane had to look down as Mrs Bailey spoke enthusiastically with her mouth full. The older woman took this for acquiescence and pressed on with her gossipy chatter.

'Yes, murdered,' she continued in a murmur.

'I don't believe it.'

'Nor should you, for it has not been proven, but the rumour exists, and where there is smoke, there is fire, they say.'

'They do,' Jane agreed, angry with Mrs Bailey for happily fanning that smoke.

'She was some dark Italian beauty – I myself never met her, but the marriage was something of a scandal, for she was a commoner, not even connected to a good family. Her name was Madolina and her detractors said it suited her because of her illness.'

'Her illness?'

Mrs Bailey looked delighted by Jane's interest. 'Indeed, my dear. They say she was mad. It was a contrary sickness that struck as it chose, creating periods of irrational behaviour. Her times of lucidity, as I gathered, became fewer and shorter until she was fully lost to the delusions of her mind.'

'How sad,' Jane said, recalling Julius's mention of his wife's temper.

'People say he loved his wife desperately, but could no longer bear her "absences", as he called them, and pressed a silken cushion to her face as she slept in one of her drug-induced stupors until she breathed no more. It was an act of love. So romantic,' she sighed.

'But as you admit, this is nothing more than hearsay,' Jane challenged, as Mr Bailey arrived amid a lot of yawning and grumbling about the early hour. 'Excuse me, I must prepare for our departure,' she said, and hurried away before another word could be exchanged.

She greeted Cecilia, who was just arriving downstairs.

'You were up early?' her friend queried.

Jane forced a smile. 'Yes, I had an excellent sleep,' she lied, 'and rose before even the birds could. I am just overseeing the loading of our bags.'

Cecilia nodded. 'You have eaten?'

'Yes, and I counsel you to hurry before the Baileys consume all that remains,' Jane jested.

It still felt like the middle of the night when she stepped out into the courtyard, but lanterns gave a thin illumination as the coachmen harnessed the horses, which were stamping and complaining at the early hour. Their breathing steamed in great wafts and the men's voices sounded overly loud, bouncing off the cobbles and stone walls in the early stillness of the frigidly cold day that was promised.

'Good morning,' said a familiar voice, and she turned to see Julius just behind her.

She gave a small nod, aware of the excitement of seeing him again thrilling through her. She stamped her feet to cover it. 'Hello again. I was told this morning, on good authority, that you murdered your wife.' She said it with a note of levity, wondering how he might react.

He barely flinched, although she sensed humour desperately wanting to twitch at the corners of his mouth as he looked at the men throwing the passengers' luggage up to be stowed on top of the coach. 'Yes, I've heard that rumour too.' He gave a low sigh. 'I rather like how dangerous it makes me sound.' He shot her a glance and now they both smiled; she enjoyed the conspiratorial sensation it provoked.

'I do too,' she admitted. 'We should arrive in Lincoln this evening, am I right?' She sniffed, reaching for Anne's handkerchief.

'Indeed.'

'I think I shall miss you, Lord Sackville,' she said, careful to betray no familiarity in public.

'And I you, Miss Granger,' he said, following suit, and she missed hearing him utter her first name. 'You have been the single aspect that has made the journey tolerable.'

'Where will you stay in London?'

'At my club in Chesterfield Street. And you?'

Jane thought of the Arts Club that she never went to with Will. 'I have a friend who owns a boarding house.'

'Whereabouts?'

'Um… Duke Street.'

'Ah, yes.' He didn't pursue it, both of them realising they were making polite conversation. He nodded toward the carriage. 'I think it looks ready for us.'

'It does.'

'But are we ready for it, Miss Granger?'

There was a subtext in his words, but Jane had to ignore it if she were not to make a fool of herself.

She smiled. 'Another day… that's all we must endure.'

They heard voices and immediately parted. Jane did not want to be seen talking softly with Julius to fuel the fires of Mrs Bailey's idle gossip, and she sensed he had the identical thought.

Once again the passengers loaded themselves into the cramped space. This time Jane chose to sit as far away from Julius Sackville as she could, finding herself opposite Charles and Eugenie Leadbetter. As usual, his nose was buried in a book, which suited Jane. She noted that Cecilia had found herself opposite Julius at the other end of the carriage, but no number of smiles or polite exchanges would entice him into discussion beyond single-syllable answers. And he soon adopted his preferred positions of closed eyes, or nose all but touching the window glass as he studied the scenery that flashed past.

And that was how it remained for most of the journey. Even the youngster dozed. Everyone was bored or lost in private thoughts, and a dull stillness settled over the travellers, broken only by the slowing of the horses at certain times when the snow became especially thick.

'Where are we, exactly?' Mrs Bailey finally wondered into the silence.

'Approaching Grantham.' They were the first words Julius Sackville had uttered since wishing Cecilia Evans good day and agreeing with her polite enquiry that he had indeed slept just fine.

And with that the carriage lurched to a sudden bone-shuddering halt, flinging everyone around until their now familiar space was untidy with flailing arms, wigs askew, legs shooting out to bruise other shins and cranky shouts of pain.

Julius was first out of the door, flinging it open angrily. 'What in hell's —' He didn't finish, but Jane could see his shoulders sag.

Everyone spilled out into the snow-topped landscape. The coach driver had pulled off his cap and was scratching his cheek. The second driver, who had been riding postilion, was badly injured and being attended by two other travellers who had been riding on top of the carriage.

Jane realised her boots were sinking a foot deep into the crunchy snow. The coach seemed to be trapped in a ditch, the men were muttering about having heard something break beneath the carriage and it was clear that the horses needed to be unharnessed immediately to fully assess the damage.

Jane gazed at the injured driver. 'He looks to be a boy. How old is he?' she asked.

The senior coachman shrugged. 'He's in training, and fifteen next summer. Aye, he's small for his age, but that be a good thing. Lightness is his luck.' He sighed. 'John Bellow broke a limb for sure when the horse reared and threw him. And the traces are broken, so we cannot attach the horse to the coach. Besides, the horse is too spooked for now.'

'What is to be done?' Leadbetter asked over the top of John Bellow's mewling and grimacing.

'Well, it's obvious the youngster needs help,' Sackville answered, taking charge. 'Coachman, you oversee unharnessing and tying up the horses. Bailey, Leadbetter and you two,' he said, pointing to the two able men who had been riding atop with the luggage. Their lips looked blue from the cold, despite their scarves. 'You four start digging us out.'

'What?' Bailey roared. 'Us, sir?'

'It's that or freeze to death,' Sackville said humourlessly.

He turned to Jane and Cecilia. 'Can either of you ladies set a bone?' he asked hopefully as the injured man moaned in obvious agony.

They both shook their heads. 'I can make a splint, though,' Cecilia offered. 'I've seen it done.'

He nodded as she rushed off, then he bit his lip. 'This cold will kill the boy even if the fracture does not... he's already too pale from pain. Mr Bailey, ask your good wife to break out that brandy flask I know she has in her cloth bag and ease this man's agony.' He returned his attention to Jane.

'How far away is Grantham?' Jane asked as she watched Bailey obediently trudge off to fetch the brandy. He glowered back at her as though this accident were her fault.

She watched Julius Sackville take a slow breath and stare out across the landscape, as though calculating the distance. Jane couldn't see how. The land was virtually flat for as far as her eyes could see, and rendered nearly featureless by the snow that tucked itself like a sparkling white blanket into every nook and corner.

'Coachman, would you say Grantham is six miles south?'

The man nodded. 'Aye, sir – mayhap closer to seven and straight ahead.'

The others gathered. They appeared comfortable with having Sackville take charge. Cecilia had now applied several splints.

'I am going to carry this injured man,' Sackville told them. 'I agree our horses are too spooked and will be more trouble than they're worth. I know the rough lie of the road. He's a slight fellow, so I will take him on my back. But in case something happens to me, I need one other person who can either stay with this wretchedly hurt fellow or go on ahead for help.'

The others looked at each other. No one seemed keen to volunteer and leave the relative safety of the group.

'I shall go,' Jane said.

'No!' Cecilia gasped. 'It is too risky!'

'Just as risky to remain here and do nothing. If Lord Sackville doesn't make it through, then no one's coming for us. His plan is sound. At least one of us will make it through to get help and it means the boy receives aid quicker. Stay, Cecilia, please.' Jane glanced at forlorn little Miss Leadbetter as Winifred's instincts screamed at her to ensure the child's comfort. 'Please, keep the child safe, and Mrs Bailey's nerves in check. We can count on your good sense and calmness. It is only a few hours. I will meet you at the inn.'

Cecilia began to shake her head.

'This man will die of exposure if we stand around debating much longer,' Julius pressed. 'We leave now. Miss Evans, will you help oversee the divvying up of the food that was packed by the innkeeper's wife for this journey?'

She nodded unhappily, unable to refuse him. She looked anxiously at Jane. 'Can you do this, my dear?' she asked.

'Better than being redundant and still,' Jane replied.

'Are we asking too much of you, Miss Granger?' Sackville enquired. She could see how much he wanted to say 'Jane'.

'You are *asking* nothing of me, sir. I have *offered* to go.'

She saw a flash of ferocity in his eyes, and interpreted it as admiration of her decision. 'Bravely said, Miss Granger.'

TWENTY-TWO

THEY TRUDGED AWAY, JULIUS APPEARING HERCULEAN WITH the ailing driver tied on to his back. Cecilia had secured the broken leg as best she could and the young man was dosed on liquor, so for the moment he was sleepy.

Cecilia had pressed a small silver flask into Jane's cloak pocket. 'A secret supply of brandy I brought for our journey,' she'd whispered at Jane's surprised look. 'You're going to need it.' Then she spoke at normal volume. 'I've packed a little food, whatever I could scrounge, that you can eat as you walk.'

Jane looked back over her shoulder and lifted a hand. Everyone left behind followed suit. Sackville had barely said goodbye to any of them.

'Is he heavy?' she asked him.

He shook his head. 'He's like a child for now, but even a child gets heavy after a while.'

'We'll make it.'

'This is brave of you, Jane.'

She shrugged. 'I thought it was what you wanted of me.'

He sent her a troubled look. 'I would not wish you in any peril. I hope you made your decision freely.'

'Of course I did. No one makes me do anything I don't want to do.'

'I'll keep that in mind,' he said dryly, and Jane wasn't sure whether to smile or feel lightly threatened. Even so, pinpricks of excitement began to tingle through her, as they seemed to do whenever she was around Sackville.

'Tell me about your husband,' he said, as though sensing they needed to be in safe territory.

'Well, if it helps pass the time...'

'It does,' he said, looking at her again, and she saw the levity was gone and the intensity was back in his gaze.

Bellow groaned.

'Your voice will soothe our patient too,' Julius urged.

So Jane began, digging into Winifred's memories and talking about William Maxwell.

'... asked me to bring money for a lawyer, and so here I am, making the journey.'

'A journey that no woman should,' Julius growled. 'It is lunacy to ask it of you. This weather is desperate!'

'So is my husband. I risk only illness; he risks having his head severed from his trunk.'

He looked away from her angrily and they trudged on in silence. There were, by Jane's calculation, at least ten minutes of awkward quiet, while they moved through a frozen wasteland with only Bellow's soft groans and the shriek of a hawk on the wing to distract from the endless desolation of sparkling white.

Jane soon came to hate the sound of deep snow crunching beneath her footfall, and the brightness that was almost painful on the eyes. Fresh snow was something about which countless wordsmiths had written lyrically, but in reality there was nothing romantic or even vaguely charming about stomping across a frozen plain when it hurt to breathe and each step felt laboured.

Snow, in her life, had always been something magical: a playground for building snowmen and throwing snowballs, a harbinger of celebration, because she associated it with Christmas festivities. But that was in another world where people travelled in heated cars on level roads, where weather was reported on the hour and no one ventured out on dangerous days. When someone broke their leg, a helicopter could airlift them to safety in minutes. This was not that world. This was a world where a broken leg might mean death.

Jane knew that she must not stop moving in spite of feeling her calves ache from lifting wearied legs that sank deep into the snow with each step. She slipped suddenly, but quickly regained her balance.

'Are you all right?' he broke into the silence.

'Yes. My boot snagged on something.'

'I'm sorry about speaking to you the way I did earlier. Truly, you and Miss Evans are the bravest women I know to be making this journey at any time, let alone in the depths of this godforsaken winter. If you were my wife, I would be immensely proud.'

She swallowed. 'Thank you. I have to save him... I have to.'

'Will they even let you see him?'

'That I don't know. But never underestimate a woman's wiles.'

He looked at her and she found a grin. Her breath was coming hard, and for the first time since they'd set out two hours ago, she could see his breathing was laboured too. They'd paused without realising it, staring at one another, and both now aware that the steam was billowing out of their mouths in audible gasps. The boy was stirring and crying out from the pain.

'From what I could see a few paces back along the road, around this bend and up a small path is an abandoned woodcutter's hut. We could take a short time to warm ourselves and rest, perhaps drink some of that warming brandy I saw Miss Evans slip into your pocket,' he said archly.

She feigned indignation, then grinned helplessly. 'Yes, please. A few moments' rest would be a blessing.'

He nodded. 'Follow me.'

The distance was longer than he'd judged, and by Jane's

reckoning it took close to another half-hour to reach the hut. By the time they stumbled through its small doorway, each of them was dragging in exhausted breaths.

Julius kicked the door closed, but the cold wind still whistled through broken slats of timber. It didn't matter to Jane. It was no exaggeration, to her mind, that in here, out of the killing wind-chill, it felt almost tropical. They lay John Bellow carefully on the hard earth and checked his splints, resecuring them despite his screamed protestations, which seemed to be sapping his remaining strength.

Jane stroked his head and could feel fever beneath her fingers. She put her gloves back on and dipped her hand into the pocket of her cloak for the brandy. She took two nips then held out the flask to Julius.

'Here, drink what you need. It's full. But I say we give the rest to John. He's better off being in a drunken sleep.'

'Agreed,' Julius said, grimacing as he straightened his arms from being in the same frozen position for hours. 'Ah, gads, but that's awkward.'

She laughed.

'You make fun at my expense?' he remarked, taking the flask.

'No, I love your language. I could think of so many different ways to say that something hurts. In fact, one word alone would convey the pain.'

He blinked and thought about this and then his eyes widened. 'I'd like to think a lady of your standing would not hear that word uttered, ever.'

'Do not be pompous,' she replied. 'Drink.'

He did as asked, taking three short swigs.

'One more,' she commanded.

He shook his head. 'I need to think clearly. Give it to him. Knock him out.'

Jane dribbled the fiery liquid into the boy's mouth; even in his pain he began to suck at it hungrily. Jane spoke soothing words to him until finally his head dropped back. He said something garbled, then drifted into sleep.

'Good,' Julius said.

'How long can we rest?'

He reached for his fob watch, flicked open the lid and sighed. 'Whatever I say will unsettle you. But I will keep an eye on the time. Do you wish to sleep?'

She could feel herself shivering. Now that they'd stopped that relentless walking, her body had an opportunity to protest in all manner of ways at the punishment it was receiving. 'I dare not.'

Julius moved to where she crouched over their charge and held out a hand. 'You are shaking.'

'Just cold,' she admitted as she placed her hand in his.

'If you would not think it improper, may I help to warm you?'

In her nervousness, she giggled.

'You laugh at me again,' he said, bemused, as he helped her straighten up.

'Forgive me.' She was thinking about all the pick-up lines she'd heard in her life. This was the best of them.

He opened his voluminous cloak and wrapped his arms around her shoulders to bring her into the immediate embrace of his body. Without any conscious action, Jane suddenly realised she had snaked Winifred's arms around the broad torso of Julius Sackville. They stood silent and unmoving... infinitely warmer, but with such heightened awareness that the hut suddenly felt suffocatingly small. Yet Jane had to admit there was nowhere else in either world she'd rather be right now.

'You smell so good,' he admitted with a soft sigh. 'What is that scent?'

'It translates, I suppose, as Ashes of Violet,' she said. 'I was given two tiny vials of it in France by Queen Mary Beatrice, who had it made up for me when I was first orphaned. My mother loved violets, you see, and the Queen, who loved my mother too, said it would remind me of her.'

'How old were you?'

'Nineteen when Mama died. I hadn't met William,' she said in answer.

'I wish I'd known you then.'

'I wonder what Mrs Bailey would make of this,' she finally said in an attempt to lighten the atmosphere, which had thickened in their tiny hut. Her cheek was pressed against his chest, and it made it easier to talk without having to look into that knowing gaze.

'I doubt she'd read innocence into it,' he replied dryly.

'Julius...'

'Yes?'

'Do you believe in fate?'

'I do.' He shifted so that he could look at her. She watched him struggle for what to say next before he moved her away from the sleeping Bellow, leading her to the furthest end of the hut, away from the light of the tiny window and into the shadows where some old logs were stacked. Jane felt the timber of the wall pressing against her back as they both accustomed their eyes to the new darkness. With Julius's arms leaning either side of her shoulders, she felt shrouded within his cloak... within yet another world: not hers of 1978, not his of 1715; a whole new world beyond time that belonged just to them. 'I believe we were destined to meet.'

Her breath felt trapped. This was it. She had permitted this situation – chosen it, in fact, by volunteering to accompany him on the lonely walk. Now he was opening up his heart to her and she could either embrace his affection or turn it away. If she chose the latter, Jane sensed that he would not bare his soul again. She could feel Winifred's fear of what was about to occur and her powerlessness to prevent it; she was also fully conscious of her responsibility for William Maxwell's life and for her Will's life, linked to the survival of the Earl. All of these people were depending on her, including Cecilia, who was probably chewing down her nails right now with worry for her.

And here she was, about to risk it all and succumb to her own weakness.

'I never felt so out of control in the presence of a man, before I met you,' she confessed.

And that was all Julius Sackville needed to hear, it seemed, for once the words were cast out and floating between them he reached to tip up her chin.

'I have to taste your lips again, Jane. It has been turning me into a man of madness to sit as close to you as I have been forced to sit in that coach, listening to the idle prattle of others, when all I can think about is you.'

Why did his earnest declaration sound a chime of love in her mind when Will's declarations never could? She doubted herself with Will constantly, and yet here, in a dim woodsman's hut with a stranger, she felt an outpouring of need from herself and, yes, unalloyed desire too... but most of all it was a yearning to love him.

'You've been like a fire burning in the corner of the carriage,' she admitted. 'I want your warmth. I need it.'

He surprised her by his slow and gentle movements, bringing his hands to cup her face. It no longer felt like Winifred's. These were *her* eyes softening to him, *her* mouth reaching toward him, *her* hands pulling him eagerly and knowingly to her lips, which finally found his. Though tender at first, once they'd tasted each other again any hesitancy fled, and their tongues began to search just as earnestly as his hands sought to undo her laces. He was kissing her neck, ears, eyelids, every exposed patch of skin... and it was clear he wanted more.

'Oh, my love,' he murmured. 'I did not believe my ice-crusted heart could ever feel like this again.'

For mercy's sake, Jane! The reprimand came through as a distant cry, but she could ignore Winifred in this moment, because Jane owned this body now and it was Jane's passion burning through it, while her host was lost.

They slid down the wall, Julius furiously unlacing the stays that held her garments so tightly to her – and she was glad he knew what to do, because she would have trembled or taken too long. Suddenly everything that had stood as a barrier between them seemed to fall away, and Jane couldn't think a straight thought. She was his. He was hers. They were desperate to become one, and it was with a deep and satisfying groan that they rode the passion that had simmered in the carriage between them. Their only witness was in the grips of a drunken sleep. *No one will know*, Jane said to herself as she buried her hands in his hair and felt the hard ground underneath her hips as they came together in a new and desperately urgent rhythm. *No one will know.*

He shuddered above her and Jane opened her eyes to witness the highest moment of his passion. Julius wore a smile of release that wasn't only physical; she knew their frantic lovemaking had changed him somehow. This was an emotional release... a farewell, perhaps, to the shadow of his wife, who followed him around like a ghost. A re-emergence into the world and its pleasures. She forgot her own needs, and pulled him close as he lowered his lips to hers once more.

'Forgive me,' he begged, sounding weak for the first time in her presence. He pushed away to lift himself up. Jane once again felt the loss of his touch like a parched man offered a pitcher of water and then deprived of it before he was sated. Julius helped her to her feet and held her silently for several long moments that, curiously, felt more loving than any embrace she had ever had from a man. 'Forgive me,' he begged again.

She pulled away. 'You are forgiven,' she whispered.

She began to retie her laces and straighten her clothing, while he did the same. It was awkward and she did feel ashamed, but she also felt like smiling. It was as though she'd just lived out a scene from some eighteenth-century bodice-ripper; she'd never sneer at them again.

'I'd better check on Bellow,' she said, desperate to alleviate the uncomfortable silence, and moved to the sleeping man's side.

Sackville stood uncomfortably by the door. 'I took advantage of—'

'No, Julius... no, you didn't.' She reached for him, held him again. 'I am my own person. I make my own decisions. I wish I could explain...'

'Could you try?'

She searched his broken expression. 'I like it so much when you call me Jane,' she began, 'because when I'm with you, I *am* Jane Granger. Winifred Maxwell is someone else. Can you understand that?' She searched his face, pleading with her eyes that he somehow might understand her cryptic words.

He surprised her by nodding. 'Curiously, I don't think of you as Winifred. That name has no meaning for me. You are only Jane to me and I prefer it that way. You are a stranger, you belong to no one, you are the make-believe woman that inhabits Lady Nithsdale.' At this, Jane gasped, and he frowned with worry. 'What I mean is that I prefer to think of you as the woman you are pretending to be rather than Winifred Maxwell. There are moments when I think I see you struggle with yourself.'

'You mean like a few moments ago?'

He nodded, meeting her gaze. 'When we are together as we were just now, I could almost believe you to be a different person.'

'Wot's going on?' Bellow bleated, still with his eyes closed, but clearly stirring.

'We must go,' Julius said, suddenly brisk and withdrawn again. He dug into his pocket and took out a card. 'We are but an hour from our destination now. We will make it, Jane, I promise you. And when we reach London we shall part. I likely will never see you again, but should you ever need me, here are my addresses – my club in London and my home in the north. I am... I am yours for —' He shook his head.

'Forever is a long time,' she said, knowing that was what he had wanted to say. It echoed in her mind that Will had once said the same.

'Nevertheless, I am yours,' he said, so softly it hurt to hear his tenderness. She didn't want him to be weakened by her.

She took the card, barely looking at it before slipping it into her cloak. She inhaled a slow, deep breath, unsure of what to say, but letting instinct guide her. 'Julius, if a woman you don't recognise should ever introduce herself to you using the name of Jane Granger, will you give her a fair hearing – give her a chance to explain something?'

He blinked. 'I do not know what you mean by that.'

She smiled sadly. 'Neither do I. My emotions are in turmoil, but you need not say anything, just make a silent promise to pay attention to a stranger claiming to be Jane Granger.'

He frowned and began to say something, but Jane moved to the door, denying him any chance to query her strange request. The pain of parting was too great, as was the shock of realising that here was the partner she'd searched for her whole adult life, but that she must now turn away from him and deny their love.

Bellow was awake for the final hour of their journey and let them know in no uncertain terms how much this trip was costing him in suffering and pain. They didn't share another personal word, but kept to polite exchanges about the distance and the weather. When the town finally hove into view an unspoken sense of missed opportunity and a deeper, less tangible loss passed between them.

At the inn they were separated immediately and Jane didn't see him again until the first group of their fellow travellers had been safely brought into the town, Cecilia and the Leadbetters among them. Jane used the intervening time to rest but not sleep, her thoughts too ragged.

Julius bowed to the two friends. 'Hello again, Miss Granger. Miss Evans, I'm glad you're safe.'

'The five hours passed easily enough in slumber, Lord Sackville. The carriages fetched us very quickly. I cannot imagine what you paid to get the innkeeper to move so many men and horses at once.'

He waved away her enquiry as if it meant nothing. 'I am going back with the men to help. But I should warn you, there are no coaches getting through. I suggest you take horses. The roads out of Grantham are a little easier on horseback. I have taken the liberty of reserving two sturdy mounts, should you wish to take advantage. They are the last pair available.'

'What about you?'

'Your journey is more urgent. Your husband awaits you, Lady Nithsdale,' he said, and she heard the underlying sorrow those words cost him. He cleared his throat and shifted his attention to Cecilia. 'I am presuming you have done enough sleeping for a while,' he said, infusing the moment with levity for her benefit. 'But at least you shall be on your way and Grantham a dim memory,' he said, not glancing at Jane, but the message was there all the same.

Jane spoke before Cecilia could reply. 'That is very kind of you, Lord Sackville. Cecilia, would you mind fetching our things from the men who brought them? Then we can leave immediately.'

Cecilia nodded and hurried off, leaving Jane alone with Julius; she had to seize what felt like it would be her final opportunity with him. 'Julius... in another lifetime, perhaps things might have been different... I know you believe in fate, but I wonder, do you believe in other worlds?'

He gave a rare smile. 'I have never thought upon it, but I should like to think in a different world we might have...' and then he stopped as she had.

Jane rushed to fill his awkward silence. 'Well, in that different world there lives a woman called Jane Granger and she deeply regrets that she is not in a position to know you better. Do not forget her. I think that's what I was trying to ask of you earlier.'

'How could I forget her? I believe she has rekindled something in me that I thought was long dead.' He stared at her and looked on the brink of referring again to their time in the hut...

'Do not say the word, Julius,' she pleaded.

'Then I shall say that I do hope we shall meet again, brave Jane.'

'As do I,' she managed to choke out, tormented by a host of new perceptions, and assaulted by feelings she dared not explore. 'I want to give you this,' she said, holding out a tiny glass vial. She shrugged awkwardly. 'I retrieved it from our luggage when it arrived. Perhaps it will be a fond memory for you.'

He could smell from the glass stopper the perfume of violets. 'But surely you need—'

'I have another, remember, back at home? May it remind you of me.'

'I will dab the perfume on my pillow every night and think of you next to me,' he said, his voice gritty with pent-up emotion.

Just then Cecilia returned and Sackville tore his gaze from Jane. 'Keep her safe, Miss Evans,' Sackville urged, pocketing the vial, his voice tight as he bowed slightly to Cecilia.

Cecilia broke all protocol by hugging him.

'You looked like you could use that, Lord Sackville,' Cecilia admitted, seeing his surprised countenance. 'That is from both of us – all of us, in fact – for taking charge.'

One of the men from the rescue party arrived and touched his cap. 'Ready for you, Lord Sackville.'

'Thank you,' he said, and ground his jaw as the man retreated. 'Well, I should best be off.'

Jane held out her gloved hand, determined to remain demure. 'It has been a pleasure, sir,' she said, and dared to twitch a meaningful smile at him.

He took her fingertips lightly and bent over to place a soft kiss upon them. 'Miss Granger, I shan't forget you,' he said, lightly reassuring her of his earlier promise.

She wanted to hug him as Cecilia had, but instead placed her kissed hand inside her cloak – as if to shield it. She permitted herself to look upon Julius once more, and fix his fine features and strapping frame into her mind's eye, because that was all he could be from now on: a mental image to cling to... a memory of a broken dream.

He nodded and turned away, and Jane watched the man she suddenly knew she loved walk away from her as she gathered up the treacherous memories of his kiss, his hands, his body on her and in her, together with his passionate words, and locked them away in a place not even Winifred could touch.

'Winifred?' Cecilia queried, hurrying alongside her as she marched behind the Angel Inn's servants to its stables. 'Are you sure this is a good idea? The innkeeper told me a snowstorm is threatening to break south of here. Should we not stay overnight at least?'

'Do not fret on my account. We have come too far. We have no choice but to press forward.'

'You *must* rest.'

'I have! Besides, I can rest in the saddle. We are hardly going to gallop, given the conditions.'

'But—'

She thought of saying goodbye to Julius, and what had resolutely pressed her to do so. 'They'll execute William, Cecilia! The Protestant usurper will —' Her friend made a hushing sound, looking around, worried that they might have been overheard. Jane dropped her voice to a hiss. 'He will ensure the Earl of Nithsdale and his head are parted.'

And then my Will shall die. She thought of him hooked up to machines, on the brink of death, and the crushing weight of her guilt over Julius suddenly crowded into that same vision. Was this now a new form of guilt driving her on and on?

Stop it, Jane! she yelled inwardly.

She let go of Julius's card and reached for Cecilia's hand instead. 'I understand if you would rather not—'

'Do not be quick to judge my intent,' Cecilia replied. 'I set out on this wretched journey so that you need never travel alone and I have no intention of abandoning you or your dear husband now because of a few feet of snow!'

Jane nodded. 'Let us not even talk about the blizzard that I fear we must yet ride through,' she admitted, looking out across the pearled and frigid landscape. 'We must leave Lincolnshire before the New Year is out and then we have one hundred more miles to London, which I do hope we shall make by carriage.'

'It is better not to think beyond the next hour,' Cecilia counselled. 'If we survive each hour, the days will take care of themselves... and so also will our journey.'

'Amen,' Jane said, beneath her breath. She sighed and looked at her friend. 'Let us ride bravely for Stamford, then.'

They walked their horses – paid for by Sackville, much to their astonishment – out of Grantham and onto the open road. He had not lied: the path ahead did look flatter, less icy. But Jane was in no mood to give herself any false illusions. The way was treacherous and Julius would have only suggested the horses because he knew she would not remain a moment longer. He probably suspected she would have set off on foot had he not made the arrangements for them.

In her pocket, where she was warming her hand, she could feel the card Julius had given her. The details were easy to memorise, but the connection with him was more important. He had touched this, drawn it from his pocket and handed it to her. At one moment they had been linked through this card – their fingers clasping either side of it. She had allowed this man to make love to her. She was engaged to Will. Winifred was married to William.

'Cecilia,' she said suddenly, 'would you laugh if I told you I have had the notion that someone else has invaded my body? I have not been feeling myself of late. I fear it has prevented me from doing everything for William that I should.'

Cecilia's expression shifted instantly to sympathy. 'Shock,

I'm told, can make us behave curiously. You could not have done more for your husband. Assure yourself there is no greater love than yours and William's. Why do you think I have accepted no offers of marriage?' Jane looked up and met Cecilia's searching gaze. 'I want to find what you two have. I want to hear birdsong in my mind when I see the man I love and I want to blush like I see you blush when William whispers something only for your hearing. I want to have that private smile you both reserve only for each other, that silent language that you can use to communicate without words across a room. And until I experience that, I am not giving myself to any man.' And there it was. Cecilia had managed to say with passion what Jane had been softly prodding her soul for since Will had asked her to marry him.

Those were the elements of a relationship that she wanted as well, and she had finally found them in a man she could not have.

TWENTY-THREE

It was the afternoon of New Year's Eve in London, and the world was on the brink of slipping into the last year of the seventies. A Moroccan restaurant, Riad, was offering up couscous as its dish of the day; most Britishers had not even heard of couscous, certainly not tasted it. But the owner, a sixth-generation Berber, was determined to bring genuine Moroccan cooking into the next decade of London's ethnic fabric.

Tonight he would entertain his patrons with traditional dancing girls balancing trays of fresh mint tea in silver pots and tea glasses on their heads as they gyrated fast and furiously, defying gravity. There would be four of them this evening to ensure a festive atmosphere. They would wear their gossamer-thin, shimmering costumes, tinkling with charms and dazzling with gold ornamentation, while their sinuous bodies moved rhythmically to the drums.

The British thought Arab girls performed 'belly dancing'! Mahmoud sighed, but if it filled his restaurant, he would have a prosperous Christmas–New Year period and that meant he could take his wife and infant children back to his Moroccan homeland for January and February to escape this vicious winter. The restaurant looked even more exotic than usual, with additional drapes and charms and terracotta tajines to create a real Berber atmosphere – not that his guests would understand such details. He shrugged. So long as they appreciated the food, he would be happy. He smiled as his nostrils were hit with the aromas of cumin and tumeric, paprika and cinnamon, and he pushed through into the restaurant's kitchen.

'Make it special tonight, my friends,' he said to the staff, as the scent of spices wafted beyond the confines of the restaurant and drifted upstairs to a vacant space that Mahmoud had held high hopes of renting out as an office. It was in a perfect location, especially for an agency – dramatic, literary, PR or even a small advertising agency. He must have shown at least one potential renter through for each week that his restaurant had operated. It was troubling that he couldn't get any of them to take on the lease, no matter how he'd sweetened the deal.

He'd repainted when they had said they weren't keen on how dark it seemed; he'd had a team of professional cleaners go through when someone else had complained of a strange smell of decay; he'd even relaid and revarnished the floorboards in a desperate attempt to make the office feel new and fresh. New lights, new doors, even new carpet on the top floor landing, but there were still no takers.

People often shivered when they walked into the office for a viewing. 'Cold in here, isn't it?' they'd remark. Mahmoud would make an excuse that the heating hadn't been on in months, but he was lying. The heating was on, yet nothing he did could get the temperature high enough for him to admit it was even warm. And when he'd called in the professionals, they'd scoffed at him because the radiators worked perfectly well whenever they were present.

He was clueless as to the meaning of this phenomenon and had begun to let the thought gain purchase that his upstairs office was haunted.

It was ridiculous, but he had no explanation for the footsteps that his staff had heard above them, or the smell of freshly ground coffee. One person had even remarked that she thought she'd heard a man's voice.

And sometimes... rarely... members of the public might walk up those stairs. The office had its own entrance, which couldn't be seen from the restaurant, but whenever Mahmoud heard someone arriving, he'd dash upstairs – hoping it was a potential renter – only to find the office empty. The most recent visit had occurred only a few days ago. One of the dishwashing staff – a pretty girl, in her late teens, with a punk hairstyle and bright smile – had been running late and told him she'd seen a well-dressed woman entering the side building clutching a lavender-coloured pamphlet. Mahmoud, frowning, duly paid a visit upstairs to an empty office, where an aroma of freshly poured coffee and a curious waft of perfume lingered.

He'd already decided that in the New Year he was going to have a holy man visit the office and bless it... just in case.

Upstairs, where the scent of Moroccan spices wafted, a small, neatly dressed man of indeterminate age stared at an old, tarnished mirror on the mantelpiece as he heard the echo of Mahmoud's thought.

'No need,' Robin murmured to the restaurateur. 'I shall be leaving now.' He returned his attention to the mirror, where a woman, with identical features to his own, stared back at him. 'Has she left?'

The woman, known as Robyn, nodded. 'She is on her way to London.'

'I'm glad.'

'Why her?'

'Why not?'

They regarded each other: one and the same, yet separated by centuries.

'Tell me,' Robyn urged.

He shrugged at his reflection. 'I found her troubling situation touching. She was conflicted and she needed clarity – the sort of objectivity that this experience might deliver her. The challenge of restoring her fiancé using life's tapestry wasn't something that her wealth could buy. It required her to move beyond everything familiar and easy in her life, and believe only in herself, for no one could know what she was facing or taking on. Besides, we both like Winifred Maxwell. We could have let Jane's life run its natural course, but I chose to interfere.'

'We're not meant to.'

'And yet we do… all the time, in little ways.'

'This is not little. This is changing the course of history. It is forbidden.'

'Whose history?'

'Any one of the cast of characters whose lives you are dabbling with.'

'I'm giving one person a chance to choose, that's all.'

'But you are changing her life – and the lives of others – by shutting down her choices. You gave her no choice!'

'I know you do not believe that. Jane is yet to make the hardest choice of all. I've given her a chance to look at her life from a different perspective. What she thinks she wants, perhaps she really doesn't. What she turns away from, she knows is what she searches for.' Robin watched his female reflection blink and hold back what she wanted to say. He smiled slyly. 'What's more, Julius Sackville could—'

Robyn hissed, cutting him off. 'Do not play with his life!'

Robin held up his hands in surrender and chuckled.

'This is not your role,' she snapped.

'What is my role?' he asked, sounding defiant.

'To offer insight when someone looks for guidance, but not to coerce.'

'She came to me, searching for answers. When someone actually looks beyond the obvious and is prepared to open themselves up to a spiritual awakening, I feel it deserves reward.'

'Do you really see this as a reward?'

'She could be bleating by her fiancé's bedside, watching him die.'

'She could die in a snowstorm on the snow-blocked roads of Britain in 1715!'

'1716,' he corrected. 'The New Year is nearly upon us all. Let it be, Robyn. Jane Granger will make her choice soon enough. Until then, Winifred Maxwell is being given an opportunity like no other and both William Maxwells could live.'

'Or die!'

He shrugged. 'That was the situation with or without my involvement.'

'And Julius Sackville?'

'I sense you have a soft spot for him.'

'He doesn't deserve this, Robin. He's suffered enough at the hands of women.'

Robin didn't answer. Hearts were hurt every day. He couldn't be responsible for every single one of them. He waited, knowing Robyn would move on.

She did. 'Maybe we should have let Winifred die instead of leaving her dormant within herself.'

'Perhaps, but occasionally it's intriguing to see what mortals will do when they're shown a pathway. Winifred needed Jane's strength to live. Now it's up to Jane and Winifred to—'

'Hello? Is anybody in here?' came a new voice. It was Mahmoud. He shook the door handle to check it was locked. Robyn heard the sound of keys rattling in the lock and her reflection in the mirror blurred and disappeared as her male self, Robin, winked out of existence.

Mahmoud burst in through the door. 'I'm warning you —' he said, to be greeted by silence, an empty space and the sound of the old mirror leaning on the mantelpiece cracking as time stood still.

TWENTY-FOUR

JANE AND CECILIA MADE IT THROUGH THE early part of the blizzard, arriving at Stamford on New Year's Eve, where even Jane could see the sense of staying put while the worst of the weather raged. On New Year's Day, after she had shared a slightly more lavish meal than they were used to – roast goose, and even a small sherry – Jane asked for paper, nibs and ink. She set to and wrote a long letter to Mary Traquair to assure her that all was well, careful that Winifred's voice came through so as not to alarm her sister-in-law.

> *... The snow was so deep that our horses yesterday were in several places almost buried in snow. In such weather we could not stir today, but tomorrow shall set forward again. I must confess such a journey I believe was scarce ever made by a woman. But an earnest desire compasses a great deale, with God's help; though if I had known what I was to have gone through, I should have doubted whether I would be able to do it...*

Jane smiled at the strange, stilted language, but that was how Winifred wrote. She was mindful also of the need to thank Mary for looking after her 'little girl', as Winifred had guided Jane to write. *Had I had her with me she would have been in her grave by this time with the excessive cold.*

A 'flying coach' was booked for the next morning, headed

first for Peterborough, where they would stop for a meal, pick up more mail and change horses. Then it was on to Cambridge, by which point they would have covered almost half the distance to London. The ostlers at the coaching inns, especially as they got closer to London, had the capacity to turn around a team of horses every twenty miles, unharnessing the exhausted animals and harnessing a fresh team in a matter of minutes. The mail would be loaded and fresh passengers speedily taken aboard, leaving barely half an hour for travellers to snatch a hasty meal and a drink.

'We'll make London tomorrow.' Cecilia quietly aired the thought that had been bouncing around in Jane's mind since she'd stepped aboard the carriage.

'Yes,' she said blandly, masking her disturbance at the notion of finally meeting the Earl of Nithsdale. She had so little idea about the man she was going to meet under such tense circumstances, and delving into Winifred's life wasn't yielding anything but the obvious. Winifred was keeping that side of herself private. While Jane respected this, given the surreal situation they found themselves in she needed her host's help, for she was afraid of letting her down in front of her husband. He was teetering on the cliff edge of a trial that would almost certainly end in death by beheading. Jane didn't need any additional awkwardness added to what she, as well as he, were already experiencing.

Why, for instance, wouldn't Winifred clue Jane into his voice, his mannerisms, his likes and dislikes? Again, she hated to rummage around in such private spaces, but access to Winifred's most intimate thoughts and memories about her husband was essential if Jane was going to get them through this.

And then what? She had no idea whether it was Winifred asking her that question, or her own scrambled thoughts. How would she know if Will had recovered... or if he was dead? How would she get back to her own life? Worst of all, what if she couldn't save the Earl of Nithsdale? What would that scenario mean to her life, now so enmeshed with that of Winifred Maxwell? Would she have to live her life out, and die, as Winifred? And would that be it?

Jane tried to wipe away a tear surreptitiously, but the ever attentive Cecilia saw it.

'Oh, my dear Winnie,' she whispered. 'I did not mean to upset you.'

Jane shook her head gently. 'It was not what you said,' she assured. 'It is that we are now close to our destination after so many trials, but I wonder how close we are to our goal. I am worried for William, for the children, our future.'

Cecilia nodded, patted her gloved hand. 'Few woman would find the courage to do what you have already achieved.'

'Cambridge!' interrupted a yell from above them.

There was a collective sigh of relief throughout the carriage. London tomorrow, and the real tests were yet to come.

Moody thoughts of Julius were banished. He had to be confined to her memories now. When this adventure somehow ended, only then would she allow herself to examine what had occurred and the feelings he had aroused within her.

The coach driver blew his horn to announce their arrival at the Golden Cross Coaching Inn at Charing Cross and it felt to Jane as though a thousand winged creatures took flight in her body. Strong hands helped her alight from the coach into the freezing late afternoon of a soggy, grey London, where any snowfall had melted, to stand alongside Cecilia, who was engrossed in directing the careful unloading of their luggage. Jane, however, was captivated by a familiar place she barely recognised. The Charing Cross she knew – the meeting point of the Strand and Whitehall and the sprawl of Trafalgar Square, the dominating art gallery, the blitz of pigeons, swarm of traffic and forever swirling river of people and riot of shops – was yet to declare itself.

Through Winifred's eyes, she saw a statue of King Charles I on his horse and close by it a raised pillory where an unfortunate man stood slumped, his head and hands locked into the stock. Jane couldn't read the placard that declared his crime, but she could see the man's head was filthy from being pelted with rotten food and she didn't want to imagine what else. No one seemed terribly interested in him, so presumably the public humiliation had passed. She knew she must not stare or look overly surprised, yet shook her head in awe at how sleepy the area seemed, how few people were milling around. Yet here was Cecilia catching her attention and saying, 'How frightfully busy it is,' and then, 'We could take a hackney carriage.'

'No, let's walk,' Jane risked suggesting. She knew their destination was perhaps ten minutes' walk away at most.

'Are you sure?'

'Yes. Why spend the money on four legs when we can get there on two?'

Cecilia laughed. 'There is something so different about you, Winifred. I swear I cannot recognise you at times!'

Her inclination was to head for the Strand immediately, because it was such a major thoroughfare for people, horses, carriages and hand-drawn and pony-drawn carts, where they would be sure not to get lost. But she sensed Cecilia – and gentlefolk like her – might choose a different route. So, unsure of what that route might be, she let her friend lead. Furthermore, she felt Winifred beginning to shiver and was aware of the vague light-headedness that seems to travel slightly ahead of fever. She hoped Cecilia, just in front of her, was too distracted to notice.

Not yet, Winnie, she whispered in her mind to her host. *You have to stay strong... just a few minutes longer.*

'Beware of these costermongers, Winnie. The lady I was talking to in the stagecoach warned me of their unsavoury habits. They'll pinch your bottom as fast as your purse.'

Jane had to laugh. She looked now at the row of barrows,

where men were yelling their wares – fruits, vegetables, fish, cordials. Each owner wore a large kerchief around his neck; she recalled from her studies that it was called a kingsman.

The two women passed by, amid a barrage of raised voices urging them to notice, to pause, to purchase. 'Comerlong, comerlong, ladies! 'Ere's yer loverly apples an' pears. Six for an ha'penny.'

Further on a different sort of produce was being sold. Jane tried not to show her ignorance. She could see coal and charcoal, but the bags of dust?

A grubby-looking man answered her silent query. 'Don't be shy, ladies, walk up and take a look. High-quality brickdust to sharp'n yer household knives. Buy it or miss it; I won't be 'ere tamorra.'

Jane would have loved to stay and watch the men, listening to their amusing brogue and their rhyming songs, which they shouted to attract attention. But she knew it was not a place where a lady of her rank should linger.

'I do hope Mrs Mills has received your letter,' Cecilia remarked, maintaining a brisk stride.

'Presumably, since we managed to defy the snow, the mail coach would have got through a week ago. Either way, our dear friend would always make us feel welcome.'

'You are right, of course. I daresay she would be sorely miffed if you chose to stay anywhere but her guest house when in London.'

Jane nodded, continuing to take in her surroundings, and suddenly aware of a mixture of strong aromas that had been sadly lacking in the small towns. She could smell coffee being ground, mixed with the not dissimilar fragrance of tobacco; meat was roasting, its smell carried on the wind with the scent of newly baked bread. She could hear animals braying in the distance, and as the streets narrowed they became more clogged with people and houses. More costermongers, with running noses and cloth caps above unshaven faces, led barrows down these streets, or lined the way ahead to make the women's path narrower still. They were again creating their own type of song, yelling their wares. Some of them were sinking draughts of ale; Jane couldn't blame them, imagining that shouting for hours on end would require regular lubrication.

Jane had lost track slightly of where they might be in the modern London of her memory but right now she was more concerned with being careful to lift her skirts. For now they had entered streets that ran with muck and the cobbles seemed permanently damp and slippery, particularly in parts where the surface damp had frozen.

She was aware of a light breeze as they rounded a corner and she caught a glimpse of shockingly bright green. Given that she'd travelled through countryside that was mostly snowbound, it was not only a surprise to see grass, but also a shock to see it here, where she was used to seeing skyscrapers.

Jane strained to see more before that tiny 'picture window' was shut to her. It was Lincoln's Inn Fields stretching northward, she realised with a sense of wonder, and she had to stop herself from giving a soft yelp of pleasure at the recognition. How amazing to be experiencing the London of almost three hundred years ago.

She had a powerful desire to run to the spot in the city where she knew in three centuries her fiancé would be lying in a coma in his hospital bed. Would she feel anything? Would there be a connection through the magic that had trapped her in this time?

Cecilia was heedless of her scrambling thoughts. 'Down here, dear,' she muttered. 'We'll move into the Strand and wider streets again.'

Jane followed, her mind still thinking on Will, convinced now that he was aware of her travelling the ley lines… they had brought her back to him, to the same city, separated from him only by time. In spite of the fact that she'd never felt further from him, here in London Jane also felt more connected. Sadly, it wasn't love in the way he wanted, but it was love nonetheless: she had loved him enough to risk her life for him.

Hope flared and with it came a fresh wave of determination.

'Oh, my dear, do not wear yourself out,' her companion warned, increasing her long stride to match Winifred's sudden burst of speed. 'Your fever could return.'

The wide boulevard of Lincoln's Inn Fields opened up, and Jane became aware of a great open green space with tall, regular houses, fresher air and reasonably ruly traffic. In the middle of the square, young men were practising archery, others playing what looked to be a form of bowls. It was a shock to her sense of what she knew of this part of London. She felt Winifred's recognition and understood that her host's parents, Lord and Lady Powis, had once possessed a magnificent mansion here, one of the first to be built during the reign of James II, the father of the exiled king in France. She felt Winifred's sorrow that the family had been forced to leave it behind for their faith and loyalty to the King.

There were three rows of fine houses, clearly providing accommodation for the nobility and gentry, while the northern side possessed a great turnstile, which opened into a densely populated area showcasing all manner of artisans – from shoemakers to milliners. Jane knew that she and Cecilia were headed southward, to where a passage would ultimately lead them through an arch into Duke Street – their destination.

'Your Ladyship!' exclaimed the tall, high-bosomed woman of middle years, clucking behind the servant who opened the door. 'I have been expecting you for two days. Good gracious, you look ready to fall over my threshold!'

'Mrs Mills,' Jane answered, drawing deeply on Winifred's memories and instincts now. 'Thank you; it is so heartening to see you again.'

'Come in, come in,' the woman fussed, closing the door as quickly as she could to protect the meagre warmth. 'Jenner, organise pots of hot chocolate and let Miss Cambry know that our Scottish guests have arrived and she must make sure those beds are warmed.'

Jane found herself ushered through a high-ceilinged hallway and up a flight of stairs that soared to the first floor, where a beautiful window flooded the landing with soft evening light. Painted wood panelling covered the bottom half of the walls up to dado height in a soft eggshell-blue colour, before a lighter colour – almost a grey cream – completed the walls. A fragrance in the air hinted that the silver had recently been polished, and mingled with the smell of beeswax that shone from the exquisite furniture.

'Thank you, Mrs Mills. We were concerned as to whether Win—, I mean whether Her Ladyship's letter had arrived before us.'

'It certainly did, and gave my heart quite a start to hear of your adventures. Is Her Ladyship feeling well, Miss Evans? She looks to be shaking with a fever. Your eyes appear somewhat glassy, my dear Countess.'

'I should not be at all surprised if she is unwell, Mrs Mills, but nothing would persuade her to take the journey slower or be easier on herself.' She turned to Jane. 'My Lady, let me draw you a tub to soak in and you can finally put your head down on a comfortable pillow again.'

Jane blinked at the notion of suddenly being spoken about as an invalid.

'Could we get some food, Mrs Mills?' Cecilia continued. 'My Lady has been eating like a bird on our journey.'

'No.' Jane shook Winifred's head, beginning to feel the presence of her host more strongly, but only her thoughts. Her strength was still sadly lacking. 'You may both bathe and eat, take some rest or exchange news, but I will not spend another minute on my needs until I have laid eyes on William.' Her voice cracked and she coughed; Jane could gauge how fragile Winifred was at this moment and could sense her two friends having to resist the urge to reach for her. 'I don't even know if he's still alive,' she croaked.

'Oh, my dear Countess, of course he's still alive. Forgive me for my thoughtlessness in not mentioning that immediately. He is awaiting sentencing, as I understand it.'

Jane took a deep breath of relief. The hardships of the journey – including the flaring up of Winifred's chilblains – had been worth it, but there was probably not a lot of time left to get William Maxwell released and to give Will Maxwell back his life.

'I shall retire briefly and have a sip of black tea with honey, Mrs Mills, and then if you would be so kind as to hail me a hackney, I must make haste to the Tower, where I gather he is incarcerated.'

Mrs Mills threw a worried glance at Miss Evans as she smiled sadly. 'Yes, of course. The Earl is confined in the Lieutenant's Lodgings. I am assured he is well cared for and in reasonable spirits.'

'Thank you. I shall tidy myself, if you'll excuse me.'

Mrs Mills nodded. 'Second floor, Miss Evans. The Countess's room is at the end of the hallway and yours is the adjoining. I shall have tea sent up.'

Jane's chamber felt palatial after the accommodation they had become used to on the journey. After drinking her tea, she sat down and released her aching, inflamed toes from her boots while regarding the card of Julius Sackville.

She had been emptying the pockets of her cloak because Cecilia had come in to voice her concern that it would not do for her to appear at the Tower in such rude attire. Jane had gladly agreed to the long, moss-green velvet cloak that Cecilia had just borrowed from Mrs Mills. It was trimmed with fur and warmer than the dun-brown one in which she'd covered all those frozen miles, and yet she was fond of the old cloak for what it represented.

Jane ran her fingers over the card, touching the letters of

Julius's name as he began to infiltrate the barrier she'd tried to create between them. She could taste his urgent kiss again, his breath on the bared skin of her neck, the promise of his touch in places yet to be bared to him.

Jane leaned on the dressing table, head in hands, hating the way she could lose control at just the thought of him and yet relishing that thought. She wanted to deny it, but she was forced to admit to herself that her feelings were now fleeing into separate camps. It was as though by living these two lives she could rightly devote one half of herself to Will and the other to a relative stranger.

Jane accepted that she was the interloper who had possessed Winifred, stealing into her life. So was it Jane who had fallen under the spell of Julius Sackville, or was it Winifred? Had he fallen for Winifred, the woman he looked at, or Jane, the woman he spoke to? She wished she could say Winifred, and divest herself of the responsibility of having given up her host's honour and of the guilt that now pressed upon her faithless heart like a bruise.

And yet Jane knew it had been Winifred who had resisted and only Winifred who'd resented it. It was why Winifred had been silent and closed to her since that stolen time in the woodcutter's hut.

'I'm sorry,' she whispered to her host. 'It was completely irresponsible. I don't know what's happening to me.'

The kiss at the inn was irresponsible. Allowing Sackville to take you was a betrayal, came a thought, like an echo through times and worlds, bursting through her fragile defence. She didn't know if it had come from Will, from William, or from Winifred. Perhaps it was from Robin... or Robyn? Whoever had reached her, the accusation stung. So, she was to blame.

But she did currently feel like two versions of herself.

There was the Jane who was with Will and her parents, her sister, her life in the twentieth century. And there was this Jane, ethereal, invisible and impressionable... or was it more correct to describe her as honest?

She'd been running from her guilt and uncertainty ever since Will put the diamond engagement ring on her finger. Julius Sackville had only had to look at her with that stormy, troubled gaze to immediately get beneath her clearly crumbling defences. Jane hoped no one was listening in on her thoughts, because right now, as she stared at his name, despite the hot, red pain of Winifred's swollen feet, she wanted nothing more than to be kissed by him again. To be unlaced, undressed and—

Damn! Could she hate herself any more? No, it would be impossible, she decided, to feel any more disgusted by Jane Granger than she did right now. She swallowed, gave thanks to Winifred's remedy of soaking her chilblained feet in water previously used to boil potatoes, and mentally gathered up her despair. She could not fail now, or lose faith in herself or the job that she was here to do. She had to throw her energy into saving Winifred's husband. And maybe, if she could get back to Will's bedside, this surreal time with Julius would be forgotten, like a dream was lost when you regained full consciousness from sleep.

That thought appealed to her. She would have no memory of Julius, or perhaps even this whole strange episode, when she woke up on the top of Uluru. Yes, that was it. She would put the guilt and helpless attraction behind her, because soon it would be meaningless.

For you, maybe, Jane. That was Winifred's thought pushing through, she was sure. *I can't fix it now*, she thought back. *So find forgiveness. I'm doing this for you and William and your descendants.*

She squared her shoulders. *Ignore the pain, Jane*, she coached herself. *Boots back on and it's time to meet the Earl.*

Cecilia knocked again and didn't wait to be asked in. 'Winifred, are you – oh, my dear, look at your toes!'

'I am looking at them,' Jane replied. 'Don't fuss. I ordered up potato water from the servant who brought me my tea.'

'I was going to say that my aunt, who was something of a specialist with herbs, believed that a mixture of the root of fennel with egg and port is a helpful remedy.'

Jane smiled. She could just imagine suggesting to her Welsh father that he paint such a concoction on his swollen toes each winter. 'Indeed? We shall worry about my feet another time. They are the least of my concerns.'

Cecilia frowned. 'The hackney is here. Would you like me to accompany you?'

Jane finished lacing her boots, then stood up and gave Cecilia a hug. 'You have been a true friend. But I think I should make this part of the journey alone. I shall be back, I suspect, within a couple of hours. I cannot imagine they will allow William the privilege of a long conversation with me. Rest. You deserve it. I am sure I will need your strength in the days to come.'

She left Cecilia watching her from the first floor landing as she glided down the stairs, grateful for the cosy velvet cloak, and thanked the portly Mrs Mills on her way out for arranging the carriage.

Mrs Mills had to bend slightly to give her a brief embrace. 'Our hearts are with you, Countess.'

Jane gave a gracious smile, realising there was no point in suggesting Mrs Mills call her Winifred, for her old friend clearly enjoyed using the title and no doubt telling others about her important guest. Nevertheless, Mrs Mills was a generous woman – the daughter of one of Winifred's mother's oldest companions.

A servant of the household helped Jane into the small carriage and gave the driver permission to depart when she was settled. Jane felt the hackney jerk forward and soon she was lost once more in the busy streets of London, alive with people, horses and carriages.

The hackney skimmed the edge of one of London's 'rookeries'; Jane could barely recognise where she was as she glimpsed a ramshackle, squalid-looking warren of lanes and alleys where overcrowded hovels accommodating dozens of families sat shoulder to shoulder with gin houses and brothels. As they passed these slums, she noted open sewers in the streets, men urinating directly into them without any coyness, and children running wild in and around the shallow cesspits. She saw a small girl selling what looked to be watercress from a basket, and another boy of similar age selling fish – mackerel, she thought she heard him bawl as the hackney momentarily drew alongside him. She held her breath instinctively while rummaging for a sweet-smelling handkerchief to hold to Winifred's face, and imagined just how easily the Great Plague of fifty years ago had taken hold amid such squalor.

The stink was so ripe, even on a wintry day like today, that it made her eyes water. She'd have to learn to control her inclination to retch, but understood now the tiny sachets of potpourri that she had seen people carry, frequently holding them to their nostrils in the streets.

She realised now how often she had complained during her study days of how grimy the London of the 1970s was. And yet, glimpsing this era, she wondered if she would survive long alone in this forbidding, dangerous and plague-ridden London of the early eighteenth century.

The scenery changed and she could finally see St Paul's Cathedral. Although it was in the far distance, and in the opposite direction to where the carriage was heading, it gave her the reassuring landmark she needed to fix her position.

Approaching faster than she wanted was the most terrifying aspect of her dangerous journey to date. She now had to meet the Earl and convince him that she was Winifred.

Would he notice her strangeness immediately? Cecilia had had no problem in accepting Winifred was sometimes 'not herself'. But Jane didn't believe William Maxwell would be quite as forgiving. Why hadn't she found a way to learn more about him, even from Cecilia? She was walking into this confrontation almost blind.

Jane felt the beat of panic in her chest, like a huge bird suddenly leaping into flight. She raised her hand to rap on the ceiling, in order to stop the driver; she had to think this through. She urgently needed to know more about William Maxwell.

But as her fingers balled into a fist, someone spoke. *Calm yourself*, the voice soothed. *The knowledge is within.*

She didn't recognise the low-pitched timbre, but she knew it wasn't Robin or Robyn, or even her own thoughts gusting around and tricking her.

Jane didn't know if it would work, but she tried. *Winifred?* she queried, hearing the thought reach out tentatively. It was met with silence. She tried again, more assured this time, hoping to somehow command her host to acknowledge her. *Winifred, speak to me!* There was no response, and by now it was too late to change direction or heart; she felt the horses slowing as the coachman announced their arrival.

This was it, Jane realised. She was at the point where her destiny and Will's would be shaped. She lowered the window and spoke to the yeoman who waited.

'I am the Countess of Nithsdale, come to visit my husband,' she said firmly. 'I believe he is held in the Lieutenant's Lodgings.'

TWENTY-FIVE

A TALL MAN OF SLIM BUILD WITH A neat, reddish beard, and a penetrating blue gaze to match his greatcoat, greeted Jane with warmth at his brazier.

'Sir George Moseley, Lord Constable of the Tower, My Lady,' he said, bowing over her hand.

She returned his gracious smile. 'Thank you, Sir George, for allowing me to visit.'

'Countess, your stoicism is to be admired. I am told you have journeyed from Scotland.' His quizzical expression suggested to Jane he didn't believe it.

'You were told no lie, sir. I left my lord's seat at Terregles the moment I learned the news from Preston.'

He nodded and said nothing, but his mouth twitched, showing his discomfort at what they both knew William Maxwell was facing.

'How is my dear husband?' she continued.

'In good health, My Lady. I assure you he is being accorded the respect and comforts due to a man of his status, although I am obliged to keep Lord Nithsdale confined alone. You understand that he is—'

'Yes, of course,' she interrupted. Winifred understood only too well the accusations against him.

'How is your family coping, My Lady?'

'We are saving the children the worst of it, Sir George. Our son is abroad; his sister is with friends in Scotland. She is too young to understand politics or why her father is not at home with her. Do you have children, sir?'

'Nine, several of them daughters.' He shrugged.

'And you would spare them unpleasantness no matter what their age.'

'Indeed.'

Jane wanted to move past the polite small talk, even though Sir George was doing his utmost to make her comfortable. 'Do we have a trial date, sir?'

He nodded sombrely. 'His Majesty is addressing Parliament in three days, My Lady.'

'And?' Jane held her breath.

He sighed. 'Can I offer you anything, Countess? A draught of wine, perhaps?'

'Nothing, thank you; I have taken adequate refreshment,' she said, although conscious that Winifred appeared pale and fragile.

'A seat perhaps… er, by the fire?'

'Sir George, I wish to see my husband.'

'I am not permitted—'

'Please, sir. Please. What can it hurt? He is a condemned man, by all accounts. You may search me if—'

'That will not be necessary.'

Jane had brought coin. 'I have money to pay for my husband's care. Please see to it that he receives all he needs.'

The older man stared at the gold guineas. Jane did not want to admit that they were almost the last of her family's dwindling savings, but she suspected he might already know that. She was also convinced he knew this was a bribe.

'I am in a hurry to see my lord husband. I'm sure you understand,' she pressed.

'Of course… of course. Well, My Lady, um, if I may take a gauge of government opinion, I suspect it is keen to show leniency.' Jane's hopes flared. 'But,' he continued, holding up a long-fingered hand to prevent her enthusiasm from spilling out too fast, 'an example must be made. Forgive me, Countess, but I fear the lords we have in captivity may have to bear the burden for the rebels who have been allowed to slip away, and for their leaders, who will not be pursued.'

'I see; so the King will wish a trial?' she asked, hoping to confirm Mrs Mills's words.

'I would not wish to steer your thoughts any other way, My Lady.'

She had to focus on William's plea for clemency.

'I have already recommended some names of advocates who might represent your husband. Lord Nithsdale has employed the services of one of these men, as I understand it. He has had several meetings with his counsel.'

He took the money she proffered. She nodded. 'Thank you again, Sir George. May I see him now?'

With just a hint of embarrassment he replied, 'Of course.' He rang a bell and a guard appeared.

'The Countess of Nithsdale is to be escorted to her husband's chamber and accorded the highest respect during her one-hour stay.'

The man bowed and Jane followed him.

'I am at your service, My Lady,' the Constable said gently behind her.

She cast him a final look of thanks and followed the guard into a cold hallway lit by cressets. She turned toward the small windows to her right and saw Tower Green beyond them, where – not quite two hundred years ago, she realised – a young queen called Anne Boleyn had lost her head. She shivered, unsure whether it was from fear, or the thrill of history. Other guards passed and nodded at her respectfully as she was led up a flight of stairs.

Jane felt a sudden desire to pinch herself as her head flooded with memories of staying with her university friend Emily in the Queen's House, as this was later renamed. She recalled that this had been the prison of many famous people in history, from Sir Thomas More to Guy Fawkes. The thought that she was seeing it as a working prison, and not as Emily's happy family home, sent a shiver of excitement through her. Just for a couple of heartbeats, she forgot about her strange and fearful situation and allowed herself the indulgence of feeling caught up in history.

Jane grabbed for the stair rail and caught sight of ravens plodding across the green. She counted four, but was pulled from her thoughts as she found herself being handed over to an older yeoman, this one emerging from a small room – the warders' room, she realised, provided for the comfort of the yeomen supervising her husband.

'One hour only,' she heard the first man murmur.

'Thank you,' she said to the man departing, then smiled at her new keeper.

'Follow me, please, My Lady,' he said, and led her across a vast room with steepled beams and huge windows made up of squares of leaded glass in the Tudor fashion. The floorboards creaked beneath her light frame as they reached the middle of the room. She felt light-headed, recalling that it was in this very room that she and Emily would often swot for exams or make plans for the weekend.

'This be the Council Chamber, My Lady,' the yeoman leading her explained – although she already knew it, knew this was where Guy Fawkes had stood and refused to give up the names of his fellow conspirators before he was handed over for torture.

The guard reached for the large iron keys that swung on an iron hoop dangling from his belt. He duly repeated what she already knew. 'You may stay with Lord Nithsdale for an hour, My Lady.' She nodded. 'If it helps, My Lady,' he added, 'you might care to know that your husband is popular with us yeomen, polite to us and generous with his coin.'

What little he has, Jane thought she sensed Winifred thinking. Most had come from Mary and Charles. She found a smile. 'I thank you for being kind to him. He is here because he is a loyal man, rather than a traitor. It is all about perspective, I fear.'

He frowned and she knew her reasoning was too subtle. 'Aye, well, there is no reason to be brutal without cause,' he replied. 'I suspect his day of reckoning is coming at him, if you will forgive my saying so.'

She nodded wearily as he turned the key in the lock.

'You have a welcome visitor, my Lord Nithsdale,' he called into the room before stepping back to allow Jane to cross the threshold.

She took a deep breath and stepped inside the chamber.

Ellen was giving Will a shave. She liked to do this for all 'her men', as she called them. Nursing had changed since her initial training; these days it was increasingly dominated by paperwork, and the management of wards was all-consuming. Handling staff and reaching targets set by management were not the reasons why she went into nursing. Far from it: the vocation, to her, was all about care.

'Caring for patients, that's what we do,' she impressed on trainees. 'Never forget it. And it doesn't matter whether they're old, smelly, drunk, deranged, confused, hostile or comatose.'

And so Ellen emptied urine and stoma bags with the same good cheer as she would show when checking a pulse or temperature. And she liked it when her patients looked and felt fresh… even if they were unconscious.

'They don't know,' one of the newest trainees remarked during handover after Ellen had asked why Will Maxwell looked so scruffy. At Ellen's glare, the young nurse shrugged. 'I'm just saying, it's not as though they can tell their armpits haven't been sponged.'

'And how do you know they can't?' Ellen demanded. 'How do you know what Will here is thinking, feeling, experiencing?'

The girl's eyelids lowered slightly, making her look even

more sullen than the defiantly pinched lips already had. 'I *don't* know,' she snapped.

'That's right, Lisa. You don't know. In fact, you don't know very much at all, given that you're a trainee of what, nineteen?' Lisa stared at her, saying nothing. 'In the meantime, you've forgotten the fundamental reason why we became nurses. What's more, you're privileged to work on this ward; most trainees never get the chance. Now, Will here – and his traumatised family – are counting on us to take care of his bodily needs because he can't. And if that means brushing his teeth or combing his hair, then it's the very least you can do.' She knew her eyes were narrowing in anger. 'And you can get rid of that pout. I presume his notes are up to date?'

'Of course,' the trainee said, still not cowed.

Ellen turned away and in doing so dismissed her subordinate with silent disgust.

There had been rounds and checks, plenty of urgent duties to get to before Ellen finally kept her promise and got around to bathing Will. It was now the early hours of the morning and the ward was at its quietest, on skeleton staff. Tina wandered up from another ward to puncture the silence with a bright voice, otherwise it was just Ellen murmuring to her mute patients.

'There you are,' Tina said. 'I thought you were on tonight; why am I not surprised to see you with that particular patient?'

Ellen smiled. 'My handsome Will,' she said gently. 'He never gives me any lip.' They both laughed.

'No change?'

Ellen shook her head as she dangled the razor in the sudsy water, flicked it and continued gliding the blades along Will's jawline. 'But I know he's coming back to us. It's slow, but there are signs. The problem is his parents have only given us days to prove it. They'll be taking him to America tomorrow.' She didn't add that she might just be going with them. So little time left to decide.

'Take a short break. Free for a cuppa?' Tina wondered, no longer interested, it seemed.

'I'll just comb his hair.'

Jane watched the tall man turn and exclaim, 'Winifred!'

But even before she saw his face, something extraordinary happened.

Winifred's spirit suddenly seemed to flood Jane's awareness with her love for this man. It roared through her, and to Jane it felt in that heartbeat that she was witnessing every good thing that could happen to a person: sunlight, warmth, safety, sensual pleasure, emotional delight, and an inexplicable joy that comes with the happiness of knowing you love this person and that you are loved in return.

And she knew in a blink that she had not felt any of this with Will, other than perhaps the sensual pleasure. Was that all that she had proposed to base her marriage upon? It was true – if she dared let herself think on him – that she had shared more passion with Julius Sackville in a few days than what had passed between her and Will in all their months together.

Worse, she knew she had felt everything that Winifred felt for William Maxwell in that final heart-wrenching kiss that she and Julius had shared.

In the couple of heartbeats it took him to cross the chamber and pull her into his arms, she realised it wasn't just William Maxwell, Fifth Earl of Nithsdale, embracing her but also Will Maxwell, American adventurer and geophysicist. The likeness was astonishing.

He was kissing her neck, her cheeks, finally her lips. 'Oh, my darling,' he said, sounding feverishly happy. 'You are here.'

Jane knew she must give herself over wholly to Winifred, keep the promise she'd been making to herself to *be* Winifred.

She let go.

*

As Ellen combed Will's damp hair, his body convulsed theatrically. She gasped softly.

'I saw it,' Tina said, without Ellen having to ask.

Ellen stared, unmoving, at Will, wondering if he would do it again. She blinked, waited, still holding the comb in his hair. 'I've never seen that before. Patients twitch, sometimes groan, but never anything so completely physical. I hope it's a good sign. Teen, go get help. Tell Sandra to page Dr Evans, or you do it if Sandra's not around. We need him immediately. I can't leave Will.'

Her colleague nodded and departed quickly. Ellen watched, determined to be there to witness any other changes or movements. She checked the time and reached for his file, quickly making a note of what had occurred and when.

'Come on, Will, come back to me now,' she murmured, convinced he was on his journey to the surface from wherever he had been drowning and not even realising how possessive she sounded of him.

William held Winifred at arm's length to stare at her, as though he couldn't fully believe she was in his arms. Jane felt deeply self-conscious about the appraisal. Would he guess? 'My, but you are a sight for sore eyes.' He hugged her again. 'How are the children?'

Jane nodded in his arms. 'I've written to Willie to tell him of your imprisonment. And our little Anne is confused, but she is well, always happy with Mary and her cousins, as you would expect. And you? You look thin.' She stood back to regard him fully.

He was devoid of wig or fine jacket, though he kept himself neat and shaven. Although the likeness to her Will was strong, she'd been tricked by shadows and low light into ignoring their differences. They didn't share the same eye colour and Will's hair was far lighter. Nevertheless, it was unnerving to see the unquestionable echoes in William's height and the shape of his head; even the pitch of his voice was dauntingly familiar. The family resemblance ran powerfully through the generations, reaching more than two hundred and sixty years into the future to paint her fiancé with similar brushstrokes to the man Winifred loved.

'Do not fret about my health, dearest. My head, mayhap, but not my health,' he jested, and grinned lopsidedly as Will might have. But the gallows humour frightened Jane. The reality of what Winifred and William were facing slammed home in her mind. *Beheading! Something from horror tales*, she thought, and then corrected herself. *No, something from the history books!* And here it was, all too real for her comfort. She felt sickened, the nausea galloping in on the prevailing fear that she was not equipped to know what to do, how to prevent this...

'William, what is to be done?' Jane could hear her personal terror reflected in Winifred's calm voice.

'I've begun my appeal by engaging the services of an advocate. You will need to pay him ten guineas.'

Jane nodded, gathering from Winifred that this was a huge sum. 'Your brother-in-law will help wherever he can, of course,' she reminded him.

He led her over to the window seat, then leaned against the sill and sighed. 'Yes, we shall surely need his finances.'

She remembered this room now. It was the actual bedroom that she had used when staying with Emily. She recalled it covered with wallpaper – a pink and green floral. It also had a dressing table where she sat now, a pine Habitat wardrobe to the side of the door and an old, single, iron bed that was painted in fashionable cream. She and Emily would sit on the floor near the fireplace and read magazines, listen to their vinyl LPs while griping about study, or plan their next shopping assault on the West End.

But right now she was standing on straw rushes and staring at a pail, one-quarter filled with foul-smelling amber liquid, where in the future a small sink would reside.

Jane turned away, overcome with memories, and looked out of the window, only to realise she was looking down from this vantage point onto Traitors' Gate. Not the living museum that she knew, but the operational water gate, still in use, bringing condemned prisoners to where they would probably spend their final days. Her gaze widened to take in the vast expanse of the River Thames. 'Did they bring you through there?'

He nodded, disgusted.

She looked to her left, trying to rein in her astonishment at yet another surprise. There was no London Bridge – not as she knew it, anyway. It would be another century before city planners replaced the ramshackle, higgledy-piggledy structure she was looking at with a more modern bridge – which was itself replaced in the early 1970s. *Is this what inspired the famous rhyme that London Bridge is falling down?* she wondered. Her surprise turned to dismay when she spotted rotting heads on pikes at intervals along the structure… the bridge looked like a revolting pincushion of shame.

But attending William gave her little time to take in the sights beyond this six paces-long, three-wide chamber in which he was imprisoned. Its roof curved in a shallow arch of beams and the stone walls were not cheerily wallpapered, but pale and plastered to protect against fire.

'The lawyer has suggested I plead guilty,' William said, cutting back into her thoughts.

She frowned. 'How does that help?'

A gust of icy air made her realise that he had kept the window open to the full force of Nature. 'William, for mercy's sake, you shall catch your death in here – and please do not jest that it might be easier than losing your head. My nerves will not stand any more of such dark comedy.'

He closed the window. 'When I feel the wind on my face, when it chills me numb, I seem to feel more alive and have reason to remain optimistic.'

It was Winifred who reached for his hand and held it

against her cheek. Perhaps Jane and Winifred were existing in concert now. Jane's host definitely felt more solidly present. She wondered if Winifred had access to her thoughts and memories as she had to Winifred's.

She knew William was waiting. 'All is not lost, my dearest. Tell me all that has happened.'

William began to pace. 'We were questioned by the Lords of Council the day after our arrival and then impeached in the House of Commons for high treason.'

'So what is your lawyer's rationale for pleading guilty?' she asked, her expression filled with confusion.

'He advises – as do the other lords' counsels – that we should claim to have acted upon our consciences and that we are prepared to face whatever penalty is allotted.'

She shook her head, alarmed. 'What madness is this? Why does he not suggest you offer to chop off your own heads and give them to the King on a platter?' Jane was impressed by Winifred's sarcasm at this harrowing time.

'*Now* who makes dark jests, my love?' He smiled grimly. 'For what it's worth, I do not agree with him and have refused to enter such a plea.'

Jane felt her breath quickening as Winifred's anxiety escalated. 'Forgive me.'

'Sentencing is set for the first week of next month.'

She began to wring her hands, joining Winifred's fear with her own. How was she going to save him? Her Will seemed closer to death in her mind at this moment than he had at any time since the attack.

'And King James?'

He gave a fresh grimace. 'What of him? The rebellion was crushed.'

She nodded miserably as Winifred's memories gave her the knowledge of James III, the 'Old Pretender', and his recent landing in Scotland. She told him what she knew. 'The fierce winter in his own kingdom added salt to the misery of failed rebellion and afflicted him with the ague. I left before I could learn more.'

'What else is there to learn, other than that he arrived, caught the fever and sailed back to France within weeks, having achieved nothing more than to commit his loyal peers to almost certain death? King George will want to make an example of us lords.'

She nodded. There was little point in pretending otherwise.

'I think we must anticipate the worst outcome, Winifred, and discuss what must be done for the children and Terregles, for your safety and the future—'

'William, stop! For the love of all things holy, stop!' Jane, propelled by Winifred's needs, fell helplessly toward him. He held her close against his chest and she was glad he didn't have to see the few pointless tears dampening his shirt. 'Why can we not appeal directly to King George? I cannot imagine he wants the blood of British peers on his hands.'

William kissed her forehead tenderly. 'His reign will be weakened by showing us mercy.'

'I do not believe that,' she persisted.

'My lawyer will not petition King George,' he said firmly.

'Then I shall.'

'You?'

'Why not? A wife, the mother of the condemned man's children; who could be more pitiful, more in need of mercy?'

'I doubt you'll find the new King of England to have much compassion for the wife or family of a Catholic peer, especially one who rose up against him.'

'We shall see. And I shall leave no stone unturned until—'

'Until it is hopeless?' He already sounded beaten.

'William. For my sake and that of the children, you must stay strong. I am entering a world I do not understand,' Jane said in Winifred's voice, believing she had never uttered a truer statement. 'If you give in, what hope have I of helping you on the outside? You must keep your mind active and engaged and your body the same. Let *me* worry about your advocacy.'

He nodded, but she could tell he didn't hold out much hope of success.

'Have you spoken with Lord Derwentwater or Lord Kenmure?' she asked. She knew these two men were powerful.

William shrugged. 'A few words exchanged early on. Since then I have been confined to this chamber, and they to theirs, presumably. We dine each night with the Constable, who is a gracious host, but we do not discuss politics or strategy at his table for obvious reasons.' He let out a sad gust of laughter. 'We discussed poetry during our last meal together.' William found a brave smile for her. 'But fear not: I have a priest, Father Scott, who visits and keeps me company, and the warders are kind; we talk often. And at least I look out onto the river and not onto Tower Green.'

Jane swallowed, though she suspected that if an execution of these so-called traitors took place, the King and his Protestant supporters would want to make it as public as possible. William and his fellow lords would probably be taken to Tower Hill for their punishment.

Jane felt the bilious, dizzying fear rising again. She had to get out of this cramped room and away from its despondency.

'The warder said I might only stay a short while, but I shall return as soon as I can with news. I've left fresh clothes with the warder.' She dug into her pockets for the tiny sack of coins she'd brought. 'Here, this will help keep your gaolers sympathetic. I have already made a judicious bribe to Sir George. I do not doubt I shall be allowed to see you again.'

He took the purse and threw his arms around her again. 'Thank you for being so strong for me. I have not even enquired about your journey – how you made it through the winter roads, how your lodgings were, or even—'

Winifred silenced him with a kiss, as Jane yielded to embarrassment and guilt. 'I am here. Everything else is no longer relevant. Only your safe return to me is what matters,' she said, guided by her host.

'I love you, Winifred.'

Jane again felt the rush of emotion her host allowed her to feel and the power of it was as inspiring as it was frightening. Will in his bed, loving her, waiting for her, was in her mind, but she hated the fact that Julius was at the back of her mind also, tarnishing that connection across worlds. Perhaps it was Winifred's weakening health that was dismantling Jane's defences.

The hackney had obediently waited as instructed, and Jane noticed nothing of the landscape around her as it rushed her back to Duke Street. By the time she'd paid the man and Cecilia was opening the door, Jane could feel Winifred's body trembling with fever again.

She stumbled into Cecilia's grip, knowing only bed rest would help her now – yet every second mattered.

TWENTY-SIX

Robert Evans glanced at Ellen, who betrayed no hurt in her expression.

'I'll ignore what you just said, Mr Maxwell. I'm sure you don't believe that one of the most senior staff on the ward would manufacture information.'

Maxwell blinked. 'I'm sorry,' he said, taking in both of them with a sweeping glance. 'I just want Will to have the best shot at beating this thing.'

'Nothing I suggest is for the good of anyone, except Will and your family. And in my professional opinion, Will's convulsion is a key sign that he's regaining consciousness.'

'Can he hear us?' Diane Maxwell wondered.

'I always believe the patients can hear us, Mrs Maxwell,' Ellen said gently. 'I talk to Will the whole time I'm working around him. How can it hurt?'

His mother nodded, smiling sadly. 'You're so kind, dear. You're right, it can't hurt, I'm sure. So what does this mean, Dr Evans?'

'I'm recommending you leave Will where he is, certainly in the short term.' They all watched Maxwell shift restlessly with annoyance, but for a rare moment he controlled his expression and his tongue, as Evans continued. 'We just don't know what the upheaval will do. Will is off life support, as you know, so this is all about him and his choice of timing. He'll decide when. We have to keep the faith and stay patient.'

'What about brain damage?' his mother asked.

'Mrs Maxwell, we can't even begin to assess that until Will wakes. And he is waking. But it's a slow process. Every person, every injury, every brain is different and reacts and responds in varying ways. Um... is there any news of Miss Granger?'

'Crazy girl's gone off on some capricious expedition that she hopes will divinely wake Will from afar,' Maxwell growled.

Diane Maxwell had apology written in her expression as she looked at Evans and his team. 'Will has been researching something called straight tracks... they're ancient. I'm not sure I understand any of it myself.'

'I've read about them,' Evans said.

'Jane's gone to a place that Will dreamed they would visit together. It's, um...' She glanced at her husband, who was wearing his familiar scowl. 'Well, they say it's a place of spiritual enlightenment.'

'She's hoping magic is going to save him, Dr Evans, not medicine,' Maxwell quipped.

Evans looked unperturbed. 'At times like these, Mr Maxwell, religion, spirituality, pagan beliefs, magic... it's all the same thing, really. We turn to one aspect of it or another at times when we're under enormous stress. I'm for whatever works, whatever helps keep you strong.' He brightened and smiled. 'Anyway, if I were to guess – because I'm sure that's your next question – I would say we shall know more in the next day or two.'

'Right,' Maxwell said. 'Now, perhaps we could have some time alone with our boy.'

'Of course,' Ellen and Evans said together, but not before sharing a glance of silent triumph that Maxwell hadn't mentioned the deadline again.

Jane blinked to gain focus. Where was she?

Cecilia's smiling face came into view. 'Welcome back, dear.'

'What's happened?' she croaked.

'Here, sip this,' Cecilia said, lifting Winifred's head, which felt as heavy as a medicine ball. 'Your fever has broken.'

'Fever?'

'A relapse, dearest. It had to happen. You have pushed yourself too hard and your body has rebelled.'

'I cannot remember... wait, I went to the Tower. I saw William.'

'Yes. That was thirteen days ago.'

It took Jane several moments to process this. But finally, as it sank in, she pushed away the glass that Cecilia held up to her face.

'Did you say thirteen?' she spluttered.

Cecilia gave a small sigh. 'I did.'

'But—'

'But there is nothing you could have done in the meantime. Be still, or you shall wear yourself out and become feverish again. Let me apprise you of what we have learned.'

Jane dutifully fell back against the pillow, but only because the room had begun to spin, as if Cecilia had commanded it to. However, she mustered the strength to say, 'Do not hold anything back.'

Cecilia gave her an admonishing glance. 'It comes to this. Sentencing has been set for 9th February,' she said bluntly. 'That is in eight days.' Before Jane could speak, Cecilia held up her hand. 'I know you want to visit William, but it has been forbidden by the King until sentencing. Of course you will wish to be present at the trial, so I urge you to use this week to get well, Winifred, dear. That journey took far more out of you than you would ever admit.'

The following week turned into a stultifying period of broths, bed baths, and restless nights and days lost to exhaustion and sleep. But within six days Jane's resilience and Winifred's determination had rescued the fragile body they shared, and once again Jane could see to her own ablutions without help or hobbling like an old woman.

The day of sentencing was ominously bleak. February was traditionally the harshest winter month and 1716 was no exception, with the temperature so bitterly cold that the skin of Jane's palm very nearly stuck fast to the iron railings when she briefly stepped outside. Even so, she made it obvious that Winifred was immovable on her decision to attend the trial.

Cecilia didn't stop trying, though. 'Apparently the Thames is frozen hard,' she said over breakfast, pouring her friend a hot chocolate.

Mrs Mills bustled in with a plate of pound cake cut into small squares and some steaming rolls. 'I've just heard from one of the delivery boys that there is an ice fair being held on the river. I shall have to take myself down there.'

'Perhaps too much merriment for me, Mrs Mills,' Jane said softly, and caught Cecilia's glare at their hostess.

'Forgive me, Countess, I meant nothing—'

Jane shook her head. 'No, please, don't even mention it. I am tired of feeling so gloomy and forcing everyone else around me to feel the same. I hope today will bring news to lift my spirits.' She was saying the right words for Winifred, but Jane heard the hollowness in them.

'The hackney will be here shortly to take you to Westminster Hall,' Mrs Mills said, moving swiftly on to practical matters.

'Who is presiding?' Cecilia asked, frowning.

'Lord Cowper, the High Steward, has been chosen as judge for the Jacobite lords.'

Cecilia nodded. A clock chimed on the mantelpiece and she shrugged at Winifred. 'I should fetch our cloaks and we must ready ourselves.'

Jane knew Winifred wasn't hungry, but she also knew her still-frail body needed as much nourishment as possible. 'I shall just eat one of these hot rolls.'

Pleasure flared in her friend's gaze. 'Good. I am happy to see you have an appetite, dear. Go ahead.'

The journey was a blur for Jane. She was unable to concentrate on anything, until she felt a sharp surge in her body as the horses slowed and the driver called, 'Westminster!'

She emerged from the carriage to be met by a man who introduced himself as her husband's counsel. She knew his name from organising the payment for representation: John Fitzwilliam. He was bewigged and berobed, his expression sombre enough to be considered funereal, Jane thought.

'Countess, I must warn you that the Whig government has persuaded the King to turn this into something of a spectacle,' he said, his deep voice adding weight to its lofty tone.

'What do you mean?' Her insides began to roil.

He cleared his throat, sounding vaguely embarrassed. 'The Hall has been cleared of its traditional stalls and is now filled to capacity with a newly erected public gallery far larger than anything we could have expected.'

Her hopes sank. 'I see,' she said, unsure of what else to say.

'The High Steward has just arrived in his coach together with his officers and will appear shortly. Countess, every one of the lords will be present, excepting Lord Winton, who has successfully convinced the government that he is insane.' He shrugged at her dismayed look. 'I thought you should know.'

Jane could not have cared less about Lord Winton, whoever he was, but she could tell William's lawyer was aiming to be thorough. Still, she loathed him for the mere fact that he had urged William to plead guilty. Surely that only helped the King to send him to the chopping block.

'May I ask what you know of Lord Cowper?'

Her dread was reinforced when the lawyer was momentarily unable to meet her gaze.

'I shall not lie to you, My Lady. Lord Cowper has a reputation as a stern judge. It is why I recommended your husband make a guilty plea, for this judge responds to admissions of guilt and especially any sense of remorse.'

She was glad William had declined to plead guilty. 'I am

afraid my husband could show no remorse for wanting the true heir to the English throne to be sat upon it rather than a German, sir.' It was Winifred expressing her defiance while Jane, horrified, could see the man's eyes glaze over. It was clear he held no hope for the Earl if he persisted with this attitude.

With nothing more to be said, he politely but silently guided her into Westminster Hall. Jane knew the building dated back to the eleventh century, but she had no time to be inspired by the architecture, for she was overwhelmed by the tiers of seats that had been hastily built on scaffolding. Half the population of London had crushed themselves into them, as the lawyer had warned. The noise was immense as excited onlookers swapped their views and anticipated the colourful theatre of death sentences passed on important people, both Scottish and English. The smell of unwashed bodies was a powerfully sour note to add to Jane's dismal mood.

People began to point at Winifred as Jane followed the lawyer's directions to seats reserved for her and Cecilia. She kept her eyes facing ahead, determined not to lock gazes with anyone but William once he was brought in. She did glance up toward the magnificent hammerbeam roof – the largest in Europe – but the sight only added to her escalating sense of terror. If the Earl of Nithsdale was sentenced to death today, her life and Will's life were over too. Nausea rose.

'Winifred?' Cecilia said, laying a worried hand on her friend's arm.

'I shall be fine,' she murmured. 'Just a moment of dizziness. I am already better.'

The Court of the King's Bench was called to order and Jane watched, darkly fascinated as the lords walked through from the Upper House and the members filed in from the Commons to take their seats. Everyone stood as the Prince of Wales was announced and sombrely took his place in what looked to be a specially prepared box. Jane's hopes were dashed further by his arrival, as it seemed to underline the gravity of the occasion, adding to her foreboding that death was about to tap Winifred's husband on his shoulder.

She heard someone nearby whisper that the footmen and ushers on duty were dressed in a new set of scarlet livery. King George, she realised, was not squandering the opportunity to impress upon the people his power and worth as their new sovereign.

Cecilia was still and silent at her side, for which she was grateful. Her companion knew Winifred too well to twitter with pointless conversation or placations at this juncture. Jane used the time to quell her rising anxiety.

Then she caught sight of a familiar face and her heart lurched. Julius Sackville was watching her from the topmost tier of the noisiest set of stands. Everyone's gaze was fixed on the doorway where the prisoners would be led out, but his was fixed on her alone. She felt tears sting. He looked so calm, as dark and brooding as a cave of secrets. She wanted to run to him, to hold him, to tell him that—

'Here's William!' Cecilia cried, elbowing her, and dragging her attention away from Sackville to search out Winifred's husband. He was second in the small line of condemned lords in their frock coats, and again she felt the familiar surge of love from Winifred, helplessly reaching out to the man she adored. From this distance Jane could be tricked again – for a moment – into thinking it was Will standing there, and her own grief raced toward her throat. She forced it back down, determined not to disgrace herself or Winifred.

Jane watched his gaze search the chamber and find her, lock on to her, in what felt like a suddenly choking triangle, because she knew to her right was Julius, completing the third angle. She dared not shift her gaze and instead simply smiled as William Maxwell gave a sympathetic half-smile with a brief, encouraging nod. He was being strong for her.

He turned away to face the Court and as he did so her treacherous gaze searched for Sackville again, but his face was lost to her and she realised he had gone. The punch of realisation that he was no longer present was succeeded by a small sigh of relief… she could devote her attention purely to William now.

Cecilia gripped her arm tightly. 'It's Lord Cowper,' and in the low hiss of Cecilia's words, Jane heard the tension that her friend was trying to control as well.

Jane let go fully of Sackville and took a deep breath for Winifred, allowing her gaze to absorb the figure of the judge, clothed resplendently in crimson, processing slowly into the Hall. At his side was the Garter of Arms, who carried his processional wand, and they were followed by the Usher of the Black Rod. Jane was grateful for Winifred's knowledge as she observed this solemn spectacle.

Atop the judge's doughy, middle-aged face and frowning forehead sat a dark brown, curly wig of such length that Jane had to suppress a nervous giggle. Were these men blind when they saw themselves in a mirror? How absurd they looked!

Oblivious to her ridicule, William Cowper, lawyer and Whig MP, Lord High Chancellor of Great Britain for the past eight years, and now Lord High Steward presiding over the sentencing, glared at the excited audience from on high. An expectant hush rippled through Westminster Hall as he awaited their complete attention. Once satisfied, he nodded.

'My Lords who are prisoners at the bar: I am to inform Your Lordships that upon any occasion which shall be offered you to speak for yourselves, you are to direct your speech to the lords in general, and so is any other person that shall have occasion to speak in this court.'

He proceeded to call out each of the lords' names – Derwentwater, Nithsdale, Kenmure, Carnwath, Nairne and Widdrington – making each sound like a death toll.

'You stand impeached of high treason by the Commons of Great Britain in Parliament assembled, which treason is contained in the articles that have been lately read; to this you have severally pleaded guilty and are thereby convicted.'

Guilty? Guilty! So, during her illness William had acquiesced to his lawyer's counsel? She blinked in heightened fear; there was clearly not going to be any further trial or discussion. She had been naïve to think otherwise. Today, the trial judge was presiding over this drama simply to weigh up the men's actions and decide how best to punish them.

Her pulse, even though it seemed impossible that it could go any faster, accelerated as she tasted a fresh sourness at the back of her throat. She watched in deep dread as Cowper permitted each of the accused to have his say. Lord Derwentwater was invited to speak first and Jane was struck by the youth and dash of this wealthy peer, a friend of Julius Sackville, who told the Court he had become involved in the rebellion purely on religious grounds. She listened to him speak passionately about his wife and children, appealing to Lord Cowper to consider them in his sentencing, and assuring Britain of his loyalty.

The crowd had now been 'warmed up' and there was a buzz of voices echoing around the Hall. Jane wondered if she'd be able to hear anything that William said. *Show remorse*, she begged him inwardly. *Thaw that hard heart of the trial judge.*

Cowper's small eyes fell on Winifred's husband. 'And what say you, William, Earl of Nithsdale, as to why judgement should not be passed upon you according to the law?'

Cecilia took Jane's hand, squeezing it for support, but her gesture only served to heighten Jane's dread, and she held her breath as she watched William straighten and nod.

'My Lords, as Scottish peers we are required to ride out at our clan's bidding, and perhaps our obedience to such fealty should be acknowledged rather than frowned upon. It shows us to be loyal peers of the British Isles, and should Britain ever need me, I would do the same. Nevertheless, I confess myself guilty of being attached to rebellion – though attached unhappily, My Lords, for I have never found that problems are solved with hostility. I am relying on His Majesty's mercy. I beg leave to assure Your Lordships I was never privy to any plot or design against His Majesty's own person or government, and was unprovided with necessaries for such a purpose; but rashly and thoughtlessly, with only four of my direct servants, joined those who went to fight from my neighbourhood, and was one of the last among them.

'At Preston, My Lords, His Majesty's general gave us great encouragement to believe that surrendering to His Majesty's mercy was the ready way to obtain it, and with repeated assurances I submitted myself, and still entirely depend on His Majesty's Commons to intercede with His Majesty on my behalf. And I solemnly promise Your Lordships, I shall, during the remainder of my life, pay the utmost duty and gratitude to His Most Gracious Majesty, and the highest veneration and respect to Your Lordships and the Honourable House of Commons.'

Jane cringed within, curiously able to feel Winifred's pride being shattered, while at the same time appreciating that William was arguing for his life. Winifred could not surely put her notions about a Catholic king on the throne above that of the life of her precious husband. In that moment, she felt something give inside her. It was Winifred, she realised, but it was not Winifred's spiritual resolve slipping so much as her religion being set aside.

And a new fire took its place. No matter what was decided today, Jane sensed Winifred was making up her own mind about how this sorry tale would end. And it certainly wasn't going to feature a grieving widow watching her husband's head being spiked for the populace to see and jeer at.

The other peers were then permitted to give their own impassioned speeches, but Jane heard none of them – only Winifred's pounding heart. The crimson-robed judge then asked each whether he had pleaded anything in arrest of judgement that might postpone proceedings.

She waited until she heard William's voice above the din of murmurs.

'I have not,' he responded.

When the last of the accused lords had pleaded in the negative, Lord Cowper waited with grave expression until a second, even tenser silence gripped everyone in the Hall. Satisfied that he had everyone's attention, he began his final address. Jane looked down. She wasn't sure she could bear to look upon the smug bastard and his horrible wig while he pronounced sentence.

'James, Earl of Derwentwater, William, Earl of Nithsdale, William, Lord Widdrington, William, Lord Nairne, Robert, Earl of Carnwath, William, Viscount Kenmure, you stand impeached by the Commons of Great Britain, in Parliament assembled, of high treason in traitorously imagining and compassing the death of His Most Sacred Majesty...'

Jane heard humming in her ears but could not listen to Cowper's self-satisfied drone. She desperately wished she could run into the cloaked embrace of Sackville and escape everything – the two Williams, Winifred's fragility, Cecilia's earnest support. Instead, she disappeared from the proceedings by withdrawing into her mind and allowing her gaze to settle on a small spider that was scuttling about near her foot.

The insect reminded her of William and Will, and her boot was Lord Cowper. In a blink her boot could descend, like the gavel near the judge's hand, and kill the spider as effectively as the axe could obliterate both men's lives. Her foot hovered above the creature – *life or death?* she wondered. It was within her power to decide, as it was within the power of Lord Cowper. They were both omnipotent in this moment, with the capacity to show no mercy or to find humanity and understand that these men were simply being loyal by—

Her macabre mind game was arrested with a fresh thought. *Winifred, listen to me*, she hissed in her mind, urging her host to pay attention. *Lord Cowper is not the man who has the ultimate power. He is merely the mouthpiece, the puppet who enacts the wishes of others. There is someone still higher: the King!*

It did not matter what sentence was handed down today.

Jane felt fresh hope surge through Winifred and she raised her eyes to fix Cowper with a stare. She knew anyone watching her might think it was one of hate. But Jane knew Winifred's unblinking gaze was daring him to do his worst.

I will not crumble, she assured him silently across the Hall. *And I will beat you. So help me, by all things holy, I will outwit that executioner's blade*, she promised.

Winifred's emotions were ringing with passion; her blood was high, her pulse pounding with newly stirred excitement. Jane wasn't paying attention, but she was aware that Cowper was completing his summing up. She could hear him sounding forth about the religion of the Church of Rome; she knew he singled out William in this part of his speech, clearly prepared.

Then Jane heard him pause dramatically. She snapped to attention, sensing a subtle shift in the audience's body language – hers and Cecilia's included – as they leaned marginally forward in tandem with Cowper while he drew a slow, single breath... almost as if drawing them under his spell.

In that breath, everyone was still. It was so quiet Jane was sure she could have heard the scratch of the spider's feet against the stone.

'And now, My Lords, nothing remains but that I pronounce upon you – and sorry I am that it falls to my lot to do it – that terrible sentence of the law which must be the same that is usually given to the meanest perpetrator of the like offence. The most ignominious and painful elements are usually remitted by the Crown in the case of persons of your quality – James, Earl of Derwentwater, William, Earl of Nithsdale...' Jane felt dizzy as he again intoned the full name of each lord. She tried not to sway. '... return from whence you came. There you must be hanged by the neck, but not till you be dead, for you must be cut down alive; then your bowels must be taken out and burned before your faces, then your heads must be severed from your bodies and divided each into quarters; and these must be put at the King's disposal...'

The Hall erupted into cheers and an explosion of voices. Jane must have swooned; she realised she had leaned weakly against Cecilia, who had caught her, but in those intervening blurred moments she had missed seeing the Lord High Steward stand and process sombrely out of the Hall.

She regained her wits just in time to stand herself, her fists white-knuckled as they gripped her gloves and her gaze searched and found William's. Amid the bedlam of the excited crowd and the guards jostling the prisoners away, he tried to comfort her with a reassuring hand in the air that did, to a small extent, steady her nerves. Her gaze whipped to the spider and she just caught sight of it scrambling away as those around her stood and moved off.

The spider is safe, Jane said in her mind, *and so will you be, William.*

TWENTY-SEVEN

According to the police officers seated in the 'drawing room', as Catelyn Granger liked to call it, a full-scale search of the national park area around Uluru was underway.

'Dozens of police, dogs, two helicopters and a huge gang of locals are involved,' the officer explained. 'Rest assured, Jane will be found.'

'Dead or alive,' Juliette murmured, and won herself a glare from her father and a look of despair from her mother.

The atmosphere was tense enough, but the telling silence that met her words forced her to be honest. 'What? Why are we pretending that we aren't all thinking the same thing?'

The senior police officer cleared his throat. 'I don't think we should be jumping to conclusions. I believe—'

'You can believe anything you want,' Juliette snapped, no longer able to stomach the frigidly polite atmosphere that surrounded these negative daily updates. 'But we know Jane. And Jane would not leave her family in this state of flux unless she was unable to reach us.'

'That's my point,' the officer said calmly. 'She may be injured.'

'She may also have been abducted.' Juliette's comment crashed against his words of hope. His expression turned to one of appeal, but Juliette was too far gone in revealing her fears to pull back now. 'Raped, murdered, left to rot in some outback cave or a shallow grave in a desert that is millions of miles wide.'

'Please,' the other officer – a woman – soothed. 'This is not helpful.'

'But it's honest, and don't tell me you haven't considered these alternatives. Just stop pretending there's a lot of hope, because unlike me, my parents trust you. They're so obedient, for Pete's sake!' Her voice finally broke and she choked back a sob. 'Excuse me…' She leaped up, leaving the room, but not without hearing her mother's soft apology.

'Forgive her, please. She blames herself. We asked her to go with Jane, but…'

Juliette disappeared upstairs filled with loathing. It was true. She did blame herself. If she'd been with Jane, her sister would not be missing. She stared at the phone extension in her room.

Come on, Jane, ring us! she begged.

Time marched to a different beat in Jane's world. On Monday, three days after the predictable yet horrifying sentence, a warrant for the Earl's execution was signed. Appeals for a reprieve had failed.

Winifred sat in the window of Mrs Mills's drawing room and looked out onto the busy street, where life continued, oblivious to her internal torment. Behind her, Mr and Mrs Mills were quietly talking as tea was being served. Their heads were bent close; Mr Mills wore a large black velvet bow at the base of his short white powdered wig to match the velvet bow Mrs Mills wore in her hair. A bonneted maid tiptoed across the fine oriental carpet and handed her master a cup and saucer, and smiled her answer when he asked if it was already sugared.

Jane wanted to scream at the domestic scene behind her and at the busy, could-not-care-less scene in front of her. Her impotence tasted bitter against the sip of tea.

News had been received this morning that the date appointed

for execution was this Friday. 'Four days,' Jane murmured. 'To save the lives of two men.'

'What was that, Winifred?' Cecilia asked, looking frightened at speaking into the near-silent pall that had settled around them.

Jane blinked. She couldn't share her latest idea with her friend, for fear that Cecilia might have her tied to the bed, claiming she'd become mad with grief.

Cecilia shivered. 'Winifred, dear, I know it is brutally unpleasant, but would you rather live with William at the Tower for the next few days until...' She trailed off, unable to finish her sentence.

Jane shook her head. 'No. How might I plead my husband's case if I were imprisoned alongside him?'

'Surely there is nothing left to plead, dearest? Why not have this time together, at least?'

'As long as William draws breath and my mind remains sound, there is hope of his escaping the fall of that axe,' she said, more to herself than to poor Cecilia.

'Darling Winifred, I fear I must be blunt with you. Yesterday I accompanied Mrs Mills on her shopping excursion and we came across a good friend of hers, Mrs Morgan, who it appears is most knowledgeable about the political climate. Her husband is a Whig colleague and fellow judge of Lord Cowper's.'

'You did not mention this yesterday on your return.'

'No, dear,' Cecilia said, her voice tense, 'but that is because I believe you are already bearing a great burden of grief.'

'Out with it,' she urged, turning away from the street scene to fix Cecilia with a cool stare. Ancestors of Mr Mills glared at her from pictures hung on the walls, and a pink and gold chinoiserie screen hid a spare commode that she hoped she'd never have to use.

'The word is that the King plans to gain popularity with an announcement that proceeds from the sale of the Jacobite rebels' estates will go toward the burdensome cost of putting down the rebellion.'

Jane frowned as she filtered this snippet of intelligence through Winifred's sharp understanding.

'They're sequestering Terregles?' Winifred's voice reflected the shock trembling through her. Jane only cared about Will, but she knew her host had to be mindful of the family's estates, her son's future as earl. Financial ruin seemed like a genuine threat now.

Cecilia nodded, embarrassed. 'I gather this is the plan.'

'Well, I thought the petition to Parliament by all the wives would save our estates.'

'I fear the arguing back and forth will take too long. Besides, though I am terrified to utter this, the general feeling is that you will fare better financially if William pays the penalty. Were he to live, you would not see a groat. They would confiscate it all and your children would have nothing.'

It was a terrifying truth to hear.

'The money means nothing to me,' Jane replied, but knew these were her feelings alone; Winifred had to balance the weight of her love for William against the weight of her love for her children, and her concern for her son's future succession. She could feel the anger of her host mixed with fear for her family.

'Dearest, please listen to me,' Cecilia urged.

'Do *not* say William is a lost cause,' Jane snapped.

'Hear me out,' Cecilia said, her voice trembling. 'You know as well as I that William's Catholic leanings and Jacobite sympathies have been a source of contention between him and the government for years. Even if the other wives can argue their husbands' cases with some success, I gather that reprieve for William is so unlikely as to be impossible.'

Jane's thoughts swam with fear, but she remembered the spider and she especially remembered her earlier notion that Lord Cowper was merely the puppet of a higher authority. 'That may be,' she said, 'but William's cause is only lost when they sever his head from his shoulders. I shall have a private petition drawn up immediately.'

'For what?'

'For presentation to the King, of course! I shall throw myself on his mercy.'

Monday evening closed in, just as sinister and black as one of the ravens she had seen on Tower Green, the night every bit as cold as the raven's sharp gaze.

With the help of her friends, she had attired herself in a black manteau and matching skirt, together with a dark cape, giving her the appearance of being in mourning. Mrs Mills had invited along her 'knowledgeable' friend, Mrs Morgan, currently heavy with child. Together, they took a hackney to St James's Palace. Jane was certain she could have cut the tension in the cab with a knife and served it on dinner plates, it was so dense... almost a fifth person, a shadow that travelled with them.

'I have a right to present the king of the realm with this petition,' Jane said into the brittle atmosphere. Her sudden remark startled the other women.

'Yes, of course,' Mrs Mills said, but her belief that this was not a wise decision was written in her frowning expression. 'It is established custom, but I suspect the courtiers may be ahead of you in this, Countess, and might think to keep the unfortunate wives of the condemned peers at bay.'

'Well, they can certainly try,' Jane said, warming to her plan. Once she'd learned after the trial about the opportunity for the kin of the sentenced men to present a petition, she'd become single-minded about it. This was a last-ditch effort to use all the legal rights available to her and she couldn't have cared less about what was seen to be dignified or appropriate.

'This is a daring move, my dear,' Mrs Morgan remarked.

'I have no choice. I must make every attempt to win my husband a reprieve,' Jane said calmly enough, ready for these last-minute efforts to change her mind. Her tone was so earnest, though, that each of her companions looked down. 'And you are familiar with life at court, I gather, Mrs Morgan? I mean, you will recognise the King, for I have never seen him.'

'Oh, yes, yes, of course,' the woman replied. 'He has the eyes of the Brunswicks, very fine hands and a long, straight nose. Forgive me for saying it again, dear Countess, but are you quite sure this is wise? You do not wish to enrage the King further, surely?'

'Enrage? No, I wish to garner his sympathies for a grief-stricken woman. But I will risk his rage, Mrs Morgan, for it surely cannot make my lord husband's plight any worse.'

She suspected each of the women was conjuring a mental picture at this moment of the terrible punishment her husband would be forced to endure for her temerity. The carriage fell quiet. Jane was satisfied that none would try to dissuade Winifred from her chosen course again. They rode out the rest of the frigid journey in silence.

Jane's feeling of breathlessness was heightened as they passed St James's Park and cantered up the Mall, to finally spy the familiar red brick Tudor masonry of Europe's least impressive royal palace. Jane's mind raced to her history: the palace had been built by Henry VIII and, if she was not mistaken, his daughter Elizabeth I was in residence here when the Spanish Armada threatened. Winifred's memories also yielded the knowledge that the very king for whom William had risked his life had been born in this palace after a long and difficult labour, in front of a sizeable audience of whispering, gossiping courtiers.

Jane snapped her attention back to the present as the hackney cab slowed to a stop. The women alighted, Cecilia aiding the tall, pregnant Mrs Morgan.

'Oh, the First Regiment Guards always make me feel so proud in their scarlet and black. Our bravest and most senior infantrymen,' Mrs Morgan whispered, 'although we do have quite a few regiments.'

Mrs Mills frowned. 'Something to do with the spacing of buttons on their uniforms, dear. That is apparently how one tells them apart.'

'And those buttons bear the royal cipher,' Mrs Morgan added.

But while her friends chattered, Jane did not permit herself even a moment's awe as she entered St James's Palace, passing by the solemn sentries in their bearskin hats, whom Jane knew as Grenadier Guards. In fact, all she could feel was relief that their quartet was duly admitted to the palace with other members of London society, and she felt her luck was still running when they learned that the King had not yet left his closet.

'Let us sit here,' Mrs Morgan suggested, guiding the women to a low-panelled chamber. 'The King will have to pass through this room.'

Jane fleetingly, absently, took in her surroundings. The chamber was painted the softest of sage greens, the carpet a magnificent mix of rich greens and purples. A trio of low windows flanked one side of the room, and before each was a broad bench seat covered in deep violet velvet. Mrs Morgan chose the central bench to make herself as comfortable as her condition allowed. The women took their places, Winifred sandwiched between Cecilia and Mrs Morgan. They passed the time observing the officials, busy about their duties, while ladies in their hooped silks and gentlemen in powdered wigs milled around gossiping, all of them waiting, it seemed, for the emergence of the sovereign, no doubt hoping to catch his eye.

Jane fixed her gaze on the door from which Mrs Morgan assured her the King would appear, while her friends talked quietly over and around her about courtiers and prominent members of London high society. She lost track of time, though guessed it was more than an hour before the door opened. She'd anticipated a tall, dominating man, so it surprised her to see a stocky figure stride into the room. The King was resplendent in a long, grey curling wig, parted severely in the middle so that the hair on either side achieved great volume. She drew a deep breath, knowing she needed to look beyond the pompous appearance of the German who held the fate of her – Winifred's – husband.

At Mrs Morgan's nudge, Jane stood to curtsey with every other woman in the chamber. When she straightened, the King was somewhat closer to their party; she was struck by his piercing blue eyes, and cheeks made extra-rosy by rouge to match the colour of his full, somewhat pouty lips.

Don't be fooled, Jane. He is sharply intelligent... The thought flitted across her mind. Had that been Winifred? Robyn, perhaps? She couldn't examine it, because a push from Mrs Morgan meant she was propelled lightly forward, suddenly directly in the path of King George I and his courtiers.

'His English is woeful. Remember he speaks French, although he prefers German,' Mrs Morgan hissed from behind her in a whisper.

Jane had no German, but she had studied French and Winifred's French was flawless. In a seamless shift, she petitioned the King in a language she knew they all shared. She wasn't sure if it was fear, or the necessary reverence, but she fell dramatically to her knees, holding the rolled paper out to him.

She could hear the gasps and murmurings around her. Sharp eyes missed nothing and her audience was predictably stunned, even horrified, by her undignified public behaviour. Jane no longer cared how they might choose to interpret her actions.

'Your Majesty, I am the unhappy Countess of Nithsdale. Please will you hear my—'

King George I had been startled initially, but once he had heard her announce herself, she noted the disgust reflected in the twist of his fleshy lips. He deliberately ignored her, instead saying something as an aside to one of the fawning courtiers.

'Your Majesty!' she said much louder, heedless now of any need for decorum. 'Please, I beg you! This is my personal petition for the reprieve of my husband, who was—'

The King was moving beyond her reach and Jane sensed Winifred's panic. Frantically, Jane reached for him, grabbing the tail of his dark, brocade coat. Was that his hem ripping? She heard others gasp, but she didn't care.

'King George!' She hauled herself forward, stretching to push the petition into his coat pocket, but he refused to stop.

Jane's ire was roused fully now. She refused to let go of the King's frock coat, while he refused to acknowledge her, and so, within moments, the pleading Countess was being violently pulled forward. Jane was no longer on Winifred's knees beseeching the King, but was prone, fully outstretched and being dragged along the parquet floor, while the sovereign remained determined to pretend he was unaware of her.

It was only when one of his gentleman advisors bent down, reached both arms around her waist and pulled firmly that Jane felt Winifred's hands slip from their grip on the King's coat. Without so much as a backward glance, King George righted his garment and continued walking, head held high.

With her face pushed onto the floor, still restrained by the man gripping her middle, Jane felt tears sting as she noticed the petition slip from her hand. Nevertheless, she saw that it was immediately retrieved by one of the courtiers and handed to another man in regal clothing.

As the King moved away, so did the people, following like worker bees on the hunt for a single flower laden with pollen. The man who had restrained her, and was now assisting her to her feet, was polite but perfunctory.

'Are you injured, Countess?' She shook her head, too shattered to speak. He cleared his throat. 'Good evening then, My Lady,' he said, giving a short half-bow and departing as swiftly as he could, throwing a look of admonishment at the clutch of three women hurrying to her side.

'Oh, my dear Countess... well, you've certainly made an impression on the court,' Mrs Morgan said, tut-tutting.

'But did I make an impression on the King?' she snapped, dabbing at her eyes, angry at showing her emotions.

'The wrong sort, as we feared,' Mrs Mills chanced.

'Are you hurt, dear Winifred?' the ever-loyal Cecilia asked, straightening her friend's clothes.

'No, thank you. Mrs Morgan?'

'Yes, Countess?'

'Who was that man who took my petition... the gentleman who reached for it after it fell?'

'Ah, that was the Lord of the Bedchamber.'

'Will he help?'

'I cannot say, except mayhap you have some angels guarding you, my dear. This evening the Lord of the Bedchamber happens to be Lord Dorset, who incidentally also happens to be a friend of mine.' Before Jane could speak, she raised a hand. 'And when I was convinced that you would not be persuaded otherwise, I took the precaution earlier today of preparing a note to Lord Dorset, for I knew he would be on duty tonight.'

'Has your letter been delivered?' Jane asked, her hopes rising from the dust of moments ago.

'Not yet. But I shall deliver it now, for I happen to know that Lord Dorset will be playing cards this evening with the Prince of Wales.'

'Mrs Morgan, I am in your debt,' Jane said, hugging the woman warmly. 'Thank you.'

'Let me run that errand now, My Lady. I think we have overstayed our welcome in the palace tonight,' she said pointedly, but not without a flash of humour in her glance at Winifred. 'Do not tarry on my account.'

Jane nodded. 'Shall we leave, ladies?'

She lowered her eyes so she did not have to face the looks of accusation and disdain from the mob of people who had witnessed her unladylike ambush of the King. She did, however, catch the eye of the Duke of Montrose, who looked as mortified as she suspected any member of society might be at her behaviour. She realised he was a close acquaintance of Winifred's, but as he approached she shook her head slightly, signalling him to keep his distance. It would be best if their friendship were not noted. Who knew what help he might lend to her petition should it be read out, and she wanted that help to be considered impartial by the King.

The next day a note arrived from Mrs Morgan to confirm that Winifred's petition had been received and read by the Prince of Wales, and that he had considered it *graciously and with kindness*. According to Mrs Morgan, he had also shown it to anyone of a *sympathetic interest*. She had gone on to note that despite the atmosphere last night, many of the courtiers who had witnessed the scene had admitted to feeling horrified by the King's rudeness, and that tales were flying around London of his boorish behaviour to a noblewoman. *It seems, my dear Countess, that you have the sympathies of London's society, rather than its condemnation. It is being said*, she continued, *that history attests the sovereign of England has never refused a petition – even from the poorest woman's hand. And the prevailing opinion is that to treat a lady of your fine quality in such a dishonourable manner is truly unpardonable. I suspect our king's reputation has been tarnished as a result of your actions last night, my dear.*

Unfortunately, Jane could not be sure whether the letter's last sentence should encourage or depress her.

TWENTY-EIGHT

JANE HAD TO WAIT ANOTHER THREE RESTLESS, hand-wringing days to learn that the general petition from the wives of the condemned men was being presented at noon to the House of Lords.

She was seated with Cecilia and Mrs Morgan in the private salon of Mrs Mills to avoid other guests. Jane had been sitting tense and simmering in one of the Flemish armchairs, but suddenly leaped up, unable to remain still. 'For mercy's sake! William shall be executed tomorrow! Are they trying to kill me too?' Jane wept on behalf of her Will, also feeling the extent of the fear and loss that Winifred was experiencing for her husband.

There was little that her friends could say to comfort her, so they sensibly kept their own counsel while she paced the edges of the richly woven rug that their hostess was adamant had originated from the Topkapi Palace of Constantinople.

'You have done everything and more than could be expected of any wife, Winifred,' Cecilia whispered, looking unsettled by her friend's constant movement.

'Have I, though?' Jane choked, moving to a window overlooking a walled garden made naked by its wintry state. Her gaze was unfocused, her thoughts reaching to a hospital bed in London, where another man awaited the fate of a different William Maxwell. 'I'm not sure.'

Jane thought of Will's father. Even when senior, experienced doctors were shaking their heads, he clutched at any thin strand of potential to keep the flame of hope burning. It hadn't occurred to her until this moment that John Maxwell, as pushy and boorish as he was, refused to give up on his son, no matter what anyone said. He had no care whether he made enemies, became an object of mockery, embarrassed his wife, bulldozed his way over the egos of others, or trampled on fragile, grieving hearts. John Maxwell intended to see his son open his eyes and smile, talk again, live again... no matter what the financial, physical or emotional cost was. Instead of loathing him, Jane accepted now that she should admire him, perhaps even follow his example, because for as long as the Earl was still alive in his cell at the Tower – a prisoner, just like Will in his coma – there was a chance for him to escape what everyone assumed was his inevitable fate.

What more can I do? she asked herself, and only realised she'd aired this thought out loud when Mrs Mills answered her.

'Nothing, I imagine, Countess.'

Her hostess must have entered the salon without her hearing. The maid had arrived also, and was now setting down a tray of steaming cups on a small oaken side table. 'Good gracious,' Mrs Mills continued, fizzing with excitement. 'London society is, by all accounts, showing an outpouring of admiration for the wife who risked public ridicule and injury by confronting the King with such daring. Here, dear, I've brought you some warmed chocolate this time. If you won't eat...' She offered the porcelain cup and Jane took it, not wishing to be rude.

'Thank you. My friends, your support is unwavering, but I fear there is always *more* one can do when a man's life is at stake. The general petition from the wives will achieve little, I'm sure.' She joined Mrs Mills and Cecilia by the fireside, sitting on the corner of a stool.

'Countess, it is out of your hands now,' Mrs Mills said gently. 'Your parents' friend the Duke of Richmond has faithfully promised that he will present your private petition today; it will carry more weight coming from him.'

'He failed yesterday,' Jane replied, glumly staring at the flames, still angry that the Duke had let them down in this regard.

'But not today.'

'There are no tomorrows. If he falters, I have asked the Duke of Montrose to step in.'

'Well, there you are, then,' Mrs Morgan said, sending a look of soft pain toward Cecilia. The pregnant woman had been silent until now, embroidering quietly in the corner nearest the window and listening to the exchange as she threaded up several needles. But now she too stood, stretching and drifting over to the hearth, picking up her cup to warm her fingers. 'Countess, you've got powerful men of the realm on your side, and doing their best for you.'

'Not the most powerful, though,' Jane corrected. 'I fear my actions of Monday evening may well push that particular man into being vindictive.'

Mrs Mills shook her head as she blew on her chocolate. 'I think not, Countess. King George now wants this matter to go away. He will not draw any more attention to you than is necessary.'

Jane put her untouched cup down and rose from her stool. The other women, who had just settled comfortably, looked up at her sudden movement.

'Winifred?' Cecilia said.

'I'm going to Parliament House,' she replied.

Her friends gave gasps of anxiety. 'To what end?' Cecilia exclaimed.

'To intercede with the lords as they enter.' Her face filled with determination. 'I will not be ignored,' she declared.

'Countess, your health is already fragile, and to wait on the frosted steps of Parliament House would be to—'

'Mrs Mills, you have been so very kind and loyal. But I have been forced to sit around your lovely fire, trying not to lose my mind with worry. While idle, my health has recuperated fully,' she lied, 'and now I shall use my newfound energy to engage the enemy again.' She cast them a look of sadness. 'I have to try,' she heard herself say desperately.

They exchanged glances and sighed.

'Then you know I will be there with you,' Cecilia said.

'So will I,' Mrs Mills piped up.

'And I too,' Mrs Morgan added, clearly not wishing to miss out on any of the excitement.

Their expedition, initially bubbling with promise, fell flat when they discovered that the relatives of the other prisoners had had the same inspiration. Suddenly Jane felt herself one of a herd. A large crowd had gathered, including many intrigued bystanders and many 'ladies of quality', as Mrs Morgan noted, who clearly did not wish to miss out on the excitement either.

Winifred tried to stand apart from the mob and appear prominent. She realised she was being treated courteously, but not one of the politicians showed overt friendliness. Lord Pembroke, who had strong connections to Winifred's family, had taken the precaution of sending her a note. The letter had arrived just moments before she and the other ladies had left Duke Street. Lord Pembroke had urged Winifred not to approach him in public – *for reasons that I am sure are obvious* – but he also assured her that he would speak in her favour in Parliament.

Jane could soon see that the ambush at the Houses of Parliament had failed, and it was probably no surprise to her companions when she made haste away from the crowd on the steps.

'I presume we shall be witnessing the debate, Winifred?' asked Cecilia as the three women caught up with her.

'You are correct. If nothing else, I intend that my presence should keep those men honest and their consciences clear.'

They headed to the public gallery of the House of Lords.

Lord Pembroke remained true to his promise and Jane listened, impressed, when the man Winifred had not seen since early childhood took the floor. He was at least threescore years old, although his luxuriantly flowing dark wig belied the grey that must surely lurk beneath. In a confident voice and with the practised air of one used to being heard with respect, he argued that the King did not possess the power to pardon prisoners accused by Parliament; he raised a motion that Parliament should present an address to His Majesty instead. Pembroke urged that this address should 'humbly desire the King to grant a reprieve'.

Jane closed Winifred's eyes in relief – the first she had felt in many days – as she heard the motion being carried. Her hopes were quickly exploded, though, when another lord made the proviso that a clause should be added: 'that the reprieve not be general but awarded only for such of them as deserve it'.

During the subsequent murmurings and nodding of bewigged heads, Jane sensed Winifred's hopes sinking. As she paid attention to her host's thoughts, she understood that any mercy won from the King would only be granted to those who turned King's evidence.

She heard distantly, through the fresh hum of alarm ringing in her ears, that the request would be made to the King tonight, on the eve of the execution of the Jacobite lords.

Winifred surged to her feet as she felt her gorge rising and, fearful of disgracing herself in a new way that London society could gossip over, she hurried from the gallery to suck in the freezing mid-morning London air, which was as frigid as it was heartless.

Friendly arms helped her to straighten, and faithful Cecilia and Mrs Mills and Mrs Morgan hurried her away from the public eye and into a hackney bound again for Duke Street to await the King's pleasure. Jane could tell from the silence in the carriage that none of her friends held much hope for William, but she would not join them in their pessimism.

Into this uncomfortable silence came a new idea, piercing her prison of thoughts like a pin to a balloon and releasing her from the mental constraints of the world she'd been plunged into. She would behave as John Maxwell had.

I hope you are listening, Winifred, she said privately as she watched a far less crowded London of 1716 pass by. *I am no longer prepared to leave our men's fates in the hands of others. There is a new plan now and I am in charge of it.* She smiled grimly as she cast out the thought. *I am taking control.*

'Stop the carriage!' she ordered, surging to her feet, her hands drumming on the roof for the driver to respond immediately.

At Welshpool, the Granger family was listening to the same pair of police officers who visited them each day. They were bringing the trio up to date with the latest developments in Australia.

'So hope hasn't been given up just yet?' Jane's father asked.

'Not at all. We spoke to the Australian police this morning,' the pretty officer – named Anne, they'd discovered – told them with a soft smile. 'It was evening in Australia, of course, so the search had been called off until morning. But they're feeling a lot more positive now that they've found Jane's possessions, which had blown away.

'The thing is,' Anne continued, 'although I don't want to give you false hope, I really do think they're optimistic. Given that there is no…' Here she paused, desperately not wanting to say the word.

Juliette helped out. 'Body?'

'Er, thank you, yes… and no sign of any struggle or injury, there's a growing consensus that Jane is alive but disoriented.'

Catelyn was wringing her hands in her lap and her husband stilled them, covering them with his hand. 'But surely they would have found her if she were wandering around?' he asked.

'You'd think so, but our Australian colleagues are going to some pains to impress upon us just how big the national park is. There's no telling in which direction she may have headed,' DC Dale offered.

Anne jumped in again. 'They're also using Aboriginal trackers.' At the look of surprise from her parents, Juliette saw Anne offer a smile again. She was certainly doing her best to lift their spirits. 'They assured us that if anyone can trace her, these locals can.'

Juliette watched her parents nodding. There was nothing else to say, so she showed their visitors out, repeating the thanks her parents could only mumble. She returned to the living room, and maybe she imagined it, but she sensed a lightening of the dread that had surrounded them since the news of Jane's disappearance had first broken.

The phone rang and all three of them leaped up as if stung.

'I'll get it,' Juliette said, making a gesture with her hands that they should remain calm. Her father nodded and she picked up the receiver. 'Juliette Granger,' she answered.

'Juliette, it's John Maxwell.'

'Oh, hello,' she said and her disappointed tone and the small shake of her head told her parents what they needed to know. She watched her mother sink back into the chair while her father turned up the gas heater a notch. 'How are you both, John?'

'Holding up. Listen, there's some news.'

'Oh?'

'Will is showing some very strong signs of waking up.'

'Really? Oh, that's marvellous!'

'It is. Of course, no one can tell me anything about the state of his brain… you know, if there's any damage.'

'No,' she said. 'Early days, I suspect.'

'I don't suppose you've heard anything from Jane?'

Juliette had taken it upon herself the previous day to ring the Maxwells' hotel and explain why Jane had been silent. His shock down the line had been palpable, but she was also not sorry that Jane's disappearance was out in the open now.

'Well, we've just had the police here and they've given us some fresh hope that she's possibly disoriented and lost in the national park. If so, it's just a matter of time before trackers, dogs, helicopters and such find her.'

'Listen... I find it hard to do all this touchy-feely stuff, but we know how much our son loves your sister. For that reason alone, we love her too and are anxious to know she's safe.'

'Well, you focus on Will, we'll worry about Jane, and hopefully our newly engaged couple can be reunited soon.' It sounded tidy and sugary, but what else could one say in this situation?

'I'll call again tomorrow,' she heard Maxwell say.

'Thanks, John. Love to Diane... from all of us.'

She hung up and turned back to her parents. 'I didn't think you'd want to talk to him.'

They both shook their heads.

'Sounded like good news, though,' her father observed.

'Yes! Will is definitely waking up, it seems.'

Cecilia had leaped from the carriage straight after Jane. 'Winifred! What are you doing?'

'Hailing a sedan. It'll be quicker.'

'To where?'

'The Tower. I must see William urgently.'

Mrs Mills poked her head out of the carriage. 'Is that wise, Countess? Will they let you see him at this late hour of his...' Jane knew she was going to say 'final day', or something along those lines, but her friend adjusted her choice of words quickly, '... appeal?'

'I have every hope they will. Money speaks, Mrs Mills, to even the most conscientious of men.' She turned to Cecilia as a sedan runner answered her friend's hail. 'Go back to Duke Street with the others and wait for me. It's midday now and I shall not be long. There are things I must say to my husband.'

Jane clambered inelegantly into the chair, while two burly men waited.

'The Tower of London, please,' Jane said, astonished at yet another new experience. The sedan's enclosed box felt like an upright coffin.

The men gripped the horizontal poles and lifted the chair and she was on the move again. She managed a quick wave to her perplexed companions before urging the chairmen to take 'the quickest route'.

They did, via back alleys and lanes that no horse carriage could navigate. They skipped over open sewers, and yelled at kids who were no doubt looking to pelt the sedan with rotten fruit or worse! She could hear the men's grunts as they hit their rhythm, moving fast because she was so light. She had seen that the sedan was ornate on the outside, even sporting a parasol that bobbed high above her to shade everything from wigs to hats with tall feathers. The side windows were blocked so passers-by could not stare in, which she appreciated. The long, springy poles afforded a bouncy ride, although she noticed that, even when her carriers were going up or down a hill, and even once down a small flight of stairs to cross from one narrow lane to another, she remained level. *Amazing*, Jane thought, *and how civilised*. She could easily make this mode of travel a habit.

But then she plumbed the depths of gloom as she remembered why she was racing to the Tower. Time was her foe, and if she were going to put this audacious new plan of hers into action, some preparation was vital, particularly with William.

Jane could sense Winifred's admiration for her scheme. It had been Winifred's idea to take the sedan and her suggestion now, as they approached the familiar lanes close to the Tower, for Jane to paste a cheerful expression onto her face. Jane understood. Smart Winifred!

She paid her bearers and stepped from the chair – a lot more elegantly, she thought, than when she had boarded. 'Wait for me, please,' she told them. 'We shall be going to Duke Street hereafter.'

'Yes, My Lady,' the eldest said, clearly happy to be paid to rest and do nothing.

She met the yeoman guards with a beaming smile. 'Good day. I bring happy news for the noble Scottish prisoners: the petition in Parliament has been passed in their favour.'

They let her pass, but Jane was not ready to let out her breath just yet. Again she was stopped at the Lieutenant's Lodgings. She was so close now to William that she refused to be prevented from seeing him. Again she dazzled them with a cheerful grin and repeated her words, this time embellishing them: 'I've been told to anticipate a reprieve for my lord husband later tonight. I can barely contain my thrill.'

'Who gave you this news, My Lady?' It was the older yeoman she'd met on her first visit and she knew he felt sympathy for her and William.

'Lord Pembroke, who argued so eloquently for the lords.' *Forgive me, Thomas*, she thought silently at Winifred's prompting.

The name clearly impressed the man, and he nodded. 'You shall have to be brief, My Lady. We were told no visitors.'

'I know, I know, but I suspect no one believed a reprieve was possible,' she continued conversationally, giving a bubbly lilt to her words and hurrying the man forward so that he would not change his mind. 'Is the Constable in his office?'

'He is not here at present, My Lady. We expect his return from the palace shortly.'

Time could beat her. She must not create any suspicion. 'How shortly?' she asked, hastening up the two flights of stairs and speaking sweetly, as though she desperately wished not to miss the Constable.

'An hour at most.'

'A pity not to see him,' she lied. 'I shan't be staying for nearly as long as that.'

He nodded. 'For the best, mayhap,' he said over his shoulder.

As they walked past the panelled anteroom set aside for the

warders who supervised William's cell, she pressed money into her yeoman companion's hand.

'The news has so cheered me that I wish you all to drink to the health of our wise and benevolent king.'

The man blinked with surprise at the coin in his palm. Winifred had wisely recommended Jane hand over an amount that was magnanimous, but not so much as to be viewed as a bribe. 'You are a generous soul, Countess.'

She shook her head with feigned humility, glancing at the man in front of her husband's door, who carried a halberd that stood taller than he did. Its axe with sharp, hanging blades on both sides looked daunting. He had not been there on her first visit. She kept the consternation from her expression, showing only warmth and gratitude as she addressed the yeoman. 'The warders have been good to my lord husband; he said so himself. I am truly grateful to you.'

The yeoman gave a short bow to her and nodded at the pikeman to step aside. 'The lads will drink to your health, My Lady.'

She smiled, watching him unlock her husband's cell. 'Please do so. Er... is this guard necessary?' she said, deliberately as an aside, as though making polite chatter, taking in the fearsome halberd he had just moved to his left as he stepped aside.

'Tower rules for condemned men,' the man – apparently senior yeoman – admitted, pursing his lips with obvious embarrassment.

'Well,' she said, loading even more brightness into her tone, 'he won't be necessary past this hour, now that my husband is to be reprieved.'

She didn't wait for his response, pushing past them both into the familiar room, where she saw a surprised William look up from a letter he was scrawling.

'Oh, my dear Winnie! I was just writing to you.'

The door closed behind her as she allowed him to pull her into a fierce embrace. Jane retreated, as she'd learned to do, and allowed Winifred to come forth. Her host's spirit had rallied since they'd arrived in London and was getting stronger by the day. Perhaps it was the close proximity to her husband, but Jane felt that Winifred was beginning to assert herself, finding her way back from wherever she had fled or been banished when Jane arrived. This was a good thing, of course. But what did it mean for Jane? She prayed that Winifred's reawakening was a sign. Were the stars aligning, the worlds rebalancing? Were the ley lines calling her, beginning to show themselves as she drew closer to her goal? Were they preparing to lead her home to a safe, healthy Will?

'By all things holy, you looked so cheerful when you burst in here just then. It must be good news you bring. I was… I was writing a farewell to the children.'

Jane thought him handsome in his vulnerability: his shirt half-open, unshaven, his hair loose to his shoulders. Indeed, the Fifth Earl of Nithsdale was still in his prime.

His face was lit by eagerness, his eyes even permitting merriment at the thought that she had come with details of a reprieve, perhaps terms that he would be glad to agree to. He searched his wife's light brown eyes and Jane watched, miserably, as the light died in his expression and his enthusiasm with it. He let his wife go and turned away, looking haunted.

'So it is bad tidings?' he groaned, clearly unsure of the signals his wife had given.

She sat down in the window seat. 'There is a possibility that some of the Jacobite rebels will be granted mercy,' Jane began, feeling her way, drawing upon Winifred's instinct of how to tread with him.

'But not I,' he cut in.

Jane took a breath. 'No, my darling, I do not believe the King will offer you a reprieve.' There was no time for niceties or fragile feelings. It was now or never; they had to be fearless.

He walked away and banged his fist against the unyielding stone of the Tower's wall. 'Nor did I expect him to,' he said, collecting himself and clearing his throat of emotion. 'Forgive me; I was fooled by your cheery expression when you entered.'

'I was feigning joy, William.'

'Why?' he said, swinging around, his face a mask of confusion.

'Because I have a plan, and I did not wish anyone to suspect anything other than the lie I have begun promoting.'

He hesitated. 'Which is?'

'That a reprieve is imminent.'

William stared at her, baffled.

Jane explained everything that had occurred on her trip to St James's Palace with her petition, her subsequent vigil outside the Houses of Parliament, and then the debate inside the House of Lords.

'So they need their scapegoat.'

She nodded. 'I suspect not only one, but definitely you. I blame myself for this. I enraged the King.'

'No, Winnie. I have been a thorn in the Protestant Crown's side for years. Our family seat on the border would be so much easier for the English Crown to parley with if I were not so wholeheartedly for the Church of Rome.' He turned away and sighed. 'Nay, my love, this is the excuse London has been searching for to do away with a prickly problem. Do not shoulder any blame, for you have done more than any other wife would dare. You have been more courageous than many men might be. I have today written to my sister Mary to thank her, and of course Charles, for their favours and kindness. I hope they will continue to show you the generosity they always have. Do you remember my mentioning Father Scott?'

'The priest?'

He nodded. 'I have been seeing him daily and have made my peace and prepared myself for death.' He shrugged. 'I have even forgiven my enemies. This is a good set of mind I have achieved. Let Willie know his father went to Tower Hill with a clean conscience and pure heart.' Jane felt Winifred's fear take flight and she helplessly rose to her feet, but William stayed her, holding her shoulders gently and pushing her back into her seat. He kissed her tenderly and Jane retreated again so that it was Winifred his lips adored as they lingered. Finally, when he pulled away, he spoke so softly it was nearly a whisper. 'You, my darling, have been the love of my life. I have cherished you since that day in the garden of Saint-Germain-en-Laye, when we first spoke. It is that image I will carry in my mind to the scaffold.'

'William, stop, I beg you!' Winifred gasped, tears stinging. Jane took charge and her host's voice sounded gritty with emotion. 'Listen to me. You agree our situation is hopeless... your case lost?'

'No need to rub it in, my love,' he said, smiling sadly and pulling her to him again, taking her hands and kissing them tenderly before fixing her with a firm gaze. 'I do not wish you to be present tomorrow. I want you to leave London this evening – this afternoon if you can ready yourself so soon. Go back to Scotland immediately, gather up what you need and sail for France with our daughter. Reunite with Willie and live out your days at the French court. I know you will be welcomed back affectionately.'

'I am not so sure of that, my dear. But do not be so hasty to bid me farewell.'

He frowned. 'It will only make it harder for me if you—'

'Sit down and hear me out,' Jane said, dragging him to the window seat.

He allowed her to pull him down beside her. She urged Winifred to hold his face. 'I would rather die than live without you.' They were the right stirring words to say.

'Winnie—'

'Hush,' Jane said, fixing him with his wife's gaze. 'You are helpless. I am not. Now, pay attention. They will be asking me to leave at any moment.'

Jane watched his expression change from bemused to intrigued as she told him of her mad plan in a stream of rushed words, not permitting him to interrupt. Finally she sat back and held her breath.

'Escape?' he breathed, as though he did not understand the word.

She nodded, smiling tentatively.

'Escape?' he repeated, looking baffled. 'From the Tower of London? Britain's proudest fortress, which has humbled far more powerful men than I with her thick walls, stout locks and hundreds of warders?'

Jane narrowed Winifred's gaze, hearing the unmistakable undertow of sarcasm. 'William, the alternative is ugly indeed.'

'I agree, but this is madness!'

'Mayhap it is, but my love, they can only kill you once. You can die trying to escape, or you can be executed on the morrow having attempted to escape... or you can let them meekly lead you like the tethered scapegoat you spoke of earlier up onto those gallows. Choose!'

He stood and scratched his head. 'Winifred, this is lunacy!' he hissed.

'It is your last chance, I tell you. Take it! I'm prepared to. I'm the one who has to perform the difficult actions. I'm the one who must hold her nerve. All I ask you to do is follow my lead. It will happen tonight.'

He searched her face again, shaking his head slightly, obviously thinking how ridiculous her plan sounded. 'It is comical,' he said, confused. 'How do you expect to get away with it?'

'Mayhap it is comical. Mayhap they will write plays and songs about it, William. But it is the childish simplicity of the plan that makes it viable. The mere fact that they will not expect it, would not even countenance such a far-fetched idea, means it may just work. What have you got to lose in trying?'

'Only my head,' he admitted dryly, 'but that is already lost.'

'No!' she whispered urgently. 'Nothing is lost. All is yet to be won if you do exactly as I say.'

There was a knock at the door and her favourite yeoman was back with a plaintive look. 'Time, My Lord, My Lady,' he said.

She nodded. 'Well, my dearest,' she said in a breathy tone. 'How excited I am. I shall write to our children today with the brightest of news.'

William played his part. 'We must wait for formal notification, my love, of the King's pardon and his terms.'

'Of course,' she said, touching his face. 'Well, my darling,' she hugged him fiercely, 'make sure you *shave* and comb your hair. You must look your proudest.' She cast William a firm look and saw the flash of understanding reflected in his glance. *Good*. 'Until later, then,' she said, pecking both of his cheeks.

As she followed the yeoman, she threw one final encouraging look over her shoulder.

Once outside, she pressed her luck. 'Sir, you have been most kind. I wonder if I might obtain your permission to bring in our close friends to visit my husband this evening?' She watched him frown. 'You see, while I am confident of our reprieve, one can never fully count on life's capricious changes. I did not wish to say anything in front of the Earl. Should Lord Pembroke have read the situation wrongly, I shall not know until it is too late. Just as a precaution, may I bring a few dear lady friends who would wish to see my husband and wish him luck?'

The man considered her words in the dim cresset-lit glow of the hallway. She waited, ensuring her eyes were wide and trusting as she regarded him with such intensity that surely he could not fail to acquiesce to her wishes.

'You said these were ladies, Countess?'

'Oh, yes, indeed, sir. Genteel ladies of high quality, who have known the Earl for much of his life,' she lied.

He scratched his beard. 'I should check with the Constable,' he murmured.

Jane already had the coin ready. This had to be handled so carefully. 'Please, Hugh.' She'd overheard him spoken to. 'Your name is Hugh, isn't it?' He nodded, staring as she again pressed money into his hand. 'Just in case. As I said, life is never certain. I would be deeply sad if my lord were unable to farewell those he loved, and these he has loved like sisters. Just a few minutes this evening. I rushed away from them today to pass on the good news from the House and fair forgot they would want to see him too. I dare not dice with a situation that could turn sour within hours.'

It was silver this time. She knew he wouldn't need to check; he would know it from its weight alone.

'My Lady, I would have to insist that these female personages be led into your husband's cell one at a time. We could not allow you all in at once.'

Jane and Winifred shared a smile. 'Of course,' Jane said, for both of them.

TWENTY-NINE

When Winifred arrived at Duke Street her cheeks looked as though the chill of the afternoon had pinched them hard with frosty fingers; either that or her fever was back. Her friends soon discovered that the reason for the Countess's high colour was an infusion of renewed energy.

'Forgive me, dearest, if this should sound in bad taste, but the visit to your lord husband has clearly improved your... um... mood,' Cecilia said.

Jane grinned, pulling off the hood of Winifred's cloak and untying the clasp, vaguely aware of how much more comfortably she moved in the body of the Countess now. *Don't get too comfortable, Jane*, she reminded herself. *Not only do you want the Earl to escape, but you want to escape too.* 'I have a favour to ask of you both,' she said, taking in Mrs Mills with her glance.

'Come into the parlour, Countess. It is just the three of us, I'm pleased to say. My other guest has departed. We'll be much cosier in there.'

'Thank you. Er, Mrs Mills, would you be so kind as to request that Mrs Morgan join us this evening? The favour I wish to ask includes her good self.'

Her hostess frowned. 'Really? How intriguing.' She glanced at Cecilia and Jane caught her friend giving a small shake of her head. 'I shall send a note immediately. Can you not give us a hint as to what is making you look so cheerful?'

'I cannot. I have the energy to explain it only once and I need us all present. And... one more thing.' Mrs Mills paused. 'Would you also kindly ask Mrs Morgan to bring her largest, longest skirt and an additional cloak?'

Her friends shared another glance of surprise.

'You want Mrs Morgan to wear her largest, longest—'

'No, my dear Mrs Mills, I wish for her to bring those items with her. I would prefer the spare cloak to be as simple and unadorned as possible, preferably with a hood.'

'Good grief, Countess! My mind is in a whirl of intrigue, but I shall do as you ask.'

Mrs Morgan must have summoned a chair within minutes of receiving her friend's note, because she was seated in Mrs Mills's parlour within half an hour, having brought with her the extra garments. When the three others had finally settled, each with a warm drink spiced with a nip of brandy, Jane took a slow, deep breath.

'I have a curious and not inconsequential favour to ask of you, my loyal supporters and friends,' she began, taking each of them in with her gaze.

They nodded, eyes wide with anticipation in the candlelight.

'Let me speak and please do not interrupt. To some extent I will be formulating my plan as I go—'

'Plan of what, dear Countess?' Mrs Morgan asked, interrupting immediately.

They saw Winifred's instant smile of forgiveness. Perhaps she could tolerate the occasional interjection. 'My plan for the Earl of Nithsdale's escape from the Tower.'

At their gasps, she raised both hands placatingly. 'Please, ladies, allow me to tell you everything – although first let me ask: are you prepared to help me in this endeavour? Without your assistance, my plan will not succeed.'

One by one they nodded, so curious that they were wholly under Winifred's spell.

Jane explained how she had told the yeoman, and thus the

rest of the warders, that a reprieve was near enough guaranteed, her express purpose being to slacken their supervision. She mentioned her bribe and how she hoped the men would drink long and merrily to the health of her husband and the King, relaxing their guard still further. She watched as the women exchanged glances and she sensed they were impressed.

'I have obtained permission to take us in, one at a time, ostensibly to bid him a potential final farewell.'

Her friends leaned forward expectantly.

'But Countess, by tomorrow everyone will know that there is no pardon,' Mrs Mills pointed out. 'The Tower will know by tonight.'

Jane nodded. 'I realise this. But I have secured permission for this visit and they will be feeling so sorry for me that it will now be a visit of genuine sorrow. The guards will not let me down, I am sure of it.'

'All right, so tell us how this plan of yours works,' Mrs Morgan urged.

'I would leave you, Cecilia, and you, Mrs Mills, downstairs and I would first take you up, Mrs Morgan, and you will be wearing that extra skirt and the extra cloak beneath your own.'

The trio of women listening stared at her and then at each other, perplexed.

'It is not so far-fetched,' Jane assured them. 'Mrs Morgan, you are tall and still so slim despite being with child that the extra garments will go unnoticed. What is more, I have noticed that you and Mrs Mills are of a similar height.' She wanted to add that right now they were of similar size too, but she didn't want to offend the stouter Mrs Mills, who was not pregnant.

'Why is that important? You have me intrigued, my dear,' Mrs Morgan remarked.

'Well, once inside my husband's cell, you will remove the additional garments to reveal the clothes you are wearing now, and after a few words with William, you will leave.'

'Right.' She frowned, and felt it necessary to repeat the

instructions in case she'd misunderstood. 'So I go into his cell, take off these extra garments,' she said, pointing to the skirt and cloak, 'then leave and go back downstairs?'

'Exactly.'

'And that is all?'

'That is your part played to perfection, Mrs Morgan. You will then hail a chair and be gone, using busy streets so you get lost in the mob.'

'Well,' Mrs Morgan said, touching her dark hair, currently swept into a bun, 'that does not sound too hard.'

Jane hoped her new friend would hold to that sentiment. 'Next it will be your turn, Mrs Mills. I will need you to arrive sobbing, holding up a handkerchief like this,' she said, demonstrating with the plain handkerchief she had taken from William Maxwell's drawer at Terregles. Jane feigned hysterical crying. 'I want your face to be entirely hidden. You must not be recognised by the guards.'

Mrs Mills regarded her companions blankly before returning her attention to Winifred. 'Why?'

'Hear me out. Once inside William's cell, after asking him to avert his gaze, you will take off your cloak and your skirt and put on those items left by Mrs Morgan.'

The women shook their heads in unified confusion. Minuscule beads of ice began to patter at the parlour window.

'Hail,' Cecilia said unnecessarily, and shivered.

Mrs Mills got up to throw a few more small logs on the fire, then returned to her seat. 'All right, my dear, let me get this absolutely straight in my mind. I am undressing out of my cloak and skirt and redressing in the discarded clothes that Mrs Morgan has left behind. What then?'

'You will leave the cell.'

'That is my part finished?' she asked.

'You too will have completed your role. I would urge you then to leave the Tower as fast as you can. Once again, a sedan is easiest.'

'And my original clothes?' she asked. 'Still lying in your husband's cell?'

'Ah, now we come to it,' Winifred said with glee, and Jane could see comprehension beginning to dawn on her companions' faces. 'Mrs Mills, you will arrive sobbing, leave your original garments behind and then emerge from saying farewell to the Earl with your face exposed and appearing perfectly composed. In fact, you will make sure the yeomen notice that you look to be a different woman from the woman who went in. You will fool them into thinking you are the first woman, for you will be dressed like her – in case anyone noticed.'

Jane cast a glance around to ensure that everyone was still following her; it sounded complicated when in fact William had assessed it right as being childishly comical in its simplicity. It was to be a process of trickery, sleight of hand – the sort of conjuror's play that forced the unsuspecting eye to see something that really was not there. Distraction – as a magician might admit – was the key to any good trick. 'Now, my lord husband will then, much against his desire,' she smiled sadly, 'put on your original set of clothing, Mrs Mills.' She didn't want to add that his broad male body would be amply covered by the clothing of her stout hostess, so she said instead: 'And your height will be extremely helpful at this point, because the length of your skirt and cloak will suit him well enough.'

'The Earl will emerge dressed as Mrs Mills went in?' Mrs Morgan said, understanding fully now.

'That is correct.' Winifred beamed, and Jane felt relief that her curious plan at least made sense to the players involved. 'He will feign sobs as though still overcome with grief, but this precaution will be simply to cover his manly face.'

There were more gasps of surprise. 'Oh, how clever!' Cecilia said, her normally reticent expression sparkling with interest. 'And so the Earl comes to where I will have a carriage waiting, presumably, pretending to be one of the women who came to visit him?'

'There you have it!' Jane said, thrilled that she had guessed at the rest. 'The guards will be in a loosened and lenient frame of mind, I hope. All we will have to do is convince them for a few minutes.'

'And you?' Cecilia asked, frowning.

'Well, I must play my part to perfection, Cecilia, for Mrs Morgan is right: the Tower will already likely know of the King's decision. Even if he does agree to pardon some, I know my husband will not be counted among them. So by the time we arrive, they will be anticipating my grief. And I will provide it, pretending to be saying a final farewell to my good husband while hurrying my maid and friends along so I can present a final petition at the House of Lords. Then the guards cannot pay the Earl's guests any undue attention.'

'I understand that gives you the excuse not to tarry, my dear Countess, but what of your husband, even if we can successfully get him out of his cell?' Mrs Mills asked.

'Mrs Mills, I am counting upon you to suggest a safe house nearby where we can conceal Lord Nithsdale. Cecilia is to wait for me, as would be proper, but she will have seen the Earl safely on his way to the safe house in a closed carriage or fast-moving sedan.'

Mrs Morgan waved a hand. 'A safe house can be arranged. But my dear, what will you be doing alone in the Tower while we are gone?'

'Pretending,' Jane said firmly.

'Let me clarify,' Cecilia said. 'We are counting on the guards, in merry moods, not to notice that two women have gone in with you to the Earl's cell, but that three have come out?'

'In a nutshell,' Jane said, looking at each in turn. 'It is daring, I agree. But it is also straightforward.'

'What if the guards do check, though?' Mrs Morgan asked, rubbing her swollen belly as her child presumably stretched. Jane, or rather Winifred, sympathised.

'I have arranged it so that the only person who might be

questioned – if at all – is you, my dear Mrs Mills, in the spare set of clothes,' she said, taking her in with a kindly glance. 'And should they do that, they would discover you are every inch a woman visitor,' Jane added.

'Countess, I think we need more help,' her hostess said. 'Let me bring my husband in on your plan. You know he is extremely sympathetic to your cause and believes the Earl should be offered his reprieve. I think if we had Mr Mills downstairs with a carriage waiting, ready to bundle your lord husband into it, then we could be more certain of a safe exit from the Tower. Mr Mills is in a far better position to find the right lodgings where your husband's whereabouts can be kept quiet.'

It did make sense to have that extra person on the ground, Jane agreed, and she knew that Mr Mills could be trusted. It was true that two men could move more easily around London. She nodded. 'All right, thank you.'

'I shall call him in,' Mrs Mills replied, looking relieved.

He was duly summoned. Mills had a calm air about him and his deeply lined face, from years as a sea captain, tended to give the impression of being permanently grave. But at the same time his sharp blue eyes appeared to hold constant amusement, and it was this genial gaze that now gave Jane hope.

'Well, well,' he said, having listened silently as Winifred and her cohort explained the plan. 'That *is* a bit of fun.' He slipped a small flattish box of tortoiseshell from his waistcoat pocket. Jane caught the flash of ivory inlay as he flipped the lid open and pinched out a tiny fingertip of snuff. The ladies waited while he inhaled this into one nostril, then repeated the action with a fresh pinch of snuff in the other. After much sniffing and blinking, he returned the box in a practised move to his waistcoat. 'And what does the Earl think of this grand idea?' he asked her.

Jane took a breath. 'He sounded as intrigued as you do, Mr Mills.'

The old sea captain chuckled. 'I applaud your pluck, Countess.'

'I admit to feeling ashamed at including your wife and Mrs Morgan in my plot, sir, but I fear I cannot carry out my plan without them and their similar height. With all my heart I believe I can get both of these generous ladies in and out of the Tower without danger. They will be seen but not recalled later in any detail. As for your good self, if you would simply wait with Miss Evans in the carriage until my husband is delivered, then find him somewhere of no consequence to lie low, that is all I would ask of you. The more humble the hideout, the better.'

'Indeed,' Mills said, sniffing again. 'I do believe I know just the spot.'

'So you will help?' Jane asked.

'Without question, I shall.' He took his wife's hand and patted it. 'I cannot have Mrs Mills cavorting around London, engaged in a daring adventure to save a good man's life, and not do the same. My dear Countess, I have the utmost respect for the Earl. And I share much of London society's dismay at how poorly the King of England has treated a noblewoman.'

Jane did not want to give them much more time for reflection.

'Oh, thank you, Mr Mills,' she said, standing up and clapping her pleasure. 'Then a slight change of plan means that I can have you waiting in a carriage for William and he can fall as a helplessly weeping wife into your arms.' She waited, then looked at each of them. 'So you all agree to help me then, dear friends?'

Under the spell of her enthusiasm and calm manner, the trio of women instantly agreed with a nod.

'When?' Mrs Morgan predictably asked.

'At once,' Jane said, pulling the plug on her final surprise. She had deliberately not left them any further time to talk themselves out of it. 'But first, ladies, let's gather up the garments we require.'

After allowing the Countess to rifle through her chest of drawers, Mrs Mills was happy to lend her a large, lace-edged handkerchief: one of the key items in their conspiracy.

'I shall also need some items from your toilette,' she said, glad of Winifred's terminology.

'Pardon, Countess?'

'White powder, rouge...'

'Ah, indeed. Here, my dear,' she said, showing Jane behind a screen to where a mirror and dressing table sat. 'Help yourself.'

Jane put what she thought she might need into a small cloth bag nearby, before returning downstairs.

'Cecilia, please send someone to hail two hackneys. We shall leave immediately. Mrs Mills and Mrs Morgan, if you would join me in one carriage...' she said. 'And ladies, if I call you by different names, don't flinch, just keep acting out the role you know to present.'

Within minutes, Winifred, Mrs Morgan and Mrs Mills were setting off in one carriage, while Cecilia and Mr Mills made their way in the second carriage using a different route, having agreed where they would secretly await the arrival of William.

Most of the way to the Tower of London, Jane ensured that Winifred chatted in a lively fashion, not permitting her companions to even think of changing their minds, or to reconsider the advisability or consequences of their plans. She had deliberately suggested they go a long way round, via a landmark she had previously only seen from a distance. When the hackney clip-clopped past the still unfinished St Paul's Cathedral, she was amazed to see that even at night it remained half church, half marketplace. Despite the latish hour and near-freezing conditions, printers sold books here and lovers cuddled.

The cab dipped further into the chaotic maze of medieval streets, some dimly lit, while others relied on the candlelight spilling out of the ramshackle buildings, particularly the ground-level spaces, many of which sheltered dicing rooms, brothels and inns.

Through Winifred's gaze, Jane saw prostitutes plying

their trade against walls, leading men down the warrens of alleys or gossiping with the other girls. She glimpsed weary nightwatchmen, trailing their lanterns around the labyrinth that was this part of London, shouting at children and others who were probably pickpockets or thieves. She saw night-soil farmers, scarves tied securely around their mouths and noses, digging out full privies and heaping the waste into their carts. The ratters were out too, whistling to their small dogs and heading into tenements to rid them of their hordes of vermin.

Yet silence gripped the occupants of the carriage as the reality of their journey took hold. They were nearing the Tower now, so Jane allowed herself to let go of her fears as she absently watched the scenery flash by.

At the approach to the Byward Tower gate, Jane could see that, even in the foreground, there was a heavy guard on tonight, but fortunately the men recognised the Earl's wife. After checking she had permission to bring in her two friends, the guards waved the driver on. The hooves of the horses echoed loudly as the carriage moved beneath the arch, and Jane experienced the sensation of being swallowed by the great stone monolith. Their hackney continued up the hill, then turned to proceed beneath the Bloody Tower, where Jane pointed to the tiny barred window of William's cell before they arrived at the Lieutenant's Lodgings.

Jane fixed both women with a firm stare from behind Winifred's eyes. 'You know what to do?' she queried, as a strange calm overtook her. They nodded. Both looked terrified, but this suited her. It was the right mood, given what lay ahead of them.

They alighted from the carriage and sent it on its way, knowing Cecilia and Mr Mills waited, no doubt with trepidation, in another carriage just outside the Byward Tower gate for their special passenger.

'Mrs Mills, please wait here, just inside the doorway,' Jane urged. She turned to Mrs Morgan. 'Ready?'

Her friend looked frightened but determined. She nodded.

'Two flights of stairs,' Jane told her, mindful of her child.

'I shall be fine,' Mrs Morgan replied as they set off.

Jane took the pregnant woman's arm to aid her. She dropped her voice. 'At the top we turn left and then it is twenty paces to William's door. Look as glum as you wish. And away from all glances,' she warned.

Jane led Mrs Morgan, their arms still linked, across the familiar Council Chamber and held her breath as they passed the guardroom. A glance inside told her that several of the yeomen's wives and children were visiting them, warming themselves in front of a lively fire. Two of the men recognised her and raised their hands in greeting, and Jane knew her money had been wisely spent. Her usual yeoman was not in the room, but he arrived now from around the corner to greet her. She nearly jumped with alarm, and stopped herself just in time.

'Countess,' he said sombrely, and slid a glance toward Mrs Morgan. 'Madam,' he said with a small bow, returning his attention immediately to Winifred. 'I am truly sorry for the news.'

Jane sniffled convincingly. ''Twas a terrible shock, indeed, Hugh. But I should have known not to presume too much upon the King's favour. All I wish now is to hold my husband one last time.'

He cleared his throat. 'The Lords Derwentwater, Kenmure, Widdrington, Nairne, Carnwath and... er, and your husband will be led to Tower Hill at midday tomorrow, My Lady. But I have won permission from Sir George Moseley for you and your lady friends to visit him now briefly.'

She swallowed, keeping her fear at bay. 'Hugh, thank you again for this small privilege.' She wanted to keep his attention on Winifred and discourage him from glancing at her companion.

He looked at her again. 'Forgive us the merriment next

door, Countess. Your coin has gladdened the warders and their families.'

'Oh, dear me, do not apologise. I am sure the merry voices of children will cheer my dear lord in these final hours,' she assured him, pushing the mute Mrs Morgan forward now. 'I have followed your instructions to bring in one friend at a time.'

Hugh nodded. He addressed the burly guard on duty outside her husband's room. 'Step aside and let the Countess and her friends pass as they choose.'

Perfect, Jane thought. 'Goodnight, Hugh... thank you again.'

He looked as though he wanted to say something more, but was suddenly bereft of words. Instead, he gave a small bow and withdrew. The door was opened and Jane hurried Mrs Morgan through, then slipped in after her and watched it close behind them.

William was standing against the wall by a small table, his shirt buttoned, his face freshly shaven as she had asked, hair combed and tied back neatly into a queue. His waistcoat was half-open and his jacket, brushed clean of dust and grime, hung over the chair. He looked as haunted as Hugh had looked moments earlier. His complexion was pale in the dim ghostly light of a single candle. For a moment they stood and regarded each other in a tense panic before Winifred threw herself toward him.

'I was not sure you would go through with it,' he whispered into her neck.

She kissed him quickly before pulling away. 'William, this is a wonderfully brave friend of mine, Mrs Morgan.'

He took his guest's hand and kissed it. 'Mrs Morgan, if this plan works, I will owe you a debt I fear I can never repay.'

Her new friend melted at his words. Jane had overlooked William's effect on women. She knew from Winifred's thoughts that her husband attracted female attention with the greatest of ease. Jane realised she had only known him in the confines of this cell, with just the two of them present. To see him now, in the context of other people's regard, was enlightening.

Mrs Morgan was clutching a hand to the base of her throat and surely blushing. 'I could hardly refuse your dear wife, My Lord. She is most persuasive, and I suspect I can now see why,' she said with a throaty chuckle as her previous fears fled. 'But now I must ask you to turn away, Lord Nithsdale, for I must undress.' She giggled, but hushed herself immediately.

Jane could barely believe that pregnant Mrs Morgan was flirting with Winifred's husband.

'William... let me run through the plan again while Mrs Morgan takes off her skirt.'

He turned his back on their companion and bit his lip. 'I fail to see how this is going to work,' he whispered, reiterating his previous concern.

'I beg you, William. You must do exactly as I say. Remember, I am familiar with the routines and men outside. I have made friends of most... right now they are drinking the ale our coin has purchased and sharing treats with their families that our savings provided. You have to trust me. We have only hours to save your head.'

He let out a sigh. 'I am in your hands, dear wife.'

'Exactly as I say,' she emphasised. 'No deviation.'

He put his hand on his heart. 'I promise.'

She looked over his shoulder. 'Mrs Morgan is ready. Now we must leave. Be ready to do exactly as I instruct quickly and without question when I return.'

'Return? From where?' He looked confused, sounded unsure again.

'Trust me,' she hissed back. Jane could feel Winifred's adrenaline surging, bringing a sort of wild energy that she knew she must keep under control or she would lose her ability to think calmly, react swiftly. The last thing she needed now was for Winifred's fragile body to fail. Her friends and her husband were entirely under her spell and one wrong move from her could prove catastrophic. She did not wait for William to respond to her words, instead taking control and hurrying Mrs Morgan from the room, while speaking in a loud, excited voice to distract the guard with the halberd and anyone else who might be listening.

'Please, please, I beg you,' she said, pushing Mrs Morgan ahead of her, 'go and find my maid quickly, as I must present one final petition this evening. I must try one last time,' she wept, her voice fully raised.

Mrs Morgan was hurried past the guardroom and no one so much as looked away from the fire. Jane saw her safely downstairs and out of the lodgings, feeling a wave of relief. 'Go!' she said to Mrs Morgan. 'Hail a sedan and get away, head home. You've been there all night; make sure the servants know it too.' She beckoned to Mrs Mills, waiting inside the doorway. Her heart was thumping now: this would be one of the most challenging parts of her plan.

'Start weeping, my friend,' she whispered, as she linked arms with Mrs Mills and started to bundle her up the two flights of stairs. Her companion obediently covered her face with her very large handkerchief and began letting out a wail. Jane could believe that Mrs Mills, slightly bent over in her distress, was weeping inconsolably. Perhaps Mrs Mills was as terrified as the others, or else she was loving the intrigue, but Jane was undeniably grateful for her acting, feeling a moment of relieved amusement as they passed the warders' room and were thrown genuine looks of sympathy.

The guard outside William's cell cut his gaze away, predictably embarrassed by the caterwauling woman, as Jane helped Mrs Mills through the door and closed it behind her.

'Keep the wails going,' she urged her companion as she glanced at a dismayed William. 'Turn away,' she snapped in her tension, and he spun around as if bitten. 'Get changed now, Mrs Mills,' she murmured to her friend, who was still performing brilliantly, allowing her cries to dull down to a softer whimper. 'Dress yourself in Mrs Morgan's skirt and cloak. Hurry, please!'

While Mrs Mills undressed and re-dressed, Jane set about the task of daubing the hastily assembled make-up, carried in beneath her cloak, onto William's face.

'Winifred, really…' he protested softly.

'Do not struggle, my love; remember your promise.'

A look of disgust pinched his face beneath her ministrations, but Jane continued to powder and rouge, and then tried to cover up William's dark eyebrows with white leaded paint she had found in one of the pots on Mrs Mills's dressing table. Jane understood it was an early type of foundation.

She finished and stood back to admire her work.

'It will not fool anyone up close, but I have no intention of letting a single guard near you. Now, William, listen closely to me.'

She explained hastily, but succinctly, that it was now his turn to act his part, just as well and just as courageously as her two companions had. Jane glanced at Mrs Mills, still keeping up a fine moaning wail, and now dressed in Mrs Morgan's cast-offs.

She nodded. 'Well done. Ready?'

Mrs Mills paused to grin. She held out the handkerchief, which Jane took.

'You know what to do, my love?' Jane said to William.

He grimaced and nodded, reaching for the skirt and cloak.

'And you'll need this,' she said, holding out the lace handkerchief, 'if you are going to convince them you're the same woman who came in wailing. You heard her. Do the same and we will have you free.'

She took Mrs Mills by the arm. 'I shall be back, William; do not tarry,' she said grimly. Jane led her friend out and hurried her past the guards, again effecting her distraught voice. 'Dear Mrs Catherine,' she said, reaching for any name that came to mind, 'I must beg of you to go in all haste and find my maid, for she does not realise the time, it seems, and mayhap has forgotten the last petition I am to give; should I fail, the situation is irreparable, since I have only this one night left to curry favour. Please, I beg you, force her to make haste, for I shall be on tenterhooks until she comes.'

Jane and Mrs Mills were able to move safely across the Council Chamber without being stopped. She almost ran down the first flight of stairs with a heavily breathing Mrs Mills, before squeezing her hand in thanks. 'You did it!' she murmured, her tone sparkling with gratitude. 'Now please, get yourself away, but first warn your good husband that his part is imminent. I thank you with all my heart.'

Her friend grinned. 'Good luck, dear Countess,' she said over her shoulder, hurrying down the second flight of stairs.

Jane could feel Winifred's heart pounding so hard it was now vibrating in her throat, but she was bravely keeping her tension under control. The hardest and most fraught part of her daring plan was yet to unfold. She turned back, fearful but determined not to falter now, and made her way again into William's cell, this time ensuring that Winifred's shoulders were deliberately sagging, and dabbing helplessly at her eyes.

Jane wasn't ready for the sight awaiting Winifred and had to stifle her host's giggle as she caught sight of her husband struggling into a skirt. Her laughter, which could easily have been interpreted on the other side of the door as a sob, had a touch of hysteria in it, and Jane made Winifred bite her knuckle to regain focus.

William turned to glare at her with a finger in the air, to forestall any sarcastic comment she might think of making, but before he could say anything, Winifred was kissing his hand.

'We're so close to finishing this, my darling. Keep faith with me,' she murmured.

His glower faded and he smiled sadly, leaning down to snatch a kiss. 'I have no choice, but in truth you make me feel far braver than I am.' He sighed. 'The warder will be along soon, with fresh candles for the condemned man's final night.'

Jane stole a glance at the twilight. This farce of hers had to be completed before any kindly warder arrived. She hurried to tie on William's cloak and then pulled the hood over his head.

'Keep the handkerchief over your face, and remember to weep like a woman does – just as you heard Mrs Mills do earlier.'

'I don't know if I can—'

'You can!' she snapped, gripping his wrists. 'Just think of how I was when I endured the miscarriages of our precious children. Remember how I wept? Keep that sorrow in mind and pretend. Believe me when I say they will not want to interrupt you – they will be embarrassed.'

He nodded in response to her insistent gaze. 'London will know I slunk away as a woman.'

'London will applaud us,' she growled close to his face.

He shook his head suddenly. 'I cannot do it.'

She stared, at once horrified but also bewildered by his words.

'Cannot, or will not?' she demanded in an angry whisper.

'Both!' he snapped. 'Do you truly want your husband to be thought of as a coward who resorted to a woman's petticoats because he couldn't face the consequences of his actions?'

'You've proved your worth as a man. There is nothing to be gained by losing your manly head!'

'I will be the clown of London.'

'Nay, my lord, you will have thumbed your nose at the Protestant king.'

He raised his gaze to hers and shook his head defiantly. 'Not this way,' he said, and Winifred recognised the implacable note in his voice as he began to undress.

Jane was even more surprised by the stinging slap she gave him than her host was. She could feel rage churning through Winifred's body, hotter than the fever that was always threatening, except it wasn't Winifred's anger, but hers.

'How fucking dare you!' she whispered with force, and she wondered if the language didn't frighten William more than her physical attack. 'Four brave women put their names, their reputations, their lives on that same chopping block as you tonight – for do not persuade yourself otherwise, Will. We too are committing treachery against the Crown, and so is everyone else involved in this secret plot to get you safely out of a gaol that no poor sod has ever broken free of before.' He stared at her in shock, her handprint still visible in the powder on his cheek. 'You are a coward if you remain. You are a Jacobite hero if you defy this king and his gaolers. We are leaving now, and I will not hear another word to the contrary.'

Jane couldn't read his expression, but the fight seemed to go out of him as he deflated his chest with a sigh. 'Forgive me.'

'This is it, Will. Be a weeping, hysterical woman for just a few minutes and you shall cheat that executioner's axe, and do much more for the Jacobite cause than dying a martyr with an audience jeering at your severed throat! Do it for our children, and because you love me.'

'I am ready, Win. Let us cheat death.'

'Come,' she said, taking his arm and pushing the hand holding the handkerchief to his face. 'Start your whimpering. Remember you are a woman who has just said her final farewell to a condemned man she loves as a brother.'

Jane felt Winifred's heart hammering so hard that it was sounding in her head as well as banging on her ribcage. She hoped her host's heart was strong enough for this excitement, but she knew by now not to doubt stoic Winifred.

She opened the door and pushed past the doorway, surprised that the yeoman outside had moved. He and three other warders were milling around outside the guardroom, blocking their path. She felt William tense.

'Head down and wailing,' she whispered.

William's weeping was surprisingly convincing and Jane began a steady stream of soothing words.

'Excuse me, gentlemen,' she said, her tone full of anxiety, pushing William and herself past the burly shoulders of the men. 'I must see my unhappy friend away from here.' Now was the moment that her trick must work; she had to confuse and distract the guards into believing this was not the third time she was repeating the request. 'Oh, dear Mrs Betty, my maid is ruining me by not coming. Please run and bring her to me. You know my lodgings. If ever you have made haste in your life, please, I beg you to do so now, otherwise all is lost.'

Maybe she should have let William practise walking in the skirt, but time had not permitted her. He was not used to the cumbersome nature of the skirt, and just as they were clearing the guardroom, about to cross the Council Chamber, he tripped. He crashed his shoulder into the wall but somehow managed to keep his curse appropriately high-sounding. Guards approached, Hugh among them.

Jane wanted to scream. Winifred was cringing within herself.

'My Lady? Is your friend injured?'

William wailed and Jane experienced what had only previously been an adage to her when Winifred's knees turned to jelly. She felt them buckle in her terror, as William's hood had slipped. She sensed Hugh coming close. That was all it would take. One glimpse at the poorly made-up face of her husband and kindly Hugh would guess what was afoot.

She let out the hysterical shriek of a woman who had reached her final level of tolerance. If she were truthful, this was no act, for Jane knew they were a heartbeat away from being discovered.

But the warders were taken by such surprise at this emotional outburst from a woman they thought of as calm and contained that they froze in their tracks. Jane pushed on in a high, breathless voice. 'Mrs Betty, please, please, I beg of you! Don't let me down now!' she entreated, clasping 'Betty' close and straightening her hood. 'If I am to save my husband, you must find my maid!' She propelled William forward, away from the immediate light of the cresset and into a pool of shadow near the stairs.

'My Lady?' Hugh repeated.

'Forgive me, Hugh; I am at my wits' end,' she said without turning. 'I must get my friend Betty on her way.'

William sobbed just loudly enough to be credible, in a high-pitched voice. Holding the handkerchief close to his hooded face, he bowed his head and made himself look as small as possible, leaning into Winifred and taking small steps, as Jane nodded her thanks at Hugh and hurried William across the Council Chamber with a sense of terrified déjà vu. She was feeling dizzy with the adrenaline that was pounding through Winifred's blood.

And suddenly they were descending the stairs. She could feel the cold London air whistling up the steps, touching her face. William was just minutes away from freedom now. They could do it! No. They *were* doing it!

He was escaping!

They half stumbled, half ran down the second flight of stairs.

'Keep crying, keep hidden,' she hissed near the hood of his cloak.

Her heart nearly stopped when they rounded the corner to find guards at the bottom of the second flight. These men had not been there before. William wailed louder and it appeared to work, for the men, on looking at Winifred's panicked expression and recognising the generous Countess, opened the door and let William out.

'To the Byward Tower gate,' she called, supporting him down the small grassed incline, his sobs slowing down now. There was no time for a farewell kiss of good luck. She could see Cecilia waiting with Mr Mills in the shadows just outside the gate, and within moments she had closed the distance and passed her precious cargo into their care. She lifted her hand to the carriage as it hurried away from the Tower into the warren of streets that comprised East London.

Jane could now hear a ringing in Winifred's ears, and knew her cheeks were burning with such a build-up of excitement and strain that Winifred threatened to vomit. They had to keep their shared joy in check.

We did it, Winifred! She wanted to punch the air.

One final hurdle, Jane, she thought she heard in her mind.

One final hurdle to leap indeed, and it was by far the most nerve-wracking aspect of her loose plan.

Jane did not have to feign her fear… having to turn around, run the short distance back to the Lieutenant's Lodgings and face climbing those stairs once again felt far more daunting than the previous occasions. She forced Winifred to retrace her steps, even though all she wanted to do was turn and run into the relative safety promised by London's dark, honeycombed streets. As she ascended slowly to the first landing, she could smell food being cooked in the warders' quarters and she was suddenly acutely aware of the combined hum of voices: chattering children, the soft laughter of women, men's heavy footsteps creaking on the boards around her. All of this detail had been lost to her while her 'sleight of hand' had been occurring. Yet now she felt anchored in the reality of the magician's craft; here was the moment when she had to pull off the climax of the trick.

She climbed the second flight of steps and felt the suffocating press of the gaol's stone walls embracing her, reminding her that it could easily become her keeper.

Once more Jane forced her brave host to cross the now-all-too-familiar Council Chamber, deliberately dabbing at their shared eyes, Jane making sure Winifred sniffled and appeared upset, but also looking as though she were gathering her wits for a last teary scene, which the wardens were surely expecting.

The yeoman with the halberd was not back at his usual position, but was lingering close.

'I can let myself in,' she said softly to him. 'This is my final farewell,' she added, so sadly he looked away, clearing his throat with embarrassment.

'I shall not disturb you, My Lady.'

'Thank you,' she whispered, and entered the empty cell.

She leaned against the door, trying to calm Winifred's pounding heart. The tension of the escape had caused a headache to erupt and she needed, now more than ever, to think clearly.

Come on! she howled to herself. *You can do this, Win! He's on the outside. He's waiting for you. He's alive. Both our Williams will live!*

Jane demanded that Winifred take several deep, slow breaths until she thought that her host felt less light-headed, and that her voice would be steady. *Here we go, Winnie. The last part of our performance.*

And now she began to act out her charade. Comical though it was, she knew all she had to do was promote the power of suggestion. The unwitting guards and their trust in the woman they had come to admire would do the rest.

'William, my love,' she said in a voice filled with heartbreak, 'hold me one last time.'

In a deep tone, the best she could effect, Jane replied, 'Hush, my darling. Do not cry. I go to my Lord with a clear conscience.'

And so Jane kept up a halting conversation with her invisible husband, acting out both parts as she moved nervously around the room. All the while she imagined William's coach moving through the back streets – or maybe they were already on foot, having given up the bulky horse and carriage to move with ease through the darkened, filthy alleys. She had no idea where Mills would take him, but surely the darker and grimier it was the better. She didn't care, so long as it was beyond the King's reach.

After approximately fifteen minutes and a worried glance over the darkening London sky, Jane felt that long enough had elapsed for William to be sufficiently distanced from the Tower. By now the threat that fresh candles would be delivered to the condemned man felt so tangible it was making Winifred's throat tight with fear. Jane straightened herself and wished her husband goodnight in a tremulous voice that did not have to be faked.

She opened the door slightly and added, looking back into the room: 'I will away, my lord, for I fear something has happened to my woman and I cannot trust anyone but myself now to petition on your behalf.' She gave a weepy smile to the empty room. 'If the Tower permits, I may try to visit later tonight. But if not, I shall be here at first light, my love, bearing good tidings, I hope.'

The guard was standing ahead of her, but with his back turned out of respect. Another man just ahead of him – the valet de chambre, she presumed – was preparing candles, slicing away at their bases to fix the wax solidly into the pewter holders.

Jane sucked in a terrified breath, looking down at the worn latch-string on the door. She had mere moments. She took her chance and wrenched it, snapping the string soundlessly and hearing the latch fall into place. Now it could only be opened from the inside.

'My good man,' she called in a wavering voice that she did not have to work at. Both men turned, but the valet noticed that her attention was riveted on him.

He bowed. 'Yes, My Lady?'

'My lord husband is saying his prayers and asked that he not be disturbed this night. He requires no candlelight for his communion with God.'

The valet blinked in consternation. 'He wishes not to be disturbed this evening… not even for a final meal, My Lady?'

'Especially not for food,' she said, knowing she was visibly trembling. 'He insists on being left alone in the dark with his prayers.'

The man bowed. 'As you instruct, My Lady.'

She glanced at the guard and he nodded too, moving to stand back outside the cell, his halberd positioned diagonally across the door to assure her that no one would pass.

'Thank you, both. I shall bid you goodnight. Do not come early for my husband,' she warned, 'for I make haste now to make a final petition.'

Hugh met her as she passed the warders' room.

'My Lady,' he bowed, 'my deepest sympathies are with you.'

She nodded, now desperate to be gone.

'Let me escort you downstairs,' he said, and Jane had no choice but to allow him to accompany her not only outside the lodgings, but back down to the gate, where a small queue of hackney carriages had gathered. He offered his hand to help her inside one of them. Jane couldn't help but feel sorry for Hugh, and she hoped he would not pay the price for her subterfuge.

She deliberately glanced up toward the window as though taking one last look at her husband. 'Thank you, you have been so kind.'

He bowed slightly again. 'Drive on!' he called to the coachman, and Jane felt the reassuring lurch of the horses as they whisked her away.

She wondered when the gaolers would discover the truth. With a curious sense of the macabre, she suddenly wished she could be a fly on the wall when it happened.

THIRTY

EVERYONE LOVED A HAPPY ENDING, AND ELLEN was beginning to believe the story of Will Maxwell might deliver just that. She squeezed his mother's hand. 'He's off life support now, Mrs Maxwell. Your brave boy's doing everything on his own.'

In fact, the room now looked positively bare, since most of the electronic equipment had been unhooked. A monitor was keeping track of his heart, there was a drip in his arm and a waste bag at the side of his bed, but to the lay visitor, Will was just resting. He was breathing deep and rhythmically now; his countenance was serene and somehow more here in the moment. Ellen had seen it before in patients; it was as though they'd surfaced from a void and were suddenly more alert in appearance, even though they were still technically comatose.

She would admit, if anyone asked, that she had never been happier for a family, secretly hoping she would be the first person Will saw when he finally opened his eyes. Ellen knew it was unprofessional to think like this, but at some stage over the course of her silent night shifts in the intensive care unit, when she kept a special vigil over Will Maxwell, she'd developed a connection that she knew was dangerous in her line of work. Her fondness for the handsome American, cut down in his prime, was known, but with each hour her affection for him intensified. She didn't care now if he woke here in London and denied her that holiday in the US, she just wanted to hear his voice. And who knew? Perhaps they might share a flute of champagne together sometime, so he could thank her properly for her care. She smiled at the daydream, knowing she was ignoring the fiancée in his life, but in her dreamscape there was no one. This was her fantasy and she fashioned it as she chose: featuring just Will and Ellen.

She cleared her throat softly and focused back on Will the patient. She could see the telltale firmness around his lips; his eyes when they moved behind his lids, though still random, seemed less 'loose'; and his expression didn't have that ghastly corpse-like slackness any more. Will was so close now.

Ellen watched Diane Maxwell's face crumple a little, but she recognised it as a meltdown of relief and happiness. The despair was retreating. She then glanced at Will's father; these days, she'd found a new respect for the man. He was tough, but she'd learned how to be around John Maxwell and not be offended by his manner. She'd been impressed when he had looked straight at her last night and apologised unreservedly for his behaviour.

'I've been unforgiving of all of you,' he'd said, 'and I'm ashamed of my behaviour. I know you've been absolutely dedicated to Will's recovery.'

She especially liked the way that, for the first time, he showed anything but robotic affection toward his wife. She watched now as Maxwell reached for Diane and pulled her close. 'He's coming back, darling. Keep the faith.'

Ellen joined in. 'Yes, he is coming back to us, Mr Maxwell. You've raised a big strong boy, Mrs Maxwell, and he's a fighter. Look how good he looks,' Ellen soothed, avoiding the dark cloud that still hovered.

Diane Maxwell couldn't avoid it though, it seemed. 'Now I'm worried about brain damage,' she whimpered. 'I'm sorry, I just can't imagine my son without his faculties.'

'Diane, yesterday we were worried whether he would live to breathe on his own... and now look at him,' her husband admonished. 'We will deal with whatever we must when he finally opens his eyes.' He glanced over at Ellen, looking momentarily anxious that he was saying the wrong things.

She nodded with a small smile of encouragement.

'You two should get some rest. I'll be on duty tonight, and you know he's my favourite, so I rarely leave his side,' she said, grinning at Diane.

His mother gulped, laughed sadly and patted her husband's arm. 'Thank you, Ellen. I think you're his guardian angel.'

She nodded, liking immensely that they'd noticed. 'Any news of Jane yet?'

'We hope she'll be home any minute,' Will's father said, clearing his throat.

Jane sat up against the leather of the carriage, oblivious to what was passing by. She barely heard or saw anything. Winifred's blood, pumping so hard, was creating enough disruption in her head to make it ache, her temple pounding with pressure, her ears echoing the powerful thump of her heartbeat. She stared ahead into the darkness, unblinking and glassy-eyed, still stunned that they had pulled off such a trick. Not only that, they'd each made their departure safely and, she prayed, without anyone being hurt or stopped.

As the great fortress, with its stout walls and sense of imperviousness, fell behind, Winifred's body began to tremble uncontrollably. The sound of her host's chattering teeth added to the internal cacophony, but Jane could only feel elation. The childish, almost comical plan had worked.

Is it over yet? she heard herself wondering.

Not yet, came the answer from Winifred. *The execution date is tomorrow. We have to see out that day and keep William hidden... and then get him to real safety.*

Real safety?

Away from England.

Scotland?

The continent. Where the Church of Rome can protect us.

Jane was drifting away on her thoughts; the peril of her own situation was only now striking her. If William Maxwell could be kept safe, then according to Robin it meant Will was safe too. But where did that leave her? She was still stranded. How would *she* be made safe? How would she and Winifred be made whole?

The carriage arrived at Duke Street and Winifred was met by a triumphant duo of Mrs Mills and Mrs Morgan.

'Oh, my dear, you were marvellous!' Mrs Morgan chirruped quietly in her ear, being careful in front of the coach driver.

The women welcomed her, but knew she must not tarry. Mrs Mills already had Winifred's bag packed. 'Here, dear,' she said, handing her a note as well. 'The sedan is waiting. Have the men take you to that address. Do not speak your name. I have asked for the sedan men to be waiting for you around the corner from here, so they will not even know which house you have come from.'

She hugged the two women. 'I do not know what to say, how to thank you both.'

'The glow in your face is more than enough,' Mrs Mills said, shushing her. 'Now go, my dear. And lie low. Cecilia and my husband are with him.'

She nodded, and gave them each a fierce hug. 'Give one of these hugs to your dear good husband for his help,' she told Mrs Mills. 'I shall get word to you somehow.'

The sedan men hurried her off and within moments she was bouncing along in the chair, this time headed to a poorer part of London; heading back, in fact, toward Smithfield and ultimately to Byward Street again, sitting in the shadow of the Tower of London.

Jane felt nausea simmering at her throat. *Why here?* Winifred's thoughts echoed her own fears.

'Sure you will be all right here, madam?' one of the chair

carriers asked, frowning at the address that she'd had to read for him. 'The entrance is down that lane.'

The three of them were standing in a street of merchants, staring down a dim alley that led to a barely visible doorway. She steeled Winifred as best she could. 'I shall be fine, thank you. I have come to visit a friend and will not be staying long.'

'Should we wait? This is a rough neighbourhood, madam.'

She shook her head, glad of the hood that covered part of her face. She did not want these men to remember her or the address. 'No – thank you for your concern.' She gave them a larger than necessary tip, hoping they might knock off early and get in their cups so their memories of tonight would be impaired.

They touched their caps to her and were gone. Jane bounded down the alley to the doorway of a squalid building that smelled of urine and something long dead. A woman in a grubby bonnet and shabby clothes, topped off by a stained apron, opened it on her knock.

'Are you Mary?' she asked.

Jane stared back, confused. 'Er...'

'Wife of Gillam?' she said, struggling with the word.

Guillaume – French for William. It was how the Earl had been addressed at the French court.

'I am Mary,' Jane said, smiling, remembering it was his sister's name. 'Where is my husband?'

'In the turret with your sister. It is small, but the quietest room I have. How long will you be staying?'

'A few nights at most.'

'Well, you will have a very good view from up there as your husband demanded,' the woman said, sucking air through her missing bottom front teeth.

'Over London? How nice. Thank you.'

'Not of London, ma'am!' she cackled. 'Of the executions of them Jacobite lords!'

Jane felt Winifred's body freeze to the rickety front step, and it was nothing to do with the temperature. Until this moment Jane had thought Mr Mills would have found William a place to be strictly incognito. But the landlady was tapping her nose and grinning.

'Well done, My Lady. None of us likes how you was treated by our king. Mayhap that is how they treats their genteel women in Germany, but not in England. You are safe here, My Lady. Among friends.'

Jane took a steadying breath. 'You are very kind,' she said, her voice shaking.

The woman nodded. 'Quiet as a mouse up there, My Lady... least until the hullabaloo dies down. You can trust us. We'll keep your secret and keep you safe.'

As exhausted as Winifred was, Jane felt new energy coursing through her fatigued and frail body as her host found a fresh skip in her step. She nearly ran up the four flights of narrow steps into the gods of this tall slum. She knocked on the door, feeling a fresh ringing in her ears, unsure of whether it was from the climb or the excitement.

'Who is it?' William asked.

'Me.'

The door was flung back and there he was, grinning as wide as he stood broad.

Emotion surged. 'You still have rouge on your cheeks.' She wept, but laughing through her tears. Winifred reached to touch his face where Jane had slapped it. 'I'm sorry I had to—'

'Hush, my love. It was necessary to startle a man from his pride.'

Jane allowed herself to be held as Winifred for a long time. Nothing needed to be said that was any more meaningful than a close embrace; two people hugging, their cheeks feeling the warmth of each other's neck, communicated it all. Besides, she had never felt more in need of a congratulatory hug in her life as she did in this moment, suspended between a husband and the wife who loved him enough to risk her security, reputation, financial status... even her life.

And all that went through her mind while in this blissful embrace was a treacherous yearning for the touch of Julius, in whose memory she lost herself while she allowed Winifred and William this intimacy.

Cecilia broke the spell between the loving couple.

'Forgive me,' she said, stepping out of the shadows of the tiny room. She cleared her throat and dabbed tears from her eyes. 'Mr Mills left earlier and now I shall leave you both too. There is wine and some bread and cheese left by the landlady for a modest supper. I will come tomorrow with more news, after the executions have taken place.'

'Dear Cecilia. What a faithful friend and co-conspirator you have been; brave to the last,' she said as Winifred embraced her friend. 'Thank you for everything.'

'Look after her, My Lord,' she said to William, nodding at his diminutive wife. 'I have never known such fierce courage or strength of will. She just took control of the situation and has been strong for everyone.'

'I am a lucky man,' he admitted, kissing his wife's hand and giving a short bow to Cecilia. 'To have both of you,' he added.

Cecilia was probably blushing, Jane thought, but it was impossible to tell in this low candlelight as she was kissed farewell.

'Until tomorrow, dear. Rest,' said Cecilia, although her little smile suggested she thought it might be the last thing on Winifred's mind. Jane's thoughts were suddenly arrested... no, no, that would not do. Surely she wasn't going to have to lie back and think of England – or Scotland, in this case?

Mercifully, William insisted she rest after Cecilia's departure.

'I am fatigued,' she admitted.

'No, you are beyond fatigue,' he noted. 'And I feel fever in your cheeks. It is time I took care of you again. You are an incredibly brave, clever woman.'

Winifred asserted herself strongly, taking the response away from Jane. 'William, I do not wish to ever let you go.'

'Be assured. I am never letting go again. I love my faith, Winnie darling, but I know I will be forgiven for saying that I love you and our children more.'

Excitedly sharing the evening's events in whispers, they sipped from a single wine glass and ate sparingly. Neither had any appetite as, inevitably, the conversation moved to the men who had not been so lucky. Jane wanted to retreat, to become an observer, but despite Winifred's determination to claim back her body she was not yet strong enough.

'William, why here?' Jane asked, her gaze roaming the damp, claustrophobic room. 'I think your cell in the Tower was bigger.'

He nodded. 'I paced it out. It is indeed a larger space next door,' he said, dryly referring to his cell. 'Mr Mills had found a place in Smithfield, but I insisted that I needed to be close to Tower Hill.'

'Is that wise?' she asked carefully.

'Truly, Win, do you imagine the Constable will think to look in the Tower Hamlets?'

She shook her head with dawning understanding. 'If you have even been discovered missing yet, he's already lost hours. I imagine he will think immediately of the docks.'

'Precisely. What's more, I think Moseley will not discover me missing until the early hours of tomorrow, and then he will most likely not even bother looking for me. He'll presume I'm already sighting the coastline of France.'

'So we lie low here, you mean?'

William nodded. 'We can sneak out in a few days when the executions are past.' He sighed, looking suddenly bereft. 'Lord Derwentwater is so young,' he moaned. 'At least I had experienced life and love.'

'He looked very composed during the sentencing,' she said carefully.

'That is because I suspect Derwentwater has more courage than all of us put together, save my darling wife. The worst is that he is not especially religious. He joined the rebellion on the anxious bidding of his wife and her family, who are pious to the point of being zealots.' He gave a grimace. 'His life was set, his future bright. Yet he threw his lot in with the Jacobites very likely against his better judgement.'

Jane felt guilt tighten in Winifred's throat. 'I met one of his acquaintances on the journey.'

'Oh, yes?'

'A man by the name of Julius Sackville. Lord Sackville, in fact. Have you heard of him?'

William frowned as he thought. 'I've heard of him, yes. Extremely wealthy man, I recall; our fathers may have known each other. I think Derwentwater mentioned he was hoping to see his friend, but Sackville was not allowed to visit. I gather he was at the sentencing – not that I know what he looks like.'

'It is sad that I too did not get a chance to wish him well in London,' Jane admitted, more to herself than to William Maxwell. 'I believe that was the only reason he was headed to London, and it was how we met.' Not wishing to discuss Julius any further, she looked to change the subject. 'And Kenmure? How does he fit in?'

William was easily directed away from the subject of Sackville. 'Kenmure is in his fifth decade and deeply involved in the plot for a French invasion; he was the representative to Saint-Germain, carrying messages between France and Scotland.'

'So he deserves to answer for his role?'

'I do not believe any of us should have to answer in the way that the English king decrees! But Kenmure chose to be involved, desperately wanted to be a leader in the plot to overthrow the English throne and allow France its sway. Derwentwater was somehow innocent, almost childlike in his swash and buckle.'

'Does Kenmure have family?'

'Yes, indeed. His tragedy is that he was appointed commander of the lowland forces when he had no military experience behind him. He was doomed to fail, and leaves behind a wife of just five years and four young bairns – three sons and a daughter.' William sighed. 'I wish I could—'

'Do not utter it, William,' she forbade. 'I do not even know where the other peers are lodged.'

He nodded. 'Mayhap their wives simply do not love them enough,' he said, trying vainly to lighten the misery threatening to settle around them. 'Come, let me sleep next to you once more, darling Winnie, so I can reassure myself this is no dream.'

They lay down together, fully clothed, in the tiny single cot, somehow finding a comfortable position as only those in love can. Not even the smell of boiled cabbage wafting up from the bowels of the tenement spoiled Winifred's and William's pleasure at being together, and out of the axeman's reach.

They rested in silence for a few minutes before his deep voice whispered to her. 'I must say, Win, my love, I had no idea you had an ear for such colourful language,' he said, recalling her anger of earlier that evening. The bed began to shake with their laughter and Jane wondered if poor Winifred would ever live down her guest's vulgar tongue.

Minutes later, Jane felt Winifred lose consciousness, drifting into exhausted sleep. She was glad of the silence, thrilled by the rhythmic breathing of handsome William next to her and the feeling of his hard, strong body curled around Winifred. She imagined longing to be back in Will's arms and hated the way the image that flashed into her mind was of Julius Sackville's hard, strong body curled around her in bed. Filled by guilt, Jane gave up all attempts to remain awake and succumbed to Winifred's deep slumber.

William Maxwell, Earl of Nithsdale, woke, startled, to the sound of a mournful bell tolling, and recalled as best he could the curious dream he had experienced. He had been drowning, or drowned. He thought he had been lying on a riverbed… seabed, perhaps? He had believed he could see light from the sun refracted and the water shifting above. He had been in darkness, but the more keenly he tried to reach it, the more the light he sought had beckoned to him from above.

The detail had already fled. Had he seen a hand reach down from the sky? Had someone urged him to grab it? His mind was too blurred. He thought he might have clasped the hand and sped, ascending at breathless speed, to break through the water's mirror-like surface. And throughout it all he had heard a rhythmic noise. He couldn't recognise it, had never heard a sound like it previously: a persistent, shrieking beep!

And as his eyes had snapped open, fearful, his lungs gasping silently for breath, he had turned, relieved, to see a familiar shape. *Darling Winifred.* The dream was gone already, slipping from his thoughts like tendrils of mist disappearing beneath the sun's warmth. And the sound he could hear was the distant toll of a bell.

Robin glanced at his watch without breaking stride and Big Ben, as if hearing his thought, chimed the hour. Time in that moment instantly aligned, as he had known it would. He smiled into a restaurant window that he passed by and his reflection, rather than showing a smallish, spare man in a striped designer scarf, actually showed a laundrywoman of centuries previous. He glimpsed Robyn looking back at him, and as the clock tolled, he knew the two William Maxwells had woken.

At the stroke of the hour, Will Maxwell found awareness. He thought he had heard a bell tolling mournfully; he reached toward it, and it felt as though he were pushing through water, searching for something. What was it? What was he seeking? His first thought was, *It's sounding my death knell.* But then he swam to full consciousness.

He was too scared to open his eyes initially. There was a

sudden overload of sensory information. The bell he thought he'd heard was the insistent beep of a machine! Around him were muted voices, busy, as though working. He knew he was lying down and the bed was uncomfortable. Light was coming from his left, but it too was dulled, like the voices. And even they had become silent now, as though the people had stepped back.

The murkiest, most distant of thoughts rode away too. He thought he heard himself whispering the name Winifred. But that disappeared as a louder voice murmured close to where he lay. 'Here he comes. Hello, handsome.'

Will Maxwell opened his eyes on a new year and an unfamiliar face.

'Will. I'm Ellen, your nurse. Welcome back. Your family's here.'

The gorgeous smile of a stunningly pretty nurse moved away, to be replaced by someone he did recognise.

'Hi, son.' For perhaps the first time ever, Will saw his father's prominent jaw tremble with emotion. He also saw that his father had aged.

'Where's Mom?' he croaked.

'Right here,' she cried, and he turned his head slowly to regard his mother. She too looked a decade older; her hair was not teased up, and her make-up was minimal and tear-stained.

In the distance, beyond his mother, stood the nurse, who smiled again at him and dabbed away a tear. He could just read her badge.

'Hello, Ellen,' he said, and winked.

She giggled and touched her heart, tapping her hand against it to show him it was pounding slightly faster just for him.

Will Maxwell grinned.

THIRTY-ONE

JANE WOKE TO THE SOUND OF A voice and realised Winifred felt gluey-eyed and disoriented, blinking several times in panic, first at the unfamiliar ceiling and then, as reality asserted itself, at the emptiness of her tiny cot.

'William!'

'Here, my darling,' he said, suddenly at her side. 'Our loyal landlady sent up some fresh water.' He offered her a cup. 'Have a drink. You must be parched.'

She sipped, still rubbing away the sleep, and watched his lean figure, stripped to breeches and shirt, move back to where he'd presumably been standing by the narrow turret window. Jane felt Winifred shiver and she reached for the cloak beneath which she'd slept, the one in which her husband had escaped. She put it on, knowing it dragged slightly on the floor, also looking around for the chamber pot. How far had she come that she not only considered a chamber pot thoroughly normal but was also happy to consider spending a very urgent penny in front of a man?

'Over there.' He grinned, noticing her urgency, and pointed to the corner, where a small screen stood.

Jane soon joined William at the turret's single window, made up of small grimy panes that slightly distorted the view. She linked Winifred's hand in his. She was a little frightened to follow his fixed gaze, knowing precisely where he was staring. Digging for her courage, she unearthed it again, and bit her lip hard to remind herself that she could do this. She'd already seen plenty of dead men on this journey. The pain flashed brightly, waking her fully, and she looked down from their all-too-horribly-clear vantage point onto Tower Green, where a mob had already gathered.

She leaned helplessly against William, her composure suddenly lost. He reached a long arm around his wife's shoulder, pulling her as close as he could, and kissed her head with reassurance.

And yet it was Jane who felt the need to offer comfort. 'You must not feel guilty,' she murmured.

'I have to admit to having woken with anything but guilt. And that is what is making me feel shame. Am I despicable in feeling relief that it is to be them and not me?'

She shook her head, sickened at the thought of what he might have faced. 'Natural rather than despicable. But had you woken within your cell at the Tower rather than here, I know you would have rallied the last of your courage and faced your executioners bravely.'

He sighed. 'I hope I would have remained stoic to the end. What if I had not? What if—'

'William, stop! You are here, not there. You cannot change it. And you cannot change the outcome of their destiny.'

'That was my destiny, though,' he persisted gloomily.

'I adjusted it,' Jane pressed. 'Let it be. That someone has cheated the executioner's axe is a triumph.'

He nodded. 'I hope the other lords see it that way.'

'We shall not have this discussion again. We all made choices, me included.'

He brushed his lips against hers, then looked away, distracted. 'Yes, but as much as this will gall you, I must bear witness to their suffering.'

'Why?' Jane asked, shrinking back into Winifred.

'It is right to do so. They were brave at Preston, stoic at the trial and now must find still more courage for a grisly death.

I can surely show similar mettle for them from a distance.'

She swallowed. It was obvious he expected her to do the same. She nodded. 'I am not sure I can bear to.'

'We both must.'

The King's secretary arched a dark eyebrow. 'He has been in a fearful rage.'

Though his mouth was already uncomfortably dry, Sir George Moseley, Lord Constable of the Tower, could not raise even a fleck of spittle to ease the lump of shame that sat like an internal accuser at the back of his throat. He gave a small, parched cough. 'I take full responsibility, of course.'

The secretary managed to raise the same eyebrow even higher, so it appeared as a small arrow pointing to his wig, which was powdered and combed back viciously from his furrowed forehead. 'He is convinced that this event could not have occurred without connivance.'

Moseley baulked, and could not find the words within him to express his surprise at such an accusation. The secretary saved him the trouble of searching for them, making a calming gesture to dampen down the Constable's rising outrage.

'Sir George, *your* loyalty is not in question, but you are required to face His Majesty and give your explanation. I recommend you say it in as few words as possible. You know the King does not like to converse in English. I shall translate for you into French.'

'Of course. Thank you,' he said, covering his feeling of disdain at having to use French in the English court by lowering his head in a polite bow.

'Follow me.'

He was led into the sumptuous chambers of the King's closet and his gaze immediately picked out the man, wearing a long, grey wig that towered so high above his head it added inches to his otherwise short figure. He was positioned near the fire, but bore a stance that suggested he was indifferent to its warmth.

His flabby cheeks were certainly aflame, but with fury. Apples of bright colour punctuated a pale, powdered face with a distinctively broad, straight Hanoverian nose. The fleshy, normally cherubic mouth looked pinched at this early hour of the morning, long before even the first birds were thinking of welcoming the dawn. An imperious glare radiated from eyes like two dark pebbles, smaller than usual, partly from fatigue, but mostly from anger – and all of it directed at Sir George, who blinked beneath this barely disguised wrath.

The King said nothing. He did not need to. The question was already posed, already waiting for Sir George's answer; it sat like a tethered monster, straining at a leash held by the King.

Moseley dropped into a reverential bow, eyes facing the parquet floor. The secretary attempted a tight smile that lifted the corners of his mouth slightly, but fell just as quickly, as if like the weight of a man on the end of a noose. 'Sir George,' he began, his voice laden with tension. 'Perhaps you'd like to give His Majesty your account.'

It was a relief to finally be permitted to speak. Moseley cleared his throat, refused himself the cowardice of glancing around and instead found the courage to fix his gaze on the angry man before him. He spoke precisely, recounting the events as they'd been reported to him by the head yeoman, pausing only while the secretary swiftly translated into French.

At no time during this translation did the King's penetrating stare leave Sir George. The room was still, pregnant with rage, the only movements seeming to be the dancing flames behind the King and the lips of the secretary opening and closing.

His Majesty fired something back at the secretary in rapid French, his tone filled with disgust.

'The King demands that the five warders on duty be relieved of their positions and not permitted to set foot in the Tower of London again in any capacity.'

Sir George considered the families of the men he would now

be condemning to poverty unless he could help them find other work. He was particularly sad at the loss of Hugh, his head yeoman – a genuinely good man, who treated prisoners with respect. While the secretary and King shared a few muttered words that were not translated for him, Moseley totted up in his mind that the men being dismissed had nearly a century of service to the Tower between them. It would be a grave loss of important experience and loyalty.

None deserved to lose their positions. Lady Nithsdale had schemed more admirably than any man, in his opinion. Her plan, so simple – comic, in fact – had fooled his men because she had seemed so helpless from the outset. A reticent woman who, though stoic in her emotions, had not showed even a speck of the cunning that she brought to the Tower behind her gentle, indeed fragile façade. Perhaps he should have guessed at her mettle, knowing of the journey she had made from north to south in conditions that would have sent most men scampering for the closest inn.

In fact, now that he considered the Countess, he could not help a vague feeling of wonder. Who could not admire her under the circumstances, especially as she'd managed to mock the king who had treated her so discourteously?

The two men had finished their murmurings and throats were being cleared.

Sir George nodded to the secretary. 'Please inform His Majesty that I, of course, formally tender my resignation.'

The King surprised him by replying to him directly, and in English. 'That will not be necessary,' he said in a mellow voice, which was disconcerting because his expression was still shaded with anger.

If his generosity in this regard was unexpected, his next words were perplexing.

'For a man in Lord Nithsdale's situation,' King George continued in perfect, though halting, English, 'it was the very best thing he could have done.'

The King turned away, and with a quick nod from the secretary, Sir George was ushered hurriedly from the chamber.

'I am afraid His Majesty does not extend quite the same munificence to Nithsdale's daring wife,' the secretary explained.

'She did what any loyal and loving wife might wish to do, but most would lack the capacity and courage.'

'Indeed,' the secretary said, sounding indifferent as he led Moseley through the various corridors back to the side entrance through which he had arrived. 'However, the Countess has injured His Majesty's pride, and her behaviour has seriously compromised his reputation at court.'

Moseley sighed. 'I am sure she did not mean anything more than to win his attention.'

'She certainly achieved that, and with it an immeasurable proportion of sympathy within the court, which has made itself felt as criticism of the Crown. If anything, Nithsdale's escape has likely saved His Majesty a headache.' A mirthless smile ghosted his face fleetingly. He cleared his throat. 'In fact, the King has been heard to say that the Countess has done him more of a favour than any other woman in Christendom, for I suspect that executing the husband would have only worsened His Majesty's position.'

Moseley sighed again. In spite of the King's anger, which he now realised was almost entirely directed at a small, beautiful woman who happened to love her husband enough to risk everything, it seemed the King and his secretary agreed, as did he, that Nithsdale's flight was a solution to a problem.

'I know you should wait for the official paperwork to be served, Sir George, but I should also inform you that Lords Widdrington, Nairne and Carnwath will be spared the King's justice. His Majesty has signed their reprieves.'

Moseley could not be sure if his shoulders really sagged with the relief he felt at this news. 'And Kenmure and Derwentwater?' he asked, hope in his voice.

The man shook his head. 'I am afraid no reprieve for that

pair, or for Nithsdale. I hope the border lord has the good sense to already be on the seas to his beloved France, for there will be a hefty price on his head.'

The Tower's constable was not concerned with Lord Nithsdale any more; the man was safe, he presumed, and if his wife was cunning enough to extract him from the country's most lauded fortress under the noses of a host of yeoman warders, she was smart enough to keep him hidden wherever they were.

No. His sorrows were now for the two remaining lords, who must confront the direst of fates. He knew Derwentwater had been feeling confident of a reprieve; he was English, after all, and so enormously wealthy and influential that he had been sure the King would pardon him and put his renewed loyalties to better use in the north.

'I had better tell Lord Derwentwater to prepare his speech for the scaffold, then,' he said, by way of taking his leave from the palace.

The secretary gave a shrug. 'They are to be executed as arranged.'

Moseley nodded. Five hours.

THIRTY-TWO

GUARDS HAD BEEN ASSEMBLED FOR HOURS, MILLING around Tower Hill and joking with the gathering crowd, keeping people away from the main platform. Jane could see it would be visible from the specially erected, railed gallery, draped in black fabric to shroud the prisoners on their last and longest walk.

Her gaze shifted to the block on the fateful platform, hulking beneath a pall of black serge while nervous tension and excitement escalated around it. It would be the focus of all attention soon enough.

A fresh wave of nausea trembled through her. It was pointless asking William to spare her this. She could pretend to faint, feign despair, run from the turret room even, but his words haunted her. There was surely something important in solemnly bearing witness to the death of these men.

'Derwentwater will be first,' William said, his voice a choked version of what she knew. It dragged her from her misted thoughts to the horrible present, and her eyes searched the platform, finding the spot where the young English earl had just emerged from beneath the walkway to stand pale but outwardly calm.

They watched him unroll a paper and read from it. In Jane's reckoning, it took less than a minute for him to say what he wanted… whatever that was. She watched, helplessly mesmerised, as the shroud was lifted, the block was revealed and the young, handsome noble walked over to it. He bent and inspected it, rubbing his fingers across its surface.

Jane felt the fear building inside her and making her lightheaded. Breath was, in fact, hard to find… it was trapped somewhere in the cage of Winifred's chest, so that it vaguely hurt Jane to inhale.

She watched with dread fascination as Derwentwater handed his parchment to a man who, William explained, was the Sheriff of London. Then the condemned lord exchanged a few words with the executioner as he pointed to the six-inch-high block.

William Marvell had hanged a number of men since the day he had been recruited from John Robbins's smithy. All of them had been villains, and he had become familiar with, and to some degree hardened to, the struggles of men desperately clinging to the last breath of life. But until this third week of February in the year of 1716 he had not been called upon to smite a man's head from his shoulders.

Now the true test was upon him.

He had never been squeamish. Animals lived and died, so did people. Today he was required only to behead the condemned rather than take them through the brutal, agonising process of being hanged, drawn and quartered. The relief at the news was evident in the breath he blew out when the Constable of the Tower had reconfirmed earlier in the morning that it was to be swift deaths for all.

'You will execute them cleanly,' Moseley had ordered, grim-faced, when they had met an hour previous. 'These are good men, men loyal to their cause. But they have defied the Crown of England and must now pay the price demanded for that treachery. One blow, Marvell. The crowd requires no entertainment.'

Marvell nodded wordlessly.

I presume, Marvell, if you swing a hammer as well as your employer asserts, that you can also swing an axe? The words haunted him. He could now swing an axe with reliable accuracy. But the neck of a man was different from a marrow or a log, which he'd found more useful for testing his skills than a pumpkin.

He watched the young lord, not even close to completing his third decade, take him in with a dazzling smile. Marvell wondered how this good-looking man, whose golden life was about to be snuffed out, found the wherewithal to smile at his executioner. He could not answer his own question, and instead watched the handsome, finely attired fellow pass his hand over the block.

The haunted look the young lord had arrived with had been chased away when he took his chance to read the speech he had prepared. He claimed that friends had persuaded him to act for the Jacobites and that he was now sorry, although he also claimed to die for his king – without mentioning which one, Marvell noted.

Now the doomed man approached him.

'What is your name, headsman?' Derwentwater asked, fixing him with a blue gaze. His eyes, Marvell noticed, were understandably widened in a state of shock.

He told him.

'And when you're not killing people, Marvell, what do you do?'

'I am a blacksmith, My Lord.'

'An honest profession.'

Marvell said nothing. He had learned that doomed men liked to speak, to make friends with their executioner. The jauntiness was usually forced and underpinned with terror, but for someone like the noble before him, it was also driven by a need to save face for his family, to have the rumour-mongers admit he looked death in the eye with courage.

'Do you have a family?'

'No, My Lord, but with today's —' He hesitated, deeply conscious of what was about to occur.

'With the price of my head?' Derwentwater prompted, as though curious to hear more.

'Yes, My Lord. With the fee I shall make sufficient to return to my village, put a ring on the finger of my sweetheart and start my own smithy.'

'Good, very good, William Marvell. It pleases me to think the chopping off of my head has a purpose,' he murmured. 'Hold your new wife close... and your children closer when they arrive. They are precious. Little else matters.'

'I shall, My Lord,' he promised.

'Now, headsman, if you don't mind, would you smooth off that protuberance on the block, lest it offend my neck?'

Marvell moved to the block and felt for the roughness, which Lord Derwentwater carefully pointed out. He obliged, chipping it away to smoothness.

'Thank you.' The young lord smiled, but his eyes had lost their glassiness now and were dull with the fearful certainty of his mortality. His voice sounded higher, nervous. He stepped closer to his executioner. 'Make it swift, please, Marvell,' he said, only for William's hearing. 'You will find a pair of guineas in this pocket. My payment to you.' He turned away to remove his coat and waistcoat, both fashioned from velvet as black as soot. 'If you would not mind...' he said to Marvell, removing his yellow-gold wig and handing it to him. 'By all means keep it. I am sure I shall have no further use for it.'

Marvell now realised that during this small drama unfolding on the platform, he had been acutely unaware of the crowd, and that was mainly because a hush had overtaken what would normally have been a noisy mob. He glanced around, too embarrassed to watch as the young lord kneeled down and began to position himself for a clean end. He took in the tense faces of the people assembled to witness the death of a man he understood to be popular with the masses. The women below the scaffolding looked sad, a few already dabbing at their eyes, while the men seemed appropriately solemn. This only made him feel more anxious. It would have been different if he were to have botched his first beheading on someone the crowd was jeering at; it would only have heightened the experience for them.

Marvell hefted the axe into his hands from where it had been resting. Derwentwater had taken his time arranging himself on his belly and placing his neck over the indented curve in the block so that he would not see the blow coming. He had also begun to murmur a prayer.

It was time.

Marvell took a final steadying moment to glance at the blade, and the way it glinted as the watery sunlight of winter caught its edge. Once again he was assured it was keen.

The blow required speed, but not too much power. His main jobs were to remain accurate and keep his weight steady to ensure a smooth swing. He could see the spot on the man's slim neck that he needed to hit and he must not be distracted by the crowd's gasp as the axe was raised. He would keep his promise to dispatch the generous lord without mess.

Marvell took a deep breath and held it as he stepped forward and raised the axe high over his own head at a perfect distance from Derwentwater.

He heard the last few words uttered: '... receive my soul!' He saw the man stretch out his arms, which was the signal he'd been given, and allowed the axe to fall.

The closest Jane had come to watching death was when their dear family dog, aged fourteen and filled with arthritic pain, was 'given his wings', as her father had described it to his teenage daughters. 'It's because we love Pirate that we can do this,' he explained, while Juliette sobbed noisily and Jane wept silently. 'He understands. He wants the release from pain, girls. He's only putting up with it for us... because we won't let him go. But now we have to.' Juliette had bawled louder, but Jane had dried her tears and nodded.

'I don't want him to suffer any more,' she'd whispered, and her father had given her a soft, sad smile.

'That's my girl. I know I can count on you to be brave.'

She had not averted Winifred's gaze when she saw Derwentwater put his hands out, presumably the signal for the executioner to deliver the fatal blow. And she had not shrieked when the circular motion of the headsman's arms brought the axe high above his head, so that it came down at great velocity, gathering strength to cleave in a single chop the boyish-looking Jacobite lord's head from his shoulders.

She knew it must have been lopped off, but didn't see it roll or drop. Jane had wondered whether she would gag when the headsman lifted it before the crowd. She'd read somewhere that, contrary to popular notion, this wasn't to earn the crowd's approval, or even as part of the entertainment. No, the head was displayed because people believed, during this style of execution, that the brain took nine seconds or so to make the right connections as to what had occurred. And in those seconds, the Crown wanted the victim's remaining consciousness to suffer the final horror of what had taken place.

Jane watched the executioner – a huge man with arms like a weightlifter's, hair tied back in a black queue and a rough beard to match – bend to lift the head from wherever it had landed. She saw him raise it by its straggly blond hair, first facing outward to show Derwentwater's dying gaze to the awed crowd, and then turned to face its own headless body.

It was then, as the head was turned, that Jane's gaze took in the crumpled features of the formerly cheerful, wide-eyed young man, and the full horror overcame her. She gagged and sent Winifred's body running toward the latrine.

'It is done,' she heard William murmur, his voice choked. 'I hope he was never told that I escaped.'

Jane knew Winifred wanted to be by her husband's side, and took a deep breath before returning to take his hand. She arrived in time to see mourners – likely Derwentwater's own retinue – mounting the scaffold, kicking up sawdust as they moved slowly and deliberately to wrap up his head. She noticed the executioner handle the head with care and obvious respect as he placed it in the white linen they held out. She wondered about the life of an executioner. Did this man suffer nightmares because of his work? Did he enjoy it? Was it a means to an end? She couldn't make out the detail of his features, but the fact that he hadn't glorified the process or made any sensation of his own role suggested to her that he possessed some degree of dignity.

Someone has to do it, she heard, as her thoughts cannoned around. She absently let her gaze fall on the people who were gently moving around their lord's body, positioning it in a black shroud that from this distance looked to be fur – a sable, perhaps. She wondered about the executioner's home life. Did he love someone? Did he tell them the truth of his work? Did he go home to bounce gurgling infants on his knees? Did he take care to change and wash so the blood of the victims never entered his home?

This will send you mad, Jane, she heard herself warn. She raised Winifred's shoulders and let them drop deliberately as she exhaled, hoping to push out the tension that had built up.

'He was so brave,' she said, squeezing William's arm, knowing he needed her to say something to comfort him.

'I hope I would have gone to my death just as James did. He was impressive to the end.' She watched his jaw clench.

'The punishment was commuted to a swift death, and for this we should be grateful. Imagine if the King had kept his promise to follow through on hanging, drawing and quartering!'

But William was not paying her sympathetic words any attention. 'Such a pitiful waste!'

'It *is* a waste, which is why talk of whether you should have faced the block is pointless. Look at them, William,' she said, pointing to the crowd. 'They have already forgotten your friend Derwentwater. They are ready to watch Kenmure's end. There was never anything to be gained by facing the King's justice.

The death of these two men is simply to satisfy an angry man and ease his embarrassment that the Jacobites achieved what they did. He is using this scaffold to make an entirely different statement from what he claims. This is surely about a German impressing upon the British that he is here to stay and does not care even to speak the language of the country he rules. And that he will crush any rebel who moves against him.'

'Then surely my escape is a further humiliation. He will hunt me down until he kills me anyway.'

She tipped Winifred's head one way and then the other as she considered this. 'Does he really care? He has shocked the people by beheading two of the most popular Jacobite lords. The fact that a third got away is irrelevant. And I suspect we might have done him a curious favour. From what I gather, my behaviour at St James's Palace won sympathy with the courtiers, while his own conduct alienated him. He'll probably be relieved not to have to execute the man whose wife has become a folk hero to London society. And the ordinary people love it when a rogue gets away with it.'

It was William's turn to sigh. 'But will he forgive you?'

She shrugged. 'Now, *that* I doubt, which is why we must leave.'

'When?'

'They will already be looking for us. However, I do believe there is some validity to the notion of permitting the blood of the Jacobites spilled on Tower Hill to dry and allowing the sting of your escape to dissipate, and the wound of my behaviour to scab over. The King wants this episode to be gone from the public consciousness. In a few days, they will stop keeping a keen eye on the docks, or on the roads north, and we can make our move then.'

'Where are we going?'

'Well, I suspect that they will be looking for the Nithsdales to head to Scotland or France, for even we know that to remain in Britain is to oblige the Crown to recapture you.'

'We should make for neither, then.'

She nodded. 'I've already been discussing this with Mrs Mills. I shall ask her to book us passage to Italy.'

THIRTY-THREE

It was Mrs Mills, not Cecilia, who slipped into William and Winifred's frigidly cold room late that night. They had decided it might draw attention if anyone recognised Cecilia from her previous visit.

Winifred was sickening again, gently pushing away William's concerned hands, when a knock sounded at the door.

The beheading of the plainly attired Lord Kenmure had been the opposite of that of the flamboyant Derwentwater in nearly all respects, other than that Kenmure also behaved calmly. Derwentwater had grabbed at this final opportunity to press his case; Kenmure, however, had declined the invitation and simply moved to the southern end of the platform to say a brief prayer.

Jane had seen the executioner nod as Lord Kenmure first kissed his supporters farewell and then appeared to refuse assistance to remove his coat and waistcoat. He did accept a strip of white linen, which he tied around his head to hold back his hair, and ensure the man beheading him had a clear view for the fatal strike. She'd watched him pass what were presumably coins into the executioner's hand and they had exchanged a few words.

She recalled now how she had begun tasting acid at the back of her throat as she had seen the man with the axe open a hand, almost reluctantly, and gesture toward the block. It had been such a polite action, gracious and gentle in its movement.

William next to her had been rigidly still. She'd found no further words of comfort to soothe his guilt.

It seemed Lord Kenmure had not wanted to prolong his personal agony, for he'd immediately obliged the executioner and stretched out his hands. The headsman, she recalled, had possibly been caught unawares by his victim's readiness and, although the axe swung just as before, this time it missed its mark. Perhaps Kenmure had shifted. That discussion would be left for debate in the inns and brothels, coffee houses, gin houses and tea salons of London. Kenmure's body had jerked on impact and a spout of blood had erupted, but the stubborn head had not toppled. She remembered how Kenmure's legs had scrabbled against the straw and sawdust and the headsman had briskly raised his axe again. The lord's head had been lopped on the second strike and the grisly task of allowing Kenmure's gaze to fall upon his own headless body had been duly performed.

Winifred had stumbled away once again to retch repeatedly into the bucket behind the screen. Afterwards, empty and weak, she had sat on the cot and wondered.

Something had felt and still did feel wrong to Jane. She had thrown up enough times in her life to mark today as different. It had been too violent. There was an instinctive knowledge within that her sickening had not entirely been in response to what she'd witnessed.

How long had it been since Winifred's last bleed? She couldn't remember. Winifred had been so sick these last moons that she'd probably put any doubts down to illness. But her bleeding must have stopped long before they left Scotland.

You're pregnant? Jane asked, but Winifred didn't answer, returning their attention to William.

'It was the necessity for the two blows required to remove Kenmure's head that unnerved you, my love,' he said, and she did not dare tell him she had closed her eyes for the second blow and was so glad she had. The only reason she had known the next strike had succeeded was because of the groan of relief from the crowd.

She could still hear that groan, even while Mrs Mills was fussing with her gloves, first pulling them off and then realising it was just as cold inside this tiny room as outside and slowly edging them back onto her pale, long fingers.

'I made sure I was not followed,' she puffed, having walked hurriedly up the stairs. 'Besides, everyone who knew you were staying with me, Countess, believes you have long fled the city. I have made sure not to dissuade them of this notion.'

Winifred hugged her. 'Why have you risked coming?' She frowned.

'For very good reason. I heard this evening that although pardons have been granted to Lords Widdrington, Nairne and Carnwath, the Crown has put a high price on *your* head, My Lord.'

Jane and William exchanged fearful glances.

'You have got away with something impossibly daring, my dear friend, but I suspect you should not test your luck. It is imperative you both leave the country.'

Jane nodded. 'You and I discussed Italy,' she said to her friend.

'Indeed we did. And I have already taken the liberty of contacting someone I know who works in the Venetian Embassy.' Her anxious gaze flicked between the pair of them. 'I am confident we can get you across the Channel into France – where you will not tarry, but will take the help that I am sure will be extended by Queen Mary Beatrice and travel to Italy immediately. I suggest you leave for France tomorrow before first light.'

'Only William leaves,' Jane corrected, surprising even herself by this remark and realising Winifred was genuinely beginning to assert herself.

They both stared at her, slightly open-mouthed.

'Is everyone forgetting our daughter Anne? Plus our family is now moving into exile. We have important hidden papers and jewels that I must retrieve if we are to be able to salvage anything for our son.'

'We can send for Anne and perhaps my sister might unearth the papers, my darling. I don't think we should risk...' William trailed off.

Perhaps he and Mrs Mills could see in the set of Winifred's mouth that she was not to be contradicted on this. It was odd, Jane thought. She was not driving this notion; she would have been more than happy to flee the country just to put some space between herself and danger so she could regroup her thoughts and work out how to get back to the London of the 1970s. Right now, it was Winifred who was asserting herself. Jane had been aware, from time to time, of Winifred's re-emergence from wherever she had fled at the time of possession. Today, however, was the first time Jane had felt as though Winifred was totally present and taking control. *Jane, dearest*, she whispered now through their shared mind, *we must fetch Anne and the papers.*

Are you strong enough?

You make me strong.

Surely you detest my being here. I would.

You have saved my husband's life with your cunning strategies and derring-do and thus my life too, and you have protected my family's future. How could I detest you?

But you are back now?

I believe I am.

Does that mean I can now return?

Who knows, dear one? I hope for your sake as much as mine that it does. Nevertheless, I have to get back to Scotland and I hope you will help me.

'Surely you cannot mean to travel back to Scotland alone?' William asked, interrupting their curious internal conversation, a note of haughtiness in his tone now. Jane could tell he was being cautious; after all, his wife had proven repeatedly that she was more than woman enough for most challenges thrown at her. And then there was that slap... and the language. She could almost have chuckled at the memory. But she sensed that he was now asserting his familiar role as head of their family, the one who made the final decisions.

'That is exactly what I mean to do,' Jane said, Winifred's voice just as firm. 'I am not sending for our daughter, who could be used against us. I shall fetch her myself and bring her to safety, along with the family papers.'

'Then I shall—'

'No, William, you shall not!' *Definitely Winifred pushing herself forward*, Jane thought. 'You are a liability now. We must get you to safety. Too many people have risked too much to keep you alive. Do not throw that effort aside for the sake of pride. You are a hunted man and we shall put you into the hands of the Venetians immediately. I shall join you within weeks, but we must secure our future first.'

She looked to Mrs Mills, who had been following this conversation in silent awkwardness.

'Right, my dears. I shall make the necessary arrangements. Please be ready to leave in the secrecy of darkness. I shall send two sedans. You will need to say your farewells here, for you will be heading in separate directions. Countess, you will return to us at Duke Street for the moment.'

Jane nodded. She was excited at the promise of moving forward. She had a sense now that her own crossroads might be beckoning and she wanted to get to the marker as fast as she could.

If she was honest, she wanted to be rid of the Earl too. He was easy to be with, even easier on the eye, but her life was complex enough. Now she just had to get through another few hours without permitting his conjugal rights, but also without damaging his and Winifred's relationship.

They embraced Mrs Mills. 'Five o'clock is the hour.' They nodded. 'There is food and wine in that hamper.' She pointed to a small basket. 'Do not be seen on the street for any reason.

You are safe in here, my husband assures me, but outside there are men who would give you up for a crust of bread. My Lord, your likeness and description are detailed in *The Flying Post*, so please heed my warning.' She took them both in with an earnest gaze.

When she was gone, Jane made a show of sighing. 'Well, I suppose we must rest,' she said, guessing it must be closing on nine, as William lit another candle. He was quiet, hurting perhaps, and Winifred protested that her husband needed comfort. She ignored it, forcing Winifred aside. 'Go ahead and eat. I had enough earlier and am not the slightest bit hungry.'

'I am not either,' he said, and turned to regard her. Jane did not need to know William better to know what that look meant.

'Not now, my darling,' she began. 'Today has been filled with blood and sorrow.'

'Loving heals,' he murmured, taking Winifred's hands and kissing them tenderly before swiftly moving to her neck and earlobes, all the while clasping her tightly. Jane felt another swell of dizziness.

I cannot, she groaned.

You must, Winifred replied.

It's between you and him. She felt Winifred melting beneath his familiar kiss. *Please, Winifred, spare me this. This is unfair. It is already too complicated.*

Jane, dear, you *are the one who has complicated* my *life. Do you believe for a moment that I wish you to share this most private of activities? Do you forget Lord Sackville and how* I *was compromised?*

Inwardly, Jane shrank at the rebuke. She and Julius had *not* been alone. How could she have convinced herself otherwise?

Winifred knew her thoughts. *Lose yourself while I attend to the needs of my husband... and my own.*

It was over quickly and Jane did disappear, but when she re-emerged to find William snoring softly by Winifred's ear, her body cupped neatly between his chest and bent knees, a question burned to be asked.

Their skin was not touching anywhere except face level and hands, because both of them were fully clothed, ready to flee. They were also too fearful to undress in the frigidly cold air that whistled around their garret window and found cunning ways into the room to chill and nip at exposed flesh.

What time is it? Jane wondered.

Probably close to two, Winifred answered.

How can you know that?

Her host chuckled. *It is a curious knack I have had since childhood. I wish I could earn money from it*, Winifred said wistfully. *I wish I could earn at all, for we shall soon be penniless in exile, and dependent on the goodwill of other Catholics in Europe.*

There are plenty of those, Jane murmured. There was a moment's pause that felt awkward.

Forgive me for making you share that intimacy.

It was the opening she needed, and perhaps that was why Winifred offered it so readily. The question hung between them – it had to be asked. *Winifred, you are more present than you have been since I arrived.*

Yes.

I'm glad. I hope it is an indication that my time to leave you is upon us.

From where have you come, Jane? I have heard your thoughts now and then and not understood. Increasingly, though, I have grasped, I think, that you are from the future. She sounded deeply puzzled.

Jane told her just how far it was into the future that she had journeyed from.

More than two hundred years forward, Winifred breathed, astonished. *I cannot imagine it.*

No. *And I shall not try to explain what my time is like*. But she did tell her how it had occurred.

And so you are going to marry Will Maxwell? Winifred repeated, her tone full of amazement.

They are inextricably linked over generations, Jane replied, deflecting the question.

How extraordinary. I should not have been able to believe this had I not been the one to experience it. However, you did not answer my question. Do you really wish to marry him? I fear I sense only reluctance in you.

I must marry him.

Why?

Look at what I have done to make it possible.

That is no answer, Jane.

She gave a moue of disdain. *You live in an age – and a society – where you marry within your class structure for the right financial and family reasons.*

I also married for love. I suspect in any age romance is imperative. What is there without it?

Love. Jane said it as though it were a word she did not understand.

Do you love Will Maxwell?

I should.

You do not convince me. Loving – the romantic way – is akin to a sort of madness. Where you would not consider your own safety; where, if the question were tested, you would die for him.

There we are then. I risked my life for Will.

You risked your life for you, Jane. It is your life that matters to you, not his.

Do not say that. It took her breath away in a punch of pain to hear Winifred's accusation.

I have said it. I believe it. I have come to know you in this odd relationship of ours. You are trying to save yourself, not Will Maxwell. If you do marry him, it will be to make your life have some meaning, not because you understand what it is to love this man.

I disagree.

That is your prerogative. But I have seen you with someone else and I have shared your thoughts about Will. They do not come close. Your fiancé is infinitely less exciting to you than Julius Sackville. You may believe you've pushed him to the back of our mind, dear one, but I share that mind and he is ever-present in your thoughts. You can still feel his touch, his kiss. You will never forget that you lay down with him.

You are wrong, Winifred.

Am I? Then why are my cheeks burning with shame... your shame?

They'd come to the point where she had to ask: *Winifred, I lack your experience of it, but were you suggesting earlier that you are pregnant?*

There was only a small hesitation. *I have suffered many miscarriages during my marriage, Jane. But I have always known when I was with child, even from the earliest moment of quickening. My sickening is usually violent.*

You are sure it was nausea from pregnancy and not from... from the executions?

Even you are sure of that.

Jane sighed. Winifred was not letting her off the hook, but she didn't want to confront any more harsh truths right now. She could feel the nausea simmering like a bog in the pit of her stomach, looking for any excuse to bubble up. Enough had been said about her and Will. It was something she certainly didn't want to confront; she was deeply unhappy that Winifred had so deftly nailed her to her lies. Will was her life raft; she had to cling to him, or lose her mind. Julius and that sequence of events that she'd hoped, down the track, she might convince herself were almost a dream, an out-of-body experience, a symptom of being trapped by magic, just didn't count. No one would ever know about them once she left here, least of all Will, and over time she could learn to pretend they had happened to Winifred, not her. Besides, it was Winifred's face he'd loved,

Winifred's body he'd craved. He didn't know Jane at all.

Well, Jane said, *I am very happy for you, and I hope there are no problems with this pregnancy – although I suspect there will be fraught weeks ahead while you travel to Scotland and then sail to France.*

I shall not think on it, but simply do.

Another curiosity surfaced. Jane was not going to ask about it, but it was released into her thoughts before she could temper it. *I thought morning sickness, as we call it, only occurred in the early months.*

In my experience, that is correct.

But you have suffered from it throughout your pregnancy?

No. Winifred sounded guarded but also vaguely sly, as though she were leading Jane down a particular path.

I do not understand.

Do you not?

Jane mentally frowned as the sense of her own words thrummed around her, daring her to make the connections, to join the dots. *It was Winifred's body he'd craved*, she repeated. Then added: *Winifred's body he'd...* She didn't need a bright light to suddenly switch on. Acid leaked along the sides of Winifred's tongue, but it was from Jane's guilt. The sour taste of realisation was the initial sensation, then a slight buzzing in her mind; she wasn't sure exactly where, because it was hotly followed by the escalation of Winifred's heart rate.

It is Julius's child? she asked, deep shock trembling from her to Winifred and back again.

It cannot be anyone else's, Winifred replied, calm but not without emotion.

Jane gave an involuntary gasp, but Winifred did not make a sound; she was tightly controlling how this conversation played itself out through her body.

You're sure? Jane pressed, hearing her redundant, pathetically grasping tone, when she already knew Winifred would not lie.

Winifred answered her anyway. *You gave your consent to Julius when I was not in a position to deny him or you.*

Winifred... I... Shame, anger, disappointment collided. *I felt as though I had no control that day.*

Clearly.

Are you angry? Another doltish question.

Angry to be carrying a child? No. Angry that it is not my husband's? Yes! Angry that I feel defiled? Yes!

She said all of this without heat, suppressing the unneeded emotion as she had been doing, presumably, since that night in the inn when Julius first kissed her. Or maybe – and as she thought it, Jane believed herself right – Winifred could not have made her feelings known then because she had 'disappeared'.

What are you going to do? Jane wondered aloud, her voice small, self-conscious.

What can I do, except have the baby and love it? It is mine, after all. I am taking the approach that this is a divine reward for my desire to be a mother again: to give life and to love that new life without reservation.

Perhaps, as you have miscarried in the past, this child will not survive.

I wish that sorrow on no woman.

Of course. She could have bitten her own tongue out if it didn't belong to Winifred. What possessed her to say something as puerile as that? Especially given that one of the reasons she'd agreed to marry Will, she was sure, was so that she could have a family of her own? *Will you forgive me?*

For what? For your insensitivity, or for my pregnancy?

Both.

Without you, Jane, there would be no husband to love and raise this new child of ours.

But Julius?

Things said aloud, and actions taken, can never be undone. Each moment of the past is just that. He was your past, not mine.

I am not a promiscuous woman. I do not know what came over me. It was as though I were someone else.

At this they both chuckled a little sadly.

Perhaps you should think on it more. None of us acts without reason. As for me, my reason is a child. I have always wanted more than two and we have had our share of loss in this regard. William has suffered enough through this period, so I hope he doesn't bother to calculate. I have no control over that, but I will face the hurdles as they present themselves. If I can bear it, you can stop pouting over it too.

Even though it was a rebuke, it was still generous; was there no end to Winifred's magnanimity?

And if it is a daughter, I shall call her Jane.

I do not know what to say, other than that I will get you safely to Scotland.

Thank you, Jane, dear. I fear it is your strength that I shall have to rely on once more.

We shall not discuss Julius Sackville again, Jane finished, hoping that really was an end to it.

Except that the time you spent with Julius will remain in your memory for the rest of your life – whichever century, whichever body you walk in.

THIRTY-FOUR

JANE HADN'T SLEPT FOR THE REMAINDER OF the night, and through those hours she had felt Winifred's spirit weakening again and her body succumbing to the ever-prevalent fragility that stalked it. Once again, it would be up to Jane to remain strong for Winifred. There was no time for argument, even though Jane could see that William still wanted one.

It was Mr Mills who slipped into their room in the pre-dawn hours to explain the plan for William's escape.

'You are to be hidden in one of the servants' rooms at the Venetian Embassy.'

'For how long?' William frowned.

Mills shrugged, but it was Jane who answered. 'For however long it takes, William. We have not taken these risks to falter at the last. We want you safe in Europe.'

She could tell he loathed being pushed around and sensed his pride asserting itself. Perhaps his relief at being alive was already giving way to his dismay at being a man on the run. She could feel that guilt had become his shadow... he still felt shame in having cheated the headsman.

'William, please, for the sake of the Jacobites who still believe in the cause, for the sake of our son who will revere your courage and for the sake of the women – and gentleman,' she nodded at Mr Mills, 'who have risked their lives and continue to do so, stay alive whatever it takes.'

He looked pained and Mills retreated.

Jane had not wanted to tell William her news, but she knew a shock tactic was needed to snap him out of his unhelpful mood.

She pulled him to the window. 'I may be with child.' Jane could feel Winifred's horror, and did her best to reassure her. 'Do not ask me how I know. Women just know and I have been through it enough times to feel—'

'But it was only last night!' he murmured, searching her face for explanation.

She nodded. 'I said I *may* be. You know how easily I fall. And for that potentially wonderful event, I want you safe. I love you, William. What can you possibly gain by risking death when you can gain so much, and do so much for the cause, by defying King George and escaping his reach? Trust me now as you did before.'

He nodded, all the fire gone out of him. She let him hold her close. 'Forgive me my ingratitude,' he said more loudly, glancing at Mills over Winifred's head. 'It is not easy to keep allowing others to take the risks.'

'I understand, old man,' Mills said.

Jane pulled away. 'Now, let us listen to what has been planned.'

Mills cleared his throat. 'There will be a coach dispatched to Dover to meet the Venetian Ambassador's brother in a few days. The plan is for you, My Lord, to pretend to be one of the footmen travelling on the coach, wearing the Venetian livery.'

'And from Dover?' Jane asked.

'Our friend at the Embassy, a fellow called Vezzosi, will negotiate with the captain of a small vessel to take you across the Channel.'

William nodded. 'Thank you, Mr Mills. I shall probably go to Scots College in Paris, where my nephews can accommodate me quietly; I cannot wait to reunite with our son.'

'What about the Scottish royal family?' Jane asked.

'I shall see them, of course, if Queen Mary Beatrice will give me an audience at Saint-Germain-en-Laye. King James may even invite me to Avignon.'

Mills nodded. 'The sedans will be here by now. Come, my Lord Earl, Countess. The adventure begins...'

Jane kissed William, Earl of Nithsdale, for what she hoped was the last time and, ignoring Winifred's sorrow, urged him to go first down the stairs. 'I shall follow in a minute or so. Be safe, my beloved,' she whispered to his back.

It seemed a reward of two thousand pounds – an extraordinary sum of money – had been put on the head of Lord Nithsdale. But even more chilling was the news from Mrs Mills that the rumour around the court was that 'the Countess's head will answer for his'.

'Lie low, my dear,' she warned. 'In fact, because one too many people knows we are friendly, I'm moving you to an address in Drury Lane where you will be far more comfortable than you were at Tower Hamlets.' At Winifred's frowning expression, her friend added, 'I could not, of course, give a fig about my reputation. However, if the authorities began watching this house I would not wish to give anyone the opportunity of snatching you when you are so close to being safe. Stay at Drury Lane for a few days and then head for Scotland. You know I will help you.'

Reunited with Cecilia and in a new chamber, she whiled away two days in hiding until Mrs Mills got news to Winifred that William had safely left the country by ship and was already on French soil. They hugged and wept joyful tears.

'We did it!' Jane said to her friend.

'You did it, Winifred. Your plan was seamless, cunning and simple. Your lord husband should be very proud of you.'

She shrugged. 'Oh, I am not so sure about that. But at least now we are free to travel. Hopefully my letter to the Duchess of Buccleuch has paved the way for our safe arrival in Scotland.'

'I am still not sure that it was a wise idea to announce that you will be arriving.'

'Cecilia, I think despite the King's public anger, privately he is happily rid of me, William and all of us connected with the rebellion of last year. There is too much sympathy for the rebels' wives, so he is not about to attract any more negative attention by pursuing me. I suspect there is no proof of my implication in my lord husband's rescue. I have not paraded myself, asked for sympathy, or gloated at his escape. The Duchess knows I will studiously remain out of the public eye, and perhaps if she can convey that to the Solicitor General in Scotland, I might be allowed to return to Terregles without being taken into custody.'

Cecilia sighed. 'Do not hear me wrong, dearest. I think the precaution of writing ahead is clever, but it could go either way. If they see you, they will have no choice but to arrest you.'

'Which is why I shall travel in disguise, wearing a dark wig.'

'By coach?' Cecilia asked hopefully.

Jane pulled Winifred's neat mouth into a cunning grin. 'On horseback. We survived our rigorous journey through the depths of winter. Spring will be easy,' she said, hoping the milder weather would help Winifred's condition.

She let the thought remain idle, knowing Winifred would soon be in southern Europe where the sun shone for most of the year and she could look forward to brighter health.

Jane's predictions proved correct, and their return journey to Scotland passed much more smoothly than their slow passage to London weeks earlier. As Winifred and Cecilia arrived at Terregles, Jane noted that William's sister had already begun packing up the house.

As they tearfully hugged, it was Jane's former accomplice, the old gardener, who gave them the chilling news.

He stood by, his head hung, waiting for the right opportunity.

After pulling away from Mary, Jane turned to regard the man wringing an old cap in his hands. 'Hello, Bran.'

He tugged at his hair, bowing. 'You be a wonderful wee sight for sore eyes, My Lady. We are all most brightened by the news of My Lord's escape.'

Jane felt Winifred's warm smile broaden. 'Dear Bran. What news here?'

'There is often a foul wind a-stirring from the south, My Lady. And today is nae different. I have heard that soldiers have crossed the border.'

Jane blinked, trying to calculate. Winifred gave her the answer. Hours. 'Well, they will find this place bare of what they search for. Thank you, Bran. You know what to fetch.'

'Right away, My Lady,' he said, bowing again. 'I shall go and get my tools.'

'Mary, is Anne here?'

Her sister-in-law shook her head. 'I did not dare risk her precious life here with soldiers possibly crawling over the house. Anne is safe at Traquair House, where she awaits her mother.'

They watched Winifred put a hand to her chest in relief. 'I shall be but a few minutes with Bran. Cecilia, pack afresh. You know we can carry little with us. We will leave for Peebles immediately.' Jane was struggling to bear the thought of virtually repeating the journey of the past winter, first into Perthshire and then to London, this time to a port with Europe beckoning. But the words coming from Winifred's mouth were Winifred's own, it seemed, and Jane deferred to her host as she felt her own confidence slipping for the first time since she'd woken in Scotland.

The women nodded. Mary held out a letter. 'This came for you too. It was sent here. There is no indication of who it is from.'

Jane took the letter and pushed it into a pocket as she shooed off both women again. 'Hurry now, we leave as soon as I return from the garden. I think I want to leave some coin behind. Just a little silver.' She grinned. 'To be cautious. Cecilia, be a love and fetch my perfume of violets, will you? I seem to have mislaid my other bottle.'

As she walked with Bran to the back garden, Jane realised Winifred was weighing up her options, sorting through thoughts, reaching toward a decision as to her best next step. Until now, Jane had made the decisions, but over the course of the journey north, she'd experienced a curious sensation that she was being squeezed out by Winifred.

It was an odd feeling to experience, hard even to explain to herself. She hadn't wanted to say anything. Ever since the revelation of the pregnancy, Jane had carried the burden of guilt. But whatever was happening within Winifred, Jane knew her host was reasserting herself in a more physical way. She was nurturing a child, she was fleeing to reunite with her husband and she wanted no extra baggage.

Jane understood that. But she had no idea how to make the final escape that would free Winifred and empower each of them to return to their proper existence.

Bran was talking; she'd barely heard a word. '"... my kingdom in Germany," the King is supposed to have said.'

She shook her head free of distractions and gathered her scattered thoughts. 'Um... yes, well, I suppose he has never truly considered England to be his home.'

'Then he should stay in Germany, My Lady.'

She laughed. 'I agree. And then what happened?' She gathered he'd been talking about the King's departure from the country.

'They say he passed a group of Jacobite prisoners, My Lady. And they were hopeful that the old saying that the royal face always carries mercy might hold good.'

She shook her head. 'They would have appealed in vain.'

'That's the truth,' Bran replied sadly. 'But we heard from a traveller who was there that an Anglican clergyman was hanged, drawn and quartered for his part in the rebellion. And he so moved the crowd with his speech on the gibbet that he attracted more converts than were scared off by his fearful punishment.' He stopped. 'Here we are, My Lady. I think it best if ye count our steps, for I cannot rely on my numbers.'

She squeezed his shoulder. 'Of course.' Together they deliberately walked, counting aloud but softly, until they reached the secret spot. 'I'd forgotten how beautiful this place is in spring. My last memory is of that terrible, frigid night.'

'When I was frightened ye might slip on the ice and fall, My Lady,' he said affectionately. 'But the earth is no longer frozen. I shall have your goods in your hands very soon,' he assured her, and bent his back to the digging.

Jane inhaled the cold air, gloriously scented by fresh grass that was growing madly. Bulb heads were just beginning to push through the earth and bright green leaf buds were fattening on the branches around her. It would be a month or more before blossom scented the air, but this hint of spring lifted her spirits and made her think about new beginnings. She was sure Winifred was thinking about the new life growing within her.

Jane was so distracted in those few heartbeats that she almost missed the figure that appeared briefly from the small copse beyond the garden. She saw whoever it was walk into the outer grounds of the property, which were given over to woodland and wildflowers.

She blinked, confused momentarily. Then she focused. *Robyn!*

Her stomach felt as though it fell away, like the unpleasant sensation during turbulence when flying in an aircraft. But how could she explain that to Winifred, who was experiencing it differently – as something more like nausea?

'My Lady?' Bran's concerned voice asked.

'I am fine. It has been a tiring adventure, Bran. And it is not yet finished for me. I was thinking about the journey ahead.'

'Would you like me to fetch you anything, My Lady?' he said, holding out the small sack she had buried with him during winter.

She shook her head. 'No, thank you. I wish to take one last tour around the property, Bran.'

He bowed. 'Would you like me to walk with ye, My Lady, lest you trip?'

She smiled. 'I will only be a few moments, Bran. Away with you. Please take that sack and ask Miss Cecilia to put it with my belongings. Tell her I am not far behind you. This is my farewell, dear Bran. I want to fix in my mind that copse, where I enjoyed many a happy picnic with my husband and children.'

He understood, nodded silently and departed, unaware of Winifred's pounding heart against the anvil of her chest. She barely felt the ground beneath her boots or the damp against her cloak as she moved deeper into the stand of dark evergreens.

Out of sight from the main house, she called out. 'Robyn?'

'Here,' came the familiar voice, and her mysterious guide appeared again from behind the trunk of a thick, gnarled yew.

'I knew it...' Her voice broke on the words. She hadn't realised that she'd been holding her breath, or that so much emotion had gathered in the space of the couple of hundred paces she had taken to get here. There was so much to say, yet all that came was something akin to a sigh, accompanied by silent tears.

'I speak only to you, Jane. It is time.'

'Time?' she asked, through her tears.

'Time to return from where you came.'

She wept harder, but still silently. She wasn't sure if Robyn saw her mumble a *thank you* to her. And she wasn't sure why, in this moment of such relief, her thoughts reached toward Julius Sackville.

You are not finished with that man, it seems, Winifred said, sounding more present, stronger than ever.

No... no, it is not that, Jane protested, pushing her hands into the pockets of her cloak to focus herself. She shook her head, the thought that had tugged at her mind suddenly lost. *Winifred, will you be strong enough?*

For the journey to London, then Gravesend and on to Europe? Of course. I shall have two children with me and my husband and son waiting for me. I have already decided, though, that I shall travel to Ostend first. I must see my sister, and I will find peace and safety in the convent with her, until I am past the dangerous time of my confinement. Be assured that I can survive whatever the heavens throw at me, dearest Jane. But are you strong enough to leave me behind?

I... She faltered. It had not occurred to her, in all the time that she'd been wishing to escape this strange existence, that she might miss it. *I will never forget you, or your courage.*

Your *courage, Jane.* Your *strength. I hope your sorrows are healed as mine are, and that you will find love and happiness in the arms of whichever man you marry. Thank you for the gift of my husband.*

Cecilia... she began.

Is none the wiser. She will not miss you, for she does not know you were here. But I shall miss you for both of us.

Jane pushed out a smile; she hoped her host could feel its warmth. She turned Winifred's head, which was glancing at Terregles, back to Robyn.

'Time is short,' the laundrywoman said.

'How do we do this?'

'You are travelling back to Peebles, I gather, My Lady?'

'Yes,' Jane answered. 'Anne is there.'

'That is perfect, for near Peebles there is a pair of standing stones located on one of the oldest straight tracks, which connects Stirling to the Isle of Iona. Druids and monks have made the journey over centuries, but you have no need to walk in the footsteps of pilgrims. You must follow my instructions and I will take you to a place of vast spiritual power, and from there, Jane, you will make your journey alone.'

THIRTY-FIVE

ROBYN HAD TOLD JANE TO MAKE HER way to this place and she sat now, within Winifred, on a large boulder, contemplating the strangeness of her life. Most curious of all, she had acclimatised to the cold. Jane couldn't imagine being in her original life, sitting on a windswept moor on the edge of winter in northern Britain, with little more than a cloak, scarf and gloves to protect her. And yet here she was, preoccupied not by the retreating claws of winter, but by the letter she was reading.

It was from Julius. She had forgotten about it until now.

My beloved Jane,

It was very difficult to look upon you at Westminster, and the cowardly part of me found it easier to walk away than torture myself. I fear, Jane, that I can never escape the memory of you, which will haunt me wherever I go.

I don't know if we shall meet again. I heard of your part in your husband's daring and brilliant escape and I swear I could not be more proud had I broken him out of the Tower myself. What a woman you are. What fire must burn in that belly of yours! Will Maxwell is a lucky man and once again I ask your forgiveness for my intrusion.

Be safe, my beloved Jane. That is how I shall always remember you. My Jane. Think kindly of me over time and perhaps the tapestry of life will not be so cruel as to deny me a chance to see you once again.

To this end I will visit Terregles in the hope that you may be there. I shall come for the last leaf-fall of autumn. By then you may know your future, and if it is with William Maxwell I shall not trouble you again. Either way, I wish you only happiness, and pray the threads that bind us might cross again. Until that time, I am yours.

JS

She was crying by the time the brief letter ended, but there was nothing more to be done. She had to go home. She would re-enter her body and become Jane Granger again... she was here right now, waiting for it.

Of course, Cecilia had erupted into protestations at being left behind at Traquair House with Anne and the in-laws, but Jane had begged her to understand.

'I promised William,' Jane had lied, and knew Winifred forgave her that lie.

'Why would the Earl want you to visit such a barren spot?'

Jane had thrown a look at Mary, William's sister. 'He visited it once as a child and perhaps he believes something spiritual occurred. He did not explain.' Mary returned Winifred's glance with one of pure confusion, and mercifully held her tongue.

'But what has that got to do with what you wish to do today, dearest?' Cecilia persisted. Her concern was genuine, Jane knew, and it was why she showed her friend none of the exasperation she felt.

'Simply this. William is certain he will not set foot in this fair land again, and for that reason has asked me to visit this place, his earliest and most vivid memory of childhood.'

Mary shook her head, as if to say she no longer desired to keep up with such whimsy.

'Well, if it is important to him...'

Jane had smiled. 'Thank you, dearest. If you would have Anne readied, we shall leave as soon as I return. I shall be gone only for the day.'

'I shall organise for young Angus, our grieve's son, to drive you there,' Mary had offered.

And so here she stood, alone in a small circle of stones. Angus had been sent to the nearby village to fetch some ale and cheese for their journey home: an excuse Winifred had helped concoct to ensure she was left by herself.

Well, not entirely by herself. Jane saw a familiar figure approaching. Robyn covered the small path, flanked by bracken, effortlessly. None of the thistles or spurs of woody plants snagged her boots or clutched at her skirt. It was as if she were passing over the land rather than upon it.

'Such a lonely spot,' Robyn said.

'Where are we?'

'The locals call it Eynsof. Mostly it has no name. You would have to have been born within a few miles to know it, and that is why I provided you with a drawn map. As to the name's meaning, I suspect it has been bastardised since ancient times. It is connected with the spiritual world and means essentially "No Beginning, No End".'

'Infinity?'

Robyn shrugged in answer.

'Why here?'

'You understand the ancient ley lines?'

'Not really. Will did try and explain.'

'And you trusted him enough to test the theory.'

She gave an uncertain expression. 'Trust had nothing to do with it. It had more to do with desperation and fear.'

'Fear of losing Will, or of loneliness… of being left unmarried?'

'All of it.'

'It strikes me as odd that you do not cut across my words, yelling that it is because of love.'

Jane regarded Robyn. 'It is such an overworked phrase, such an overwrought emotion.'

Robyn appeared unmoved. 'And yet it is the emotion that preoccupies the lives of probably everyone you know. And arguably most of the lives of the people in the world you come from.'

Jane said nothing. She was tired of this argument. She was tired of her test. She had done her best for Will.

'You mentioned we are on a ley line?' she said, keeping her voice even, but changing tack firmly.

'Indeed. We straddle a track that connects Montrose on the east coast of Scotland with the Inner Hebrides isle of Iona. It runs through places of great spiritual significance, including the Fortingall Yew, Glen Lyon, and Tobermory on the Isle of Mull, which translates as the Well of Mary.'

'Is the track as powerful as the one running through Ayers Rock?'

Robyn smiled as one might at an innocent. 'No, dear Jane. And it is why you need me here with you.'

'Are you taking me back?'

'Yes.'

Jane could feel the relief sighing through her host.

'How?'

Robyn dug into the small knitted pouch she wore slung diagonally across her body and from it retrieved a tiny vial. 'Winifred, I must ask you to drink this. And I am addressing Winifred, Jane, because it is her permission I seek, not yours.'

Jane took a breath. *Go ahead*, she said to her host, wondering if Winifred were able.

It felt surreal. Winifred required no further encouragement and seized her moment to reclaim full control of her body. Jane felt herself being squeezed out, the vacuum filled effortlessly by Winifred, taking control of her limbs, while Jane retreated. Initially Jane felt a flash of irritation at the sense of yielding, but then she gave herself up to it as she knew she must.

She had no sense of time, could not tell whether seconds or

minutes had passed. But when she regained her awareness, she had a curious feeling of weightlessness, as though floating in a bubble. She could hear Robyn's voice, but it sounded as though it were speaking down a long, tinny tube. It reached into the hollow where she existed with a metallic ring.

'Winifred?' Robyn asked.

'Yes?' Winifred replied.

'Bienvenue,' Robyn said, welcoming her in French. She had obviously known it would make Winifred smile.

'Benvenuto may be more appropriate, given that I am fleeing to Italy.'

'Have you ever been to Italy?'

Winifred must have shaken her head, Jane thought.

'Well, do not fear. You will fall in love with Rome. It is more exciting than Paris, and William will, I suspect, prefer it.'

'I wonder why.'

'I shall let you and him discover. Thank you for being such an indulgent host to Jane.'

'She has more than repaid my kindnesses,' Jane heard Winifred reply in her usual magnanimous way.

'I understand she has left you a special gift.'

Jane sensed that Winifred must have looked down at this point. She couldn't tell whether her companion was simply embarrassed at the forthright way of Robyn, or whether she felt genuinely shamed. She would never know, for Winifred did not reply and Robyn did not press her.

'The contents of this vial will not hurt the child.'

'Will they hurt me?'

Jane thought she heard Robyn chuckle. 'They will free you of your burden. You will sleep, but only briefly. Drink them now, for Angus will not be long in returning.'

Distantly Jane heard the sound of swallowing and remotely felt the sensation of drowsiness laying itself around her. She felt inclined to travel with it, ride the slope into unconsciousness, but Robyn's voice was with her.

Come with me now, Jane.

I don't know how to do this.

Yes, you do. Let go. Remember the wind on Uluru? Remember how it pulled at you, urging you to let go? That's me now. I am the wind. I am asking you to trust me and to let go.

Robyn, will everything be as it was?

Nothing ever is.

Shall we meet again?

I cannot say.

Can I meet you again? she pressed, not really wishing to, but determined to get a definitive answer to one of her questions.

Can you? Probably. Should you? No. Will you? I have no idea.

How would I? She refused to let it go.

A crack through the mirror, came the nonsensical, typically whimsical answer.

Take me home, Robyn. Farewell, dear Winifred.

When Jane regained her wits, she could feel herself bumping and thumping over a deeply ridged surface. Impossible though it seemed, she was being driven in the front seat of a vehicle; she could tell that much. Opening her eyes to slits, clear harsh sunlight hurt her head. She could see only the burnished red of a central Australian desert, interrupted by scraggy, greyish eruptions of gorse-like bush.

She slid surreptitiously to her left and turned her head slightly to regard, through her still-slitted vision, whoever was at the wheel. He was dressed in a washed-out, flinty, grey-green uniform that echoed the vegetation they were passing. His arm reached over and pushed a bottle at her.

'Drink!' he said, fully aware of her scrutiny. 'Get as much water into you as you can.'

'Who are you?' she croaked.

'Jimbo. One of the rangers. One of the dozens of rangers who've been out looking for you.'

He was half grinning at her: rich coffee-coloured eyes above a generous mouth full of white, well-spaced teeth that would never need flossing, she was sure.

'Sorry,' she said to him.

'What the hell happened, mate?'

Mate? 'I don't know.' Well, at least that was the truth. Now came the lies. 'I did the climb…' She swallowed several gulps of water. 'I climbed, the wind came up out of nowhere… and I can't really remember much else.'

'You've been gone days, mate. Do you know that much?'

They were thundering along. She recognised nothing.

'Where are we?'

'We're on the road out of the Olgas.'

'The Olgas!'

'Yeah, though how you got there is beyond me. You walked about fifty kilometres and you're saying you don't remember any of it?'

She shook her head, stunned. Robyn had brought her back. Given the time and distance, fifty kilometres off was an amazing feat.

'I'm sorry,' she repeated.

The car radio crackled, and he grabbed it and began explaining that Jane was 'compos' again. The scrambled voice on the other end seemed to make sense to Jimbo, but it was a torrent of nonsensical sound to her. His side of it was equally unrevealing.

'Yeah… yeah… nah. Nah, she's got no idea, mate. Yeah… yeah, right. Aw… 'bout thirty minutes?' He said it as though he were asking a question, even though she realised he was answering one. It was a quirk of Australians, she'd noticed. She liked it. They were so easy to pick because of it.

He threw the radio back into its holder. 'You feelin' okay? Not goin' to spew or anything?'

She barked a laugh. 'I'm feeling relieved. Thank you for finding me.'

'Yeah, well, you should have sunstroke, mate. You had us all guessing. Your folks must be tearing out their hair.'

'You didn't give up on me... thanks.'

'Nah, trackers don't give up that easily. A few days in this weather is dangerous, though. Even one of us rangers would find it tough and we have all the equipment.' He gave her a look, scratching his curlyish, rich brown hair, which had golden tips in some places. She was so glad it was Jimbo who'd found her.

She laughed. 'They breed us tough in Wales, I guess.'

'They must do, wherever that is. What did you eat, drink?' He scratched his head again.

'I think I had some food and water with me,' she lied. 'That's right. I had bread from the breakfast, fruit, bars of chocolate. I had a water bottle – I do remember that now,' she said, clearing her throat and sipping more water from his bottle to cover the gargantuan fib.

'Ah, that makes sense, then. I mean, three days without food is tough for someone not used to it, but without water it's impossible.'

She hoped he would let it drop, but she also realised this question was probably going to be asked a hundred different ways as soon as she hit civilisation. She might as well finesse her story now, get it sounding plausible, because only a lie was going to work.

The truth was ridiculous.

THIRTY-SIX

LONDON WAS MISTED WITH THE KIND OF nearly invisible drizzle that rarely tempted an umbrella, tending more to show itself as tiny crystals on the shoulders of dark overcoats and irritating the hell out of women.

Jane smoothed down her damp, darkly golden hair, which had immediately frizzed in the misty atmosphere, and stared at herself in the mirror. She realised it was still something of a novelty not to see Winifred looking back at her. She'd lost weight. *Can't complain about that!* she thought, with a small spark of triumph flashing in her eyes. She could now see the apples of her cheeks – her mother's term, not hers – sitting high and round, pinched slightly with a blush of colour that was not make-up, but nervous anticipation. Jane licked her dry lips. She'd not bothered with colouring or glossing them; she wanted to be able to kiss Will without having to apologise for the gluey sensation and coloured residue every man must loathe when kissing lipstick. He'd always said that her lips were perfect cupid bows and that they had been searching for his lips all of her life. She blinked slowly at this memory. Will had enough romance in his imagination for both of them.

Whether it had been the weeks as Winifred, or just a new mindset, make-up and fashion felt suddenly trivial. This was how she truly looked. And she liked her face, especially now that she had it back. The gene pool had been kind to her and she knew she was pretty in every conventional way: an oval face, symmetrical features, well-shaped teeth, and eyebrows that were neither bushy nor invisible, arched in an artist's sweep above eyes that people invariably mentioned for their startlingly pale grey. She knew her eyes attracted people to her – made her seem, sometimes, 'otherworldly'. That used to please her. It didn't now… not since she'd experienced otherworldliness first-hand and knew how cruel and bloody it could be.

She didn't want to remember any of it, and yet her time as the Countess of Nithsdale remained vivid. Moving through London in 1979 now felt strange, the city almost clinical by comparison in its cleanliness, though she didn't believe a single Londoner would agree with her! In spite of the filth, the disease, the poverty – fortunately little of which she'd had to experience personally – the London of the early eighteenth century had felt infinitely more romantic than the careless, hard-nosed metropolis of today. Jane had reflected more than once that if you fell over during the afternoon rush hour, then heaven help you, because you would surely be trampled by commuters streaming down into the bowels of London, desperate to be rushed away to the south's green belt and released from the city for a few hours. It was dog eat dog down there in the Tube stations, where no one made eye contact until the first soupy gust of wind told commuters that a train was imminent. It would roar toward them, pushing the air before it, which gradually flowed over waiting passengers like a warm metallic-scented breath. Only then would gazes connect, and more often than not in a gladiatorial look. *Where will the door stop? Can I get on before you do?*

Yes… even if flushing toilets were now, in her opinion, the single greatest advance in human technology, she realised that she was genuinely missing the polite, elegant lifestyle of the eighteenth century. Why had she thought that women were subdued, whispering creatures whose single preoccupation was marriage? She could name so many of her contemporary friends who suffered that angst. No… women of that time just knew how to achieve their influence while working behind the façade of that polite, tea-sipping atmosphere.

Now she was assaulted by music in the street – New Romantic, punk and other styles jarring with the deeply smooth harmonies of the Carpenters. It had seemed fabulously modern just a short while ago, but now, after her experience in history, it almost saddened her that her children – if she ever had any – probably wouldn't learn the piano in quite the same way as Winifred's memories told her Anne would have, nor would a daughter of hers easily learn to dance the quadrille – would she even want to? Would she sew well? Jane wondered whether she would teach any daughter of hers from a young age how to set about managing a large household. She had glimpsed a world where the phone was yet to be invented, and now she was living in a world where it seemed plausible – if you believed the technology experts – that people would soon be able to make calls on a phone that could be carried around in their pocket! Really? The art of letter writing would surely be lost, she thought, remembering the two notes from Julius Sackville, in his sloping handwriting, which she'd memorised because she'd been unable to bring them back. They were buried at Peebles on an ancient ley line, along with the precious vial of Ashes of Violet.

Her parents had met her at Manchester Airport, expecting to whisk her back to Wales in a couple of hours on the motorway. But they didn't seem surprised when she refused and demanded they hit the motorway for central London. They'd even packed for that eventuality.

The journey down was tense. Her mother was still too shocked to speak with any fluency and simply clung to her in the back seat, holding her hand as though she never intended to let it go again. Her father wouldn't let go of her arm, which he held gently on her other side, so she was flanked by watchful parents, determined not to lose sight or contact with her. Even Juliette seemed unable to let go of her, constantly flicking her gaze into the rear-view mirror to glance at her sister with a haunted expression while she drove.

How could Jane explain any of it? She couldn't. So she stuck to the well-crafted lie, which she'd massaged and got pitch-perfect in her mind on the flight home. There had been a brief press conference in the Northern Territory where Jane had been able to fudge her way through with a dazed look and lots of shrugs and *I really can't remember*s. She haltingly explained, in enough detail to please the hungry press, what she could recall of the build-up to her 'event', as she termed it, on Uluru. Beyond that moment of the rogue wind, she allowed the story to trail into a no-man's-land of lost memory.

A medical team had performed a thorough examination, to pronounce her in surprisingly robust health despite her trauma, although a lack of food and water meant she was showing signs of dehydration and weight loss. She was thankful that her body was looking fragile, or the mystics of the world would have been howling that she was some sort of phenomenon, she was sure.

And now here she was at the hospital, exhausted, keenly aware of her body's shortcomings while it got used to having her animate it again. She had begged a few moments alone in the bathroom to gather her thoughts.

Will had woken yesterday, apparently. He was still quite groggy, as Juliette had warned.

She'd already run the gauntlet of meeting his parents in the hospital reception, had briefly trotted out her story and had allowed herself to be hugged and kissed then passed to the next person. She was glad that the coincidence of Will waking up and her discovery at the Olgas on the same day was not resonating with anyone present. She alone understood the inherent magic of that coincidence. Winifred and William would hopefully be reunited and safe. She'd saved William's life as she'd been charged with doing, and as a result her Will had been given the gift of his rebirth.

How tenuous life is, she thought, as she tried to coax her honey-golden hair back into a smooth, silken sheen. This was how Will liked her to wear it: free from her preferred ponytail, so he could knot his fingers in it absently while watching a movie or smooth it tenderly while lovemaking.

Her reflection seemed to shiver before her and she thought for a fright-torn moment that she saw Julius behind her, staring at her with that dark look of slight injury he wore so well. She'd imagined it. A blink later and all she could see was her reflection, and the peppering of freckles around her nose that make-up would normally hide. The light tan from Australia helped add an artificial glow of health.

'Julius,' she whispered to the mirror, 'you have to leave me alone now.'

Juliette pushed through the door, which protested with a creak. 'Jane? What are you doing? We're all waiting. The nursing team say he's sitting up, ready for the family to arrive.'

'Does he know I'm here?'

Juliette shook her head, grinning gleefully. 'We're all holding our breath with excitement. Diane's already discussing wedding dates with Mum. They're out of control, but they're so happy, Jane. I mean, this really is a happy ending and there was a time – I will admit – when I didn't think we were going to have it.'

Jane swallowed. She couldn't tell her sister how nervous she was feeling; she dared not tell her parents that her experiences in a different era had changed her; she certainly couldn't tell Diane and John Maxwell that she had been a harlot and unfaithful while their son lay near death.

She nodded. 'I know what you mean.'

Juliette stepped fully into the bathroom to hug her. 'It wasn't until I thought we'd lost you that I realised how much I love you, Jane.'

Jane was startled by the admission but allowed herself to be hugged, returning the gesture with feeling. 'I... I've missed you all too and I'm sorry I seemed so preoccupied with my needs.

It felt so important at the time to go to Australia.' Her sister nodded and sniffed. 'Good grief, Juliette, you've gone soppy on me.'

Her sister's eyes were misted. 'Yeah, well, don't get used to it. Come on, let's get you two kissing again.' She grinned. 'You must be so excited.'

'Yes,' she said, overly bright. 'I was in here pinching myself.'

'Dr Evans wants to say something to you first. He wants you to go in alone.' Jane frowned. 'Let him explain.' Her sister dragged her out into the small reception area of intensive care.

Jane smiled when she saw the nurse she recalled as Ellen beaming at her.

'You're back,' she said, coming forward to surprise Jane with a hug. Everyone was in a huggy mood, apparently. 'Seems your magic worked,' she whispered for Jane's hearing only. 'Lucky, or I was going to ask him to marry *me* instead,' she jested.

Jane pulled back, determined not to cry, but feeling her chin wobble. She nodded, swallowing hard, determined to hold herself together. 'The magic asked a lot of me.'

'So I gather.' Ellen gave a sympathetic smile. 'Dr Evans has asked the two families to hold back. We think it will be overwhelming for Will if everyone is staring at him.'

'I couldn't agree more. I have to be honest: I wasn't prepared for today to be quite so emotional.' She couldn't tell Ellen that she was thinking of an entirely different man from an entirely different century. 'I want to see him alone.'

'He spoke briefly to his parents yesterday.' Ellen stepped closer again. 'He's been resting ever since and we've kept everyone away. Obviously the Maxwells are champing at the bit to get to his side again, but Dr Evans spoke to them before you arrived and warned them that Will could experience what we call an overload. Come on, come and speak to Dr Evans and then you can have some private time with Will.' She looked back at the anxious relatives. 'Excuse us, everyone. Won't be long.'

Evans was waiting for them in the corridor. Jane could see Will lying asleep and caught her breath. Her promise not to cry was broken. He looked angelic lying there, so still and golden and heartbreakingly handsome. But her fears were borne out. She was not as thrilled to see him as Juliette had been to see her. The man she wanted was not lying in that bed. How would she ever find the right words to tell him this when he had been on a long and challenging journey to come back for her... as she had come back for him?

Julius, she wept inside as tears rolled down her cheeks, and everyone quite likely – and quite reasonably – presumed they were tears of joy.

'Hello, Jane,' Evans said, beaming. 'Welcome back. We're very relieved you're safe.' He surprised her with a brief, fierce hug too. What was in the air today? 'Wow, you're as tiny as a bird. No wonder you blew off Ayers Rock.'

'Have you seen it?'

'Seen it, climbed it, signed my name at the top. Amazing experience. Not as dramatic as yours, though.'

'No, that's for sure,' she said, her full meaning lost on him.

'Jane, I have to tell you, he's still a bit blurry.'

'I'd be surprised if he wasn't.'

'No, I mean, we are not yet able to measure damage.'

'Oh, I see. He's talking, right?'

'Yes. But he's confused.'

'He recognises where he is, though?'

'He knows he's in hospital. He knows he was injured. He remembers nothing of the incident. He recognised his parents, but he's had no contact with the family since. It's only been hours. He's been sleeping for most of them.'

Ellen squeezed her arm. 'He made us laugh this morning, recalling a story of his childhood when the family was clustered around his bed at Christmas time, because he was so ill they brought the party to his bedroom rather than leave him alone upstairs.'

Jane grinned. 'And he threw up over Great Aunt Esme,' she finished.

Ellen giggled. 'He's a good storyteller.'

Evans smiled encouragingly. 'Ready? Go slowly with him. Perhaps best not to let him know about how we lost you for a while.'

Jane gave him a wry glance. 'Yes, I might just keep that to myself for now.' She wondered why they hadn't mentioned that Will had been asking where she was. But the thought was lost as she was shown into his private room by Evans. Ellen followed them.

Gone were the machines that Jane recalled from the last time she'd been here. Will's hair remained a bright blond, but looked somehow darker and duller after all his days prone in a bed. His eyelashes, tipped with gold, lay against the tops of his cheeks just as she remembered from mornings waking up next to him. He too had lost weight and his face had sunk slightly against his teeth. There were longer hollows where once small dimples had pressed into his flesh when he grinned. He looked every bit as beautiful as he always had, but now he appeared as a haunted echo of the sometimes impossibly cheerful, ever-smiling person she had been enamoured with.

She was doing it again. *Enamoured, entranced, had fallen for.* Never *loved.* Winifred had nailed her on it; even Robin had remarked that she never spoke of love in connection with Will. Her heart was pounding, but from anxiety at being found out for the impostor she felt sure she'd become.

Did she belong here? Or did she belong in 1716? Who was she?

'Come on, Will,' Ellen was saying as she shook him gently. 'You have a very special visitor.'

Jane felt redundant. She stood at the end of his bed and gripped the railing, watched him run his tongue over his lips as he surfaced from his doze. He gave a soft groan.

'Lovely Ellen. I think I have to marry you,' he mumbled

drowsily to his nurse, not opening his eyes. Ellen smiled adoringly at him before sending her an apologetic look.

'All normal,' Evans assured her. 'Sleep heals. He's going to feel drowsy for a while yet.' Jane nodded her understanding. 'Yesterday he was lucid for about twenty minutes. This morning for ten. Every day will be different.' He shrugged. 'I'm afraid it's not maths. Will is going to come back to us in his time frame, not ours, but he is definitely present and with us again. That's the main thing.'

Ellen glanced her way. 'You try, Jane. It's your voice he needs to hear. We're hoping that you, of all people, are the one who will really bring him back into himself.'

She disguised her reluctance by forcing herself to replace Ellen at Will's side. And finally she was confronted by the biggest question of all.

Is this what you want, Jane?

Who asked that? It sounded like Robin, but she was probably going slowly mad, tormenting herself like this. Why was she second-guessing her actions, her motives? *Look what you've done to be here!* she yelled at herself. *This must be what you really want, or why would you have gone through that harrowing experience?* Yet her alter ego, or whichever other voice was doing battle inside her, was equally insistent. *Be honest. Tell him!*

'Try, Jane,' Dr Evans urged. 'Let him hear your voice.'

She cleared her throat, realising her cheeks were wet from her tears. 'Will…' she began hesitantly. Ellen had joined Dr Evans at the foot of the bed and both of them were smiling encouragement, nodding that she keep going. 'Hey, Will,' she tried again, wiping her cheek. 'It's me, Jane. I've missed you. Come on, wake up fully for me.'

Will stirred, eyes blinking but not opening fully. He croaked a response, but she didn't catch any words. She glanced at Ellen. 'Normal,' Ellen repeated gently, hands pressing the air in a reassuring gesture. 'Go for it, Jane.'

She touched him. He was warm through his hospital gown. She remembered this shoulder beneath her fingers, knew the gnarls and indents well and exactly how the flesh covered them. She was familiar with a silvery scar just where her thumb was placed; that was when he'd fallen while mountain climbing, and she knew this was the same shoulder that ached a bit in winter, because it had been broken during the same fall in the Rockies.

'Will, wake up!' She shook him gently. 'It's Jane. I'm here. Everyone is!' She glanced at Ellen; knew what the nurse thought she should be saying. She took a breath and leaned close to him. 'I love you, darling.' It sounded as feigned to her ears as she knew it was in her heart. She swallowed her shame, but she realised no one else in the room had heard the false ring in her tone, least of all Will, whose eyes opened.

He blinked a few times.

'There he is,' Ellen said. Jane had always wondered why hospital staff spoke inordinately loudly, but she realised now they were trying to get a patient to focus, or to impress something upon the patient's loved ones. 'Morning, Will,' she said brightly, coming around to the other side of his bed to give him a solid shake.

He was properly awake now, rubbing his eyes. 'Hi, Ellen.'

'There,' Ellen said, and pointed Jane to the plastic beaker on his small bedside cabinet. 'Give him a drink,' she urged. 'Drink up, Will. You need fluids.'

Jane obliged, reaching for the beaker, which had a plastic straw embedded into the lid. Evans helped Will to raise his head, while Jane put the straw to her fiancé's lips and nodded with a smile. He sipped, bright blue eyes fixed on her. She'd forgotten how most women melted beneath his gaze, which had an underlying innocence to it. That look impaled her now, as he sucked on the straw.

She smiled, at last feeling some of the tension fall away. Lovely Will. She knew how much he loved her. She knew that nothing mattered more to him than for them to be married, starting a shared life with a shared name and a shared passion to have a family.

'I've got enough love for both of us,' he'd quipped when he first popped the marriage question, and she'd looked at him, made a bit uncomfortable by the speed at which he was moving. 'I promise. You do love me, you just haven't caught up with it yet. I'm well ahead of you, darling. I know our love is the sort that inspires poetry and stories.'

She'd laughed at that. He'd always been able to make her smile, and humour made it easy to love someone, didn't it?

'I'm struggling for what to say,' Jane confessed to him. 'I thought we'd lost you. I went to Uluru for you, Will. I knew it would bring you back to me. The ley lines... I have so much to tell you,' she said, breaking her promise not to refer to her adventure and then pulling back from any talk of magic and spiritual awareness. She couldn't imagine how it would sound to the man of science and the down-to-earth nurse on the other side of the bed.

'Uluru?' he mumbled, the straw gripped between his neat teeth.

She nodded, giving a watery smile as the wretched tears betrayed her again. 'Yes.' She laughed. 'I was gripped by your magical madness.' She saw his puzzlement. 'Anyway, you're back, and so am I.'

Will sighed and lowered the beaker to clutch it loosely in his hands. He blinked and frowned slightly. 'Er... sorry. Who are you, again?'

Jane's breath caught and her mouth opened a little. 'Um...' She threw a look at Ellen, who didn't return it. Ellen's gaze was fixed on Will. Evans was pulling at his beard, pondering, but not giving Jane eye contact either.

'I should know you, shouldn't I?' Will said, his expression regretful.

She swallowed, but nothing went down. Her throat felt parched. 'It's me, Will.'

Shame ghosted across his features, momentarily reordering their perfect arrangement. 'I'm sorry. Dr Evans said it was a head injury and things might be blurry. Did you say your name is Jane?'

She nodded, stunned.

He frowned and, like a child might, he seemed to strain to think about this name. 'There's nothing.' He shrugged. 'I don't know you. I mean, I obviously should…' He looked distraught. 'But I don't know you from a stranger on the street. I'm totally in love with Ellen, though.' He grinned, his sentiments boyish, meant to be fun. He could have no idea how this hurt.

It sounded so harsh, said like that. She sat back and the shock of his words made it feel as though she were collapsing from the inside out.

'We were getting married,' she strained to say. It came out as a choked whisper.

'No.' He looked shocked. 'I… I… don't know about that,' he added, contrite. 'I'm so sorry, I don't remember.' His distress intensified. He began to shake his head, looking at the doctor and Ellen for help. His blue eyes puddled into pools of anxiety and he held his head in the long, splayed fingers she remembered caressing her, teasing her. How could he have forgotten? 'I've been trying through the night, but I really can't remember much since university days.'

'What?' Jane couldn't help herself.

'Don't push it, Will,' Evans soothed. 'Memory is a fickle thing. Your brain is healing. There is every likelihood that getting back all those memories could take a little while.' He glanced at Ellen and Jane knew some unspoken signal passed between them.

'Are my parents waiting?' Will asked, his anxious gaze trying to avoid Jane's mask-like expression.

'Yes, sweetheart,' Ellen said. 'Would you like me to bring them in?'

He nodded. 'Just them.'

Ellen sent Jane a look of deep sympathy. She came around the bed to squeeze her shoulder. Nothing was said.

'Do you want me to go?' Jane said to him, an edge in her voice. She knew it was wrong to bully, but until now her thoughts had been occupied with her return and her confusion had been about whether she wanted to go back to all that was familiar. It had never occurred to her that someone might take that away from her – least of all Will.

He shifted his glance back to her at last and she saw deep pain reflected in it. 'I am so sorry. You're very beautiful, but I'm a bit lost.' He frowned. 'I don't think I'm the sort of person who would pretend.'

'You're not that sort of person,' she replied. 'Your total honesty used to make me uncomfortable sometimes.' They smiled sadly at each other. 'You loved me enough for both of us.'

He stared back at her and shook his head. 'I'm sorry.'

'I am too,' she said gently, clearing her throat before she stood and kissed him lightly on the forehead as one might a child. 'Be well, Will. I'll send in your parents.'

He caught her hand. 'Jane?'

She raised her gaze to meet his.

'You said something about ley lines. I'm really interested in them. In fact, I'm sure I'm interested in Earth vortices.'

'I know you are,' she said, stroking his hand. 'You're also quite a well-known geophysicist and geologist.' He stared at her with a slight hint of amazement in his eyes. His expression was warming now that they were off the sticky subject of not knowing her from the hospital cleaner. 'You have a quirky take on earth formations.' Jane smiled. 'I think you've always seriously wanted to explore the spiritual connection that exists between the old straight tracks and the great Earth vortices.'

'I do,' he said, letting out his breath with a sigh. 'At least I think I do.' He chuckled and they swapped a glance of regret. 'I read about the ley lines in a *National Geographic* when I was a child. I think I've always wanted to accept that they held a sort of... magic, but no one else would believe me.'

'I would,' Jane said, and, without wondering whether to do so or not, bent down and let her lips brush his tenderly. 'Goodbye, Will.'

He squeezed her hand. 'Thank you for understanding, Jane. Maybe in the future...?'

'Maybe not,' she said gently. 'Don't feel bad. It's changed both of us.'

Ellen was back with Will's parents in tow and Diane was already leaking tears; perhaps the nurse had told her of the disastrous reunion. John gave her a look of sorrow.

'He needs time,' he murmured to Jane as they passed each other. She nodded, putting on a brave smile.

In the anteroom her parents opened their arms again to hug her and commiserate. She knew her soul-searching was only just beginning.

THIRTY-SEVEN

Jane's parents returned to Wales for the week, promising to come back the next weekend, but both their daughters remained in London. Jane insisted on checking back into the hotel where she and Will had been staying, but she surprised everyone by making no effort to go to the hospital, instead giving Will the space that Dr Evans felt might be wise. She spent the days following that terrible afternoon of realisation being shuffled around by Juliette.

Her sister planned peaceful day trips to galleries, museums, Kew Gardens… anything that would distract Jane, but not allow London to crowd her. They avoided the Underground, took taxis everywhere, ate picnics in the park and went to bed early, drifting off to reruns of old sitcoms. They ate in unpopular restaurants, frequented out-of-the-way cafés, and roamed the top floors of Liberty and Hamleys, John Lewis and Selfridges. But the girls were not buying, just killing time.

Killing time. *Is this how it's going to be?* Jane wondered, as she watched Juliette choose the food for a picnic lunch from the fridges of Marks & Spencer.

'Ham and salad roll?' Juliette held it up.

Jane shrugged. 'Fine.'

'Okay, let's find some non-alcoholic cider to go with it,' her sister said, leading the way to the beverage section.

Jane followed dutifully, killing time… killing her thoughts… killing her chance.

She blinked as Juliette considered the soft drinks.

What chance?

'No apple fizz,' Jane heard her sister mutter. 'How about boring mineral water?' She didn't wait for Jane's response, but put a bottle in the basket and pointed to the biscuit aisle. 'Chocolate biscuits – a must.'

Jane didn't answer. She'd have preferred fruit, but really it didn't matter. Nothing mattered any more. That was the real problem for her. She was numb and she didn't care about anything. Not even making Will love her.

Hadn't she really come home to prove to herself she didn't love him? Yet he'd beaten her to it and reversed the situation. It was a relief, but it also hurt. Now what?

As they queued, she fixed Juliette with a stare. 'I can't make him love me again,' she said.

'What?' Juliette pursed her lips as she understood. 'Jane, it's barely been a week. Give him a chance.'

'Why? Why force what's not there?'

'You don't know it's not there.'

'There's a saying I heard in Australia: not knowing someone from a bar of soap. I'm the bar of soap, Juliette. And he doesn't even know which brand! He likes the nurse, Ellen, more than me. I don't blame him or her, I'm just saying…'

'Two pounds forty, please,' said the girl behind the counter.

Juliette handed over a five-pound note and the girl passed her the change and gave Jane a plastic bag with their lunch inside.

Juliette bundled Jane out of the store. 'You've got to stop this.'

'Stop what? It's everyone else who has to stop. Will doesn't know me. I'm a stranger. And frankly, I get it. He feels like a stranger to me too.'

'Jane, don't go there. You haven't given him a fair chance.'

'To remember me?'

'Of course to remember you.'

'And then what?'

Now Juliette looked at her as though she were dim.

'Do you think we just slip back into being Will and Jane?' she continued.

'Why not?'

'Because it's not going to be like that, Jules. Damage has been done. Even I don't feel the same. And if Will came back to me now, I would be the one hesitating.'

'You were always the one hesitating!' Juliette accused.

Jane looked around but no one seemed to care about the two women arguing softly in Covent Garden.

'Listen,' Jane began, 'I haven't told you or Mum and Dad yet, but I spoke to John Maxwell on the phone last night.' Juliette's gaze narrowed. 'Will wants to go back to America. Ellen is going with them as his private nurse for a while.'

'Oh, that's just John—'

'No, it's not just John. This was Will's decision. John and Diane are as distraught as our parents over it all, but obviously they want to do what's best for their son. I think it's the right decision.'

'So you're just going to let him go?' her sister asked, incredulous.

'What do you want me to do?'

'Fight for him.'

She shook her head, knowing how much she already had fought to keep Will alive – not that anyone in this life would ever understand. 'He doesn't know me. And Juliette, he never knew that I didn't love him enough.'

Juliette's mouth opened like a fish ripped from its pond and struggling for air. 'You're crazy. Crazy with grief, Jane. You're not making sense.'

'I am. I'm seeing everything so clearly. It was Will's love that kept us together. I'd never known what it is to be made breathless by someone, until…'

'Until…?'

Jane panicked. 'I mean, until now I didn't realise that he never did make my heart pound, or my breath catch.'

'Jane, stop this. Will is such a gorgeous guy. Everyone loves him.'

'Everyone, but me. I love him, but not in the way I should. Not in the way that makes me want to give my life for him.'

'Now you're being dramatic. No one gives their lives for—'

'They do. There are women who would risk their lives for the man they love.'

'Only in movies and books.'

Jane shrugged. She knew better. 'Nevertheless, that's the love I want. I want his kiss to make me see stars, I want to never be apart, I want to know that I have so much love for him that I can't live without him. I don't have that with Will, Juliette; I never did. But because I was lonely, or insecure, or just bored with not having someone special, or fearful of being left on the shelf, I thought *his* devotion was enough. Will, bless him, loved me just as I've described... but now he has nothing to give and we have nowhere to hide. Don't you see? Will deserves better than me for a wife – he deserves to be adored. He's brilliant and funny and ridiculously handsome. The stars have fortuitously aligned to give me a chance not to make a big mistake. To save us both from me.'

Juliette threw her hands in the air. 'You really did go bonkers while you were in Australia! You're making me angry listening to you.'

Jane smiled sadly. 'I've always made you angry.'

'What are you going to do?'

'I'm going to Scotland.'

'Oh, come on. Jane—'

She handed her sister the picnic supplies. 'I'll ring Mum and Dad from King's Cross Station.'

'But why are you going?'

'There's someone I have to see.'

'Jane, please...'

But she'd already moved away. She blew a kiss to Juliette before turning and disappearing into the throng of Covent Garden, without giving herself a chance to consider the madness of this spontaneous decision.

She ended up ringing her family from a pub in Perthshire and tried to explain, over the tears of her mother, that she was searching for something important.

'But what, darling?'

'I can't explain it, Mum. But I know when I find it, I'll be happy.'

'Oh, Jane. I don't know what happened to you on that Australian rock and I don't know why this has happened to Will, but I wish you would come home and just let us look after you.' Catelyn had dissolved into a flood of tears and Hugh, who had been listening in on the other phone, took up the conversation.

'Jane, it's Dad.'

'Dad, please try to understand. I have to do this.'

'What, though? We don't know what it is that you've gone off to do.'

'I'm searching history,' she said bluntly. 'It's a project I'm doing. There's someone I have to hunt down.'

'Oh? Well, why didn't you say so.' He turned away to address her mother. 'She's doing a research project.' Jane heard muffled voices. 'I don't know,' her father answered distantly. 'Probably an extension of her degree. She spoke a while back about doing some more study.' He returned to her. 'So you're studying in Scotland, is that right?'

'Sort of. I'm starting here, at least.'

'Well, how long will you be gone?'

'I don't know, Dad.'

'All right. That sounds vague, but so long as you're keeping occupied. I'd hate to think you were lonely or depressed.'

'The opposite, Dad. It's giving me purpose.'

'Well, good. Let us know what you need.'

'Is Juliette there?'

'Yes, hang on.'

'Mum, are you there?'

'Yes?'

'Let me talk to Juliette alone.'

Her sister's voice finally arrived. 'Jane?'

'Are they both off the phone?'

'Yes. What the hell is going on?'

She fed the phone with another pile of coins she'd had ready in a neat stack. 'Jules, I'm going away for a while. Listen... I know this sounds crazy, but can you remember a name for me?'

'Which name?'

'Sackville. Julius Sackville. Born 1680. Look him up sometime.'

'What am I looking for?'

'Nothing in particular. *Just remember the name*. And if you get curious, look him up.'

'You know, you're making very little sense. In fact, we're worried for you all over again.' She knew the tone in her sister's voice, knew Juliette wanted to accuse her of being unfair, seeking attention.

'Promise me.'

'Julian—'

'Julius!'

'Julius Sackville. All right! Got it. 1680. I've written it down. Satisfied? When will we hear from you?'

'Not sure. And Jules...'

'What?'

'I'm not going mad. I'm not depressed or suicidal. Quite the reverse. And I love you.'

'Wow... are you taking drugs?'

Jane laughed. 'Love is a drug,' she said.

The quip immediately eased the tension and she heard Juliette laugh. 'Call us.'

Jane put the phone down, smiling. She felt better in this moment than she had expected to, but maybe that was because only she knew it was goodbye.

THIRTY-EIGHT

JANE STOOD IN TRAQUAIR HOUSE, AND ALTHOUGH it had changed over almost three centuries, it still felt familiar. Her pulse had begun to race with fresh hope as she'd slipped out of the tour group and come back to the chamber where she had first slept as Winifred. She had fully expected the door to be locked, but the knob had turned and the door had given at her gentle push; obviously, today's owners didn't expect the public to ignore their sign asking visitors not to walk down this end of the house.

The room was still a bedchamber, only modernised. However, old pieces remained, including the exquisite French dressing table and its mirror, which she remembered using to study her reflection as Winifred. Now Jane Granger looked back at her – or was it the ghost of Jane Granger? She certainly looked wan. She could see the ribbed shape of her breastbones in the 'v' of her T-shirt and her arms looked vaguely skeletal. Her cheekbones, of which she'd been proud when she'd first returned to London, now protruded a fraction too sharply, and she could trace the outline of her skull because it was fleshed too thinly these days.

She heard laughter from the front of the house, where her fellow tourists were probably making their way back down the driveway. How long would it take before she was noticed as missing from the group? When they did the head count on the minibus? She had maybe half an hour at most, probably less.

Robyn was not here. Why had Jane thought she would be?

Desperation, guilt, shame, hope. Everything had coalesced to plague her over these last haunting weeks of searching herself for answers. Jane knew she'd made the right decision not to pursue Will, but her internal longing confused her. Nevertheless, she'd made a fateful move the day before yesterday, striding away from Juliette, and that had led her on the long railway journey and today's tour of stately homes in Perth. She'd had to walk through two others before they'd arrived at Traquair House and all the familiar sights and names had stirred her longing again. She felt anger at herself for reaching for the past so desperately, and yes, inescapably, anger – despite her best intentions – at Will for letting her down after she'd gone through so much.

It would have been so easy if she'd fallen into his arms as he woke up and they'd both whispered words of relief to one another and their families had sighed happily. She might have waived the pomp and ceremony and married him the next day, because then she wouldn't have had to confront this.

'This what?' asked a familiar voice, and she swung around, seeing no one.

'Robin?' She couldn't hide the tension in her voice, or the excitement that exploded within.

'Anger serves no purpose.'

'Where are you?'

'I warned you that magic always demands a price,' he said, and she followed his voice to the mirror, where she could see him clearly reflected. 'Your price for using the magic to restore Will was having to give him up.'

'I saved his life,' she said, not knowing what else to say. 'I wish that he had saved mine.'

'He did, Jane, by not recognising you.'

'Will he ever remember me?'

He shook his head. 'No. But I cannot tell if he would have

fallen in love with you all over again. That would have been up to you.'

'Robin, I'm lost.'

He nodded. 'And you've come searching for an answer?'

She took a breath. 'Yes. I want to be like Winifred and William. I have experienced that love now and I know Will and I never had that.'

'Why have you returned here?'

'Don't make me say it.'

'Oh, but I must.'

She blushed. 'Because of the letter.'

'From Julius Sackville.'

She sat on the stool in front of the dressing table and stared at her curious companion. 'He said he would visit Terregles at the end of autumn. By then he believed I would know my husband's fate.' She knew the exact words by heart: *By then you may know your future.*

'And what do you think he meant by those carefully chosen words?'

'I suppose that if we were still married, still happy, he would never trouble me again.'

'And if not?'

'He did not say.'

'Well, it's academic, Jane, because in 1716 Winifred and William *are* still married.'

'Where are they?'

'Blissfully happy in Rome.'

She swallowed. 'And the child?'

Suddenly, for the first time since she'd left Winifred's body, Jane understood the second reason for her unhappiness, her sense of dislocation, her inability to integrate back into her old life and particularly her sense of loss. She'd allowed people to think it was connected with Will; privately, she'd believed it to be about Julius. But only now in uttering that question did Jane realise that it was also about the child she and Julius had created.

Robin gazed back at her and hesitated...

'Winifred had suffered many unsuccessful pregnancies before you met her. She miscarried again on the rough voyage to Belgium, where she was heading to see her sister, Lucy, who was by then Mother Prioress at the convent.'

'Oh,' she said, unsure of whether she felt relief or hopelessness.

'It was for the best,' Robin said with a stern look. 'Rather complicated otherwise.'

She nodded, her cheeks burning afresh. And now, the question she was desperate to ask. 'Robin, can I go back?'

He hesitated again.

'I accept that there will be a price,' she said, trying to keep her voice light-hearted, but Robin didn't return her levity. 'Julius spoke about the tapestry of life – as you did once. In the letter...' She took a slow breath. 'Well, he hoped the threads of that tapestry that bound us might cross once again.'

'Is that what you hope too?'

She looked back at the mirror forlornly. 'I have to be with him. I have to.'

'You could never see your family again.'

'I understand.'

The mirror shimmered and Robin appeared before her, suddenly real. She gasped. 'Do you, Jane? Do you really want to grow old in a time before you were born?'

She could feel the thrum of the magic around her, but she remained calm as she nodded. 'I want to grow old with the man I love. Isn't that what the great tapestry of life is about – the many threads of love? The relationships that weave their way into the future to form the lives we live?'

'Yes, someone said a similar thing once,' he said, unable this time to repress a little smirk.

'I want to know the love of a man who is loved in return. I didn't have that with Will. It was a one-sided love affair and he deserved better, and it could be why life has reworked his part of the tapestry. And I want to be Jane Sackville... can you take me back to his time?'

'Julius Sackville was enamoured with Winifred. Are you sure he could love *you*, Jane?'

She shrugged. Robin could certainly tap into her fears. 'I can only hope. I think if he met me there would be a chance for us. Isn't that what love is all about? Hope?'

He nodded. 'Well, if you're absolutely sure, we must leave immediately.'

'Robin, there is nothing for me in this life but disappointment everywhere I turn.'

'Understand this. The only reason I will help you to unpick the tapestry of your life and rework the threads is because I fear I should not have tampered with it in the first place.'

'But you did, and I am grateful for it. I have no regrets other than the pain I've brought my family.' She thought of her parents' dismay as she'd explained she was going travelling again, refusing to answer their questions. 'I wrote a long letter to them on the train and posted it as soon as I arrived in Perthshire. I told them everything that I choked on trying to explain when I rang them... as I knew I would. It was too difficult. But if you take me back, I'm going to write another letter in the past for them in the future. I shall tell them not to let me make that trip to Cornwall in 1978, and then I shall never meet Will and none of this will happen.'

'Now you're confusing me.' He wagged a finger. 'And this is why we must not tamper with people's lives and their destiny. Changing history is dangerous. I doubt you will be there in 1978, Jane, because you are now choosing to change the course of *their* lives too.'

'Then I'll save them pain.'

Robin was kind enough not to pursue it by reminding her they'd have to live through her loss anyway. Instead, he shrugged at her. 'Transference of your whole self is going to be painful.'

'I'm ready for it,' she said gamely, hoping she was.

'Well, you know where to go next?'

'The standing stones.'

He nodded.

THIRTY-NINE

THE JOURNEY BACK IN TIME WAS ONE of breathless agony, to which Jane had to give herself over completely. There was no thought, no light, no dark, no sound, no purchase on anything except the pain that wracked her body, hurt her mind and caused her to scream into a silence where no one could hear her. She had no idea how long it endured, but gradually Jane came back into herself, trembling and damp with exertion at first, then slowly steadying her breathing, calming that hammering heartbeat.

When the panic of transference had passed, she raised her head to see that Robin was now Robyn and they were standing in the gardens of Terregles. She could tell that the house was now shuttered and locked.

'Welcome back, Jane,' said Robyn, draping a cloak over Jane's naked body.

'That hurt,' Jane gasped.

'You were warned it would, if you were to come through fully as yourself.'

She winced, looking up at Robyn from the ground where she had landed. 'I feel changed.'

Robyn reached out a hand to help her up and rearrange the warm cloak. 'You *are* changed. You belong here now.'

Jane shaded her eyes against the sun, which was now full and warm. Summer was announcing itself; time had moved on in 1716. 'So the house is deserted?'

'Locked up since the Maxwells left, although I suspect the son will return to claim it in due course, when he is old enough, because the King didn't want it. For now, William's sister and her husband have put everything in order.'

Jane nodded. 'I hope a few of Winifred's clothes remain.'

'Come, I know a way inside.' Robyn beckoned.

And it was no longer Winifred's feelings, only Jane's emotions surging with relief and delight to be back at Terregles. She'd only been here briefly, yet Winifred's feelings of home and love had coloured Jane's, and now it felt familiar and welcoming, even in its deserted state. She remembered Sarah and dear Bran – where were they now? She was sure she could find them soon enough.

With Robyn at her side, she walked through the house, opening shutters, flinging up windows, pulling back drapes – at every opportunity allowing the beautifully soft Scottish sunlight of a summery afternoon to leak back into a house that she remembered had been filled with love.

'I'm going to take off every dust sheet. It's going to be a fully working house again.'

'You're that confident he will come?' Robyn asked.

'He will come.'

'And if he doesn't?'

'I don't regret being here, if that's what you mean.'

'You'll make a life here?'

'I have no choice. You told me that yourself. I have friends in London – Mrs Mills, Mrs Morgan. Oh, they don't know we're friends yet, but they will. There's dear Mary and Charles at Traquair… even Mr and Mrs Bailey, or Mr and Mrs Leadbetter, if I'm desperate!' She giggled.

They ascended the stairs, the old dark timber creaking beneath their feet, until they reached the landing, where separate portraits of William and Winifred hung. Winifred looked back at her with a serene expression, soft golden hair clasped back, curling gently behind her ears.

Jane kissed her fingers and placed them on Winifred's image. 'Hello, darling Winifred.' She blew a kiss to William. 'Will, how fare you?'

'Well done, Jane. You already sound like you belong.'

She sighed, smiling contentedly. 'I do belong. Here they are, my closest friends, with me still.'

'You'd better write to Mary and concoct a reason for being here.'

Jane nodded. 'I'll say I'm an old friend of Winifred's, for only an old friend would know where money is stashed.' She chuckled. 'I shall need to be frugal, though.'

In Winifred's room, which Jane had not seen previously, she discovered her friend's wardrobe intact and was assured she would never want for clothes, as they were of similar size. She looked around at the simple, but elegant, furnishings and could see Winifred's fine and slightly French taste reflected here more than in any other room she'd visited in the house. Two floor-to-ceiling mullioned windows let in golden afternoon light to bounce off papered walls depicting tall and dramatic soft green foliage with pale flowers. A central carpet echoed the colours in a delicate floral pattern and covered burnished parquet flooring, to finish at the four-poster bed, which was set into a wall recess. Jane recalled William's bed and this was its feminine twin, with finer finials and rich, cream-coloured, silken draping. Beneath the dado, the plasterwork was picked out in sage green and cream while heavily gilded French mirrors either side of the bed and between the windows made the room feel bigger, lighter. It was altogether feminine and beautiful. She sighed. Winifred was still with her.

Robyn beckoned again. 'Come. I have something for you,' she said.

Jane tiptoed softly across the carpet, hardly wishing to stir the air of Winifred's room, until she stood by the walnut dressing table. She watched Robyn lift the lid on a small wooden box that was so simple in design she could see the marks from the maker's chisel.

'Willie made this for his mother,' Robyn said, answering her question.

'It's unsettling the way you hear my thoughts,' Jane admitted.

'Only your questions,' Robyn confided. She reached in and pulled out what looked to be a bundle of stained, folded papers, but Jane recognised them instantly.

'Julius's letters!' She took them greedily, held them to her chest. 'Thank you. It means so much to have them.'

Robyn nodded with a half-smile. 'I knew it would. And this,' she said, dipping again into the box and retrieving a small glass vial.

Jane had to bite her lip to stop it from trembling, refusing to weep. 'Winifred's perfume,' she breathed.

'You buried the perfume and letters together on the ley line at Peebles. They belong with each other and now they are back with their rightful owner.'

Jane closed her eyes and sniffed the bottle stopper. The familiar scent that Winifred had called Ashes of Violet filled her senses, and with it came an image of Julius, his expression bruised, struggling – the one he'd worn the day she'd glimpsed him in the Court.

She gave Robyn a kiss. 'Thank you. Now he is with me, even though he is not present.'

And so began four months of living quietly, with only Robyn for company and to teach her everything about living as a gentlewoman in the early Georgian era. If anyone asked, Jane had learned to spin the story that she was a very close friend of the Earl and Countess and they had given permission for her to make use of the house. She had taken the precaution of writing to Mary and Charles at Traquair to ensure they understood that she was living at Terregles, but that she was occupying a small cottage rather than the main house. Soon she was corresponding regularly with Mary, who sounded pleased that someone was looking after the family home. She was sure Mary would have written to Winifred and that made her smile, for she knew if she could, Winifred would want to meet her. Perhaps… who knew, she may one day visit Italy and introduce herself properly. But not yet… not until autumn had come… and gone…

Jane remembered where Winifred had buried some of the Maxwells' silver, and used this coin to buy seeds to plant vegetables. She learned from Robyn about simple animal husbandry so that the purchase of a cow and chickens meant some staples could be guaranteed. She learned how to bake bread and live without anything more technical than a wheelbarrow. Bran was back in her life – it seemed he'd never left – and was happy to come down from his new home in the highlands to help run a small household again for Her Ladyship's friend, and look after the land. Jane even bought a horse, so that she didn't feel entirely trapped at Terregles. Life, despite the grandness of her surroundings, was simple in her cottage and she understood, while learning with Robyn's help to darn socks at night by candlelight, or engaging in her latest passion, spinning wool from stores on the Maxwell property, that she had never felt as happy or fulfilled as she did in living this plain life.

Jane assured Robyn that, although she was often alone, she never felt lonely, whereas with Will she had often felt isolated and guilt-ridden.

Nevertheless, it came as a bright pain when, one morning, Robyn announced that it was time for her to leave.

'But why?'

'I must,' is all her friend would say. 'This is the right time.'

'Now, perhaps, I shall be lonely beyond understanding.'

'You will be fine, Jane. You have carved out a most pleasant existence for yourself. And perhaps that existence may change as time moves on, but for now I know you are capable of taking care of yourself.'

She knew she couldn't force Robyn to stay, but when they hugged farewell Jane had a teary moment.

'I do not regret being here, Robyn, but I will miss you.'

'Perhaps,' her friend said, and gave her a reassuring smile that Jane didn't understand.

A few hours later, Jane was in the side garden of the main house, selecting herbs for the rabbit stew she had had in mind since Bran had arrived with a brace, which was now hanging in her pantry. With the colder weather that autumn had brought, it seemed appropriate to start cooking more heartily.

She blinked into the setting sun and could see a rider approaching. At first she thought it might be Robyn returning, having changed her mind, but then Jane remembered that Robyn had left on foot.

As the figure drew closer, she could make out the shape of a man. Jane straightened up and smoothed Winifred's skirt, wondering what this messenger's arrival might signify. Was it news of young Willie's return to the house, or Charles, Winifred's brother-in-law, paying a visit?

She shielded her eyes to try for a better look – and swallowed hard. The figure of the man was achingly familiar. Not daring to believe it, Jane held her breath as she watched him dismount at the main gate and begin leading his horse up the main path to the house. His hat hid his features, but she knew it was him. He'd kept his word, even though he had no idea whether she had even received his letter.

Since Robyn returned it, she had carried it around with her like a talisman. And now she reached into her pocket and touched the stopper of Winifred's perfume to her wrist. She moved around from the side garden to stand at the front of the main house and let out the breath that had been caught in her chest. Her heart sounded like a drummer without rhythm; she took a slow, deep breath to calm her racing mind.

This was the moment. In fact, the next few heartbeats would decide her fate forever.

'Good afternoon,' he said, giving a small bow. 'My name is Julius Sackville.' The voice drifted over her like a balm. This was no illusion; it was really him. He was even wearing the same riding coat.

'I know who you are,' she said, linking her fingers to keep her nervous hands still.

He regarded her, frowning. 'Forgive me; have we been introduced?'

She smiled. 'In a manner, we have. You are a friend of Lady Winifred, are you not?'

He cleared his throat. 'Yes. Is she in residence?'

'I am afraid not, Lord Sackville,' and she could see the surprise in his expression that she knew his title. 'The Earl and Countess are now living abroad permanently. I am a close friend of Winifred and my understanding is that she will not be returning to Terregles, not even for a visit. Perhaps you've heard they are fugitives?'

He looked down. 'I have.' She could feel his disappointment batter against her senses like a tidal wave of sorrow. 'Er... forgive me,' he said, trying his best to cover it. 'I promised Winifred that I would visit next time I was in these parts.'

'And I am sorely glad you have,' Jane said, trying not to blush.

He studied her. 'I feel embarrassed not to know your name, miss.'

'Oh,' she smiled, 'it is I who must apologise, sir. But first, may I ask if you remember a conversation with Winifred when she asked you to pay attention to a friend of hers who might introduce herself to you as Jane Granger?'

He blinked slowly. 'I do,' he said, his throat raspy.

Jane looked down. 'She asked you, if I'm right, to spend some time getting to know this woman, to give her a fair hearing... at least, to give her a chance to explain something. I believe she tried to impress upon you that it was important that you did.'

'Winifred did not say her friend would be so beautiful.' He waited. 'You are... Jane?'

'I am Jane Granger, Lord Sackville. And I have been waiting for you throughout the summer. And now that autumn is riding in hard, I hoped with all of my heart that you would come.'

He stared at her, aghast. 'How did you know this?'

'Because of the letter you sent me.'

She watched him think on her words, as though replaying them carefully in his mind. 'I sent a letter to *Winifred*.'

'No, Julius. You thought you were writing to Winifred. But you were writing to me. Your letter spoke to Jane. And you once said to me in a woodcutter's hut that you only thought of Jane when you made love to Winifred, because she seemed different to you if you called her Jane. I have travelled a long way to be with you. And I have waited for you.'

The lovely face, tanned by summer's rays, blanched before her. 'How can you know this about me... about Jane? I don't understand.'

'Because, confusing as it surely is, I *am* Jane. It was always me, Julius.'

Consternation wrestled with despair in his expression. 'You toy with me, miss. And with my broken heart.'

'No, Julius, my love. I shall explain everything if you'll promise to hear it. Winifred asked you to hear Jane out, to give her a chance.' Jane held out a hand to him. 'It is wonderful to see you again.'

His manners forbade him from doing anything else but bend over her hand to kiss it politely. Yet as he did so she knew he inhaled a scent that made him pause. She felt the hand holding hers shake. 'Ashes of Violet,' he murmured, his voice gritty with emotion and memory.

Jane pulled the vial from her pocket. 'I keep this close because it makes me think of you when I smell the fragrance. I wear it only for you.'

He looked at her, unnerved, unsure, desperate to understand. 'Jane?'

'I came back for you. Please give me a chance to explain. I need you in my life again. I need to feel your kiss...'

'Again?' she heard him murmur, and trembled as she felt the tentative and gentle caress of his lips. In that moment she knew that the right threads had crossed and knotted together in the tapestry of her life.

'I love you,' Jane said, and, for the first time in either life, she meant it.

EPILOGUE

JULIETTE GRANGER HAD READ AND REREAD THE separate – secret – letter her sister had posted from Perth, desperately trying to make sense of the words. Her parents had accepted the details in the letter that Jane had sent to them and resigned themselves to the knowledge that their daughter needed time, but Juliette suspected whatever Jane had written to them had skipped over the truth.

I am going where I can be happy. Where I know that a man who loves me and whom I love just as madly waits for me.

Where that was, Juliette had no idea. She presumed Australia, for where else could Jane have met someone between Will's coma and waking up? It had been six weeks now since that letter and spring was giving way to early summer warmth, the Irish Republican Army was promising reprisals and strikes were being threatened. But Juliette was in a summery frock and sandals and she had a new man in her life. Although it was early days, it felt like the real thing. She couldn't remember a happier time, and she was starting to realise that Jane's decisions would no longer affect her or her future. *Jane says she's happy*, she told herself as she waited in the foyer of the Victoria and Albert Museum. *Now it's my turn.*

Her flat sandals sounded gritty on the grey and white tiles, and echoes of other footsteps sounded around her. People spoke softly, but their voices carried and bounced against the hard surfaces, especially their laughter. A woman gave a high giggle and Jane followed its sound, but was immediately diverted back to the main doors, where she could see Pete arriving.

Pete was in furniture design, which made him interesting, and she loved his softer creative qualities, but the downside was that he was always dragging her into museums, even on a delicious day like today.

She tapped the face of her wristwatch and he arrived laughing, giving her a big kiss and pulling a rose from behind his back. 'Picked it for you this morning.' She gave a smile of pleasure. 'Got me plenty of looks on the Tube,' he admitted dryly as she kissed him again.

'Thanks – now I forgive you for meeting me in a stuffy museum on a summer's day!'

'It's not officially summer, and I shall take you to a park for a stroll and a cuddle and an ice cream, and whatever else your heart desires, very shortly. Besides,' he said, looking up into the glorious rotunda of the V&A's wedding-cake-like, Italianate lobby, 'how could you ever call this stuffy?'

'Are you going to lead me round early eighteenth-century fabrics or something tedious?' she bleated, with a deliberate whine in her tone.

'As a matter of fact, no, but well done on getting the era spot on!' he congratulated, dark eyes twinkling. 'I have a surprise for you. It's bizarre.'

'Bizarre?' she repeated.

'Early Georgian; totally whacky, I promise… when you see it, you're going to pinch yourself.'

'All right, I'm intrigued.'

'Second level. Come on.' He took her hand. 'It's such a crazy coincidence. I have to show you – it will only take a couple of minutes – and given all the worry you've been suffering over your sister, I thought it would make you smile.'

'My sister?' she said at the top of the stairs. 'Is this about Jane?'

He nodded. 'Sort of. Just something amusing for you.'

Juliette followed her boyfriend into light-filled galleries and was grateful he didn't pause to explain the gilding on furniture, or the Chinese silk of such and such a fabric that was nearly five hundred years old, or the majestic commode so exquisitely carved, blah, blah.

She realised they were moving through chambers and passing through centuries from earliest to modern.

'This way,' Pete urged. He sounded genuinely amused. Juliette read that they were now entering the Georgian age; they'd just been walking through an exhibition about domestic décor. It held zero interest for her, but she could imagine how learning about home furnishings down the centuries would thrill Pete, so she would indulge him. She was sure only love would have enabled her to do that!

He led her to a cabinet on the furthest wall, passing various chairs, tables, drapes and small vignettes of clustered domestic goods denoting different rooms in an early Georgian household. There were also households of different social levels, so museum-goers could draw an impression of domestic life during the reign of George I in every setting from a London slum to a fine rural household.

'Here!' Pete finally said, sounding triumphant. 'Make what you will of that. I'm sure that's the name you told me. Sackville, right?'

Juliette peered at where he pointed to two small oval paintings on china. Her gaze was drawn to the man first. He had dark hair and dark-looking eyes with an intense and brooding gaze. He was not smiling. In fact, he looked unhappy to be posing, but he could not, despite his serious expression, hide the fact that he was a handsome fellow. He was dressed quietly in a long, dark frock coat, she imagined; she could see nothing below mid-chest. A silk cravat was tied loosely at his throat and he wore no wig; his hair was tied back neatly, she noted. She got the impression he had been painted standing in front of a stable. But her gaze was already sliding over to the woman in the painting next to him, seated in a garden setting. She had an infant on her lap and she was smiling.

Juliette blinked and caught her breath. The resemblance of this woman to Jane was unmistakable.

Pete was talking, although she only realised that now.

'... you see. *Jane*, it says.'

'What?' Juliette murmured, her throat suddenly as dry as a desert. Her gaze followed where his finger stabbed urgently.

'*Lord Julius Sackville, c. 1720. Lady Jane Sackville (née Granger) and the Honorable Miss Juliette Sackville, c. 1720.*'

The information accompanying the pieces went on to explain that painting on china was common in this era and that noble families often had small portraits of themselves commissioned for posterity, but Juliette wasn't reading any of it. Her gaze fixated on the names. Julius, Jane, Juliette. Née Granger! Married to Sackville. Sackville was the name that Jane had impressed upon her – Julius Sackville, in fact. She felt dizzy.

'Say something, Jules.'

But Juliette was still staring at the likeness of Jane, who looked out from the china oval with a serene smile.

'I'll leave you be a moment,' Pete said, sensing his girlfriend's response was not amused awe but genuine shock.

'It's her,' she breathed. Juliette placed her hand against the cabinet, her fingers touching her sister through the glass. 'Jane... I can see him. Julius Sackville. You made me promise,' she whispered. 'I've found you both.'

She didn't realise she'd begun to weep silently. Pete was back, concerned.

'Oh, sweetheart, I didn't mean...'

'No, no, you did the right thing. This is so exciting. But now I have to find out more. I need to know where these were found.'

'It's the summer of 1979. You know it can't be her, right?' he said, smiling bemusedly.

'Sure,' Juliette lied, straightening. 'Come on, let's get some sun. You said something about ice cream?' she said, diverting him. As Pete wandered away, Juliette made a private promise that she would return and learn the provenance of these china paintings once owned by Lord Julius and Lady Jane Sackville.

You look happy, Jane, Juliette cast out in her mind, and as she took a final glance at her sister she could have sworn she caught the fragrance of violets.

ACKNOWLEDGEMENTS

It is accepted that truth is often stranger than fiction, which is why the true story of the Earl and Countess of Nithsdale at the Tower of London is so powerfully romantic and helplessly attractive to a novelist. Nevertheless, I have taken liberties in this tale and twisted reality to suit my story. I must assure my readers, however, that some of the most incredible passages of the tale – those connected with brave Lady Winifred – are based wholly on facts learned from the history tomes.

I wrestled long and hard with how to write this story – should I try to recreate the language of the era, ignore it altogether, or attempt a hybrid form? Again I came back to what I am, and that's a storyteller. For me to risk cramping the tale with clumsy attempts to deliver the dialogue in a wholly early-Georgian style seemed pointless. Instead, I have aimed to give readers a simple 'sense' of the style of speech, but mostly I've kept it modern so both sides of the story can flow.

Help came from unexpected quarters and perhaps the most exciting was a visit to the Tower of London, where I fully expected to be a common-or-garden tourist as I braved the autumn rains. I'd seen the Tower many times previously, particularly in my youth, but felt it was necessary to see it again, this time trying to imagine it in the early 1700s. What I didn't expect was to meet the Constable of the Tower – Sir Richard Dannatt, former Brigadier General of the British Army – and his wonderful and generous wife, Pippa, who welcomed me like a member of their family. Not only did I eat a scrumptious home-cooked meal in the dining room of the Queen's House, but I also had the rare opportunity to see the very chamber of the Tower where William Maxwell, Earl of Nithsdale, spent his final days in England, and from where he was meant to be escorted to his hanging, drawing and quartering. The room is now a spare bedroom – cosy, cute and thoroughly everyday. But to see it meant everything to me for this novel. I'm indebted to the Dannatts for allowing me to tread in the footsteps of the real William and Winifred, as well as countless kings and queens of the realm. I walked the rooftops where Elizabeth I took a daily stroll on her parapet when kept at the Tower, and I explored the bowels of the Queen's House (previously the Lieutenant's Lodgings) where Sir Thomas More suffered at Henry VIII's behest. None of these areas are open to the public, so it was a rare privilege. I enjoyed a private showing of the Crown Jewels and was a very special guest during the Ceremony of the Keys... I almost gave a royal wave to the shivering tourists. And all of this came about because of my agent, Charlie Viney, who not only pointed me to a book about the history of the Tower of London that prompted me to pursue this story, but also made it possible for me to meet the wonderful Dannatts. Thanks, Charlie, and for your energy and love for this story.

Everywhere I turned required research, which took me from the Guildhall Library in London to Saint-Germain-en-Laye just outside Paris. Even though I was working in London at the end of the '70s, I was not paying enough attention in my late teens to know what all the locations looked and felt like in much detail, and I dared not rely on memory. So thank you to David Bieda from the Seven Dials Renaissance Partnership, a charity that has invigorated that area of London, for his assistance with historical details. Any historical errors are mine alone.

Sincere thanks to Stephanie Smith for her guidance as she edited, and especially to Emma Dowden for her fabulous work, and to the team at HarperCollins for embracing this new style of fantasy from me so enthusiastically.

I'm thrilled to see this new edition now published by Penguin Random House Australia.

I am deeply grateful to my husband, Ian, who gave so much of his time to the research of this book and took as much pleasure as I did in finding out nuggets of information, whether it was trawling through the London Museum or the V&A, or reading everything on the Battle of Preston, or even making contact with the present-day family at Traquair House in Peebles, where Winifred enjoyed happy times.

The Tower of London is, for most of us, a cheerful tourism experience. But over the course of researching and writing this book, I came to appreciate what a forbidding, frightening place it surely was in centuries past for anyone brought beneath Traitors' Gate as a 'guest of the Crown'. What Winifred – as a gentlewoman of 1716 – achieved cannot be underestimated. Her defiance of the Hanoverian king alone was astonishing, but the courage she found to take the action she did surely ranks her as one of the most romantic heroines of all time.

Enjoy!

F

[illegible]

[illegible] now published by Random House Australia.

[illegible] husband, [illegible]

[illegible] London [illegible]

[illegible] House in Peebles, [illegible]

[illegible]

[illegible]

ABOUT THE AUTHOR

Photo credit © Shaun Li from Capture the Present

Fiona McIntosh is an internationally and million-copy bestselling author of novels for adults and children across several genres, including fantasy, historical fiction and her popular Detective Jack Hawksworth series. Fiona roams the world for her research and lives between Adelaide in South Australia and Wiltshire in England.

fionamcintosh.com

Bedford Square Publishers

Bedford Square Publishers is an independent publisher of fiction and non-fiction, founded in 2022 in the historic streets of Bedford Square London and the sea mist shrouded green of Bedford Square Brighton.

Our goal is to discover irresistible stories and voices that illuminate our world.

We are passionate about connecting our authors to readers across the globe and our independence allows us to do this in original and nimble ways.

The team at Bedford Square Publishers has years of experience and we aim to use that knowledge and creative insight, alongside evolving technology, to reach the right readers for our books. From the ones who read a lot, to the ones who don't consider themselves readers, we aim to find those who will love our books and talk about them as much as we do.

We are hunting for vital new voices from all backgrounds – with books that take the reader to new places and transform perceptions of the world we live in.

Follow us on social media for the latest Bedford Square Publishers news.

@bedsqpublishers

facebook.com/bedfordsq.publishers

@bedfordsq.publishers

bedfordsquarepublishers.co.uk